Praise for the novels of Claire Cross

Third Time Lucky

"Witty, whimsical, reflective and romantic, *Third Time Lucky* should tickle your funny bone, as well as touch your heart."

—Tanzey Cutter, *Old Book Barn Gazette*

"A screwball comedic romance that stars several interesting characters. Claire Cross writes a warm, witty and often wild novel that shows the expanse of her talent." —Harriet Klausner

"Do you feel lucky when you get more than you expect? If so, I strongly recommend this book. I rarely laugh out loud while reading, but this gave my smile muscles a good workout while engaging my brain. The writing is snappy and refreshing . . . This was my first Claire Cross and I plan to pick her up again when I need a good laugh." —*All About Romance*

"Laced with a good deal of humor. Ms. Cross creates characters that will alternately have you laughing and sniffling. [She] makes the transition from writing historical romance to contemporary romance seamlessly and without apparent effort. Writing with a completely different style, [her] creative voice still shines through. I thoroughly enjoyed this emotional, riveting tale." —*Romance Reviews Today*

continued . . .

Double Trouble

"A fun, funny, *Sex and the City* kind of tale."
—*The Romance Reader*

"For a fast-paced, captivating story of romance, family relationships and following your heart, *Double Trouble* is not to be missed."
—*Romance Reviews Today*

The Moonstone

"Consistently tickled my funny bone."
—*The Romance Reader*

"Claire Cross has a great sense of humor and it shines in this book. Her characters are vivid, her plots exciting and her book's a delight. *The Moonstone* is full of romance and humor. Who could ask for anything more?"
—*The Literary Times*

"Magical . . . enchanting . . . hilarious. Ms. Cross continues to win loyal fans by gifting them with fresh plots and fast-paced tales."
—*Rendezvous*

"Are you hungry for a marvelous book? Well, look no further than *The Moonstone*. Written with wit, pathos and charm . . . characters rich in personality sparkle with humor and sensuality . . . delightful, delicious and delectable."
—*Under the Covers Book Reviews*

Once Upon a Kiss

"Delightful."
—*The Toronto Star*

"A work of art. Take a bow Claire, this is stunning."
—*Bell, Book and Candle*

"Like a sorceress, Claire Cross spellbinds her readers and carries them on a magical journey . . . fresh and exciting, passionate and sensual." —*Rendezvous*

"Extremely absorbing . . . this enchantress turns this book into a magical reading experience." —Harriet Klausner

The Last Highlander

"Excellent . . . Claire Cross has a way with words." —*The Literary Review*

"You'll love this story . . . splendid." —*Bell, Book and Candle*

"Superb . . . I can't remember reading a novel I enjoyed more. The lead characters immediately steal your heart . . . sensual beyond belief. An exciting delight and a marvelous read; clearly one of the year's best." —*Under the Covers Book Reviews*

"Ms. Cross has that rare gift of creating books that are both plot and character driven. Long after the last word, you'll bask in the afterglow of this fascinating story." —*Rendezvous*

"Fantastic and refreshingly unique . . . will hook audiences from start to finish." —Harriet Klausner

And don't miss Claire Cross's novella, written as Claire Delacroix, in

To Weave a Web of Magic

Third Time Lucky

Claire Cross

BERKLEY SENSATION, NEW YORK

THE BERKLEY PUBLISHING GROUP
Published by the Penguin Group
Penguin Group (USA) Inc.
375 Hudson Street, New York, New York 10014, USA
Penguin Group (Canada), 90 Eglinton Avenue East, Suite 700, Toronto, Ontario, Canada M4P 2Y3
(a division of Pearson Penguin Canada Inc.)
Penguin Books Ltd., 80 Strand, London WC2R 0RL, England
Penguin Group Ireland, 25 St. Stephen's Green, Dublin 2, Ireland (a division of Penguin Books Ltd.)
Penguin Group (Australia), 250 Camberwell Road, Camberwell, Victoria 3124, Australia
(a division of Pearson Australia Group Pty. Ltd.)
Penguin Books India Pvt. Ltd., 11 Community Centre, Panchsheel Park, New Delhi—110 017, India
Penguin Group (NZ), Cnr. Airborne and Rosedale Roads, Albany, Auckland 1310, New Zealand
(a division of Pearson New Zealand Ltd.)
Penguin Books (South Africa) (Pty.) Ltd., 24 Sturdee Avenue, Rosebank, Johannesburg 2196, South Africa

Penguin Books Ltd., Registered Offices: 80 Strand, London WC2R 0RL, England

THIRD TIME LUCKY

Cover design by Masaki Ryo.
Cover art by George Long.

PRINTING HISTORY
Jove mass market edition / November 2000
Berkley Sensation trade paperback edition / August 2005

Berkley Sensation trade paperback ISBN: 0-425-20375-1

This title has been registered with the Library of Congress.

PRINTED IN THE UNITED STATES OF AMERICA

10 9 8 7 6 5 4 3 2 1

For Konstantin—
who let me borrow his Freddie joke.

Prologue

He was nervous, straining for his first glimpse of the city like the unseasoned traveler he wasn't. But this flight was different. He was reminded of another flight, another trip with change as his destination.

Another uncertain reception. That he was invited was no more reassuring this time than it had been the last.

It had taken him almost thirty years to come full circle. In a way, it was odd to be no more certain of what he would find now than he had been then.

The aircraft dipped low over the Atlantic and he pressed his face to the cold window, watching as they dropped closer and closer to the sparkling chop of the sea. In the last possible moment, lights flashed at the end of a runway conjured from nowhere. The tires hit the ground and he was thrown back in his seat by the force of the thrust reversal.

Home.

Or the closest thing to it.

He was the kind of man who took his time making decisions. He liked to mull over every facet of the problem, examine his options fully before making a choice. But once he had decided, he was always impatient to forge ahead, perhaps to reach the next conundrum.

This was no different. He was now anxious to have the inevitable behind him. He was already gathering his leather knapsack—his only piece of luggage—from beneath the seat ahead as the familiar announcements rolled unheard over the passengers. He was standing in the aisle as soon as the aircraft halted beside the terminal, his toe already tapping.

He wasn't the first off the plane by dint of his seat assignment, but he quickly outpaced his fellow travelers in the terminal. His long strides and lack of checked baggage made him the first to snag a taxi. The cab's wild lunge into the traffic suited his own need for haste.

It wouldn't be long. He forced himself to lean back in the vinyl seat, to note the changes in the city that had been the first he had ever known. It was different.

Of course. Everything changed, even here—though at least here, he wasn't responsible. He thought the city had looked better before—more green, less concrete—but then, no one had asked him and no one would. He shied away from both his last memory of this place and his recent preoccupation with compare-and-contrast, and let his thoughts skip ahead to the house.

What kind of reception would he find? Lucia had been angry, deeply angry, when he had left fifteen years before. She wasn't the kind of person to forgive and forget—which was why her invitation had been such a surprise.

He wouldn't put it past her to get even. Lucia had an ability to wait for her moment, probably a skill cultivated on the stage she loved. Waiting for her cue, as it were.

Either way, he'd know as soon as he opened the door that was never locked. (Had that changed? He wondered. Surely even tiny Rosemount couldn't still be immune to petty crime.) If Lucia had cooked for him, he was forgiven.

Unless even that constant had changed.

He frowned as they sped away from the city. He rolled down the window, taking a deep breath of the salt-tinged air. Funny how he hadn't been able to leave the ocean completely—and equally funny how different it was on the other side of the country. The warm winds that caressed Seattle brought rain and tolerance, optimism and an easy pace.

This wind had a bite to it, an edge that separated the wheat from the chaff and drove the timid inland. Like his grandmother, this wind permitted no illusions. It could buff a tough soul to a sheen or flay a tender one alive. It even drove the colors of sky and sea to the cold end of the spectrum, to glacial blue, to the mauve of frostbitten fingers, to rock and wave and winter.

The air felt clean in his lungs, invigorating for all its cold. It seemed to clarify his thoughts, as it always had, and he inhaled it greedily, profoundly grateful that it hadn't changed.

Then the cab took the exit and he found himself sitting forward to study the familiar streets, his pose in marked contrast to his usual inscrutable composure. The houses had changed, one after the other having surrendered their charm to renovators. They looked strikingly similar, where once they had been quirky and unique.

People apparently had no ability to appreciate what they had, no matter where they were. Not only was change inevitable, but change for the worse seemed to be the prevalent trend.

But Lucia's house stood as a sentinel to the past, at least from the outside. He felt himself smile at the sight of it. Old, slightly decrepit. It looked as though it had always been there, slowly disintegrating, and always would be. He could imagine that the house would erode, like a mountain, be worn down over the centuries by wind and water until it joined with the earth once more.

It was probably more cluttered than ever inside, the corners even more tightly stuffed with improbable objects. Lucia was a pack rat extraordinaire—or at least she had been. And her taste in bric-a-brac ran to the theatrical, just as it did in clothing and manner. Lucia collected used stage props. The treasures of her collection were lit and posed for maximum effect. Her collection could not possibly have remained static for fifteen years.

He paid the cab and stood on the curb for long moments after its engine had faded away, simply staring at the house, remembering the first time he had seen it and the awe that he had felt that they were to live here.

He had been sure that there had been a mistake. Now, he felt an echo of that certainty, the house giving no sign that he was welcomed or even expected.

The slate shingles were still slipping around the chimney, though they never seemed to fall off. The copper eavestroughs were more dented than he recalled, the ivy grew higher, the twisted evergreens on either side of the entry had nearly obscured the door but didn't look any more healthy than they ever had. The garden was dead, just as it always had been, a sign of his grandmother's disinterest in one facet of the world.

There were no half measures with Lucia. All or nothing was how she played the game. He had had all and never realized it until he had nothing from her. All was definitely better, regardless of what price she demanded.

He had missed this place.

He had missed her.

It was a dangerous and unwelcome realization, a chink in his armor of self-sufficiency and one that hopefully he'd be able to hide.

He discovered that the door was slightly ajar, not that uncommon an occurrence with Lucia. She was untroubled with mundane details. Once he would have pushed through the door without a thought, but on this day, he hesitated, wondering whether he should knock.

It had been so long.

But she had summoned him.

He gripped the old brass handle, his thumb rolling over the welcome familiarity of its smoothness, and pushed the heavy door all the way open. The hinges creaked with a predictable whine and he guessed that no one had oiled them since he had done it last.

He stepped over the threshold and gave himself the luxury of a moment unannounced within the foyer. He found himself relieved at the familiarity of it all even in change. The two models of crucified thieves were definitely new acquisitions, but they stared down at him with glassy eyes only Lucia could have thought to touch up with Vaseline.

And they complemented the snarling taxidermied lynx that perched on the bannister. The great cat was looking a bit woebegone, its fur more patchy than he recalled. The decor of the foyer might have made anyone else hesitate but it made him smile. He shut the door behind himself, petted the stuffed lynx—some of its fur clung to his hand—and called her.

The house cast his cry back at him.

But it was a big house and its sole occupant was getting older. Convinced she hadn't heard him, he dropped his bag at the foot of the stairs and headed for the kitchen. The swing door creaked beneath his touch and admitted him to Lucia's sunbaked, spotless refuge.

She hadn't cooked.

Disappointment made his steps falter, but he hadn't come this far just to walk away from a fight.

In fact, he was looking forward to it. The door to the greenhouse was ajar, revealing his grandmother's location. She would be puttering with some exotic beauty of a plant, talking to it, replanting it. She would be absorbed in her task, characteristically giving it her full attention.

Or at least pretending to do so until he "surprised" her.

It could have been twenty years before. He could have been coming home from school, running through the house with Sean, snagging a snack in the kitchen, bumping into everything and being scolded by his grandmother for some boyish transgression.

But that was before.

There had been no point in shirking her then and there wasn't any now. He called to her again from the threshold of the greenhouse. A trickle of water echoed from a hidden fountain, but no one replied.

She wasn't going to make this easy.

He should have expected as much.

The air in the greenhouse was oppressively humid, so thick with moisture that it seemed to push against his skin. Some plant filled the air with a noxious odor and he guessed she had found a new oddball for her collection. The sunlight was filtered through leaves of a thousand shades of green, the heat making him want to shed his jacket.

He followed the path, his footsteps crunching on the pea gravel. That plant's smell grew stronger and made his bile rise. The vines overhead had grown even more lush, their little mouths open and glistening as they waited for flies and spiders. The expectant look of them always made him shiver.

He rounded a corner of shrubbery, more than ready to argue with her choice of specimens, then stopped.

His grandmother lay on the stone pathway, sprawled where she had fallen. Her red garden clog had slipped from her foot, revealing a thick ankle blue with veins. Her face was greyish, her eyes were wide and unseeing, her mouth open in what might have been dismay.

It was blood he smelled, *her* blood.

It ran across the stones and glistened darkly in the sunlight; it stained her dress where a knife had been driven into her throat. The swirl of colored glass around the handle caught the sunlight. The blood was drying on her flesh, her chest did not rise and fall.

He was too late.

He stared at the knife, numbed by the memory of the little shop in Venice where he had found it. He'd known as soon as he'd seen it that it would be perfect for Lucia. A stiletto for a letter opener would suit her style and her sense of humor.

He'd thought it would be the perfect peace offering.

But it had become something else. And he knew all too well that there were no coincidences. Someone had chosen this weapon with care, someone who didn't want him reconciled with Lucia.

It was all too obvious who that was. The past rose to choke him. He backed away.

A police siren began to wail. It grew louder with alarming speed. He felt the trap closing around him.

It was happening again.

But not by his choice.

He bolted, as graceless as the gangly kid he once had been. He grabbed his bag from the foyer and lunged into the thin sunlight, leaving the door swinging behind him.

He ran, putting as much distance between himself and trouble as he could. It was only a matter of time but he would claim every minute he could. Sweat ran down his back and he shivered in the cold of the wind, but he ran until he couldn't hear the siren.

And then he ran further.

When he finally stopped, he stood by the sea, miles from the house. His chest hurt, his feet were sore, his face was wet with tears he hadn't known he'd shed. He dropped to a crouch and pressed his shaking fingers to his temples, listening to the thunder of his heart. He closed his eyes and saw Lucia again.

He rubbed his face with his hands, feeling more alone than he had ever since he left this place.

He was sure he'd been seen, sure he couldn't just catch a plane back to the coast and escape as he had the last time. Oddly enough, however, he didn't want to leave.

He took a deep breath of the wind and savored the icy stab of it. Lucia deserved better than another lie. He'd come too late to tell her the truth or, more accurately, that opportunity had been stolen from him. The unfortunate fact was that the past would ensure that no one believed him now. Someone was counting on that.

But there was one other person who knew the truth. One other person who might believe him.

He wondered what had become of her. He stood and watched the skyscrapers in the distance light up against the dusk like stars in the twilight. He wondered whether she *would* believe him—she would only have his word this time.

He wondered whether she would help him. She had had her own reasons for helping before, and he wondered what had ever come of those. He hadn't asked, maybe he hadn't wanted to know.

Maybe he didn't have a choice anymore.

He hefted his bag and began walking toward the city.

Lucia Sullivan waited a full twenty minutes—twenty minutes that seemed to stretch clear to eternity—before she moved. Nicholas was long gone, his footsteps faded to silence, but she didn't trust him to not return and check.

The boy had always been too conscientious.

Meanwhile, she congratulated herself not only on a job well done, but the splendid good timing of that police siren. It warbled into the distance now, a happy coincidence that had served her purposes well. Nicholas could have looked too closely, found her pulse, some hint of her breathing, or the line where the stage makeup ended below her chin.

That would have ruined everything. She was good, but a perceptive eye could see through the very best effect. The sun had come out from behind the clouds at the worst possible moment and, as much as she hated to admit it, her skills weren't quite what they used to be.

Which was the point.

Her lips thinned as she considered Nicholas's response to the police siren. Fear didn't suit him, particularly a fear of the law.

But despite a twinge of compassion, Lucia wasn't going to change her plan. The boy had to learn from his mistake.

For Nicholas—her favored grandson, a child so honest it had pained Lucia to watch his dawning realization that the world would not play on his terms—had *deceived* her. She wasn't inclined to let that slip, not now that she had the opportunity to twist the knife in the wound.

No pun intended. The use of his gift had been an inspired choice, she thought, though stagecraft demanded that the blade be sawed off. It would never be the same again, but that was a comparatively small price to pay.

Lucia intended to teach him to never make such a mistake again. Tit for tat, as that fool woman Donnelly liked to say. He wouldn't miss this lesson of what could have been lost by his choices—and if it was harshly granted, well, that was small restitution for the heartache she had endured.

Fifteen years was a long time. She wasn't getting any younger.

Lucia sat up and grimaced at her body's reminder of that. She had a splendid set of aches for her troubles and she sat for a moment to catch her breath before getting to her feet. Her heart was running a bit too fast.

She'd never given in to anything without a fight and Death wasn't going to have an easier time of it.

She wiped some of the raccoon's blood from her face. There was no substitute for the real thing, all stage concoctions aside. And the smell had been the coup de grace.

Lucia had no qualms about killing a wild creature for the greater good. One less raccoon wouldn't be noticed, and even if it was, the garbage-rummaging beast certainly wouldn't be missed.

She snorted, retrieved her garden clog and pushed to her feet.

A restorative cigarette was called for, then a hot bath. Maybe she'd even treat herself to a brandy after she put the greenhouse to rights. It would have to be a quick one though.

There wasn't a moment to waste. Sooner or later, Nicholas would be back.

And the stage for Act Two had yet to be set.

Chapter 1

I was drunk on the night it began.

But then, that's not really true. It wasn't so much beginning as continuing, though I didn't immediately get that part.

As far as whether this whole mess should have ended already, or whether it should even have begun in the first place, well, that's an entirely different issue. I'm sure my mother has an opinion about it, and I'm equally sure it's not one that I want to hear. You're welcome to ask her, but don't say I didn't warn you.

Beginning or continuing, though, there was no doubt that I was pickle-dee-dee. I had the world on a leash—one of those pink rhinestone-studded specials that even poodles find embarrassing—but I had felt that way before Veuve Clicquot and I made our acquaintance. A critical distinction, even if it was a bit blurred in that moment.

You see, getting drunk was a first for me.

Now, don't be too incredulous. You have to respect your genetic weaknesses, in my opinion, otherwise they'll ambush when you aren't looking. I had resolved long ago that I would never join the family gallery of lushes.

But this had been a special, special day and my partner Elaine does have her persuasive moments.

It was about eleven on a Tuesday night, not a respectable time to be dancing on air and champagne bubbles, but there it was, and there I was. Fa la la. All the proper brownstones scowled down at me as though they would rat on me in the morning, when all their proper occupants—who were now properly tucked in and properly sober—had risen to properly face another day.

There's something irresistibly frivolous about pink champagne. It *looks* like a party in a glass—Barbie's victory drink of choice—and it does the fandango on your tongue in starlight slippers.

Make that sequin-studded fuschia slingbacks.

Which was why Elaine insisted we had to have it. No mere sparkling wine or even those pedestrian golden bubbles would have done for us. No, sir. Only rosé champagne was good enough to celebrate such a coup—though it was humbling to learn just what a cheap date I was. All those years of guzzling herbal tea had taken their toll—one tall, skinny glass of froth and I was completely wasted.

Fortunately Elaine is made of sterner stuff and had no quibbles with polishing off the rest of the bottle. No chance of our treat going flat. She even looked sober after it was gone, which might have been sobering with any other companion. But I've known Elaine long enough to understand that she's not one to waste any of life's goodies—she even laughs when I call her a regular little martyr to the pleasures of the flesh.

But that's another story.

We had succeeded where others have failed and lo, it was very good. Lady Luck was smiling down on us and nothing could ever go wrong again. Life was full of opportunity and possibility, success was ours for the taking. All those years were finally paying off.

Have you ever flailed away at a dream? You begin because it seems such a terrific idea that success is inevitable—not to mention all the fame and fortune that will fall into your lap as a bonus-pak—but you learn the error of that thinking in a hurry. It gets tough, the dream loses its luster and eventually, you run on the refusal to admit you're wrong.

Which doesn't pay well, in case you aren't sure. I've eaten more mac-and-cheese over the past few years than I'd like to think about and I'm not talking homemade cheese and noodle comfort food like Mom used to make. I mean the kind out of the box.

You can make it with water, you know, and it's not all bad.

Sometimes it's startling how far we'll go to conquer dreams, even further than we might have guessed ourselves. But then, the alternative is even less pretty than mac-and-cheese fusing overnight with the unrinsed pot.

The urge to avoid failure is powerful stuff indeed. Even as you smile that big confident grin and slog onward, in some hidden corner of your heart you wonder how long it will take you to fail, how long it will take your dream to fall so far into the scrap heap that there's no hope of salvaging it at all.

And if you have a family like mine, well, there's the added bonus of a line of helpful souls constantly calculating the odds against you, just in case you get the math wrong.

I *always* get the math wrong, much to the amusement of my three brothers who snarfed up all the math genes before I was even a glimmer in anyone's eye. For example, on this particular night, after being ambushed by success and bamboozled by the champagne, I over-tipped the cabdriver and made a friend for life.

Maybe not quite that long. The moment I steadied myself enough to stand without clinging to the roof of the cab, he was gone, leaving the Last Generous Tipper in Massachusetts wobbling on her heels in the middle of the street. Good thing all the neighbors were safely tucked into bed, because I must have looked like a dope trying to reach the curb before I caught it with my chin.

I decided, right there on Mr. McGurvey's chemically enhanced golf-course-green boulevard, to avail myself of the one mythic perk of being self-employed. Everyone otherwise employed assumes that working for yourself is an excuse to lay around, sleep in, catch up on the soaps, scoot out of the office early and take many many lunches-of-no-return.

Ha. Truth is, my boss is the worst slavedriver ever—and she's me. I've put in more hours, nights and weekends, working for myself than any legitimate employer could have demanded. I've bedded annuals and double-dug roses and moved trees and laid interlock.

I've built decks, for God's sake, when workers disappeared into that great void where contractors seem to go without warning or return. I've tiled porches and walls, caffeinated myself for another night of drafting plans without the decadent luxury of sleep, then marched out the door to do it all again.

I've talked a blue streak that I didn't know I could, I've weasled better terms from skeptics, I've supplied impromptu therapy for divorcées removing "all signs of *him*," I've endured the caprices of women who can never make up their minds.

And it was finally paying off.

The pink bubbles tingling through my veins couldn't touch that giddy feeling of triumph, though they did give it a hefty boost. I did a little softshoe on the sidewalk and tripped over my own feet. Fortunately, those champagne bubbles broke my fall—the drunk, as any cop will tell you, have no bones at all.

I felt pretty cocky once I had scaled my neighbor's drive to the sidewalk and even imagined that I approached the house with a measure of my usual insouciance.

As if. Somewhere someone is snorting their beer at the idea of me even having insouciance.

The thing is, if I *had* had any, it wasn't destined to last long.

I was about twenty feet from the porch, admiring the little crocuses poking their yellow heads through the soil and congratulating myself on doing a decent job of installing a porch light with a sensor. The light was on, so I hadn't completely screwed up the wiring, though Number Two Son—my brother Matt—would have issues with my uncompensated, unauthorized improvement of a leasehold facility.

And then I saw him.

There was a man sitting on my porch.

Watching me.

Even stinko, I was pretty sure I lived alone. And I knew I hadn't invited any guests to join me for an intimate yet casual nightcap. It wasn't my style.

Those bubbles abandoned me, though that didn't leave me any better equipped to run or to fight or whatever it is you're supposed to do when some guy waits for you in the dark and you have to get past him to sanctuary.

He seemed prepared to wait for as long as it took me to make up my mind what to do.

There was an outside chance that he was a champagne-induced illusion, but if so, he was a pretty substantial one. And he showed no signs of fading into oblivion. In fact, he stared steadily back at me as though I shouldn't be surprised to find him there at all.

The stillness of him reminded me of someone, someone I wanted desperately to see again, someone I knew I should never want to see again. I took a couple of steps closer and, yes, it's true, my heart really was in my mouth.

Because it couldn't be *him*. He'd been gone too long and I'd gone cold turkey on waiting for that apology years ago.

But Nick Sullivan was sitting on my porch.

Waiting for *me*. And I suddenly felt all the smooth assurance of sixteen again.

I gaped at him, like the lovesick idiot I once had been, and my heart started to pound hard. A bubble of hope invited the champagne bubbles to cha-cha, and the happy couple took to the dance floor.

Which left my fogged brain trying to wrap itself around the concept of Nick coming to look for me.

Me.

I had been warned for years and years that the Sullivan boys were trouble with a capital T, that they were no good, that they were not the sort of people my sort of people should know. And I had bucked popular opinion all those years ago, believing that I knew better, that I knew Nick, that he wasn't as bad as everyone believed. I even thought that we were friends.

Then he proved popular opinion dead on the money.

He wasn't supposed to be here—he was supposed to be in Seattle, running a wildly successful adventure travel company. Okay, so I had been curious enough to find out about that, and maybe I had checked out his web site and maybe I had even looked for him once or twice in airports.

But I was supposed to know better. I was supposed to remember how he let me down.

How he disappeared without a word.

Funny how just finding him there on my porch made me forget all of it. I was ready to concede that there could be an explanation, that I had misunderstood him, that he had a really good reason for walking away.

Even if fifteen years is a long, long time.

The artfully installed porch light threw a golden glow onto one side of Nick's face, leaving the other side in shadow. He looked mysterious, but then, he looked mysterious and unpredictable in full sunlight. He was still long and lean and devastatingly handsome; those Black Irish looks still hadn't failed him. And he still had the most steady gaze of anyone I've ever known.

But there were changes, albeit subtle ones. He was bigger, his features were harder, he had perfected the art of mimicking sculpture. Nick wasn't a lanky kid anymore, he'd become a man, one even more difficult to read than the teenager had been. He looked older, of course, but then so did I.

That realization put my feet in motion once more. Nick hadn't wanted me fifteen years ago—he sure as hell wasn't going to want me now. The only good thing about that was that I was pretty sure I didn't care.

It would have been nice to be completely positive, but head and heart were definitely at odds here. The champagne wasn't helping, nor was the sense that everything was finally coming up roses for me.

Fortunately, I'm a mind-over-matter kind of girl and I knew I could frost Nick right out of my life again. I flipped through my keys and strolled to the steps.

"Hello, Nick." I kept my voice even, as though I came home to find men on my porch all the time, even men who had been missing in action as long as he had been.

I even managed a cool smile—the one I saved for those women who could never make up their minds—and had exactly two seconds to congratulate myself on my composure before I looked up and saw that he wasn't fooled.

The trouble with Nick was that he was *never* fooled. I wanted to stick my tongue out at him, but that was the bubbles making me think pink.

"Hey, Phil." He was probably the only man alive who could make my hideous name sound like a benediction. He still had a voice like rough velvet and it still made parts of me tingle.

Even if I might have preferred otherwise.

I gritted my teeth and marched up the steps, grateful that I didn't stumble. He was the only one who ever called me Phil, and probably the only one who could have done so and lived to tell about it.

But then, there had been a time when I would have forgiven Nick Sullivan just about anything. I snuck another look. There were tiny laugh lines around his eyes and he had too much of a tan for this time of the year. He had probably been off somewhere exotic, I realized, then felt immediately very homebound.

Worse, an unadventurous workaholic who didn't have time to take vacations and couldn't have afforded them if she did. There was a reminder that I didn't need.

"Hey, yourself." Oh, nice business crisp voice. Well done. He actually flinched. I fit the key into the lock, though not as neatly as I might have liked. "What are you doing here?"

"I needed to see you."

Once upon a time, I would have thrown myself at Nick's feet for a bone-melting claim like that. I tried to resist temptation, but couldn't help taking another look. I had to see whether he was serious or not.

A smile touched his lips. Just a little crooked smile, the one I remembered, the one that made any woman with a pulse notice how firm his lips were, how sexy his smile was, how it made his eyes gleam. My knees threatened to give out on me, though for the sake of my pride, I blamed the champagne for that.

I gripped the door frame with all the insouciance I could

muster. He looked at me, really looked at me, and his smile broadened slightly. I knew my resolve could quickly be in very serious trouble.

"Ever heard of the phone?" The dead bolt punctuated my question with a satisfying, decisive roll of brass.

It was perfectly simple. I was going inside.

He wasn't.

I was *not* running away, though it sure felt like it.

"That's how I found you." Nick eased to his feet, evidently coming to a different conclusion than I had. "Not too many Philippa Coxwells in town, fortunately for me."

Fortunately? Why fortunately?

My heart skipped a beat—hope is one impulse that refuses to learn from experience. It was in the air that night and I suspect it runs in my blood. I stomped on hope hard and knew damn well it didn't surrender.

I could feel Nick drawing closer and knew that if he touched me all those barricades against him would come tumbling down. I blocked the door with my body and briefcase, and eyed him the way I imagine a rabbit eyes a hungry fox. "What do you want, Nick?"

He frowned quickly, then pushed one hand through his hair, leaving the dark waves in a tangle. "I need your help, Phil." Before I could go crazy speculating about that, he looked me square in the eye. Something quivered deep inside me.

"I need some legal advice and I didn't know who else to ask."

Well, romance is alive and well, but has left the galaxy in search of greener pastures.

Every champagne bubble simultaneously went flat.

See? crowed the know-all voice deep inside me, a voice which sounds a whole lot like my mother's.

And that, even more than his words, made me mad.

"You need *what?*" I dropped my briefcase inside the door,

too divested of inhibitions to hold back. I flung out my hands and he took a step back. "You think you can just show up, after fifteen years, and ask for free legal advice in the middle of the night?" I poked him in the chest to make my point. "Ever heard of business hours?" Another jab. "Ever heard of Legal Aid? Haven't I done you enough favors for a lifetime?"

"Phil, take it easy." He spoke quickly, soothingly, as though I was unpredictable. He caught my jabbing finger and folded it into the warmth of his palm. His expression was so earnest that my mouth went dry. "I know this is a surprise. If you don't want to help, I'll walk away and never bother you again. Five minutes of your time, counselor, tops."

Counselor. There's one word I would love to never hear again.

I glared to the best of my abilities, ignoring the SOS signal my captured hand was telegraphing back to mission control. "You need a lawyer so you just show up on my doorstep in the middle of the night and expect a hearing?"

"Phil, this is different."

I caught a glimpse of the vulnerability that lit his eyes. Maybe it had been there all along, but he looked suddenly so battered and uncertain that my heart went out to him.

My hand was already there.

Now, I am the greatest sucker in the world. Elaine keeps saying she'll get me a trophy. I fall prey to more cons than my pride will let me admit—most involving pictures of starving children.

And it's not just strangers who sucker me. Everyone in my family dumps their emotional payload on me. I've listened to thousands of Elaine's tales of romantic woe. I've got more secrets in my stash than a sane person would know what to do with.

Even I'm not sure sometimes.

But you've got to draw the line somewhere. And Nick had let me down. I watched his thumb slide across the back of my hand and knew I should be remembering that. I should be walking through that door and locking it against him, I should be denying him anything I could deny him.

It was a lot harder than it should have been.

"Just hear me out, Phil." He shrugged and that smile appeared again, though this time I noticed that it didn't reach his eyes. "This time I don't want to just let the law have its own way."

Unsuspectingly, Nick gave me the ammunition I needed to turn him down. If he had been asking me to listen as a friend, or for old times' sake, or if he had made any kind of reference to emotion at all, I might have buckled.

But Nick had made the mistake of bringing it back to the law again.

It was the theme song of my life and the tune grated on my ears. If the only reason he had come looking for me was because I might be a lawyer, then he could get in line with everyone else who was disappointed in my choices.

I pulled my hand out of his and reached for the door. "You came to the wrong place."

"How can that be?" Well, if he needed a map to the nerve he had hit, I was more than ready to give it to him. "You must have been called to the Bar by now. If nothing else, Phil, you get stuff done. Last time I saw you, you were accepted to all the best schools and choosing where to study."

"And I was totally miserable over it, if you recall."

Nick looked surprised and I knew he *didn't* recall.

That stung.

"But, you must have become a lawyer!"

I propped my hands on my hips. "I must have become a lawyer, because that would be useful to you? Just like I was useful to you before? And the possibility that I might be *useful* is the only reason you're here? I'm not a kitchen appliance, Nick!"

"No, Phil, you've got it wrong." His voice dropped low, down to resistance-is-futile-land. "I'm here because I trust you."

That was tempting, but he said no more and I wasn't going to fish for the thanks that was so long overdue. "I can't help you this time, Nick. I'm not a lawyer."

"Phil, that's nuts. How can you not be a lawyer?"

"I'm not, and even better, it's all your fault."

Now, Nick looked irked, and in a way, it was a relief to see his composure slip. "What the hell is that supposed to mean? Everyone in your family goes to law school."

"But you were the one who told me to stop living other people's dreams and follow my own." I shrugged. "So, I took your advice." I pushed open the door and started to follow my briefcase.

His eyes widened. "What?"

"I'm a garden designer." I smiled. "And a damn good one."

But if I had expected him to be annoyed by this revelation, I'd bet on the wrong horse. Nick's frustration faded into admiration, as dizzying a sight as I had ever seen. He smiled at me, as though I'd hung the sun and moon, then reached out to brush a fingertip across my cheek. That old magic crackled between us, and my face tingled from his touch.

"Good for you," he whispered.

Nick has always had the most amazing eyes—a perfectly clear green that seemed to slice right through your soul and ferret out your secrets. He was looking at me as though I was a new discovery, as though he had never really seen me before, as though he was ready to launch a prolonged exploration of my terra incognita.

It wasn't all bad, as sensations went. I wasn't the only one who took a step closer.

Just between you and me, I really thought he might kiss me

then. Maybe it was that sense that everything was coming up aces as of today, maybe it was the hope of that desperate sixteen-year-old speaking up once more.

And, okay, for a minute there, I let hope out of its cage.

Call it a moment of weakness.

His eyes narrowed slightly, and suddenly I wondered how much he did see. Scary thought. I turned and fumbled with the key, cursing myself for forgetting how perceptive he was, for being dumb enough to let my guard down. I felt the heat of a blush from nipples to hairline.

"Sorry, can't help," I said quickly.

And I ran.

Well, not exactly ran. More like lunged (or perhaps tripped) across the threshold of my apartment, forced a smile, said good night and shut the door on that sharp gaze.

Then I leaned back against the door, considered the crack in the ceiling that I'd been meaning to fix, and felt like an ass.

Everything was jumbled up inside me, but at least I should have held the conviction that I had done the right thing.

I didn't have any such thing.

I reviewed the bidding. Nick was trouble, everyone had always said so, and though I hadn't believed it for the longest time, he'd proven the truth of it to me in the end. It doesn't come much more cheaply than a thank-you, but he hadn't ante'd up. I was old enough to know better than to trust him again, old enough to not expect anything different from him, old enough to have learned from my mistakes. I certainly shouldn't have been charmed by the brush of a warm fingertip.

Which explained, of course, why I felt so *mean*.

I took a deep breath and crossed to the kitchen. The answering machine light was flashing. Maybe I'd been too hard on ol' Nick. Maybe he had picked up the phone earlier in the day.

Did I just want to hear his voice again?

Not wanting to go there, I stabbed at the replay button. I rolled my eyes as a familiar, slightly slurred voice filled my kitchen.

It wasn't Nick.

"Philippa? If you're there, pick up." A long pause followed, then Mom took a sip and I could guess of what. "Well, I certainly hope you're not working late again. That's no way to find a husband, Philippa, all cooped up in that terrible office of yours. And what an area it's in. Surely you could have found something more posh, something with affluent neighbors where you might be *seen* . . . Oh! Maybe you're on a date tonight."

Mom's voice warmed in a most predictable way. I leaned against the counter and pinched the bridge of my nose. So maybe my life had two familiar theme songs, both of which grated on my nerves.

"Now wouldn't that be a wonderful surprise. Does he have money? Did he take you somewhere nice? I want to hear all the details. I certainly hope he comes from a good family, Philippa, for you do have less discrimination than any young woman I've ever known."

Mom's voice rose slightly and she settled in for a rant. The woman could fill my tape from start to finish, just ruminating through my endless potential and considerable list of shortfalls.

"Which is probably why you're not on a date at all!" She exhaled indignantly. "You're probably out *gallivanting* around with that partner of yours."

I've always wanted to know how to gallivant. It sounds like fun. My mother would not seem to be the kind of person who would really know.

She was right about Elaine, though. Elaine probably wrote the book on gallivanting. I'd have to ask for instruction.

"That Elaine is a *tart,* Philippa, the worst kind of trash and you'll never find a decent prospect while you consort with the likes of her . . ."

I hit the stop button. "She's my friend," I firmly told the machine, which was just about as effective as telling that to my mother and a lot less stressful. I rewound the tape without listening to the rest of the lecture.

Maybe my life *was* a bit thin in the romantic department. Maybe parting badly with Nick once didn't mean we should part badly again.

Maybe I am the world's heavyweight champion sucker.

But maybe I owed him something, both for the years of friendship we had shared and for giving me the courage to buck my family's expectations. Maybe I was curious as to why he had come back, let alone why he thought he needed a lawyer. And maybe I *could* help him. Osmosis, you know. I've picked up a lot of legal guck, albeit unwillingly, over the years.

I rubbed my fingertips over that glowing spot on my cheek. Maybe it was all just a rationalization to have my own Dream Date Ken look at me one more time as though I was the most gorgeous woman alive.

So, sue me.

I was all thumbs with the dead bolt, but finally opened the door and shouted into the night, neighbors be damned. "Five minutes and not a second more!"

He hadn't gone far, not quite a block. The streetlight silhouetted Nick with yellow light as he turned slowly to face me. I had a sense that I had surprised him—for once—and it made me cheeky.

I tapped my watch. "Get it in gear, Sullivan. I'm already counting."

I saw his grin flash and felt a giddy rush that had nothing to do with champagne. He strode back to the door with startling speed and caught my hand in his before I could step away.

His eyes shone and I could smell the tang of his cologne. Oh, it was a good one. My toes curled in my shoes and my heart went pit-a-pat. He pressed a fleeting kiss to my knuckles like an old-fashioned courtier.

"I owe you big for this, Phil," he murmured in that black velvet voice and I felt drunk all over again.

Chapter 2

I was thinking that this hadn't been a really four-star idea. Lady Luck had her limits after all—or maybe it was more accurate to say that I wasn't too sure of mine. I put on the kettle and surreptitiously rubbed my tingling knuckles, stealing a glance at Nick through my lashes as he took off his leather jacket.

Yum.

Naturally, I couldn't think of a single clever thing to say. If there's a jarring little fact of life that I could do without, it's that people from your past can send you straight back there just by crossing your field of vision. Maybe it's worse for people like me who've deliberately traveled a long way away from their past, who've redefined themselves and their lives. Maybe not.

It is annoying, though.

And it's the reason why I had left Rosemount with nary a backward glance. Who wants to be a plump, unpopular and uncertain teenager again? Not me. Been there, done that and burned the evidence. Encountering people from Rosemount High puts me right back in Fat Philippa's skin. There's a lot of it to spare, but the view doesn't much suit me these days.

It never did really.

But it's tough to put distance between the kid you were and the woman you want to be when every five minutes someone is commenting on how far you've got to go. So, I left Rosemount and I only go back when it's absolutely necessary.

Which is a little too often.

This flashback backlash was a hundred times worse with Nick, the closest I had come to having a friend in high school. The "dynamic duo," he used to call us, but we really were the "outsiders." I was fat and he was short—and he was bad blood, to boot, as well as a comparative newcomer. Which of course was why I deliberately befriended him in the first place.

Once a sucker, always a sucker.

But now he was in my kitchen, an incongruity if ever there had been one. Nick hung his jacket over the back of his chair, then stretched out his long legs and crossed them at the ankles. He was wearing jeans and suede desert boots, a teal green t-shirt that clung to his muscles and ensured I had no doubt how truly magnificent a male specimen he was.

Funny, I never realized how warm that kitchen could be. I resolved to talk to the landlord about the heating being too high. Nick practically filled the room, which suddenly looked very feminine and too small for two people.

I fussed with the teapot and remembered when he had suddenly grown taller. Really suddenly and really tall. He must have sprouted a foot and a half in a year. And whenever someone asked, he had explained, absolute deadpan, "The return policy expired, so Lucia decided to feed us after all."

Probably half of Rosemount believed him. It was too easy to

imagine that the boys' grandmother and reluctant guardian would have declined to feed them.

According to rumor, she hadn't, after all, been thrilled to take them in.

"Dragon Lady" Lucia was the subject of a tremendous quantity of discussion in Rosemount. In fact, if she ever moved away, gossip would completely dry up—or at least, cease to flourish as it currently did. And her neighbor, Mrs. Donnelly, would lose preeminent status among the gossipmongers.

Lucia was supposed to be a witch, or rumoured to at least have the Evil Eye. She obviously didn't give a damn what anyone said about her. She had been known to spin around and shout "boo" at children who boldly dared each other to follow her. That would be more funny if she hadn't scared the living crap out of me more than once.

When there was nothing else to fiddle with, I kicked off my heels as though I was much more comfortable in Nick's presence than I was, and chucked my suit jacket over the back of a chair. I didn't sit down, but leaned back against the counter, supposedly waiting for the kettle to boil.

I caught him checking out my legs and was so snared in my Fat Philippa past that I was shocked at his obvious appreciation. I turned back to the kettle, well aware that he was still looking.

"You've changed, Phil."

"It's been a long time." I had a hard time catching my breath, but tapped my watch. "Time's a-wasting."

"Yeah." He drew a line on the tabletop with his thumb, giving me the sense that he was trying to hide something from me.

That would have been a first.

I opted to help, all the better to get him on his way before I forgot everything I was supposed to remember about him. "So, why did you come back?"

"Lucia invited me."

"I thought you weren't speaking." Events of all those years past hovered at the periphery of our conversation but neither of us were ready to talk about that.

"We weren't." His lips twisted, his expression revealing his inexplicable affection for Lucia. He had always been nuts about her, though God only knew why. "Not that such details would stop Lucia from having her say."

Then he tapped a finger on the table. "But she didn't have a chance to tell me what she wanted, Phil." He looked up, his gaze stark. "She was dead when I got to the house."

Dead?

I opened my mouth and shut it again, not knowing what to say. I couldn't imagine Lucia dead. She was vital, I had to give her that, and possessed of the strength of ten immortals.

I tried again and this time managed to croak out something. "Dead tired?"

"Murdered."

Now there is one of those words you don't much expect to hear in the normal course of conversation—unless, of course, your name is Hercule Poirot or Jessica Fletcher.

Mine isn't.

For a minute, I knew I'd heard him wrong. This was my kitchen, after all, and not usually a hotbed of sordid tales. "Murdered? Are you sure?"

"No doubt about it." He looked very grim. "I found her in the greenhouse."

I forgot my shyness and sat down opposite him. "But Nick, *murdered?* Maybe it was an accident. She could have fallen. Or had a heart attack."

He looked skeptical. "And jabbed a knife into her throat in the midst of it?"

I had to admit that seemed unlikely.

"She'd been stabbed with a little stiletto that I bought for her when I was in Venice." Nick rubbed his face with his hands, as though he could scrub the memory of the sight away. "I thought she'd enjoy using it as a letter opener. It's a nasty but ornate little thing."

It sounded like something Lucia would like, but that still didn't give me a clue what to say.

"Murder's not something you get wrong, Phil. There was blood everywhere and . . ." His throat worked and I reached across the table to touch his hand. He closed his fingers over mine, hard, and looked away.

I had to ask.

Because this brought the past squarely into the present, and easily explained why he had come to me.

"Did you do it?"

"No!" The look he gave me could have cut glass. "Why would I kill her?"

I tried to remain objective. "You two did have that fight."

"Right, so she might have cheerfully killed me, not the other way around." Nick shook his head. "She was the one who was so angry."

Because he had lied to her. The past hovered a little more insistently, but didn't get any air time all the same.

"So, why did she invite you back now? Why would she bother?"

"I don't know. Maybe because I sent her that gift and reestablished contact between us." He flicked me a glance that spoke volumes. "I didn't ask a lot of questions."

But he came.

He cleared his throat when I didn't say anything. His voice dropped lower as though he was confessing a secret. "I missed her."

If anyone could miss Lucia, it would be him. Nick had always been a bit unconventional in his tastes—and he had always had that rapport with the Dragon Lady.

She did have a soft spot or two. Even I'd seen it once, and Lucia and I were far from pals.

"So, who did it? Who would have wanted to kill her?"

"Who *wouldn't* have wanted to kill her?" he muttered. "Probably most of Rosemount would have been glad to do the honors."

"Oh, come on. Lucia was a bit"—I had to search for a diplomatic word choice—"*opinionated,* but . . ."

"More than a bit opinionated, Phil. They didn't call her the Dragon Lady for nothing."

I hadn't thought that he knew about that moniker. He pushed to his feet and paced the length of the room and back. I was weak enough to enjoy the view.

"I think she pissed off everyone in a fifty-mile radius at one time or another." He shook his head and that smile touched his lips again, his next words so quiet that I barely heard them. "She probably kept a list in her phone book, just to make sure she didn't miss anyone."

I didn't dare laugh. It was probably true.

"But she was killed with a gift from you, right before your expected return." I was thinking out loud. "It can't have been just anybody. That's too many coincidences. And who would have known you were coming?"

Nick looked up, his expression wary. "She would have told one person, for sure."

I knew we were thinking exactly the same thing. His younger brother, Sean, might as well have pulled up a chair and joined the conversation.

"Are you going to let him do it?"

"Not this time." Nick shook his head with finality. He sat backward on his chair again, his expression intent. "But I don't know what to do to make this come right."

"Which was why you came here."

"Old instincts die hard." He grimaced, then met my gaze steadily again. "Being in Rosemount meant I should talk to you."

I had a lump in my throat the size of Texas. "For legal advice."

"Maybe not just that." He reached out and took my hand this time, running his thumb across the back of my hand and putting an army of tingles on the march. "When did you become a girl, Phil?"

The mercury in the kitchen inched up a little higher.

I watched his fingertip on the back of my hand. It was true that I used to wear a lot of sweatshirts and baggy clothes, trying to hide mass behind fabric. I guess it wasn't very feminine.

"Fifteen years is a long time."

"Yes, it is." He sat back abruptly, his eyes narrowed, and my abandoned hand felt suddenly cold. He pushed both hands through his hair and the romantic interlude was clearly over.

I knew I'd spend hours thinking of all the brilliant things I could have said, if only I'd thought of them in time. Maybe that had sounded like an accusation to him.

In a way, I guess it was.

"I must have left fingerprints all over the place," Nick muttered, his thoughts clearly moving on. "It's not as though they're not on file. Mrs. Donnelly probably saw me go in and out."

"That old busybody."

He was on his feet before I even saw him move, and paced the length of the kitchen like a caged tiger. "They're probably looking for me now."

"Did you call the cops?"

"How could I? You know what they would think."

Yup, I knew what they would think. What's bred in the bone comes out in the flesh. Another Sullivan good for only locking up and throwing away the key. Here's our boy again, back to his old tricks. This time, let's make it stick.

"So, what are you going to do?"

He shrugged into his jacket. "I'm going to make sure that justice is done."

"The trick is that you'll have to stay out of jail to do it."

He almost smiled. "Got it in one. You were never one to mince words." His gaze swept over me. "Same old Phil, but in shiny new packaging." I blushed, though I wondered what I looked like to him.

He looked good enough to eat to me. Those little lines around his eyes deepened when he smiled and I could see now that there was a little bit of silver at his temples. I remembered that I hadn't had dessert tonight.

But then, I wasn't that kind of woman.

I wondered whether maybe I should be.

We stared at each other as the steam from the kettle filled the kitchen. I was telling myself not to offer to help, he was probably telling himself to leave, but something had stirred to life between us—something that made us a little less anxious to part ways this time.

The kettle boiled and I got up to make the tea. He paced the length of the kitchen again, clearly impatient to do something. I was encouraged that he didn't choose the walking-out-the-door option.

"I heard the sirens before I left. Someone must have called the cops when I went into the house."

"Mrs. Donnelly being helpful again."

He grimaced. "It must be all over the news by now. Phil, I shouldn't have come here. You shouldn't be involved, not again."

His concern awakened a nice, warm glow. I flicked on the radio, because it was close at hand and I wasn't ready for him to walk out of my life again. I fiddled with the dial and honed in on a station just in time to catch a musical ditty.

"All the news, all the time," sang the chorus.

Nick stopped to listen, leaning against the counter right beside me. Even when he wasn't moving, he seemed to vibrate with an inner urgency.

Like a volcano on the verge of eruption. I stared at his hands and wondered whether it was fatal to be around this particular fault line. My mouth went dry.

What if the wheel of fortune *had* finally rolled around for me? It was a heady possibility and it wouldn't have taken anything less monumental to make the company move into the black this week.

I've always believed in luck and always done my best to lure some my way. I've been avoiding ladders and skipping number thirteen, petting all black cats and tossing salt over my shoulder for as long as I can remember. A long time ago, Fat Philippa figured she needed all the help she could get.

And now I had a sense that things were going to pay off big. It was either intuition or indigestion. What if my ship had come in? There might very well be a pair of ruby slippers lurking in my closet, just waiting for me to put them on and dance like Ginger Rogers.

What if the stars were lined up so perfectly that any fool with a glass of champagne in their belly could make a wish and that wish might come true?

Okay, so I wished. I'd wished this particular wish a few times before, twice to be accurate. You know what they say, third time lucky. Besides, it can't hurt to keep your options covered, can it?

A toothpaste commercial was followed by news of two airliners nearly colliding somewhere over the Midwest and testimonials of a variety of aviation experts.

We stood and waited, and now I know how it feels to have bated breath. I was certain each story would be about the horrific murder of a darling older eccentric in sleepy Rosemount.

But the newscaster rolled through a succession of stories that became progressively less violent and sensational. The news finished with the rise to glory of a high school girl's volleyball team, obviously the warm and fuzzy human interest story. The music rolled, followed by a few commercials and the ditty.

Then, the newscaster started with the same lead story as he had the previous half hour.

"They haven't *found* her yet!" Nick breathed. "How can that be?"

"Maybe it's too soon. When were you there?"

"Around six, right after my flight got in." He shook his head and headed for the door. "I've got to go back there."

"Are you nuts? You just said you weren't going to let Sean do this to you."

"Well, I can't just let her rot there."

"So, you'll walk in and incriminate yourself. Brilliant move."

His words came through gritted teeth. "I can't abandon her there. It's not right."

The words were out before I could stop them, some part of me reaching out to do a little bit more than just wish. He looked so upset and it seemed such a small thing to do. "Then, I'll 'find' her, not you."

"What?"

"I'll discover the body." He looked at me as though I had gone insane. I was half certain that I had, but smiled valiantly. "Favor for a friend. That's all."

"That's nuts." Nick propped his hands on his hips, skepticism personified. "What possible reason could you have for being in Lucia's greenhouse at one o'clock in the morning?"

"None. But I could have an excuse at, say, eight in the morning."

"How?"

"She could have hired me."

"Lucia has the tightest purse strings of anyone alive." He frowned at his own use of present tense but kept using it anyhow. "She'd never pay anyone to design her garden."

"Older people get whimsical. And who's to deny that she called me?" I was on a roll, slipping on my sales persona without even realizing it myself. "It could just be a consultation. No one will know but me and Lucia, and she's not going to tell."

He shook his head and I couldn't begin to guess his thoughts, though the heat in his eyes was enough to fuel Greater Boston for the month of January. "What makes you jump in to help, Phil?"

I shrugged, uncomfortable with his scrutiny. I'd die before I admitted I did this more for him than anyone else. "It's just the way I am."

"I know. But it's not the way *I* am to let other people solve things for me. You're not going there and that's that."

Ah, male pride. You've got to love it. I turned back to the kettle. "Then go yourself. I hear the food's better at the county jail these days."

I felt him glare at me. "Phil, I appreciate your offer, but I don't think your going there is a good idea."

"While your going there is a great one?"

He started to pace again, then pivoted as inspiration struck. "I could make an anonymous call."

"You could, but they'll track the number."

"Then, there's no other way." He headed for the door.

"What if they *have* found Lucia and are waiting for you to return to the scene of the crime?" I asked sweetly when he was halfway across the threshold. "Isn't that supposed to be the great weakness of murderers? They can't leave well enough alone? You could walk right into your pal O'Reilly's arms. I'm sure he'd love it."

Nick spun to face me. "Tell me O'Reilly isn't still there." I shrugged apologetically and he swore. "And if *you* walk in?"

"I've got a cover story. Innocent bystander. It's perfect, Nick, so you might as well admit it."

"I don't want you involved."

Oh, nothing like a little male protectiveness to make a woman get all mushy inside. I did my best to hide my response. "Sadly, you haven't got any other options."

We stared at each other for a long moment and I could virtually see him going through the alternatives, assessing and discarding each one in turn.

He shut the door firmly, then shook his head. "All right, Phil. You're on." He stuck out his hand to shake on it. His thumb slid over my hand in a slow caress that could have stopped my heart cold. "Looks like I owe you again."

It wasn't quite the thanks I had once hoped for, but it was pretty good stuff.

"We do this on my terms, though." His expression set stubbornly. "I'll meet you there."

"Oh, that's a great idea. And I used to think you were a smart guy." I rolled my eyes. Maybe I wasn't playing too gently with him, but he couldn't have expected sweetness and light after all this time. "How is being seen lurking around the house going to help you here?"

"I won't be seen."

"Because you'll will everyone to be blind? Have you learned voodoo while you were gone?"

"Phil . . ."

"Please, Nick. We're talking about X-Ray Vision Donnelly here. I'm sure she keeps a ledger of all doings at Lucia's place." I flung out my hands. "And how are you going to get there? Do you really think renting a car with a credit card with your name on it in order to drive to Rosemount is a brilliant idea? If you take the bus, do you think no one will see you?"

"I could walk there."

"Mmm. Start now and maybe the commuters won't all notice you trudging along the shoulder."

"So maybe I'm not thinking too clearly." His shoulders sagged as he rubbed his brow, and I touched his arm gently.

"You haven't had a great day, have you?"

His hand closed over mine and we stood there together in silence. Finally he gave my hand a little squeeze of thanks, then deliberately put some distance between us.

"And you always said you didn't have a devious mind." He leaned against the counter, arms folded across his chest. "Okay, Phil, tell me your plan."

"I'll drive. You can tag along if you want, but you'll stay in the Beast."

"The Beast? Sounds Biblical."

"It's our beloved company truck. Don't you name your cars?"

"Never had one." While I blinked at that, he turned away. He picked up one of the business cards from the stack I keep on the counter, always at the ready.

His obvious approval pleased me a lot more than I should have let it. "Your own partnership? Or are there more Coxwells in the garden than I knew about?"

"Just me in the garden and yes, it's a partnership. Elaine Pope and I. She does more interior stuff. I'm the plant woman."

"How's it going?"

My chest puffed with pride and I couldn't have stopped my smile to save my life. "We signed a deal today that will make us profitable for the first time."

He must have heard the satisfaction that was practically oozing out my pores because he smiled too. "Oh, I remember that day. There's nothing like moving into the black."

I tried to sound casual, but probably failed. "You have your own business too?"

As if I didn't know every damn detail.

Nick shrugged and his smile faded to nothing. "I had an adventure travel business. I just sold it off to the competition."

That surprised me, but he didn't give me a chance to ask anything more. Interrogation interruptus, that was Nick all over.

He waved my card at me. "Your family must be proud."

I rolled my eyes. "As if. Do you remember my family?"

And he laughed. Nick has a great laugh, though he doesn't let it loose very often. It seems to roll up right from his toes and flow over everything in its path. "Some things never change, do they Phil?"

I hoped that he wasn't just talking about my family. "No, they sure don't."

Our gazes caught again and I caught my breath at the look in his eyes. His smile faded and he stepped closer, lifting one finger to touch my cheek. He was looking at me again, really looking, and I felt like the eighth marvel of the world.

"Maybe that's a good thing," he whispered in that whiskey voice. He hesitated only a moment, as though giving me time to duck away, then leaned down and kissed me.

You know, some things are eroded by yearning—once delivered, they fall far short of the accumulated height of expectation, whereas on their own, without that yearning, they might have made a decent showing. I had wondered how Nick would kiss for about twenty-five years, off and on, and his kiss might very easily have been a disappointment.

It wasn't, not by a long shot.

His kiss was gentle, yet hinted at strength, it was firm without being hard, it was passionate without being pushy. Mostly it was persuasive, a promise of potential, a tiny taste of what this volcano could offer to those who dared to slip over the side.

His kiss nudged awake the starlight that had dozed off in my veins, then hitched a ride to Venus.

I could have kissed him for a week, but he suddenly stepped back and looked away.

"Meet you at your office at seven," he said quickly, more quickly than he usually spoke.

He pocketed my card and was out the door in a heartbeat. I had the sense that he was on the run from me, which would have been pretty funny if it had been the case. Without so much as a backward glance, he was gone into the night, swallowed so completely by the darkness that he might really have been a champagne fantasy.

But my lips burned.

Fantasies have never managed that. I locked the dead bolt and looked at that crack in the ceiling again, telling myself that this was no big deal. One kiss did not a future make.

Ha. My heart told me to check on those ruby slippers before I gave it up so easily.

But no, reason must prevail. I was just going to do a small favor for an old friend, and that would be that. Some favor, discovering a body that had been laying in the sun for a day or so. I wrinkled my nose at that prospect. But it was perfectly mundane, get in, get out, back at my desk by lunch and probably never see Nick again. My pounding heart missed a beat and I tasted him on my lips once more.

But maybe not. He had come to me, after all. He had confided in me, too, and I knew how reticent he was.

And he had kissed me. Fa la la.

I danced toward the bedroom, in no doubt that the world was my oyster. I knew I was going to dream about Nick Sullivan.

If I managed to sleep at all.

He walked.

He had no clear idea where to go, at least for the short term, but it didn't matter. He had learned over the years to sleep when he could and get by without when he couldn't—and there was no way he'd be sleeping tonight. He did his best thinking while walking and he had a lot of thinking to do.

He wasn't ready to think about Phil Coxwell just yet.

He still couldn't believe that Lucia was dead. Even though they hadn't talked for years, he had known she was there. He had felt her presence, like a vigilant if temperamental guardian angel.

At least he had always thought that was what he felt. He still was aware of that force of will, which only proved how much he had kidded himself. Perhaps it was his own conscience. It certainly wasn't Lucia.

Because she was dead.

He thought about change.

He shoved his hands into his pockets and lengthened his stride. Cars flew past him, headlights sweeping over him as the cars hurried from here to there. Everyone was in a hurry, everyone had somewhere to go and something to do, everyone was filled with purpose. Everyone embraced change and "progress."

Everyone but him. He'd seen change, he'd witnessed the so-called progress that had spun from his influence and he didn't like the view. He had thought he was doing something good but it was just an illusion. It had gone terribly wrong.

And it was his fault.

It seemed that no good deed of Nick's ever went unpunished. For years, he had tried to protect Sean from the results of his own misdeeds, from the potential consequences for both of them.

He had tried to protect Lucia from the truth about her favorite grandson. The price of his last lie had been his own relationship with her, a treasure which he had valued less than he should have done.

And when he had finally returned to mend fences with his grandmother, it had cost Lucia her life. Sean had always been one to make the most of the barest sliver of opportunity.

While he had paved a personal road to hell with good intentions.

Not that he could do much about it now. He turned up his collar against the wind. The money from the sale of his company would always feel dirty in his hands, tainted by what had created its value. He spent it because he had no other options, but he didn't enjoy these fruits of his success.

More than once, he had come close to giving it all to a charity, some organization that fed children in the third world or paid for vaccinations taken for granted in the first. But he had been to too many of those countries and seen too many of those charitable dollars end up in pockets they were never intended to line.

The money was his millstone and it might as well have hung around his neck.

He was a steady walker, used to covering a lot of ground with a minimum of effort. His feet were tired by the time he reached Cambridge, a gift from the relentless concrete. He headed for Mount Auburn Cemetery and the relief of greenery.

Even at night, there was a sense of spring in the buds on the trees and the bulbs bursting from the earth. The signs of rebirth invigorated him, and made him think of Phil. A garden designer. He could imagine her doing that, putting her mix of gentleness and severity to good use in a garden.

Her character would have been wasted on the law.

If she had been with him now, she could have told him what every plant was, how it would bloom, how big it would become. She would have infected each description with her enthusiasm and passion.

She would have made him smile. Even picturing her here, talking about plants in the dead of the night, did make him smile. He believed she would have done it.

By the time he had settled against a cold stone to watch the moon rise, he was inclined to be less hard on himself. There was one thing he had done that hadn't gone wrong in the end. Phil blamed him for setting her on the course to making her own choices. He didn't remember telling her to do so, but that was beside the point.

He liked the rare sense that he had been a catalyst for change that had proven positive. He watched the moon tear itself free of the horizon and cast its glow on the silhouette of Boston, enjoying the knowledge that he had been at the root of a good change.

He wasn't an habitual smoker, but occasionally indulged when the moment was right. He wished he had a cigarette now, to turn in his fingers, to watch the red glow of the ember, to blow smoke rings at the stars.

Lucia had taught him to blow smoke rings. It would have been a fitting tribute to her. But he didn't have a cigarette and he wasn't likely to find one here.

He did without, as he so often did without so many things.

He had had his last butt in Chile, lost in the solitude of a national park that went on forever. He had been on a camping trip with half a dozen others, packed into an ancient blue minivan. The park was cut by a gravel road apparently untraveled by anyone other than themselves, because they drove for hours without seeing another vehicle or human.

Their truck had overheated at twilight and the local driver had opened the hood to study the engine. It seemed a peculiarity of South Americans, this conviction that just looking at the engine would make it spontaneously repair itself. And the more people who stared, the better. He had seen buses in the Andes broken down and drawn to the shoulder, their entire payload gathered around to eyeball the engine in silence.

He had joined the driver that evening, they had exchanged grim prognoses in Spanish, then the cook had climbed out to offer his pack of cigarettes. The three of them had stood there beneath a brilliant canopy of stars, smoking, collectively willing the engine back to life.

It hadn't worked, but neither would have any expression of frustration. When the last cigarette was ground out under a heel, the three of them had pulled out the toolbox and set to work.

That moon had been bright enough that they hadn't needed a flashlight. In contrast, this moon fought valiantly against the electrical glow of the city, but was still diminished to a distant glow. A night-light in the celestial bathroom. Even the stars were so dim here.

But one star winked at him, as though it was telling him to buck up. It made him think again of a certain auburn-haired woman, one who had no trouble sharing her thoughts.

Phil had always been off-limits, both because she was his friend, and because she was sweet on his brother. Not that Sean had ever reciprocated in kind. Consoling Phil when Sean treated her badly had been just part of the big brother cleanup and protection plan.

Hadn't it?

And she had gone along with Nick's own lie to protect Sean from his own mistake, keeping the secret for Sean's sake.

Hadn't she?

But if she had, why hadn't anything ever come of it? He had half-expected Sean to have capitalized on Phil's complicity, to have used her affection for him against her. He had more than expected her to be either with Sean and miserable about it, or abandoned and embittered.

But she seemed to have completely forgotten Sean.

Or was that just Phil's tough talk?

He didn't know and it irritated him more than he knew it should have. After all, even dreading a confrontation with his brother, even suspecting that his brother might be with Phil, he hadn't been able to stay away from her.

Phil had always had that effect upon him. It was the way she listened, the way she wasn't afraid to speak her mind, the way she made him feel at ease.

He had thought that was because they were friends, a tentative balance at best between teenagers of different genders and one he had worked hard not to upset.

But if Phil was yearning for his brother, how could she kiss him as though she would eat him alive? She was the most honest person he had ever known, and her passion couldn't be a lie.

But was she making do with one brother because the other hadn't shown? There was an ugly possibility and one that had occurred to him when her lips clung so sweetly to his. He'd stood in for Sean more than enough times in his life. The sense that he was doing it again had sent him running from Phil like an idiot.

The brothers had always looked similar, close enough in appearance that some people confused them. In manner, they had been like night and day, but few got friendly enough with the Sullivans to detect that. Both had been useful situations once.

At least to Sean.

But not this time. If Nick kissed Phil again, he'd make sure she knew which brother he was.

Speaking of the devil, he supposed he had avoided the inevitable long enough. Eventually the dirty work has to be done. He abandoned his imaginary cigarette and went to work.

He was, admittedly, curious.

He found the address in the North End without a lot of trouble, although the building's windows were all in darkness when he arrived there. The street was close enough to Hanover Street to be a bit busy, which suited him.

Sean's was #2, according to the white pages, and he managed to get a look at the array of buzzers by the door on a stroll-by. Three buzzers, three floors, "Sullivan" beside the middle one. No mysteries there. He found a niche between the buildings opposite and hunkered down between the shadowed trash cans to wait.

He was rewarded just after three. The arguing couple didn't attract his eye initially, until the man raised his voice in anger. Nick's head snapped up at the familiarity of that drunken slur. He straightened silently, his eyes narrowing as his brother gave the woman a push up the stairs that was just a bit too helpful.

He noted with some satisfaction that he and his brother didn't look that similar anymore.

The lights came on in the second-floor windows a moment later, the small, dark-haired woman rushing to pull the blinds. Sean peeled off his coat with a deliberation Nick knew to be wary of, his gaze fixed on the woman.

She didn't get the last blind down quickly enough. Nick flinched as his brother struck her shoulder. Hard. She cried out and Sean shouted something. He hauled down the blind and turned on her again, a menacing silhouette.

A neighbor's light flicked out, as though that person chose deliberately to not be involved.

Nick did not share the neighbor's reservations. It was time his brother learned something about repercussions.

He strode to a pay phone and called 911. He reported a domestic squabble, described what he had seen and gave both the address and Sean's name.

When the dispatcher asked for his own, he hung up.

He waited for the squad car to arrive, lurking in the shadows with his hands balled in his pockets. He wanted desperately to intervene, but Phil's implication that he wasn't thinking straight rang in his ears.

She was probably right.

The cops came fairly quickly. He waited until they took Sean away, his brother loudly protesting innocence all the way. He'd be out in no time, Nick knew it. The woman wept on the stairs, disregarding the earnest advice of a policewoman.

He'd done what he could, but he didn't feel a lot better. He couldn't solve this, though it was a step in the right direction. The squad car pulled away and he stepped into the thinning crowd on Hanover. He walked, more quickly now, with even less destination. The night was getting colder, but anger kept him warm.

By dawn, he'd dealt with the worst of his frustration. He fingered the card in his pocket, checked the address and turned toward Phil's office, anticipation lightening his step.

Chapter 3

Morning came early and it was not a pretty sight. The Widow Clicquot had proven to be a vengeful piece of work. My head was pounding when the alarm went off. I vaguely remembered saying to Elaine that the label didn't make the woman look like a party girl. It was dark and cold, as though the weatherman had forgotten it was supposed to be spring. I groaned a lot, got out of bed and faced the bathroom mirror for the bad news.

And it was bad. My eyes were puffy in that oh-so-attractive I'm-an-eighty-year-old-alcoholic kind of way. Luck was wounded in a gutter and would die a painful death the moment Nick got a look at how scary mornings could be.

So much for second chances.

Now, I am *not* a morning person, not by any stretch of the imagination, and a mere five hours sleep treads dangerously close to hell in my worldview. Heaven, in case you're interested, involves sleeping in until at least eleven, lounging around in silky pajamas, and perusing horticultural catalogues. I added Nick, naked and enthralled, to the image and felt somewhat perkier.

Elaine insists that my reluctance to face a new day is due to a "tragic" deficiency of caffeine in my bloodstream. Elaine runs on the high-voltage stuff—she's a double espresso before bed kind of girl, and probably sleeps like a baby.

Only fools underestimate her.

I refuse to get on the coffee bandwagon, since I won't come within spitting distance of any addictive substance, whether it's legal or not. Last night had been an exception and even the bubbles were on the side of negative reinforcement this morning.

Now, chocolate is beyond the jurisdiction of this addictive substances injunction. A rare exception. Maybe a loophole. Or somewhere there had been a precedent. I know the fundamental right of every mortal to eat chocolate is in the Geneva Convention.

If it isn't, it should be. The precise legal rationale is unimportant—see? I told you I wasn't cut out for that stuff—but the chocolate is not. It must be bittersweet, it must be of European manufacture, and access to it must not be impeded.

Otherwise things can get ugly.

Many foods have been banished from my kitchen and diet because of their betrayal of me in those dark teenage years—auslander potato chips, expat donuts, juvenile-tried-in-adult-court home fries—but my relationship with chocolate is beyond such restrictions.

Our love affair borders on the divine. All transgressions can be forgiven for one's soul mate—as long as it remembers its place. I handle chocolate as a controlled substance, since prolonged exposure results in extreme lateral growth. One chocolate bar every month and not one bite more is my allotment.

Fantasies fortunately don't count.

I buy the chocolate on the first of the month, as regularly as clockwork, and ogle it in the fridge for as long as I can stand it. Once it's gone, I'm S.O.L. until the first rolls around again. Under this agreement, the chocolate I do eat is forbidden to land on my hips.

Thus far, treaty terms had been maintained by both sides.

On this bleary-eyed morning, I surveyed the healthy contents of my fridge and knew I couldn't face yogurt. I was sleep-deprived, hungover, and—remembering this part a bit too late to do anything about it—en route to discovering a slightly stale corpse.

And meeting Nick again, maybe without the sparkle of Fortune's smile.

Nervous? You bet. Sustenance for the soul was due.

It lurked in the back of the fridge, a glorious truffle-filled Belgian confection that I had hidden from myself but knew damn well was there. This month's chocolate orgasm. I pounced on it before it could get playful, inhaled half of it before I had realized what I had done.

Discipline returned and I savored the rest in the slow motion it deserved, to heck with the three weeks remaining in the month. It was chocolate bliss. I rolled each bite around my mouth in a near-swoon, and by this one deed, made myself ten minutes later than I already was.

It was worth it.

The crumpled gold foil brought the inevitable panic, but I reminded myself sternly that my luck had changed. Just to prove the point, I opted for my little black Chanel suit, because the skirt has a mercilessly sleek fit. One wrongful meal and I'll pop the zipper.

And this morning, I didn't even need control tops. Time for a victory dance. It looked good—but then, black is my best color. Besides its slimming effect, it makes my hair look more red. The sapphire blouse makes my eyes look more blue than they really are and yes, I had a bit of color in my cheeks this morning despite my aching head.

Because I was triumphant. My luck had turned. I could eat chocolate for breakfast! I could push the books into the black with a single contract! I could kiss Nick Sullivan!

I was Woman. I was Invincible. I roared in the bedroom and probably was responsible for the thump of my upstairs neighbor falling out of bed.

I put on my lipstick in two expert swipes, grabbed my keys and jacket, jammed on my heels and ran for the door. There was a cab ambling down the street, evidently looking just for me.

I could get used to living like this.

I flagged the cab down and settled in, relieved to find my tiny calculator in this purse. I could *calculate* the tip to the precision of eight decimal points, instead of winging it and mucking it up.

As a bonus, there, tucked in the tiny side pocket where I should put my keys, was a pressed four-leaf clover. I remembered finding it one day in the back lot of the office, growing through a crack in the concrete of all things, and had pressed it just on general principle.

Tough luck, I'd said to Elaine and laughed.

Now it made me smile again. But maybe luck was tougher than we tend to believe. I smoothed the pressed leaf and eased it back into the pocket. I felt a thousand times better than I should about life, the universe and everything, even when the cabdriver took the corner on two wheels.

He was obviously anxious to be rid of a cheap tipper like me.

So, the yard was abandoned.

It wasn't really surprising at that hour of the morning, but I was disappointed that Nick wasn't there waiting for me. He'd come, though. He was the kind of guy who kept his promises.

At least he used to be.

Doubt wiggled its toes.

Let's take a moment to set the scene. The head office of Coxwell & Pope is not the most glam place in the world. There's a gravel lot in front of the relentlessly functional square building of taupe brick, which dates from the late fifties. It's a building that says "no frills" in its every line.

It had been built by a paving company to house the owner/manager/salesman and his secretary, as well as all their files. That company's backhoes and pavers had once parked in rows along the side of the highway. I remember seeing them as a kid on our trips to the city. The big yellow monsters with their jagged teeth had been a landmark of being "almost there," or in the other direction, of "nowhere near home." In those days, this had been a no-man's-land of cheap real estate.

No-man's-land had moved much closer to Maine since then. Now the lot was smaller, the land on either side having been sold off when the paving company moved on. Far from being beyond the reach of civilization, we were nestled in the midst of a gasoline alley that stretched from Boston almost all the way to Rosemount.

The small, fenced back lot was perfect for our baby backhoe and minimal inventory of interlock paving stones and interesting rocks. Mostly we used it as a staging area, buying what we needed shortly before installing it rather than keeping inventory. Our business was very susceptible to personal taste, which meant that any inventory would have had to be enormous to be useful.

I preferred letting the big companies and tree farms keep the inventory—and pay for it—until I knew I needed it.

Our office rubbed shoulders with a fried chicken place and an obscenely expensive nursery. Both Elaine and I had sworn off chicken shortly after we took the office three years before—the smell of the fat all day and most of the night is enough to put anyone off deep-frying for good—and often joked about poaching customers from among the nursery's well-heeled clientele.

What was good about our location was its visibility. We had a beautifully big sign, with flowing green text that proclaimed Coxwell & Pope to be purveyors of exquisite garden design and landscaping. When we noticed all the Land Rover Ladies taking a good look at the sign from next door, obviously not wanting to risk their fancy shoes on the gravel, we had added our phone number to the sign. It was cheaper than paving the lot and we have had a few calls from Back Bay.

Including Mrs. Eugenia Hathaway, my personal favorite and patron saint of the Land Rover Ladies. Except she has a Jag, in a lovely hue of emerald.

Mrs. H., though, was our ticket to profitability and possibly to a whole lot more.

The back gate was still locked up, the Bronco Beast—also embellished with logo—sat cold and hulking beside the office door. It looks completely decrepit, but it's not as old as you might think. I guess hard living has aged it beyond its years. All the office lights were out and the sky was pale pearly grey. Determined to see the bright side, I resolved that I could get some work done on those sketches while I waited for Nick.

The fat for the chicken was already heated up—I could smell it and my stomach was not impressed. Fried chicken for breakfast is not an appealing concept any day of the week. I was thinking that the yogurt might have been a good choice after all as I did the key shuffle.

Which was why Nick nearly gave me a heart attack when he stepped out of the shadows.

I squealed his name.

He looked as though he might have laughed at me under other circumstances. “You were expecting someone else?”

“Of course not.”

He looked just as yummy as he had the night before, which didn’t help me find my composure. The dark shadow of a day’s beard only made him look a bit more mysterious, his eyes more startlingly green. My heart, having jumped, now lodged solidly in my throat.

Worse, I felt myself blushing. I figured I’d blushed more in the last twelve hours than in all the years since I was Fat Philippa. “I didn’t see you.”

“That would be the point.” Nick shoved his hands into his pockets, his gaze assessing. “You were the one who said I shouldn’t be seen.”

“Right.” I opened the back passenger door of the Beast and managed a smile. “The windows are tinted, so if you stay down, we can stick to that plan.”

Nick climbed in and looked around himself with some surprise. “Do you think you could have found anything bigger?”

I bristled that he dared to criticize my baby. “It’s useful.”

Nick snorted. “Where does the stewardess sit?”

“Very funny.” I slammed the door and got in behind the wheel—a neat trick in a straight skirt but one I had mastered—and started the engine.

The truck grumbled to life, coughing and farting its way to a throaty rumble that made the keys jingle in the ignition. The Beast is well-seasoned, pretty much reliable and possessed of enough quirks that it commands affection.

“Seriously, I’ve flown on smaller aircraft.” Nick leaned forward between the seats. "Is that a *cup holder?*" His expression effectively communicated his disdain, and I—who dearly love this snorting behemoth—was insulted on its behalf. "Why on earth would you need such a gas-guzzling monster?"

I met his gaze in the rearview mirror. "We move trees. We plant shrubs by the dozen and perennials by the thousand. Sometimes I even have to deliver stones to the crew. A bicycle, however environmentally responsible, wouldn't quite be up to the job. And I don't think we could afford the comp for the rickshaw drivers."

Nick leaned back, looking cool and dangerous. I eyed him in the mirror and felt as though the Marlboro Man had slid into the backseat to lecture me on biosustainability.

Before I was even awake.

"But you could get a new one. It would have to be more efficient than this. How many miles do you have on this thing?" He leaned forward again, peering at the odometer, which had stuck many moons ago at 162,000 miles.

"New trucks cost a lot more."

"Capital investment. Put it on the books."

"That won't pay for it." I shook my head. "Tell you what—the next time we win the lottery, my first acquisition will be a shiny new truck."

I got a raised eyebrow for that. The Beast was running as smooth as silk now that it had warmed up.

Maybe it was showing off and defying Nick's attitude.

"But every time you take this puppy to the corner for a coffee between then and now, it adds a little something special to the atmosphere."

"I don't drink coffee."

"Phil, we have to be responsible with the planet . . ."

"Global warming is good for my business."

Nick looked shocked for one satisfying moment, before he realized I was joking. Then he leaned forward to argue.

"Don't tell me again." I held up a hand. "You don't even have a car and never have had one."

"Don't need one." Nick's eyes were cat-bright. "But if I *did,* it would be a fuel efficient little number, not something out of a Mad Max movie. Do you know . . ."

Enough was enough. I slammed the truck into reverse and would have peeled some rubber if there'd been any asphalt in the lot. As it was, the track slid sideways, grappling for traction, and spewed up a lot of dust before it lunged onto the road with a roar.

Nick swore and disappeared from my rearview mirror. I heard a thunk and allowed myself a smile.

"Oh," I said, eyes wide in mock innocence. Scarlet O'Hara is one of my best imitations. "Didn't you have your seat belt fastened? Sometimes I just forget how powerful a great big gasoline-sucking pollutant-spewing vehicle like this can be."

"Very funny, Phil," Nick growled. "Glad you've had a good night's sleep."

I didn't think it was the time to reveal that I had lain awake half of what had been left of the night, replaying that kiss. "Don't come complaining to me. You could have stayed on my couch."

He sat up straight, probably as surprised as I was that that suggestion had fallen from my lips. Clearly, malicious aliens had seized control of my tongue. I shut up and drove, the silence telling me that I wasn't going to weasel easily out of that flub.

Nick sounded grim when he finally spoke. "How exactly would that keep you from being involved?"

I felt my cheeks get hot and concentrated on the road. It was dead straight and empty, so required my relentless attention. "Where *did* you sleep?"

"I didn't." He looked out the window, his expression somber. "I just walked."

My heart squeezed. He looked very lonely and very tired and the sucker impulse is tough to quell. He had to be running on empty. "We could stop and get a coffee."

That earned me a sharp glance. "Let me guess—drive through at a burger joint? Do you know what those people are doing to rain forests? And never mind the impact on populations here and abroad with their artery-clogging menus . . ."

I pulled over in the parking lot of a donut shop and hit the brakes, then glared at him in the rearview mirror. "Let's get something straight, Nicholas Sullivan. I am doing you a favor. Now, you can keep the lectures and we can go to Rosemount, or you can spout your opinions from the curb as you try to hitch a ride. Your choice."

Nick folded his arms across his chest, a hint of a smile touching his lips. "And when did Phil Coxwell start talking so tough?"

I gave him a look of mock ferocity. "You said my baby is ugly." I patted the dash of the truck soothingly, as though its feelings might be hurt. "Them's fighting words."

"This truck is your baby?"

"You better believe it."

Nick grinned then, the smile softening his features and the twinkle in his eye banishing my annoyance. "I surrender. I could use a cup of brew, regardless of where it came from. It can't be worse than the worst ever."

I pretended I wasn't affected by his smile. "Which was?"

"Tepid water and used coffee grounds, strained through a sock, somewhere in Bhutan."

My eyes widened, but one glance told me he wasn't lying—about the sock or the location. Once again, I felt suddenly stay-at-home, the most unlikely companion possible for a man who traveled the world with enviable ease. "I don't even know where Bhutan is."

Nick's expression had become distant, his thoughts on the other side of the world. "It's east of the sun and west of the moon. The last Shangri-La." His gaze locked with mine so suddenly that I jumped. "More pragmatic travelers connect through Tibet. Bhutan's in the Himalayas. You should go sometime. You'd love it."

"Why do you say that?"

Nick leaned forward, bracing one elbow on the back of the front passenger seat. "The colors, Phil. Last time, we went in March, because there's a religious festival around the solstice. We sat for three days watching priests, all in costumes and masks, dancing and chanting. The crowd waved streamers and pounded their feet on the bleachers, the sound of the drums and cymbals got right into your blood."

He shook his head. "You end up with children on your shoulders who you don't even know and at the end everyone is dancing together, caught in the moment. It's magical and marvelous."

The focus in Nick's eyes shifted back to me, but they stayed the same turbulent green. He looked at me, then the warmth of his fingertips landed on my shoulder. This time, I couldn't blame the heat in his eyes on either lighting or champagne.

His hand rose, his fingertip ran across the curve of my bottom lip. I didn't even care if he smudged my lipstick.

In fact, I was hoping he'd smudge it with his mouth.

His gaze dropped to my lips as though our thoughts were as one. He leaned in a bit closer and I couldn't resist. I reached out one hand and touched the stubble on his jaw, yearning for another kiss.

Just to see how much was champagne and how much was real, of course.

But Nick pulled back as though he had been jerked by a string. He scowled out the side window and his words turned brusque.

"You'd love it, Phil. It's actually more colorful than your kitchen." All the affectionate warmth had been banished from his tone, his comment that of a stranger. "You should go sometime."

It was hardly an invitation.

Trust Nick to make sure that I knew where I stood. Honesty was this man's terminal disease.

I turned off the ignition with a flick of my wrist and reached for the door handle, trying to lighten the moment. "I don't know if I'd be up for exotic destinations if I had to drink the coffee."

"The sock was clean!" Nick protested, clearly relieved that I offered the chance of retreat. "But the coffee was horrible. It was a sign of desperation that we drank it anyway."

"I think we can do a bit better than that today."

"I'd hope so. It would be pretty scary if the glories of civilization couldn't do better than tube socks for filters." Nick watched me, but the intensity was gone from his eyes. "You don't think they have any of those double chocolate numbers, do you?"

I feigned shock. "Wait a minute. Aren't you the guy who just lectured me on environmental friendliness? Shouldn't you be asking for tofu and twig filling?"

Nick nodded with mock solemnity. "A man's got to know his weakness. Double chocolate donuts are mine."

"Uh huh." An army of brothers had taught me to establish quantities *before* shopping for food. "When did you eat last?"

"Yesterday. Airline food." Nick grimaced. "And I use the noun loosely."

I laughed despite myself.

I splurged on half a dozen double chocolate donuts. Nick fell on them like a ravenous wolf. I declined his offer to share—

which probably relieved him—and entertained myself with the driving.

And it was fun. There was no one on the road ahead of us, at least not going in the same direction we were—no one except a sleepy little russet Honda. It was puttering along, clearly not a morning car, or maybe not driven by a morning person. Yet I, a non-morning person myself, was feeling frisky. And it wasn't even eight o'clock.

Must have been that chocolate bar.

I pulled up right behind the Honda, imagining that the Beast exhaled a puff of smoke at the little car's back bumper. The driver slowed down and put the right turn signal on. I waited, but he or she didn't turn anywhere.

It was my cue to pass.

The sounds of donut destruction halted. "You're not going to do this," Nick admonished, but he was wrong.

I didn't answer, just gauged the oncoming traffic, which was pretty heavy. The Beast was ready to rock, pistons a-pumping, sparks a-firing.

I chose my gap and floored the accelerator, easily passing the Honda and swerving back into the eastbound lane with the breadth of two baby hairs to spare. I had a fleeting glimpse of the woman in the oncoming silver Lexus, who looked as though she had swallowed her teeth.

The Beast swayed hard on its shocks before reestablishing its balance—there was that heady sense of an almost-roll—and I felt better than I had all morning.

A long way ahead, another car lurked in my lane. I smiled a predatory smile and touched the gas, urging the Beast on. Clearly I had missed the fun of driving to Rosemount by plodding along in the rank and file of the evening commuter exodus.

Oh yes, if nothing else, I can drive.

The first thing I asked my brother James when he won the job of teaching me to drive was how to squeal the tires. He refused, supposedly on principle, but I figured he didn't know how to do it. Eldest son, you know, scion of respectability etc. etc.

So I asked Matt—Number Two son—and he ratted on me to my father, who promptly suspended my driving lessons for six months "until I learned some decorum." Father is big on the carrot-and-stick scenario. Punishment always figures largely on his agenda. I guess that makes him a good judge, a better conservative and a downright splendid church father—if one of the "you're all going to hell and good riddance" variety.

Not that I have any issues with that.

Zach, of course, being youngest son and household rebel was up for squealing tires, though he cheerfully admitted that he didn't know how to do it either. We figured it out together, along with how to make nice regular figure-eights on the iced-up Rosemount High parking lot. It was fun, even if we did pay dearly for our transgressions once discovered.

Zach, though, is nuts. I never drove donuts on the ice on Mary Lake. I'd drive out with him, because I was sure he was going to plunge through the ice and die a cold wet death and there would be no one around to save him but me. How exactly I was going do that wasn't clear to me at the time.

Fortunately he never did break through the ice, so I never had to figure it out. But then Zach is the proverbial cat of nine lives, the one who always lands on his feet.

The silence prompted me to glance in the rearview. Nick looked a bit green around the gills. His fingers were dug deep into the deluxe vinyl upholstery, his donuts forgotten. "Do you always drive like that?"

"Pretty much." I wrinkled my nose. "Maybe driving aggressively is my weakness."

"And you use the verb loosely."

I pretended to be insulted. "Would you rather walk?"

"Very funny." He polished off the last donut and checked the corners of the box diligently for strays. "I'll take my chances."

We laughed and the sky pinkened in the east. We might have been old friends riding along on a mission, but that kiss that hadn't happened rode along with us like an unwelcome passenger.

And so did the one that had.

My mind was going faster than the Beast, trying to sort out all the potential repercussions. Nick never did anything by accident, after all. Did ducking a kiss this morning mean that he was worried and distracted, or that he had no long term plans for hanging around?

Either way, I would find out pretty damn quick once we got to Rosemount.

Like it or not.

Chapter 4

Rosemount is an old New England town, founded in the late seventeenth century. The town looks out to sea, its back braced against a low hill, a site that accurately reflects its indifference to the country behind and its interest, at least once, in Old Mother England. It has a stern and grey demeanor, like an ancient spinster, perhaps one who enjoys rapping her cane to make sure everyone is listening.

The town had originally been named Whalers' End, a tribute to the first source of its income. After a maritime accident—the wreckage of which still provides stalwart divers with adventure—the name had been considered bad luck and had been changed to the more sedate Rosemount. There still weren't many roses, although the hill behind could have been said to be a mount.

A little one.

Maybe a dowager's hump.

Boston had once been so far away as to be effectively of another world, and there were still residents who would prefer it stayed that way. The automobile had changed Rosemount, just as it had changed the rest of America. A mere fifty-minute drive from the northern outskirts of Boston ensured that the fishermen of Rosemount had been gradually replaced by commuters.

The more practical among the town's citizenry saw this transition as a good sign. Diversifying the local economy was key to survival in a changing world. After all, fish were an integral ingredient in Rosemount's fishing industry, and everyone knew the stocks were dwindling.

In fact, an ongoing argument as to who is responsible for the sorry state of the fishing business—local opinion favors alternatively big business, the Japanese, those Canadians or the government, depending on the wind—can be joined at the Merry Widow pub right downtown, if ever you're so inclined.

Despite its relatively small size, there's a big division in the town—between old residents and new, between fishermen and professionals—a division perpetuated by their differing perspectives regarding development.

The town's older houses have been restored and renovated, primarily by commuters with fat wallets. A strict historical society ensures that the mood is kept intact for a burgeoning tourist trade. The newcomers want "quaint," a New England town from the past with picture-perfect views and gregarious locals. Unfortunately, since most of them have demanding careers in the city, they expect this local hospitality to come from the old-timers.

The old-timers, predominantly fishermen, just want to get on with the increasingly competitive business of wringing a living from the sea. They don't want to paint their boats in cheery colors or hang gingham curtains in their smaller, older seaside houses. They don't have the time to plant nasturtiums or the interest to greet every visitor like an old friend. And they are, by and large, a crusty and colorful bunch, content to be who they are rather than worry what they look like.

The economic disparity between the two groups does little to ensure reconciliation—though in the summers, when revenue flows like a good rain, tensions are slight. Old-timers grumble of the intrusion of tourists, but do so under their breaths. More and more of them each year take those tourists to see the whales, or divers out to the wreckage, loading down their boats with something other than nets bulging with silvery fish.

There are those who don't quite fit into either camp, the Coxwells and the Sullivans being two such families. Maybe that's what drew Nick and I to each other. We were never going to mingle with either group and even as kids, we knew it.

The Coxwells were counted among the old-timers by dint of the date of our arrival if not our traditional occupation. My great-grandfather acquired our property as a summer retreat around the turn of the century, when such coastal cottages were in vogue.

The family myth was that he had complained mightily of the cost of renovating Grey Gables, for the house had then been the dilapidated residence of the local doctor and far too small for my great-grandmother's ambitions. She had apparently brooked no argument—she had been smitten with the house, no less her vision of how it should be, and nothing less would do.

I would have liked to have known her.

And, Henry Coxwell, being a prominent Boston lawyer, had had deep enough pockets to satisfy his wife's demands despite his legendary grumbling. They had four kids, so their marriage couldn't have been all that bad.

It was my father who had moved out of the city completely, concerned by the wave of change in the sixties and the future of his three impressionable teenage sons. Small-town life, fresh air and a Republican vote are the solutions to whatever ails anyone, in Father's frame of reference. My mom had always hated the rambling old house, but her opinion had been overridden.

It's an unshakable fact of the Coxwell household that Mom's opinion seldom counts for much, if a fact that only I seemed to notice. To be sure, she never rails against the unfairness of it all, at least she never has in my presence. It takes two to tango and my parents' mutual expectations seem to mesh, however unacceptable I find them to be. Maybe Mom was of an age and an era where women adjusted themselves to such unilateral spousal decisions.

The constantly dipping level in the sherry decanter at Grey Gables hints otherwise.

If nothing else, my parents have provided a picture postcard of everything a marriage should *not* be.

But on this trip, I didn't take the turn to my parents' house. I did feel a twinge of requisite guilt and resolved to not even tell them I had been here. Grey Gables is on an old-timers' street, lined as it is with massive horse-chestnut trees, the sports cars and utility vehicles in each drive belying the aura of another era.

I drove instead to the other side of town—always said with the tone of it being the "wrong" side—where New Money had built flashy shrines. It was here that the investors in the whaling ships and those intrepid merchants of the colonial era had erected sweeping houses, most of which looked out to sea. It was here where those who made fortunes in the twenties built their abodes, and often lost them shortly thereafter. It was here—albeit closer to the highway—that the new suburbs had been slapped up in the decades since Rosemount became a commuter town.

And it was here that the Sullivans had staked their claim. They actually hadn't arrived much later than my family, but their history decreed how they would fit in and where they would live.

The Sullivan house pre-dates its fellows, looking for all the world like an old-timer house tragically misplaced. Everyone in town knew that Nick's grandfather had bought the house from some disreputable rogue who had died trying to lose his fortune. Despite his untimely end, he'd done a pretty good job and his widow had had to sell the house to see him buried. His name, not inappropriately, was forgotten, or at least eclipsed by the notoriety of the Sullivans.

There wasn't a soul in town who didn't have an opinion about a family who had made their money running booze during Prohibition—much less one who had forgotten.

The house perched on the biggest and best lot on the street, a house not intending to be ignored. In fact, the street itself seemed to be the driveway of the Sullivan house. The house was brick—another whimsy of a heavy purse in a neighborhood of clapboard—and had so many turrets and gables that it looked as though it had been transplanted from the other side of the Atlantic.

I had once heard a local roofer call the Sullivan house "the job from hell." He had done nice work though, despite his whining, and I didn't doubt that he sent prospective clients around to check his handiwork.

And they would come too, grateful for an excuse to gawk.

There was something about the house that invited rubbernecking, even beyond that of the history of its occupants. It had an eerie aura, that house, and seemed to crouch at the end of the street like a venomous toad. There were reasons why kids dared each other to ring Lucia's bell on Halloween.

And reasons they ran for the hills if she answered.

Even as an adult, I couldn't even look straight at the house. I keenly felt its disapproval as I pulled into the driveway and turned off the ignition. The silence of the early morning filled my ears and the hair on the back of my neck prickled. I hesitated, Lucia's death seeming much more real from such proximity.

I was half-expecting Nick's grandmother to step out the door, blowing smoke rings and giving me heck for daring to park here.

But she didn't.

And she wouldn't ever again. I suddenly felt very sad not to have known her better as well.

Nick reached for the door handle and I noted his gesture. I hit the button for the rear "childproofing" power locks.

They even worked.

"You're supposed to stay out of sight."

"I changed my mind."

"That's a woman's provenance and as far as I can tell, you're not on the team."

Nick glared at me in the rearview mirror. "Very funny. Let me out."

"No."

"You can't do this, Phil. It's just going to get you involved in something that isn't your problem."

"I'm already involved."

"And I'd like that to stop right here."

"Why?"

He frowned out the tinted window, not answering.

"What's changed, Nick?"

He cast me a dark glance and wiggled the door handle. "Are you going to let me out of this monster, or do I have to come over the seat?"

He wasn't going to answer me, which was significant enough to get me wondering. Was this protectiveness the legacy of that kiss? That was something I could ponder later, after this was done.

But I couldn't help thinking it was another sign of changed luck. They do say that the third time is the charm.

"Do you think the front door will be unlocked?" I ignored Nick's fuming as I gathered my bag. I should have brought my briefcase, or a notebook, or something that would look more official than a purse.

"Phil, don't do this."

"Too late, I'm doing it. Will it?"

Nick shrugged, hardly pleased. "It usually is."

"Where's the greenhouse?"

He held my gaze for a charged moment. "You're not going to change your mind, are you?"

"I finish what I start."

Nick might have sworn under his breath, but his lips only tightened briefly. "I had forgotten how stubborn you can be." Before I could be insulted, he sighed. "I wish I had a really good reason to disagree with you."

"But you don't and you're smart enough to know it."

"Point taken, but I don't have to like it." He shoved a hand through his hair, giving himself that restless and rumpled look again. "The greenhouse is at the back of the house. Just straight through the kitchen. You can't miss it."

"Right." I reached for the door handle.

"Phil?"

"Uh-huh?"

"Be careful, will you?"

I tried to not be touched by his concern. I really did.

I slammed the door and hit the key on the remote to lock all the doors, taking some satisfaction in the fact that Nick was indeed out of sight. Maybe I just had a weakness for this man because he listened to me, a rare enough occurrence in my life. I walked to the front door, hoping I looked more confident than I felt.

I was, after all, going to discover a body. One that had been waiting for a while.

In the sun.

I decided not to think about that. No, I would act as though I was here for my own pretence of a reason. I had been summoned to redesign the gardens of one Lucia Sullivan, so I'd concentrate on assessing what was here already.

Have you ever had the feeling you were being watched? Well, I had it in spades that morning and the gooseflesh to show for it. It wasn't a benevolent gaze either—someone was sending major "go away" vibes.

The Force was not with me.

I ignored it. I checked out the garden, giving my best impression of a consummate professional. There wasn't much there. Nick was right to say that his grandmother didn't care about gardens.

Yet it wouldn't take much to make a difference. Low maintenance seemed to be the obvious choice—bulbs, perennials and self-sowing annuals.

What this long bed in front of the house needed was a burst of color, maybe yellow or buttery cream to highlight the russet of the brick. Maybe both, all jumbled up together.

No, bolder than that. This was Lucia's house. She was not a woman who was afraid of bright color. (*Had been* afraid of color, I corrected myself silently.) This garden called for magenta and brilliant yellow, orange and purple, some red tossed in for zing. Yellow crocus, red-fringed tulips, hot pink tulips, maybe a few crown fritillaria. They were showy things, a bit vulgar, and would be just the ticket.

I walked slowly, making a good show of assessing as I went. Yes, and a border of tarda tulips, always cheerful, easy to maintain for those non-gardeners to whom this house seemed to belong. They could become a pest, but there was lots of room for things to run amok here.

Then, we could follow with some asiatic lilies—as long as they were out from the shadow of the house, they'd thrive—really tall ones in a mix of improbably hot colors. Some cosmos in dark pink, coreopsis in vivid yellow, and red, red poppies. Let the self-seeders fight it out. The place would be a jungle of color in no time at all. By the third summer, it would be completely out of control and over the top.

Perfect.

I winced in sympathy for the neglected cedars framing the door and decided killing them would be a mercy. A nice, neat spruce—no, a pair of dwarf ones, one on either side of the walk—would frame this great old doorway perfectly and add some order to the chaos I was already envisioning.

One glimpse of the door and reality returned. The expanse of wood seemed to defy me to even knock. It turned out that I hadn't really done a good job of distracting myself. Those watchful vibes—along with the dismissive ones—seemed to treble in strength.

But it was just a house. And pretty much an empty one. I stepped up on to the porch and tried to slow the hammering of my heart. I checked my watch as I thought I should and was surprised to find it not quite eight.

Was it too early to look plausible? But I was here now, for better or for worse.

I rang the bell.

The ringing echoed through the house, making it sound huge and hollow. Tomblike, ha ha. Not surprisingly, there was no answer of running footsteps. I shifted my weight from foot to foot, trying to act as though I expected to be greeted. I checked my watch again, knowing that there could be any number of prying eyes checking on my presence.

Maybe it was the neighbors I felt watching.

It was stupid to have come so early. No one met gardeners at this hour, especially if they weren't commuters, and there would be questions about my timing. I cast a glance to the right, noting the fine array of crocuses in the neighbor's bed. A cat watched from the porch, a Siamese, its eyes narrowed in suspicion as it watched me. The hair rose on the back of my neck.

The very fact that the cat was out hinted that its owner was awake.

And knowing Rosemount, watching.

It was Evelyn Donnelly's house, so I shouldn't have even doubted it. I thought of the ledger she must keep and swallowed a smile.

I rang the bell again and tried to look a little bit more impatient. Perhaps curious. Definitely surprised.

Certainly giving my best performance.

I looked to the left and the right more deliberately, peeked at the shrouded window, checked my watch again.

Then I noticed the brass door handle.

It was an old handle with a handgrip and lever for the thumb, the parts where hands had repeatedly touched it now worn smooth. I stared at it, thought of cop shows and mystery novels, and knew that if Nick had been the last one to come into this house, his thumbprint would be waiting right there to condemn him.

That made all of this very real.

Lucia had been murdered. Nick had been set up. And he would be charged for a crime he hadn't committed.

Again.

But this time, there would be no respite. His thumbprint would condemn him.

After all, it would be right in the files.

Before I could think too much about it, I grabbed the handle and smeared my thumb across the lever. I could almost hear my brothers scream in outrage at this tampering with evidence—they probably all simultaneously and inexplicably broke out in hives—but it was done.

And the door suddenly swung inward with a creak. It moved so abruptly that someone might have opened it from behind.

I jumped back, but there was no one there. There might as well have been, because that sense of presence was stronger than ever.

And that presence did not approve of *my* presence.

I shivered. This place deserved every bit of its creepy reputation. There used to be stories of people who had hung themselves in the basement, of women locked in the garret who clawed at the windows until they starved to death, of vengeful ghosts that stalked this house's halls.

I refused to glance back at Nick even though I could feel his gaze upon me. He wasn't supposed to be there, after all. I stepped over the threshold, hoping I looked untroubled by the prospect of what I knew lay ahead.

"Yoo hoo!" I cried cheerfully, knowing damn well that the neighbors might have spectacular hearing. "Mrs. Sullivan? It's Philippa Coxwell, just keeping our appointment. Are you here?"

Oh, Lucia was here, and I knew where—not to mention in what state—even though the house wasn't telling. I hesitated, as any visitor faced with such circumstance might do.

"Mrs. Sullivan? Hello?"

Well, there was no delaying it now and no point dallying over what had to be done. Straight through the kitchen to the greenhouse, just as Nick had said.

Sunshine was playing on the old oak cabinets in the kitchen, making the distant room look like the light at the end of a tunnel. Head down, away we go.

I didn't look to either side, just trotted down the hall, pulse thumping in my ears. The kitchen was pristine, only a single brandy snifter left on the counter. I paused on the threshold of the greenhouse, swallowed, then opened the door with a flourish and strode into the sunlit room.

The greenery brought me to a screeching halt. The place was bursting with exotic blooms and tropical flowers, pampered beauties that could never have been cultivated by someone without a green thumb.

It seemed that Lucia's indifference to plants extended only to the outdoor, pedestrian varieties. I almost smiled, having no trouble reconciling that to what I did know of Lucia.

She was a former opera singer, so only the prima donnas would do.

And they were glorious—the doorway was flanked by a bright yellow allamanda heavy with trumpet blooms and an anthurium with blossoms so bloodred they didn't look real.

I forgot my mission for a moment as I stared in admiration. A massive columnea grew down most of the wall that had once been the exterior wall of the house, its orange and yellow flowers gloriously illustrating its common name of Goldfish Plant. The leaves looked like dark green water flowing over the brick wall, water chockful of goldfish.

Incongruous, but effective. Certainly it was dramatic.

Pure Lucia.

There was only one white-blooming vine and it was one that I couldn't name, its trumpeting blossoms fringed on the ends of the petals. Obviously Lucia thought the bloom interesting enough to put up with its lack of color. Just beyond that, the bird of paradise held its orange and blue blooms to the sunlight.

And all I could smell was the yellow plumeria. Okay, I felt a little triumphant that I had nailed Lucia's color scheme in one. This place was like a Hawaiian shirt of giddy color.

I wandered a little further on the wet gravel pathways. Apparently the overhead sprinkler system was automatic, and came on in the mornings. The plants themselves had already dried from their shower and the sun was quickly baking the gravel dry as well.

I rounded a corner, and caught my breath at the display of paphiopedilum orchids. They all had mottled leaves, all held one exquisite blossom skyward, all were tucked back against one wall in orderly rows. It looked as though someone either spent a lot of money on plants or did their own propagation.

How strange for me to have something in common with the Dragon Lady.

The orchids looked like little dragons of a kind, with their mouths open and their tongues out, waiting for a yummy morsel. Of course, they weren't carnivorous.

But the nepenthes overhead most certainly were. Myriad pitcher plants grew down from planters suspended from the ceiling. Their gaping wet mouths were the one thing they all had in common regardless of their sizes and coloring.

No wonder there were no bugs in here.

But they reminded me why I was there.

I set to work, but it took only a few moments for me to discover that there was nothing in the greenhouse, nothing but marvelous flowers. It was a bit colder than I would have expected for most of these varieties, but then it's been a while since I did much with hothouses. I scurried through the room again, but there wasn't so much as a trowel out of place.

There certainly wasn't a corpse. I would have noticed that.

Which meant someone had lied to me.

The light belatedly went on.

Someone had tricked me. And Fat Philippa had fallen for the lure, willingly becoming the butt of the joke one more time. How many times would it take me to learn? My face heated in recollection of a thousand high school taunts, a dozen tormentors laughing when I stepped right into the humiliating trap of the day.

I had been tricked by the one person I trusted—even knowing I was bucking the odds to bother. I never would have guessed that Nick could be so mean.

Or that I could be so stupid.

But I already knew that his brother could easily be that mean and they were, for better or worse, two of a kind. I spun on my heel and marched out of the greenhouse, slamming the door hard behind myself.

Once a sucker, always a sucker.

I could have sworn the damn house laughed.

He should have warned her.

He sat in the truck, fidgeting with impatience, and was convinced three different times that his watch had stopped.

He could feel a thousand eyes on Phil's Beast. It wasn't exactly the most inconspicuous vehicle she could have had. It was also emblazoned with her company logo and phone number, a detail he hadn't expected. Stress, grief and a lack of sleep hadn't left him as sharp as he liked to be.

There was something else at work too.

He'd felt it the night before but dismissed it. This morning, in full sunlight, his attraction to Phil couldn't be so easily denied.

And this unexpected protectiveness was a thousand times worse. He didn't want Phil to go in that house, he didn't want her to expose herself to a scene he'd never forget, he didn't want her to be embroiled in his problems again.

He wanted to take her to Bhutan and had very nearly said so.

He was losing his edge.

But he could see Phil there so easily. He could picture her putting up with the trials of travel with good humor, showing the same delight of discovery that had once motivated him to travel. Her kitchen was filled with the same jubilant use of color, the same disregard for convention in pairing this with that, the same joy of being alive that he associated with certain cultures.

He traveled alone as a matter of principle, or at least kept to himself when in a group. Travel was his private domain and he had never even considered the possibility of a travel companion.

Let alone a woman. A lover.

Phil. Who had once been head-over-heels crazy about his brother and might very well still be.

He should remember that detail.

Instead he relived his first sight of her in fifteen years. Something had quickened in him as Phil walked unsteadily up her driveway, something that wouldn't have been surprising with any other woman on the face of the earth.

But in association with Phil, lust was an unwelcome accomplice. She was the only person beside Lucia he could trust and the one he had trusted with a greater measure of the whole truth. She had kept his secret, whatever her reasons. He owed her respect—not lust.

But when had Phil become a girl?

It seemed like a ridiculous thing to think of a woman more or less his contemporary and he had felt like an idiot as soon as he had asked her, but still. Phil had always been a jeans-and-baggy-sweatshirt-teenager, with a mouth and a half.

She had always been a bit plump, had a zit or two, and wore her heart on her sleeve. He knew she had befriended him purely to get closer to his brother, but she was such good company that he couldn't take offense. Knowing that she adored Sean, even from afar and anonymously, made her the kind of girl who could be a pal instead of a pursuit.

The kind of girl a guy could easily call "Phil."

Now he couldn't believe that he had ever thought her safely genderless. That primal part of him had noticed the sheer length of her legs and the way her skirt hitched up when she got into the truck. And he'd watched those legs as she stabbed at the gas pedal, even when she drove like a lunatic and a desire for personal longevity should have ensured he was watching the road.

He'd studied her surreptitiously in the rearview mirror, searching for some clue that she wasn't really the Phil he knew. He'd never seen his Phil wear any makeup, let alone a lipstick that made her lips look so soft and tempting. Her reddish tangle of hair—which had so often been impatiently snatched back in an elastic—now swung against her jawline in a smooth auburn bob, the cut accentuating the creamy length of her neck.

It wasn't so much that she had slimmed out, for she still wasn't built like a model—he thanked the gods for that—but Phil carried herself with confidence, she dressed with the same verve that colored her words and her kitchen. She was as comfortable in her own skin as she had once been awkward, and she was unabashedly feminine.

The result was as sexy as hell.

If Phil hadn't recognized him so obviously, he might have assumed she was the older sister of the Phil he had known, or a distant cousin with a passing similarity of build.

But this *was* Phil, for all the changes in her appearance. Funny, straightforward, blunt and clever, honest and caring. The same Phil, but blossomed. She had always been cute, but never seemed to do much about it. A guy had to look to see it, at least in those days. Phil had always had a little secretive smile that was femininity squared.

Come to think of it, that smile had often surprised him, too.

And he'd always wanted to kiss it off her lips. As teenagers who were friends though, he'd been pretty sure she'd deck him if he did. Even then, he had been certain one kiss would change everything.

So, he'd been half-right.

The scary part was that now she was looking at him as though she was thinking much the same thing. It bothered him, it bothered him a lot. Because even if Phil didn't have him confused with his brother—the jury was still out on that one—he thought he knew her well enough to understand that she didn't play by the same rules as he did. Phil would expect the traditional commitment route: trip to the altar, house in the 'burbs, 2 cars in the garage, 2.2 kids and a golden retriever.

That wasn't Nick Sullivan's style. He was mobile, uncommitted, content with what he could carry and no more. He didn't do long term. Never had. Never would.

Some things really don't change.

His every instinct said "run like hell" but he was stuck here, hiding in Phil's truck like a coward, waiting for her to finish what he should have insisted on handling himself. As a man who lived for the moment, this was a moment he'd pay good money to see done.

He certainly wasn't doing a very good job of leaving no mark of his presence, but then he should be used to screwing that up by now. He scowled and focused on the heavy oak door, willing it to open.

He should at least have warned Phil about the house. He should have told her about the costumes, the stage props, the collections. The stuffed lynx over the door had been known to startle the occasional visitor and those thieves, well, a psychoanalyst could have made a career out of Lucia.

Phil had never been across the house's threshold—no one who was not blood or a favored acquaintance of Lucia's entered that place. She would be surprised, disoriented, maybe even frightened. The realization almost sent him vaulting over the seat, his own best interests be damned.

But Phil *hadn't* screamed.

Which, in a way, was worse.

The house brooded silently, as it was wont to do, keeping its secrets to itself. He had become so used to it that he became jaded to its eccentricities. In fact, there had been a time when he naively thought everyone lived like his grandmother, surrounded by improbable souvenirs, posed and positioned for maximum effect.

What was taking her so long? He wanted to pace but the truck wasn't quite that big. He drummed his fingers.

Phil had to be in the kitchen by now, surely? He checked his watch and found that precisely two minutes had elapsed since she crossed the threshold. What if she was sickened by what she found?

He should never have let her go.

He gritted his teeth and gave her one more minute.

Just one. The second-hand sweep in his watch moved with paralyzing slowness. He lasted a full thirty seconds, then started to climb into the front.

But Phil came out of the house in that very moment. To his astonishment, she looked as cool and as composed as when she entered it. She shrugged and ran her fingers through her keys, an elegant lady disappointed.

He sat back, realizing belatedly that Phil was playing her role, part of a cover story he had pretty much forgotten. But she was evidently made of sterner stuff than that—and a lot less transparent than he remembered. She smoothly slid behind the wheel, started the truck without a word and backed out of the driveway. The only hint that something was amiss was the way she squealed the tires when she shifted into drive.

She said absolutely nothing.

It was as though he had become invisible.

"Well?"

Phil cast him a glance in the rearview mirror that could have frozen his marrow. Her lips tightened and she looked back at the empty road ahead, still without speaking. She turned onto the highway and hit the gas pedal so hard that Nick fell back against the seat.

When he sat up, they were merged into the increasing commuter traffic and headed toward Boston again.

"Aren't you going to the police station?"

"No."

There was trouble in that word, big trouble. He had heard women embue a single word with volumes of meaning before and he knew he'd likely hear it again before he died.

But this time, he didn't know why the woman in question was so angry.

"What do you mean? That was the whole point of this little charade." He leaned over the front seat. "We need to get the cops. Lucia's dead!"

"I don't think so."

Phil changed lanes with a savage gesture, nearly dispatching a Chevy to the ditch. The driver honked at her, she lifted her chin and put the pedal to the floor. The truck began to rattle, but Phil showed no signs of easing up on the gas. She ducked and weaved between the commuter traffic, her grip so tight on the wheel that her knuckles were white.

He debated the merit of distracting her while she drove like a madwoman. Then she nearly peeled the side off a Cherokee and it didn't seem as though they had a lot to lose.

"What's going on? Phil, what did you find?"

That captured her attention, though he had a sense that wasn't a good thing. One dark brow raised, those snapping baby blues meeting his in the mirror again. "Exactly what you thought I would."

Her voice was low and dangerous, a trait he had never associated with Phil before.

But then, you never knew how people were going to deal with a shock like finding a corpse.

"Look out!"

She had already seen the old Ford limping along ahead of them. She checked her mirrors, changed lanes and circumnavigated the Ford with such daring that the Bronco nearly rolled over and played dead. She left a couple of inches to spare and the Ford's driver looking as astonished as Nick felt.

He was tempted to cross himself, as the women passengers in tiny mountainous countries were prone to do, particularly when buses executed death-defying hairpin turns.

Instead he braced his elbows on the back of the front seats. He kept his voice calm as the truck hurtled toward Boston, sounding as though it would self-destruct before they got there. "Phil, it's okay if you're upset. Just talk to me. Tell me what happened back there. Tell me what we're doing."

"It's okay?" She sputtered for a moment, her eyes flashing. "I'm sure it is *okay*. I'm sure you'd love for me to lose my temper. I'm sure you'd enjoy being able to laugh at the success of your little trick."

She hauled the truck over to the shoulder suddenly and hit the brakes with such ferocity that they squealed. The truck fishtailed to a stop, raising a cloud in its wake and he got a much better look at the windshield than he might have preferred.

Phil spun to face him, her eyes blazing. "Get out of my truck."

"What?"

"You heard me. Out!"

"I heard you, but I seem to be missing a few pages from the script here." So much for calm. His voice rose. "What in the hell is going on?"

"What's going on?" Phil's eyes flashed and she jabbed her finger at him. "I thought we were *friends*, Nick. I thought you were someone I could trust. And you know what? I just found out that I was wrong. Dead wrong. I found out that you're just like all the rest of them, not above a little trick on Fat Philippa."

"What trick?"

But Phil was on a roll, his question trampled beneath the stampede of her words. "What did you expect me to do? Did I miss some booby trap? Or was it enough that I was terrified going into that house? Did you rig a camera to capture the moment on film forever? Maybe you can get together with all the boys and have a chuckle over how you fooled me into making a fool of myself, maybe . . ."

He interrupted her tirade. "Phil, I didn't . . ."

"Spare me the play of innocence," she said coldly. "Lucia isn't dead. There's no rotting corpse in the greenhouse, and I'm sure there never was. The paphiopedilum orchids, however, are in full bloom and the plumeria smells divine. So, why don't you go and phone your grandmother, have a cup of tea, enjoy your homecoming and forget that we ever knew each other."

He didn't know what had happened, but he didn't like what was happening now. He held Phil's gaze, willing her to believe him. "Phil, I didn't play a trick on you."

"Bull." She glared back just as steadily. "Get out of my truck."

"Just give me a chance to explain."

Her eyes widened. "Why you couldn't just come home and leave me out of it? I'm sure I don't want to know."

"Phil . . ."

"Don't you dare suggest that you wanted to see me. If that was the truth, it wouldn't have taken you fifteen years to bother." There was heat in those words but she didn't give him time to think about that.

She leaned past him, reaching to open the door of the truck and showing a breathtaking stretch of leg in the act. "Get out."

He'd never seen Phil angry and could have done without it. She was completely composed, her voice flat, her eyes cold. In a way, it was much worse than if she had screamed and shouted. The traffic whizzed past them as they stared at each other.

He didn't get out. "All I want is a chance to explain."

"Then tell someone who gives a damn. Your account with me is overdrawn." She pointed again to the door.

He knew better than to force the issue. He'd argue from the

shoulder of the road. He got out of the truck, but had no chance to lean back in and make a last appeal.

Because Phil slammed the truck into gear and floored the accelerator, swerving back onto the highway in a daring merge that spewed loose gravel all over him. The open door swung wildly, then slammed of its own accord. He coughed and, when the dust cleared, stared after the hulking silhouette of the truck.

It didn't seem that Phil even looked back.

He blew out his breath and ran a hand through his hair as he reviewed the bidding.

Lucia wasn't dead in the greenhouse. There was no way she could be. He knew Phil was telling the truth—and there was no other reason for her to be so angry.

Which meant someone had cleaned up after he had been there. Come to think of it, he had left the front door wide open. It couldn't have been the cops, or they would have been all over the house.

Wouldn't they have been?

But then, what did he really know of police procedure? Maybe this last half hour would have progressed very differently if he had gone into the house instead of Phil.

He would have bet good money his brother knew the answers to most if not all of those questions. He should probably visit Sean, demand an explanation and see this resolved.

But that might be exactly what his brother would be expecting. There was nothing that could be done for Lucia at the moment and he wasn't inclined to make things easy for his brother, at least not this time.

Let Sean wait. Let him worry. Let him wonder.

He had more important things to do. He found himself straining to make out a hulking green silhouette rollicking down the road ahead. Phil's truck was already indistinguishable from the line of commuters.

But the hurt in Phil's voice was going to haunt him for a long, long time, unless he fixed this. She was wrong—they *were* friends.

It stung that she thought him guilty of the kind of cheap trick Sean had once pulled on her. But then, it seemed, he hadn't left things as pristine behind himself as he had always thought.

If he was going to walk away now without leaving some kind of scar behind him, then he had to straighten this out and make sure Phil knew the truth.

He could only hope that by the time he caught up with her, she would have calmed down enough to at least listen to him.

It was a long shot, by any accounting.

Once upon a time, in a pragmatic New England town where skepticism held sway and all things unseen had bad PR, a magical transformation took place. That this went unnoticed by most isn't surprising, but doesn't make the event any less important to the participants.

One participant in particular.

You see, there was a girl in this town, a girl who had never fit in and never failed to disappoint her family, a girl who by the ripe old age of fourteen had decided that things would pretty much stay that way for the rest of her life and that maybe, just maybe she even deserved the things that happened to her.

Though it was her nature to be as cheerful as a ray of sunshine, this epiphany made her sparkle a little less. She took consolation in simple sugars and starches, not the wisest choice in hormonally rampant teenage years, and she had both the thighs and the pimples to show for it. The other boys and girls taunted her, because she was so trusting that she made an easy mark for their malice and so plump that they never lacked for ammunition.

They called her Fat Philippa, which hurt, just as they had known it would. She knew that no worldly means could bring about her acceptance, so she did what she could. She pressed four-leaf clovers and followed rainbows, she avoided cracks in the sidewalk and tucked a rabbit's foot into her pocket.

And one day, just when she might have given up, her efforts bore fruit. On the cusp of her fifteenth birthday, her body was making a metamorphosis of its own, her ample figure developing some dips and curves that showed some promise for the future.

She was sure that no one noticed—until Sean Sullivan invited her to the senior prom.

Sean was a dashing rogue of a football player, well deserving of the hero's role in any fairy tale. He was a boy who all the girls whispered about and one who starred in any number of teenage fantasies. He certainly starred in several of our heroine's, though she would have died if anyone had guessed.

Yet, as though some otherworldly force drew them together, he had invited her to the prom. Things were coming up roses, her ship was in, the future looked bright. That the prom was to be held on the night of her fifteenth birthday was the perfect guarantee.

Her mother was pleased by this social coup, even if she didn't quite approve of Sean himself. She insisted that our heroine have a proper dress, borrow her pearls, learn to walk in high heels, twist her hair up into an elegant chignon, wear lipstick. For a brief shining moment, she was Cinderella heading to the ball, albeit looking more like her mother than she might have preferred.

The first transformation was physical, a change in her appearance that convinced her not only that she was lovely, but that magic could happen to her.

Magic, though, is sly stuff and never waiting where one expects it. It plays by its own rules and darts through shadows, pouncing on the unsuspecting. That's certainly what it did on this ill-fated night. Our heroine discovered too late that Sean was using her, just as everyone else had used her, that he had invited her so that she could provide amusement for others when his trick was revealed.

She was his admission to the closed ranks of the popular set. He hadn't noticed anything about her—except that she made easy prey. They mocked her and excluded her from the moment she crossed the threshold—when he laughed harder than the others, she knew the truth.

She fled their laughter in tears. And here it is that magic had its say, for she encountered none other than Sean's brother, a quiet loner. She was at her worst, trapped in the harsh light of an all-night diner and nursing a cold cup of coffee because she didn't want to go home and admit the truth. He came in, saw more than she wanted, and sat at the next table. She spoke to him because he looked lonely.

As is so often the way with those who have nothing left to lose, the act of taking that chance changed everything and ensured that she won a great deal.

To her surprise, Nick was more interested in listening than talking. He drew the humiliating story from her in dribs and drabs, and then he gave her an unexpected pearl of wisdom.

"Trust," he said as he stirred his coffee, "is a gift, and one that shouldn't be wasted on those who don't deserve it."

And our heroine realized then that she had played a role in her own tormenting. By trusting the crowd over and over again when they only proved themselves untrustworthy, by taking the bait of an acceptance which they would never truly give, she offered them a willing target.

A target she could remove, simply by refusing to trust them any longer. Instead of playing the role of victim, she could choose to step off the stage.

Magic, as anyone knows, does its work in threes. This then was the second element of her transformation, the awareness that she alone held the key to change her own life.

And this sense of empowerment, this talisman so critical to the triumph of any heroic character, restored both her smile and her inherent optimism. She might have declared her birthday night worth-

while at this point, but Nick insisted on repairing what his brother had destroyed.

He wanted her to have the magical evening she had anticipated.

So he took her home, to his disreputable and eccentric grandmother, a woman who always knew what to do. If our bedraggled heroine was startled by the sight of the former opera singer in a Chinese red silk robe, her cigarette in an ebony holder, her eyes lined with black reminiscent of Cleopatra, she hid it well.

For her part, Lucia Sullivan took one look at the hopeful young girl, blew a smoke ring, and discerned a great deal more than anyone might have liked.

A more unlikely fairy godmother could not have been found in the forty-eight contiguous states, but that was the role Lucia played that night. She cranked up the Victrola, lit the fairy lights strung around her overgrown patio, and proceeded to give waltz lessons. She was big on feeling the music, instead of responding to it, and an exacting teacher. She abruptly pronounced herself exhausted and insisted that Nick dance with our veritable princess instead.

That was the moment when the starlight slid into her veins, blending with the music in an ancient alchemical formula due to all girls in their teenage years.

For it was there, on the Sullivan patio, on the night of her fifteenth birthday, that a part of this young woman awakened for the first time. She felt strong and beautiful, she was in command of her fate. The view ahead was blue skies and sunshine all the way.

When she looked into the eyes of Nick Sullivan, her breath caught in a tingly new way. She noticed suddenly the strength of his arm around her waist, the resolute grip of fingers on hers, the alluring scent of his skin.

She realized she had not only mistaken the frog for the prince, but worse, not even noticed the prince at all.

Until now. A dragon awakened in her belly, contenting himself for the moment with a growl that rolled straight down to her toes, shooting sparks all the way.

Nick helped her pick the biggest and brightest star for her birthday wish, for luck. She wished—quite predictably—that this magical night would never end and maybe for a bit more than that. As long as that night endured, she was Cinderella, caught in the arms of her prince, dancing barefoot beneath the stars, hoping against hope that midnight would never come.

But even after the clock did strike twelve, Philippa Coxwell was never the same again.

Chapter 5

So, maybe I overreacted.

But maybe I didn't.

I'd just been jumped by a bogeymen that I'd thought was banished forever. Blindsided by the one person from my past who I trusted—and who I clearly *shouldn't* trust. The person who had, in fact, told me not to trust people who didn't deserve it. It hurt like hell, and dredged up a lot of painful memories I could have done without.

Fat Philippa was right there in the Beast with me and I wanted her gone. She must have been the one who was crying because I gave up that crap ages ago. I told you that people from Rosemount had a way of screwing up my rhythm and Nick apparently was no exception.

Years of having it all together, years of making myself what

I wanted to be, and everything shot to heck in less than twenty-four hours.

Some run of luck.

I recounted my crimes, just to ensure I didn't forget them. My first taste of success and I had celebrated by breaking my cardinal No Alcohol rule, blowing my chocolate allotment for a month in ten minutes, and agreeing to be a sap for Nick Sullivan.

I was clearly the kind of person who did much better facing adversity. If my luck *had* changed for the good the day before, it had made a course correction for the worst. The consolation prize was that I'd soon be fighting uphill again, playing the role of the underdog that I was born to play.

All the same, I could have spit sparks. I could just about *feel* that chocolate bar breakfast rising in lumps on my thighs. It probably would have been faster just to smear it right on my butt, since that was where all those calories were going to end up anyway.

Things had gotten out of hand.

Undoubtedly a little dark cloud was tugging along behind me as I marched into the office. There was no sign of Elaine, but that wasn't too astounding after the night before. And it was still early. I dropped my keys on my desk, started the pot of coffee which Elaine would surely need, then stared at the drawings on my board.

Even the orderly arrangement of the shrubbery for Mrs. H's garden didn't appease. I tried very hard to imagine the white tuberous begonias against the slate blue-grey of the hosta in the shade against the house, the little white outline around each hosta leaf perfectly accentuating the fleshy white begonia blooms.

Instead I saw Nick's surprised expression.

And my anger eased enough for me to acknowledge a teeny

tiny niggle of doubt. Why would he turn up now, just to play such a juvenile trick on me?

Why would he bother?

I hadn't exactly given him a chance to explain.

But then, did it really matter? Either he was playing a trick on me, or he had shown up on my doorstep because I might be useful to him.

Like a kitchen appliance.

I snarled and stuck a pencil in the sharpener, letting the little motor chew it down to a stump.

Then I sacrificed another one, because the demise of the first felt so good.

As though to prove that when things go bad, they can always get worse, the phone on my desk rang. I hesitated to answer because no good news comes at work early in the morning.

Another contractor sucked into the void. Nope, it was too early for Joel to be sure of that. Elaine couldn't be calling in, because she wouldn't expect me to be here. In fact, no one would expect me to be at work at this ungodly hour.

Except one person.

I allowed myself one sigh and picked up the phone. "Coxwell and Pope. Hi, Mom."

"Philippa? Is that you?"

Okay, I winced. Just a little. Then I sat down and braced for the worst. Some days are meant to go bad and there is nothing a mere mortal can do to stop them. Might as well ride along and check out the view.

I counted off on my fingers—Nick, trick and Mom. If all things came in threes, I was due for a break. I knocked the wood of my desk for good measure.

"What's up, Mom?"

"I was going to ask you the same thing, dear. You didn't call me back last night."

"I got in late."

"You could have called this morning."

"I just got here."

"Well, we haven't talked for a while. How is your little business coming along?"

That tripped a warning wire. Nothing good could come from family curiosity about my work. Scorn I'm used to, curiosity could only be a harbinger of trouble.

"Fine." I was proud of how neutral my voice sounded. "Why do you ask?"

"I had no idea you were expanding beyond Boston." My mother's voice hardened and I had a bare inkling of trouble before it hit. "But Evelyn Donnelly mentioned that she saw you calling on Lucia Sullivan this morning."

Mentioned. I refrained from commentary on Mrs. Donnelly. I did, however, doodle "busybody" on my scratchpad and give the word eyes and horns. "Did she? I didn't know you two were friends."

Mom snorted. "She's hardly of our class, dear, and as you might imagine, I was embarrassed that she felt so *familiar* that she could call me out of the blue. The woman is common, but then, what would you expect from new money?"

Mercifully my mother was running full steam ahead and I didn't have to comment.

"But I was concerned—as a mother, of course—that she said you looked troubled when you left. Are you worried about things, dear? Your little business not holding its own?"

Oh wouldn't she just love that! Another failure on my part would give the Coxwell clan something to cluck about for years, a little mortifying tale that could be dragged out for everyone's entertainment each Thanksgiving, Christmas and Easter dinner.

As though they didn't have enough of those.

"Everything's fine, Mom. In fact, we just signed a project yesterday that might interest you . . ."

"What interests me, Philippa, is your future. Are you seeing anyone?"

Elaine stepped into the office, looking sleek, blond and expensive. She did a double take when she realized I was there, then looked at the wall clock, clearly incredulous.

"Holy shit," she mouthed. Everyone's a critic.

I mouthed "mother." Elaine winced. She pointed her fingers at her temples and crossed her eyes, effectively communicating her state after our celebration.

I fought against a chuckle and pointed to the brewing coffee. Elaine feigned falling to her knees in gratitude. Then I remembered it was time for me to say something. "No, Mom."

"Then that's obviously why you looked so miserable this morning at Lucia Sullivan's!" A triumphant and fairly inevitable conclusion, at least from my mother. "What woman wouldn't be upset to see her life stretched out before her, empty as far as the eye can see?"

"Well, actually, Mom, anyone would be troubled when their appointment wasn't kept."

It took two heartbeats for me to realize my mistake.

"An appointment with Lucia Sullivan? To do what?"

I stuck to my cover story. "I do gardens, Mom. You know that."

"Well, I'm not surprised she wasted your time. You can hardly expect better from the likes of the Sullivans. Are you so desperate that you have to take work from her? What will people think if you do business with people like that?"

I put down my pencil with some impatience. "Lucia's a bit eccentric, Mom, but that's hardly a thing to hold against someone."

"Eccentric is the least of it, Philippa. I forbid you to take any work from Lucia Sullivan. You just don't know how it will work out."

"I'll put plants in her garden and a sign on her lawn. She'll pay me and we'll both go on our merry ways."

"I doubt that! She's a wicked, wicked person, Philippa, and if you know what's good for you, you'll stay miles away from her."

"Wicked?" Seemed a bit strong to me.

My mother heaved a sigh. "I suppose it's only because you're such a nice girl that you don't know this, but Lucia—" She struggled for the words and gave it up with a sigh of frustration. "Well, Lucia takes care of things."

"Things?" I sat back, intrigued and mystified.

"Yes, things! Unwanted *things.*" My mother waited, but I didn't get it. "Oh, Philippa. For girls who get into trouble."

"She's an abortionist?"

"She's *not* a doctor. She's one of those women who know things, who mix potions and make charms."

I half laughed. "Are you trying to tell me that Lucia is the witch of Rosemount? That's an old lame story."

"Everyone knows it! Why she and Evelyn had an enormous argument right in front of the town council. Lucia gave Evelyn the evil eye when the council ruled in Evelyn's favor." My mother's voice dropped. "And one of Evelyn's cats died the very next day."

I was skeptical. "Mrs. Donnelly's cats are ancient."

"Not all of them."

"It could have been sick."

"You're making excuses, Philippa. The cat was perfectly healthy until the council meeting."

"How do you know?"

"Why are you defending her?"

I changed the subject, abandoning that particular breach in the walls. "What was the argument about?"

"Lucia wanted to make her greenhouse bigger. It would have gone almost to the lot line and been two stories high. It would have blocked Evelyn's sunlight completely and for what? She probably intended to grow marijuana or something."

Years of exposure to my father have ensured that my mother shares not only his abhorrence of marijuana and conviction of its ills. It is the demon weed and root of much evil in the world, according to Judge Coxwell.

The irony, of course, is that neither of them have a clue what it smells like and once told Zach to quit burning incense in his apartment when he came home from college redolent of weed.

So, I let that one go.

"I certainly hope you aren't involved in that project! Why, the whole town was up in arms about Lucia's plans, not that she gave a hoot what anyone thought."

"I didn't know anything about it until you told me, Mom."

"Really?"

"Honest and true."

Mom barely paused for breath before making a maternal leap straight to Guilt Central. "Well, you should have come to the house, dear, since you were right here in Rosemount. A cancelled appointment would have given you time to stop for breakfast. And, after all, we haven't seen you in so long . . ."

"Well, uh, things are really busy at the office right now." I waved frantically at Elaine, then mimed a drowning woman. Elaine chuckled but picked up the phone, using our established trick. We had three lines installed, a fact which could be terribly useful in such moments.

The office phones rang in unison as Elaine's call was routed to the second line. Elaine put her receiver on the desk, the twinkle in her eye not nearly fair warning.

"Philippa!" she wailed. "Get the *phone,* would you? God, there's no crap wrap left in here and my panty hose are around my ankles! *Philippa!*"

Elaine's voice undoubtedly carried right down the phone line to Rosemount, just as she had planned for it to do. I was dying to laugh. My mother was outraged.

Of course.

"Philippa! Is that your partner? My goodness, but I'll never understand how you managed to link up with such a vulgar woman. She clearly doesn't come from a good family and you mark my words, Philippa Coxwell, bad breeding will out in the worst possible way . . ."

"Mom, I've got to get the other line."

"First I have to tell you the important part, Philippa, and there's nothing more important than your family and your future. You tell that to that common piece of baggage in your Ladies' Room."

"Philippa!" Elaine wailed again. The phone rang and rang. I had a very bad feeling about what was coming, though I tried to ignore it.

"Mom, I've got to go."

My mother continued undeterred. "Philippa, I've arranged for Jeffrey McAllister to take you out."

"What?" I forgot the ringing phone and sat up straight. "You fixed me up?"

"Well, I could hardly wait for you to find yourself a date. Honestly, Philippa, a person could come to the conclusion that you had no interest in men at all."

Oh, there was a leading opening—I was ready to be gay just to get out of this, but she didn't give me the chance.

"Fortunately, I know that that's not the case. Why, it seems like just yesterday that you were making moon eyes at that Sullivan boy, what was his name? He was trouble, just like all those

Sullivans are. I told you but you didn't listen and wasn't I proven right when he went to jail? *Jail,* Philippa!"

Mom inhaled in horror at the memory of that close brush with infamy and I seized the moment to make a timely diversion.

"Who is this guy?"

"Oh!" Mom's voice warmed. "Jeffrey McAllister is that nice young lawyer who joined the family practice."

A lawyer—could things get worse? I had been a fool to imagine that Mom had given up on her subversive matchmaking. She'd invited me to dinner more times than I could count when "nice young men" just happened to be in attendance. When I twigged to that trick, she enlisted dutiful Number One Son James to perpetuate the ruse. I stopped accepting his wife's dinner invitations too.

Now, Mom was going for the jugular.

"A nice, clean-cut young man, a lawyer with a future and charming manners—surely it can't be too much of a burden for you to meet the man and share a meal together."

It occurred to me that a man could be a serial killer and would be an eligible bachelor in my mother's view if he had one good suit and a conservative haircut.

"That's four," I muttered. "Bad things are supposed to come in threes." I braced myself for two more bad events.

"Stop mumbling, Philippa. You know, these young lawyers work so very hard and get lonely in the city. I'm sure he'd just love some feminine companionship. Perhaps you should cook him dinner tonight. Philippa, you might at least come up with a decent casserole. Or get something catered and pretend you made it. Just a little white lie, because after all, the way to a man's heart is through his stomach. And he's such a nice boy, and from a perfectly respectable family . . ."

"I don't need a date, Mother."

"Oh, *Mother,* is it now? Well, the thanks I get for trying to ensure your happiness."

"I don't need a date."

Mom's tone turned arch. "Because you're seeing someone already? What are you keeping from me, Philippa?"

"Nothing." Sullen and sixteen was looking like a good behavior pattern to me right now. The office phone was still ringing and it was ganging up with the champagne residuals to give me a serious headache.

"You see. You *do* need a date. Jeffrey will pick you up at noon for lunch."

"Mother! I don't do lunch!"

"Everyone who matters does lunch, Philippa."

"I have a business to run!"

"Jeffrey's very punctual, so I suggest you be ready. You never have a second chance to make a first impression, dear."

"I'm not going," I said, but the dial tone wasn't responsive to my opinion.

I treated myself to one small obscenity, then tossed the receiver back into the cradle. The office phone rang only a moment longer before Elaine hung it up too.

"Sorry. I thought I was pretty good for improv." She leaned one hip against my desk. "Still no match for the wiles of Mom, huh?"

"I should have known it would only be a matter of time."

"What?"

"She's fixing me up with a *lawyer.*" I looked my partner in the eye. "He's the first, but he won't be the last."

"You say his occupation like it's a disease."

"Trust me, it is."

"But think of all the lovely money." Elaine grinned. "You could get a few nice rocks for your collection, if nothing else."

Elaine is so open about her mercenary tendencies that it's impossible to hold them against her. She loves pretty things, pretty *expensive* things, and makes no bones about it. More than one man has bought her a bauble with a few brilliant carats just to bask in Elaine's smile.

Or maybe to enjoy other favors. I don't ask. There are some things I just don't need to know.

The men come, the men go, the gifts pile up. Heartless and gorgeous, Elaine hits men before they even know what's happening, gets what she wants and leaves them gasping for breath. She does so with such charm that more than a few of them come back for more. It's not her fault that so many of them hope to change her.

Because if nothing else, Elaine plays fair—she never pledges love, she never offers more than she's willing to deliver, and she is brutally honest with her conquests.

She hadn't found a man yet who could bear that honesty for long. I was kind of looking forward to witnessing that match.

If it ever happened.

"You've got me confused with you," I charged with a smile.

Elaine shrugged, then rummaged through the drawings on her desk. "Well, you can throw any strays my way, if you like. Lawyers make a decent buck. Have you seen the Villeroy & Boch catalog?"

"Over there. Hey, how about Bachelor number one?" I felt remarkably generous date-wise under the circumstances. "Noon today. Lawyer. My father's new junior partner and he does pay well." I recounted Mom's list of Jeffrey's assets, then spread my hands. "He's all yours."

Elaine flicked a glance my way, the quickness of the move not hiding her interest. "Lawyer, hmm? Has this paragon of masculine virtue got a name?"

"Jeffrey McAllister."

Elaine looked up quickly, her skin paling beneath her foundation. The phone rang before I could ask, then there was nothing beyond Mrs. Hathaway's fears for her prize hellebores over the course of the landscaping project.

Maybe I was working my way through a second set of three mishaps. The view was definitely looking more familiar—but then, I do well facing adversity, just like I told you before. It's feeling lucky that throws my game.

But now I was right back in the trenches. Mrs. H. was officially my numero uno concern, thanks to that lovely new contract, and I was ready to do anything to ensure she was thrilled to her toes with Coxwell & Pope.

Which was why I was in the Beast within minutes, heading for the Hathaway house to move those hellebores with my bare hands, if need be.

Time for a little client TLC. I was toying with the idea of not coming back to the office until after lunch, but already knew I wouldn't do it. There'd be hell to pay if I insulted Father's new protégé.

And the truth is that what's bred in the bone does come out in the flesh. I am my mother's daughter, for better or for worse, and the older I get, the more I see her patterns of behavior in mine. There's no getting around it—there are some things I just can't do. Being rude is one of them. I'm becoming my mother in some ways, a terrifying prospect for me which would delight her.

Tell her that, and I'll have to hurt you.

He reached the perimeter of the city, more dusty than he had been since arriving at Timbuktu. But that dust had been red, this was a more pedestrian brown.

Not that Timbuktu could have in any way been mistaken for the avenue of rampant consumerism that led to Phil's office.

Her office was on the outskirts of suburbia, presumably because land was cheaper here. The Coxwell & Pope building was small and stand-alone, a glorified double garage with cheap siding and a fenced yard behind. The front lot was gravel and the windows were coated with the resulting dust. It wasn't fancy, but he had almost tasted her pride this morning.

He could relate to that.

The city was closing fast, though. A few nurseries lingered on either side of the four-lane road, their buildings hinting at a recent past when they were still out in the country. More than one had yuppified and gone upscale—Nick guessed the others wouldn't last, at least not in this location. Looking toward Boston from Phil's office, burger joints and gas stations jostled for position, the signs of a few big discount stores rising above the rest.

Soon the fields behind would be filled with tract houses. Nick grimaced, not wanting to imagine the greenery divided into little lots, their driveways choked with mini-vans. People had to live somewhere, but he was starting to wonder what they'd do when the whole country was paved from sea to shining sea.

Those donuts had long since exhausted their usefulness, the sun was high and he was ravenous. That's what he got for eating sugary junk. It was burned through in nothing flat. Maybe he hadn't missed those donuts as much as he had thought.

On the upside, his timing was perfect. He'd kidnap Phil for lunch.

The Beast was gone, though that didn't necessarily mean that Phil was gone with it. There was also a dinged pickup truck parked in the lot. It looked to be of the same vintage as the Beast and had once been red. The lettering on the side proved it too belonged to the business.

The bed was filled with an array of shovels, plus a gizmo with an electrical cable he couldn't name. Stone samples were cast on the dusty cab seat and the windows were open. A golden retriever sprawled on the driver's seat assessed Nick with wise eyes, its tail thumping as soon as he spoke to it.

"Big schmoozer, aren't you?" he teased, scratching the dog's ears. "You'd unlock the doors and give it all away, if you could, tough guy." The dog leaned into the scratch with obvious delight, whimpering a little when Nick continued on.

A sleek small BMW nestled beside the truck, the shiny silver paint incongruous with the truck's heavy patina of dust. Company calling, he concluded. There was also a turquoise Geo, an efficient vehicle of which he heartily approved.

The chain-link gate to the small yard behind the building gaped open now, no longer padlocked as it had been this morning. He spotted a man in workboots, jeans and a red tank top sorting through the interlock and stones. It was a bit chilly for such summer wear, but the guy had the build for it. His tan gleamed gold and his hair was bleached fair, his physique testament to how many of these rocks he had moved.

No sign of Phil there.

A quick survey of the street revealed that the Beast wasn't making a reappearance. The golden retriever had propped its chin on the rolled-down window of the truck, its dark gaze fixed on Nick.

"Some watchdog," he told it. "Not so much as a growl."

That tail beat against the seat again.

He rapped once on the office door before striding in. He had only a heartbeat to notice that the office was not only as cheerful, colorful and chaotic as Phil's kitchen, but that Phil wasn't there.

Then he had a definite sense that he had interrupted something.

After all, the knockout blonde looked ready to murder the guy in the suit who was glaring right back at her. Neither even twitched when Nick entered the office, and the air was snapping.

The blonde was turned out to perfection, all sleek curves, a suit that screamed of New York and jewelry that could blind a man when it caught the sun. The guy looked to be her parallel, his suit impeccably tailored and his shoes polished to a shine. His watch was enormous, an overengineered piece of machinery that its bearer probably only used to check the time.

Despite sharing expensive taste, these two clearly weren't getting along.

"I was looking for Phil Coxwell," he said, using his best smile to no discernible effect. "But maybe this isn't a good time."

The man spared him a disdainful survey. Nick held his ground and stared back, not needing French cuffs to have any confidence in himself.

"I would suggest you call later." The other man's gaze lingered on Nick's dusty jeans. "Philippa and I have a lunch appointment, so she will not have time for you before our return."

"Maybe we should ask Philippa what she thinks about *that.*" There was just enough edge in the blonde's voice to make the other guy look her way, but she smiled so graciously that he couldn't possibly have responded in kind.

Nick immediately liked her.

"Elaine Pope," she said, her smile warming as she offered her hand. "Philippa and I are partners."

"A most unfortunate circumstance for Philippa." The guy snorted. "No wonder her family wants her to give up this excuse for a business."

Right. Phil had hinted that her family wasn't proud of her accomplishments and this one's choice of words supplied the fact that he was not blood-related.

Was Phil dating this jerk? The thought made his stomach churn with more than hunger.

Elaine bristled, her eyes snapping fire as she turned. "Really?" she inquired sweetly. "Why would it be sensible to abandon a profitable business? Surely any parent would want their child to succeed?"

"Surely any parent would want to ensure that their child consorted with the right class of people?"

"You are such a pig!" Elaine stepped forward as though she might deck him and Nick couldn't blame her.

All the same, bloodshed was better avoided. He shot Elaine a warning glance and stepped closer, letting just enough skepticism filter into his tone. "And that would be where you come in, right?"

The other man's lips thinned. "I hardly see how my role is of any pertinence to you."

"But you have no problem making Phil's decisions for her without knowing her opinion or what the circumstances of this business are."

Elaine eased closer to Nick, their alliance negotiated, signed and set in stone.

"I understand and appreciate what her family wants for her."

"But what about what Phil wants?" He deliberately kept his tone mild, since his opponent was itching for a fight. "Doesn't that count for anything?"

The other man almost smiled. "Some people cannot be trusted to make responsible decisions for themselves." He coughed lightly. "It is clear from Philippa's family's confidences that she is one of those unfortunates."

Elaine made a choking noise, but Nick laid a hand on her arm. "Who *are* you?" he asked, incredulous that anyone could be so pompous.

"And who died and made you God?" Elaine demanded.

The man in question smiled coldly. "I am Jeffrey McAllister, the new legal partner of Robert Coxwell. Anyone of any merit—" his look excluded Nick and Elaine from such company "—knows that Judge Coxwell is the most esteemed legal mind in the greater Boston area. Philippa and I have a lunch engagement."

It was interesting that Phil's credentials were solely her father's credentials.

McAllister sniffed once more, his nose wrinkling as he looked over Nick. "Though I can hardly imagine that an explanation is owed to the *help*."

It was too good of an opening to ignore.

"Me?" Nick shook his head as though the idea was ludicrous. "I don't work here." He folded his arms across his chest. "I'm Nick."

He didn't explain further, as though his first name was ample explanation in itself. Truth be told, he was enjoying the sight of McAllister trying to work out the possibilities. Those lips unpursed enough to round in dismay.

"Surely, you cannot be a *customer!*"

"No, not me." He flicked a glance over suit, shoes and watch, then let his smile turn predatory. "I just stop by for *Phil.*" Nick waited for the other man to blink quickly, a number of times in quick succession.

He had always known that the Coxwells were uptight, but if this guy was any example of what Phil put up with from them, she had his heartfelt sympathies.

"What can I say—Phil and I are close, *really* close." Nick shot a look at the avid McAllister, then picked up a china catalog as though he hadn't a care in the world. "Nice plates," he said to Elaine, clearly settling in to wait and looking as though he did so all the time.

Her smile flashed, approval of more than his taste in china in her eyes. "You have good taste."

"Um hmm. Can you put it in the dishwasher?"

The other man made an exasperated noise but they both ignored him. Elaine perched on the desk beside him. "Oh yeah, it's great stuff. Very practical." She flipped through the pages. "This looks more like you."

"Nice." As though he knew anything about china . . . or cared. "What if I drop it?"

"Well, it's porcelain, so it's tougher than china."

McAllister cleared his throat, unused to being forgotten, but Elaine turned her back on him. It was no accident to Nick's thinking.

Elaine warmed to her theme. "If it does break, though, even if you can't find the pattern locally, they have an eight-hundred number to track down stuff for customers."

The lawyer tapped his toe.

"No kidding?"

"No kidding." Elaine smiled. She was pretty, in that manicured blond, high-maintenance kind of way that did nothing for him. City girl. She needed the bright lights and modern conveniences to survive.

She'd be a lot of trouble if forced to backpack.

Whereas Phil, well, Phil struck him as the kind of woman who would cheerfully put up with a lot, enjoying the good bits and ignoring the bad.

With her family, it sounded as though she had lots of experience.

"It's expensive for a reason." Elaine's words dragged him back to the conversation at hand.

"Huh." He fanned through the catalog, not in the least bit interested in its contents. He felt McAllister fuming and was honest enough with himself to enjoy it.

"I demand to know what reason you have for seeking Philippa out," McAllister finally sputtered.

Nick and Elaine glanced at him as one. Nick waited, one beat, two, then shrugged. "I told you, she's special to me."

"How *special?*"

Nick smiled slowly and lowered his voice, as though he was recalling her many charms. "Oh, Phil is about as special as a lady can be."

Truth be told, Nick *was* thinking about Phil's charms. She'd put a lot behind her and come out fighting. He was beginning to sense how hard she'd had to buck her family's expectations at every turn to chase her own aspirations. She was making a success of her business despite them all.

And this pompous ass had been sent down by her daddy to tell her what to do next.

He knew whose side he was on.

"Funny," he said with a telling glance. "She's never mentioned you."

Dull red rose up the back of the other man's neck. "We've never actually met."

"Ah." He nodded as though that explained everything, because it did explain a lot. "You just thought you'd show up and take her to lunch? Let me guess—was this your boss's idea?"

"No, her moth . . ." McAllister shut up, his keen legal mind discerning that any further confessions could be used against him.

"Wow, I haven't had anyone's mommy set me up in a long time," Elaine mused.

"Hardly a surprise," the lawyer snapped. "Women tend to be protective of their sons."

Nick looked between the two of them and wondered what had happened before he got here.

Or whether something had happened a long time before that.

Elaine's eyes glittered coldly. Then she summoned a smile and sauntered over to the more chaotic of the two desks. She threw Nick a quick, conspiratorial wink. He noticed that that desk was stacked with gardening magazines, half-rolled drawings and one cold cup of something pink that might well be herbal tea. There was lipstick on the rim, lipstick the same pale hue that made Phil's lips look so soft.

Phil's desk.

Nick's heart began to pound as he recalled the way Phil had turned, the curiosity in her eyes when she had asked him about Bhutan. He could see the wonder lighting her features, the yearning to see the world's wonders for herself.

That was part and parcel of what made Nick travel—the need to see and smell and experience for himself—though he had lost his grip on that lately. The look on Phil's face had awakened his dormant urge to explore, as well as giving him a sudden tug of commonality with her.

Which was why he had almost kissed her again.

He wished now that he hadn't pulled back. He stared at the lipstick stain and relived the taste of Phil, the smell of her skin, the warmth of her against his chest. He might have come back to apologize and set things straight between them, but he decided then and there that he wanted one more taste before he left.

Just to make sure he hadn't imagined how good it was.

With an effort, he managed to track what Elaine was saying. "You know, just the other day, Philippa was talking about you, Nick." She lied so smoothly that he almost believed it was the truth.

Maybe, given his current thoughts, he just wanted to believe it was the truth.

He told himself sternly to not even go there.

Elaine poked beneath a hardcover book left open and frowned in apparent concentration. "She had the cutest pictures of the two of you on vacation, you know at that nude beach?" She cast Nick a wide-eyed glance and he nearly laughed out loud at her improvisation. "Well, Philippa didn't let me see all of them, of course"—Elaine even managed to blush a bit—"but oh, that sunburn must have *hurt* . . ."

"What?" McAllister made a strangled sound. "What nude beach? What vacation? Her family said nothing about Philippa having a past!"

"Everyone has a past," Nick said calmly. "At least everyone interesting does."

Elaine laughed. McAllister spun to point an accusing finger at Nick. "You're the bad influence on Philippa. I demand to know who you are! I demand to know the full extent of your relationship. *I demand to know what the hell is going on here!*"

Phil chose that moment to make her reappearance.

The Beast farted in the parking lot and ran on after the engine died. The three of them turned as one to look. Phil hauled open the door, her hair in disarray, her lipstick gone and her cheeks kissed by the sun. She was wearing flat shoes and there was a smudge of dirt on her skirt, as well as more than one run in her stockings. She looked hurried, hassled and happier than Nick had expected.

He thought she looked fantastic.

Chapter 6

I pulled into the lot at eleven fifty-five, and couldn't help but notice the gleaming silver beemer beside Elaine's econo-box. The man was punctual, as predicted by Mom Radar.

And I was filthy. I'd had to dig up those hellebores myself. I'd run my stockings and had soil under my nails, I'd almost certainly eaten my lipstick and probably had some earthy souvenirs on my suit. You've got to love black for practicality.

But Mrs. H. was delighted. And making my client happy had made me happy.

To be honest, getting my hands into the dirt always makes me happy. I like the feel of the soil in my hands, I love seeing all the life teeming within it. The hellebores had been breathtakingly healthy, though they would shock with being moved. Mrs. H. had hovered like an anxious mother hen when I dug up the plants and we made a little bond there that surprised me.

Here I had thought she was all about show, but she loved those hellebores, possibly more than her own children. Maybe they were more deserving of her affection. Not my question to ask.

But I could relate to her concern for those plants.

Mrs. H.'s hellebores were in bloom, of course, being as they are one of the first hints of spring's arrival. Hellebores like the sun in the spring but not in the summer, so they're fond of corners like the one she had chosen. Here, a hardy hydrangea was cut back to a foot or so and still slumbering, but in summer, it would be a good six feet across and shelter the hellebores beneath its shade.

The hellebore has a striking flower with five petals. Mrs. H.'s all had huge white blossoms—the classic Christmas Rose—but you can find purple and pink hellebores, even chartreuse ones. The petals hang on over the summer, and turn green while the seed pods grow from the center. The plants have lovely leathery dark green leaves and are beautiful all year long.

In the spring, though, they're pure magic.

Once Mrs. H. was convinced that I wouldn't kill her babies, we talked about adding some bulbs to showcase them. There aren't too many choices that bloom that early in Massachusetts, but some snowdrops would echo their white and green show. Or crocuses, either in giddy yellows, like Gypsy Girl, or purples like Prince Claus, or early buttery-hued C. *ancyrensis*.

My instinct was to go with both the snowdrops—the early, green-accented Flore Pleno would be perfect—and the purple crocus, maybe adding a second purple crocus patterned differently, like Barr's Purple. We could save the hydrangea—it was a lovely white-blossomed Annabelle—to shade them all in the summer.

It got her thinking about color, which was a good thing because she was uncertain about it. She struck me as a woman who liked subtlety, who wanted the garden to look simple and uniform until you crouched down and really *looked.* She was going to love those blue hostas with the fine white outline on each leaf.

There's something satisfyingly complex about garden design. Just as a choreographer has to make a beautiful whole from the movements and shapes of the individual dancers, so must I put together living things, nurture them, anticipate them, and arrange them to their own advantage through at least three seasons of the year. When a garden design works, I feel not like a creator but a facilitator.

And no garden ever feels done to me. It never can be done, because the participants aren't static. The plants grow, they thrive or they falter, the weather favors one this year and another the next. The spotlight has to move seamlessly to highlight each one in its seasonal prime, providing a shifting and interesting show.

I still visit my "completed" works—the contract might be complete, but the living sculpture of the garden never will be—and suggest a trim here, another perennial there, an addition of a little toothy-leafed plant to brighten that corner.

It's proof of my theory of incompletion that every garden I revisit surprises me in some way. It never matches my vision of how I expected it to grow—sometimes because of the plants themselves, or sometimes because the owner became a new choreographer and began making changes of their own.

And like all good dances, there's a measure of magic in the mix. Unpredictable events make the magic. Plants don't always bloom according to plan, or even in the color stated on the label. They surprise me constantly—and they amaze me in their endless variations.

My talk with Mrs. H. got me all fired up about getting back to the office and working on those plans. I was whistling as I climbed the steps to the office, feeling much more my usual self, skeptics be damned.

Maybe I wouldn't have to endure a lunch date after all. Though I hadn't planned to look like the frump special, it could certainly play to my advantage. If Jeffrey recoiled from my less than perfect state, then he could eat lunch alone.

I fully expected him to do just that—I mean, he was working for my father.

I didn't, however, expect Nick to be there.

But he was leaning against my desk, looking at me as though I held the keys to the universe. His arms were folded across his chest and he was pretty dusty, which made me feel a teensy bit guilty about kicking him out of the truck.

He also looked as though nothing short of a nuclear bomb would get him out of the office without having his say first.

Even that was touch and go.

My mouth went dry and my footstep faltered. And that meant that I was in trouble already. After all, I had been positive I'd never see him again, that he'd just hop back on a plane and head back to Seattle. Or somewhere even more exotic.

I told myself not to read too much into anything.

He must want something from me.

Before Nick could say anything, I turned to the only other man in the office. Jeffrey looked as I had expected—all turned out in Brooks Brothers, tall, lean, handsome and breathtakingly predictable. He seemed horrified by my appearance. Nick might prove tough to shake, but Jeffrey could be sent running in a hurry.

Elaine, oddly enough, didn't look inclined to pitch relief.

"You must be Jeffrey." I stepped forward to offer my hand, dirty nails and all. "I'm Philippa Coxwell."

But it was Nick that caught my hand and stepped between us. He looked dangerous, disreputable and—as much as I didn't want to admit it—bitably sexy. If my heart had been on a diving board, the lurch it made would have been a glorious belly flop into the pool.

So much for immunity.

"Phil, we've got to talk."

My habitual weakness for this man was making an encore that I could have lived without. "We *did* talk."

"No. You've got to hear me out."

I tried to pull my hand from his grip and lost. Still I tried to be sensible. "Why?"

"Because I don't want you to be angry, especially not with me." His voice dropped in the way that made my knees turn to butter and he smiled that little smile I loved. His thumb moved persuasively across my hand, leaving a heat wave in its wake. "It would be one thing if I deserved it, but not this time."

I tried to look unswayed.

"You're my oldest friend, Phil. That's not something worth chucking away over a misunderstanding."

Oh, he was good. My defenses were crumbling fast—it was time to bail. "I *did* understand you. You thought I'd be useful to you, but hey, I'm not." I forced a smile that was supposed to be perky. "Happy trails, Nick. See you in fifteen years, maybe. Maybe not."

I tried to step past him but didn't make it. His hands landed on my elbows and he looked annoyed as I'd never seen him before. "I'm not my brother," he insisted, then bent and kissed me.

It was a bone melter of a kiss and put our only previous effort to shame. Every sinew dissolved right on cue. His tongue slid across my lips and I opened my mouth to him, and then it was too late.

The man tasted better than chocolate.

Which is saying something.

In fact, I could give up chocolate for kisses like that—and

probably lose ten pounds in the process. I forgot whatever it was we were arguing about and didn't care.

I don't know how my hands got in his hair, but it was thick and well worth grabbing on to. He smelled like sunshine and wind and made me hungry for something I'd never much had a hankering for before.

I don't know whether Nick meant to shut me up or to persuade me to agree with him or just to set my undies on fire, but he accomplished all three in record speed.

I was dizzy when he lifted his head and had to hang on to his shoulders to make sure I didn't fall over.

His expression was no less intense than before. "Phil, I didn't lie to you. I didn't set you up. I'd never do that to you."

Oh, the standard was lost and the battle against temptation going very badly.

"Never?" I even squeaked, to my eternal shame.

"*Never,* Phil." Nick tucked a strand of hair behind my ear and I guessed we were both remembering a certain dark night. A lump came up in my throat and I had to admit that Nick never had treated me badly.

Well, other than disappearing into the distance without a word of thanks some fifteen years before.

Besides that.

"I'm sorry you were upset this morning," he said quietly. "That wasn't part of my plan."

I wanted so much to believe him. Call it a weakness. "But what was your plan? What happened?" I remembered a bit too late that he had tried to stop me from going into the house.

What did he know that I didn't?

He smiled that dangerous little smile. "Why don't we go for lunch and talk about it?"

"You were upset *this morning?*" Jeffrey squawked, looking every inch my father on the verge of a hissy fit.

Sadly, forgetting about his presence hadn't been enough to make him disappear. A-la-kazam.

"Are you involved with *this* man? My God, Philippa, are you sleeping with him? Why didn't anyone tell *me?*"

Too late I realized I'd be hearing about this kiss—and various admonitions associated with my behavior—until hell froze over.

And probably for a while after that.

"Oh shut up, Jeffrey," Elaine said with surprising scorn. I wasn't expecting her to come to my defense. "Much as I hate to break the news, the world does not revolve around you."

Jeffrey turned on Elaine, animosity in his eyes. "You haven't changed, but now you've changed Philippa. I'm not surprised! You just wait until I tell Judge Coxwell. You just wait until her family gets wind of this. You'll be shut down so fast that you won't have time to blink, and it'll be just what a hussy like you deserves."

Elaine's face turned scarlet. "Oh, I thought you were an ass before, but this . . ."

"Hey, hey, hey," Nick intervened, raising one hand. "Deep breath all around. Let's calm down before someone gets hurt."

Elaine folded her arms across her chest, as sullen as a spoiled princess denied her golden ball.

Jeffrey's gaze fixed on Nick's hand, where it rested on my elbow. He spoke through his gritted teeth, a neat trick he had probably learned from my father. "Philippa, I have made reservations for twelve-fifteen at Sabatino's. If you intend to accompany me, we shall have to go now or Victor will be forced to surrender the table."

I had a much better offer. "I'm sorry, Jeffrey, but my mother never told me about her arrangements until this morning. And I'm, uh, busy for lunch today."

Jeffrey's nostrils flared. He really was my father thirty years younger. "Your father expects me to take you to lunch. I intend to take you for lunch, and I intend to do so today."

Because it was a great career move.

Be still, my foolish heart. "I'm not going, Jeffrey." I smiled for him. "Be honest with yourself—you don't really want me to."

His gaze flicked over me once, lingered tellingly on the run in my stocking and mud caked on my shoe. "Don't be ridiculous," he insisted with gallantry that was far from convincing. "Of course, I want to take you to lunch."

"Good choice, Philippa," Elaine declared, then affected Jeffrey's upscale accent. "You have to watch the class of people with whom you consort. I wouldn't date him either."

Jeffrey looked fit to explode. His hands clenched and he looked daggers at Elaine.

Who smiled.

"Gad!" Joel stepped out of the shadows at the back door and I jumped a bit because I hadn't realized he was there. "I should come inside more often. I had no idea life was so interesting in here." He leered at Nick's butt, then turned an appreciative eye on Jeffrey. "And such fine scenery—" he lisped, then rolled his eyes and shivered in apparent delight.

I winced at what Joel called his Drag Queen voice—because he only uses it to make people uncomfortable.

It works.

Joel pulled out a chair, then propped his chin on his hand and gazed at a horrified Jeffrey in apparent adoration. "I'll go for lunch with you, cowboy." He winked. "How else can I make your dreams come true?"

Jeffrey turned as red as a beet and I tried not to laugh. His mouth opened and closed a few times, and when he did speak, he was far from coherent. "Why you, but you, you're, you're . . ."

"A flaming fag," Joel provided with gusto. He opened his

eyes with mock astonishment. "But why are you so surprised, big shooter? Aren't *you?*"

Jeffrey went white. Elaine made a choking sound that might have been laughter.

Joel lifted one hand to his mouth in feigned dismay. "Oh, my goodness gracious golly me, you mean you're *straight?* Why I would never have guessed . . ."

That was apparently enough for Jeffrey. He offered a jumble of apologies, then fled to his car. We all watched out the window as he seemed to have problems with working the remote on his key chain.

"You know, Joel, that was a bit mean," I said, because I felt that somebody should.

"He had it coming," Nick said grimly, not surrendering my elbow.

Elaine wasn't content to leave well enough alone. "Figures you drive a wanna-beemer!" she shouted, holding the door open with her foot. "A real lawyer would have the big sedan!"

Jeffrey straightened with dignity and bestowed a cold glance upon her. He surveyed Elaine's Geo pointedly, then looked back. "Your car suits you—cheap and disposable."

Yeow! I'd obviously missed something good.

But then I realized what it had to be. I suppose that it was only a matter of time before this happened. Elaine had dated every eligible guy on the Eastern Seaboard—sooner or later, I had to find one of her castoffs.

Or at least, my mother did.

I gathered that she and Jeffrey had not parted on good terms.

Elaine's chin lifted. "Well, at least I'm not pretending to be more than I am. Honesty might be worth a try, McAllister."

"Honesty?" Jeffrey propped his hands on his hips and practically barked. "Here's some honesty—I worked hard for this car and everything I have, whereas you milk everything out of someone else. You don't think this car is good enough because I'm driving it, but if someone *gave* it to you in exchange for services rendered, you'd snap up the keys without another thought." He hauled open his car door savagely. "How's that for *honesty*, Ms. Pope?"

He didn't wait for an answer, but revved the engine and squealed the tires as he left. If nothing else, Jeffrey hadn't been one of Elaine's usual no-fuss-no-muss affairs.

Nope, there was scar tissue there.

"Shit," Elaine whispered, so low that we were obviously not supposed to hear her. "I hate it when he's right."

Then she turned back with a bright grin that didn't hide how unsettled she was. "If you're going for lunch, could you be back one-ish? I've got to scoot out to the Montgomerys' then and play with floor samples."

"You didn't say you knew Jeffrey."

Nick became very interested in the floor pattern, but Joel listened unabashedly. "You didn't ask." Elaine slammed a sample book closed on her desk, sat down and blinked intently at her Day Timer.

"I'm asking now."

Her glance could have been lethal. "Then, don't."

I took a step back, not used to her speaking sharply to me. Nick's hand moved to the back of my waist and its weight was reassuring.

Elaine surveyed her kingdom, then flicked a finger at Joel. "Get your boots off those catalogs, my lady fair. They're off to a client and I won't have your dust on them."

Joel shivered dramatically before he complied. "Oh, I love it when you get feisty." He blew Elaine a kiss and she swung her hand at him in a playful swat.

"Shoo!"

"I get a tax credit for working with the emotionally impaired," I told Nick, sotto voce. "Though usually they're slightly better behaved."

"Something about *that* man that brings out the worst in us," Elaine declared, jabbing one finger toward the departed BMW.

"Are you even gay?" Nick asked Joel. "Or were you just scaring the locals?"

Joel laughed heartily, speaking in his normal voice. "It's all painfully true. I'm the token poof. Every design company needs one—we decided I could play with the rocks just to challenge expectations."

"And you love it," I reminded him.

"Don't let him fool you," Elaine growled. "Joel's eye-candy for Philippa and me, and even better, he's calorie free."

Joel grinned and spread his hands, guilty as charged and proud of it.

"Your dog?" Nick asked, indicating Joel's truck.

"Jezebel." Joel beamed with pride. "Isn't she the best?"

"Maybe not the best watchdog, but she has a good temperament."

"Mess with me or the truck and you'll change your mind but quick."

"Jez is very loyal," I confirmed.

Elaine was drumming her fingers and I knew she'd change the subject. "Oh, Mommy Coxwell will be furious that her matchmaking didn't work," she mused. She wasn't much for dogs—which was why ol' Jez hung out in the truck or yard instead of in the office—and usually changed the subject away from Joel's darling. "Shall we mount a defense for you, Philippa?"

"Especially if she hears you chose the riffraff," Nick added. I looked at him in surprise, but he clearly knew what my mother thought of the Sullivans.

But then, she's not the most subtle creature.

Elaine smiled, genuinely this time. "Welcome to the club of undesirables, Nick. Judging from your performance so far, you're going to fit right in."

"But he definitely complicates the mix with that whole sexy angle." Joel rubbed his chin thoughtfully. "Speaking of which, I'd give that kiss a seven point seven, Elaine. What did you think?"

"Well, it was a good approach." She frowned, mocking the concentration of an Olympic judge as she surveyed us. I felt a blush rising from my toes. "Excellent delivery."

"Great follow-through." Joel agreed. "But don't you think we could have seen some more creativity with the hands?"

"That's enough," I tried, but might as well have spit into the wind.

"Oh, maybe," Elaine agreed. "But it was a public setting. I give him bonus points for not being too pushy under the circumstances."

"You two are unbelievable." I tugged Nick's elbow. "We have to go, right now, otherwise the lines will be huge."

But Nick didn't move. "We have to know our score, Phil." A wicked glint lit his eyes. "How else are we going to improve?"

Improve?

Joel hooted and applauded. "Points for attitude!"

"You're all nuts." I turned to leave, but didn't get out the door quickly enough to miss hearing the conclusion.

"Seven point nine, Joel," Elaine decided. "Couldn't be a shade less."

"Average score, seven point eight." Joel winked. "Not bad for a new team of contenders."

"Does that mean we take the gold?" Nick asked, apparently serious, and I gave up hoping the floor would swallow them—or me—whole. I tried to haul him forcibly out for lunch, but he was about as movable as a set of concrete steps.

Joel scribbled as though he was tallying scores, then poked at Elaine's calculator. He shook his head sadly. "I'm sorry, Nick, just the silver."

He assumed the attitude of a sportscaster, seizing a letter-opener for his "microphone." "The East German team is tough to beat, don't you think, Elaine? They've got discipline and the endurance to really pull through in the end." Joel offered her the end of the letter opener.

"You're right, Joel. Training is a lifestyle for them." Elaine nodded sagely. "From the age of ten, they make tremendous sacrifices. It's tough for our American kids to compete when the playing field isn't level . . ."

"I could have you all committed and get some kind of volume discount," I suggested, but everyone ignored me.

"I demand a steroid test," Nick insisted.

Elaine nodded. "You know how they are! Did you see the shoulders on their so-called women's swim team?"

"And the chest hair!" Joel added, before the pair of them started to laugh. Their routine collapsed without further ado.

Joel stood up and offered his hand. "Hey, Nick, I don't know where you came from or who you are, but I like you. You ever change teams, you give me a call."

Nick shook his hand. "I think I'm a lifer."

Joel sighed theatrically. "All the good ones are."

"I don't think so." Elaine gave Joel's butt a pinch.

"See what I have to put up with?"

"It's a damn shame," Nick agreed.

I tugged his sleeve again. "Will you come on already?"

"Ready when you are." Nick slipped his arm around my shoulders, heading for the door as though I had been the one holding them up. I caught the scent of his skin and felt suddenly flustered. I wasn't used to Nick touching me so easily and I certainly hadn't been touched by very many men overall.

Clearly I was out of my depth.

Again.

And I was a mess. Dressing for success would certainly help me summon a bit of composure. "I should change my shoes. These flats don't look good with the suit."

"Why, because I'm going black tie?" Nick rolled his eyes. "Forget your heels, let's walk. It's the company that counts, Phil, not what shoes you're wearing."

How was I going to resist a man who said things like that?

He grabbed my hand and pulled me out the door, sparing a jaunty wave for Elaine and Joel. "I am seriously on low fuel, Phil." He eyed the line of fast-food restaurants dubiously. "Take me someplace where everything doesn't come with fries and I'm all yours."

My heart skipped a beat, even though I knew he was just making a joke. "I know just the place."

Chapter 7

Don't tell anyone, but ethnic food is my secret weapon. You won't catch me snagging a burger—or anything else—from a typical fast-food place. That kind of food is fast, all right. It makes a beeline for my butt, settles in and is just about impossible to aerobicize away.

Trust me on that one. The only things worse are donuts.

But the rest of the world uses more discretion when filling their plates and their bellies than we often do. Give me lots of legumes and not much meat, give me whole grain bread so thick and chewy that I forget about butter—I never *completely* forget about butter, but I suffer temporary amnesia if the bread is good enough—give me beans and lentils and couscous and spinach pasta, give me vegetables until I can't eat another bite.

Give me Indian and Thai, Szechuan and Hunan, Spanish and Moroccan, Italian and Greek. Give me big salads and interesting combinations of flavors, give me color and spice. This kind of food is guilt-free and filling, and it's even gorgeous to look at.

There are always a few things to avoid, but they're obvious ones—I'm not a dim sum fan, and I don't eat anything deep-fried, I pass on most sauces because they're sugar city. Steamed rice, preferably brown and chewy, is my carb of choice, and I lean heavily toward vegetarian offerings, turning a blind eye to the pleasures of fat.

I *love* Indian food. I love the colors and the smells and the complex artistry of it. I love how it looks and how it surprises your tongue and how many different combinations and permutations of everything there are. I love spicy accented with sweet, maybe some sour. I even love the names of everything—string the names together to make a caravan to the unknown.

And when it comes to conjuring a little bit of nirvana in the kitchen, Chandra is the best.

Her restaurant is small and never crowded, a bit too far from the colleges for students and a bit too redolent of wondrous curries to attract the suits. It's decorated in dirtied vivid hues that Elaine would never put together but that work all the same. They make me wonder whether my vision could ever stand to visit India.

Or maybe I was just thinking that way because I was with Nick. He'd probably been there a hundred times. I didn't ask.

Chandra changes the look often, mixing and matching her collection of plates and linens. Today our table had a cloth of giddy pink edged in gold embroidery, topped with another laid diagonally in a yellow that would make your eyes pop all by itself. It shimmered against the fuschia, then hummed when the waitress set plates of persimmon red on top. The table on my right had a green cloth as its base—it was exactly the hue of avocado paste and was vibrating quietly where it came close to the pink.

Lucia would have loved it.

I thought about tucking something bright pink among the greens of Mrs. H.'s hellebores, just for fun.

I followed my usual menu strategy and enjoyed the wealth of possibilities for their own sakes. I chose what I would eat carefully, then drank lots of water and enjoyed every single bite. Eating slowly is another one of my state secrets.

So is *savoring*.

Nick meanwhile hoovered his way down Chandra's sumptuous buffet twice before he stopped for breath.

"This"—he punctuated the word with an intense green look at me—"is really good. You are officially an angel of mercy." He ran a piece of nan bread around the rim of his plate to catch the last of some sauce, then closed his eyes and did a little savoring of his own.

I watched him, then just about jumped through the ceiling when he suddenly opened his eyes.

"What's in this? There's a spice I don't know in this curry. It's darker, maybe deeper. What do they use?"

"She, not they. Chandra." I sipped my water. "And I have no idea."

"She doesn't share her recipes?"

"I've never asked."

He was clearly incredulous. "Why not? This is fantastic."

"Well, I don't cook, so there's no point." I shrugged. "I just come here."

If I had been trying to deflect his attention, I'd just failed. Nick propped his elbows on the table to give me his undivided attention. Butterflies on pins have nothing on what I was feeling in that moment.

"How can you not cook? *Everyone* cooks. What do you eat?"

That steady look should come with a warning label. "I make

toast and herbal tea. I nuke broccoli. These are the extents of my culinary talents."

He snorted, threw his napkin on the table and picked up his plate to return to the buffet. "No wonder you've lost so much weight. You've got to eat, Phil."

It took me a minute to find my voice. "I *do* eat! That's my problem!"

But he didn't get it. "You're not eating much here. And you ate nothing this morning." He shook his head. "You'll fade away to a shadow, Phil. You need to take care of yourself."

"For God's sake, I'm hardly anorexic."

He looked skeptical. "Women take these fashion magazines too seriously. Phil, it's healthy for a woman to have some meat on her bones, not to mention that it's sexy for a woman to have curves . . ."

I lost it.

"My curves have curves! And I can't just eat whatever I want. My God, Nick, if I learned to cook, I'd be nibbling all the time and would be as huge as a house." I was shouting and I didn't care. "I have the slowest metabolism on the planet! Do you think it's easy to watch every bite, to count every calorie, to pass on everything I love just to make sure I'm never Fat Philippa again? Do you think it's easy for me to sit here and not inhale five thousand calories of goodies?"

He sat down and looked at me hard, his foray apparently forgotten. I ran out of gas and stared at my plate, embarrassed that I had admitted so much so publicly.

And so loudly.

"I'm sorry, Phil. I had no idea that you were doing it on purpose." I felt him studying me but I avoided his gaze. "I guess I put my foot back into it again."

I pushed a bit of chicken around my plate and sneaked a

peek. He looked contrite but that old wound was oozing one more time.

"Hey, Phil."

Oh, danger danger, there was that black velvet voice again.

"Talk to me."

"I've said plenty."

Nick leaned across the table and caught my hand in his. "You look terrific, don't imagine otherwise. I always thought you were as cute as hell."

"Liar."

He shook his head. "No, you've got this little smile that used to make me nuts." I looked up, ever hopeful, and he smiled. "Yep, that's the one. It's as though you know something good but you're not going to tell. I used to think of it as your Mona Lisa smile."

Okay, so I was charmed. Maybe I'm easily charmed.

Maybe I still found Nick pretty irresistible.

And it was definitely getting warmer in Chandra's, though that wasn't because of the curry. His admiration made me get all hot and bothered.

"I thought you were going back to the buffet." Not a smooth segue, but it would do.

"I was going to." He watched me, earnesty personified. "Do you mind?"

"Why?"

"Well, it's rude for me to play the human vacuum while you're exercising such self-control."

That was it. Asking whether I minded was the sweetest thing any man had ever done.

I was officially all his. "No, I don't mind. I might be pea green with envy, but I don't mind. I'll live vicariously."

We shared a smile.

"I just got lucky, Phil. I was born with a fast metabolism." He shrugged and stood up, lingering a moment, his expression deadpan. "Either that, or it's Freddie."

"Freddie? Who's Freddie?"

"My pet tapeworm."

I just about snorted my allotted teaspoon of mango chutney over that.

"I figure I picked him up somewhere near La Paz, en route to the Inca Trail and Macchu Picchu. It was a bad trip, between the altitude sickness and Freddie settling in. Now, though, he keeps me lean and mean."

Nick winked and returned to the buffet.

Freddie the tapeworm. It was sick, but kind of funny. I was still shaking my head when he came back.

"So." He set another steaming and heaping plate on the table and I didn't even care. "Does your mother often fix you up with types like Jeffrey?"

"I think she's getting desperate."

"For?"

"Grandchildren, maybe. For me to enter the blessed state of holy matrimony, certainly."

"You sound less than thrilled."

I shrugged. "So, maybe I'm a romantic. Don't shoot."

He chuckled but before he could launch another personal question, I changed the subject. "What do you think happened with Lucia?"

He sobered immediately. "I don't know. She was there yesterday, murdered in broad daylight." His gaze searched mine. "You're sure there was nothing?"

"No corpse, no blood, no Lucia. It's not the kind of thing you miss."

Nick didn't smile. "What did it smell like?"

I thought about that for a moment. "Like a greenhouse.

Lush and humid, you know." I shook a finger at him as I recalled. "The plumeria was in bloom—the place was filled with perfume."

He poked at his food. "How hot was it in there?"

"Actually, it was a bit cooler than I would have expected. Some of those plants, not the orchids so much but the nepenthes and anthurium, like it hot and humid. I was surprised that someone who would bother to have them wouldn't have turned up the heat—but then, they were blooming, so they must be happy. Maybe whoever discovered Lucia turned the heat down because they didn't know better."

"Or opened the windows to get rid of the smell."

I was confused. "Of the flowers?"

"No. Of death."

I didn't think I needed to know that. "What do you think happened?"

"Well, obviously someone killed Lucia. Maybe they were still there when I got there. At any rate, it seems as though this person wanted to make it look as though I had done the deed."

"The knife."

"And the timing." He frowned.

"I thought you heard a police siren?"

"I did. I was thinking that someone called the police to ensure I was caught red-handed, so to speak, but then that would mean that the police had found Lucia."

"Maybe they did."

"Um. But it's pretty weird that there was no one there this morning. Did you see any signs that they'd been there?"

I shook my head. "Everything was pristine. Maybe too pristine. Maybe they were watching the house."

"Waiting for me to come back? Maybe." He turned his attention to his meal. "Or maybe they just relied on Mrs. Donnelly to keep them posted."

"Which is funny, since she and Lucia evidently just had a big fight."

He looked up in surprise and I told him what my mother had said.

"That's interesting." He grimaced. "Sounds like Lucia though."

"You don't think she had anything to do with the cat dying, do you?"

Nick shrugged. "I'd like to say no way, but I don't know. Depends how angry she was. She might have put a little can of salmon out in the garden, one that had been embellished a bit."

I shivered. "That's not nice."

"Those two have always been at it, ever since the cats found a way into the greenhouse."

"What difference did that make?"

"Mrs. Donnelly didn't let them out to play, Phil. She doesn't like cleaning litter boxes, but the cats were never excited about Rosemount winters. The greenhouse must have felt like the lap of luxury."

I pushed the rest of my lunch away. "Oh."

"Yeah, oh. The smell was out of this world. Lucia went ballistic. The only thing that stopped her from making cat stew was that I found the hole and blocked it. But war was declared."

"Do you think sometimes that people just don't have enough to do?"

He smiled. "Definitely."

"I guess it's a good thing you stayed in the Beast."

"Why's that?"

"Well, she certainly let my mother know in a hurry that I'd been there."

Nick looked up suddenly. "No kidding?"

"No kidding."

He pushed his own plate away impatiently. "I don't like this."

"I don't like it either, but that's not going to change my mother calling me." My joke fell flat.

"Not that, Phil." He pushed one hand through his hair and sat back to watch me. "I should never have looked you up again."

If he was looking for a way to ruin the mood, that was a good choice.

"Well, it's a bit too late for that." My tone was a bit snippy. "What are you going to do?"

He folded his arms across his chest. "It doesn't matter."

"What?"

"No more, Phil. You shouldn't have been involved as much as you were. I came back today to apologize. I'm sorry I got you involved, then and now. From here on out, this is my problem."

"Well then, don't let me keep you."

He leaned forward, his eyes dark. "You're ticked off at me."

I blushed, though I should have expected him to call a spade a spade. "So, what if I am? Doesn't sound as though you'd care."

"Well, you're wrong. I do." He lifted one eyebrow. "This is supposed to be a reconciliation lunch."

"So you can wander off into the sunset, guilt-free?"

His features set determinedly, revealing nothing of his thoughts. "Nothing but a footprint, Phil. It's my motto."

"And the name of your business."

He looked up with sudden interest and I knew I had slipped. "How did you know that?"

"Someone told me," I lied and flushed the color of the table linens. Time to redirect traffic. "You're not going to take the blame for what Sean did this time, are you?"

Nick picked up his fork again. He began to clean off his plate, but he looked grim and there was no enjoyment of the food in his manner.

And he wasn't answering me.

"Tell me, do you always play the grand inquisitor?" I asked.

"What's that supposed to mean?"

"You ask all the questions. You pry all sorts of information out of me, yet you won't tell me anything at all."

"It's better that way."

"For who?"

He cast the fork on the clean plate and pushed it away. "Why are you angry with me?"

"Who says I am?"

He studied me for a long moment and I tried not to fidget. There he went again, assessing, analyzing, replaying the conversation. I wasn't surprised when he nailed it in one. "You're mad that I said I shouldn't have looked you up."

He was right and he knew it, so I saw no reason to admit the truth.

Nick leaned forward and traced one fingertip on the tablecloth around my own fingers. He didn't touch me but still made me very aware of his proximity. I figured that pulling my hand back would make me look skittish, so I left it there. But I stared at the rhythmic movement of his tanned fingers as he traced around my hand and around and around.

"Maybe I should clarify," he said quietly. "I shouldn't have looked you up and gotten you involved in this. I regret that, because I don't know how this is going to shake out, and I don't want you to feel any repercussions. You were right—I wasn't thinking straight last night." He gave me a sharp glance. "But I don't regret seeing you again, Phil. You're the first change I've seen in a long, long time that was for the good."

"And what does that mean?"

He studied me. "That you're still you, you're still the same person I remember, but you've made yourself into who you want to be. It's a change that's both honest and courageous, and I'm glad I got to see it."

His thumb moved across my knuckle and we said nothing. I tried to figure out the last time anyone said something so nice to me.

The thing was that I wasn't quite ready to let Nick Sullivan sail out of my life again, whether he said those kind of things or not. "So, what are you going to do next?" I tried to ask casually, but it didn't work.

"Let it go, Phil." Nick pulled his hand back and watched me carefully. He was establishing distance between us and I knew what that meant.

But I wasn't going to make it that easy for him to check out and leave the keys on the TV. You see, there comes a point when you know what you want, or at least you're curious enough about it to take a chance. You can't just sit around and wait for wishes to come true. Sometimes you have to reach out and snag that star, maybe stuff it forcibly in your pocket.

He'd said a lot of nice things to me, he'd come to me for advice and he'd come back to make sure we didn't part badly. He might very well be just erasing a footprint, but he was pretty worried about ensuring the job was done right.

I took that as encouragement.

"Speak, oh inscrutable one. I'm just curious."

"Why?"

I shook my head. "There you go again."

He leaned forward, bracing his elbows on the table. "I'm going to visit Sean." He was watching me very carefully again, looking for all the world like a wily and unpredictable dragon, one desperately trying to look innocent.

One who you might make the mistake of thinking was

asleep—right before he pounced and gobbled you up, breathing a little fire in the process.

Maybe he was looking for a little encouragement of his own.

"Want a ride?" I offered before I lost my nerve.

His eyes glittered. "Missing my little brother?"

I laughed. "Hardly."

Nick didn't laugh with me. "But you were always sweet on him," he said with a caution the words didn't deserve. "It would only be natural for you to want to see him again."

"Right. I gave up wanting to see Sean gelded a long time ago."

Nick was suddenly leaning across the table. "I don't understand. You were nuts about him."

" 'Were' is the operative word, Nick. It didn't last long. He treated me like garbage and that was the end of that."

I started to get up but Nick wasn't ready to let this drop. He stood so that I could get out between the tables, an effective roadblock if ever there had been one. "But you cried your way through a whole dispenser of napkins that night."

He smelled really good and it made me tingle to be so close. All the same, I pretended my heart wasn't galloping for the finish line. A woman's got to have some pride.

"Because I had been such a dope, Nick. Not because my heart was breaking or anything melodramatic like that. It's not as though I really knew anything about him—we'd never even talked before he asked me out. I guess that should have been a big clue." I rolled my eyes. "Honestly, Nick, I'm not that stupid about men, despite what my mother thinks."

He thought about that, and I wondered why this was so interesting to him. "When did you last see Sean?"

"I don't know. Probably around the same time I last saw you. Why do you care?"

A twinkle lit his eyes. "Just curious."

Trust him to dig out my secrets and keep his own. I decided

that he'd had enough amnesty on that one. "You think I'm still sweet on him." I patted his hand. "God, it's cute when you're protective."

I'd bet good money that no one had ever called Nick Sullivan cute before and his expression told me I'd rolled snake eyes.

"Cute?" He practically spat the word out on the table. "I don't think any such thing . . ."

"That's right, you're not thinking." I scooped up my purse and waved to Chandra for the bill. "I wouldn't want to be Sean when you show up to talk to him."

His features darkened. "If he hurt Lucia . . ."

"And he probably did. So, here's my free bit of legal advice. It would be in your best interests to have a witness of this little interview, Nick." I gave him a knowing look. "We both know what a lying snake Sean is and you'll want a third party to confirm what was said and not said."

He stepped back, his eyes narrowed. "Just how well do you know my brother?"

"As well as I need to." He looked unpersuaded so I leaned closer. "Nick, he would never have let you do what you did if he had a scrap of decency in his soul."

"He'd learned to expect as much." He shrugged. "I taught him to."

"Ha. Some people take and some people give, Nick. It's wired right in. If it hadn't been you, he would have expected a gimme from someone else. It's just the way Sean is."

"Phil, you don't need to go with me."

Ah, the lone wolf, hunting his prey alone, regardless of what price he might have to pay. "You're right. He might not even be there."

"He'll be there."

"He might have a job."

Nick shook his head. "I doubt it."

I knew my curiosity showed. "How would you know?"

"I dropped by already, but relax, counselor. He doesn't know it. And I'm guessing about the job. It wouldn't be his style."

He didn't say anything more, which I figured was my cue to exit stage left. I'd made an offer that I thought he couldn't refuse, but I was wrong.

Live and learn.

"Well, I've got to get back for Elaine."

"I know." Nick laid claim to the bill before it hit the table, conjuring a fifty so fresh it might have been printed in Lucia's basement yesterday. I had a fleeting glimpse of the inside of his wallet and it was fat with more crispy new bills.

"I'll get this." He looked me dead in the eye, as though he'd dare me to ask. "It's not nearly the thanks I owe you, Phil, but it will have to do."

So, I had the thank-you I'd waited so long to collect. It didn't feel nearly as good as I'd thought it would, but there you go. I'd been pretty blunt about my interest, but whatever interest he might have had had gone AWOL.

The reconciliation lunch was over.

"Well, take care." I started to cross the restaurant, knowing damn well I shouldn't have expected better but disappointed all the same. I was not going to look back.

"When do you think you'll be cleared up?"

I spun to find Nick right behind me and nearly lost my balance. He caught my elbow and steered me toward the door. "What?"

"To drop in on Sean. I'd like to get that recipe from Chandra first and you probably have some things to tie up." Nick frowned at his watch. "Would three be too early for you?"

I gaped at him and he smiled slowly, raising a fingertip to my lips. "Speak, inscrutable one. Yes or no?"

"Why are you changing your mind?"

He smiled and I had the distinct sense that dragon was preparing to have a little dessert. "Does it matter?"

"Yes."

His smile broadened, and his gaze dropped to my lips. I could feel the warmth of his hand on the back of my waist again and I liked it just fine. "You're very persuasive, Ms. Coxwell."

I didn't even have the wits to step away, though my voice did sound a bit high. "Three's good."

He nodded once. "I'll see you then."

And just to add to the surreal sense of the moment, Nick bent and brushed his lips across mine. His fingers fanned across my back and urged me closer. It wasn't as good as that last kiss—mostly because it didn't last long enough—but it still made me dizzy.

Not so dizzy that I didn't knock wood on the way out, though.

Chapter 8

Nick directed me to a street in the North End and I had to squeeze the Beast into the only spot we could find—it was not a lot of fun. He went straight to a town house that had been divided into apartments and leaned on the bell for #2.

I wondered when he had last talked to Sean as the bell echoed distantly.

Nick rang again when there was no response, then someone snarled over the intercom. "Whatever you're selling, I don't need any."

"Sean, it's Nick."

There was a long pause, so long that I thought he'd leave us standing there until hell froze over. Then the security lock on the door clicked. Nick pulled it open, ushering me in, and we climbed the stairs.

Sean was standing at the top of the flight, hands on his hips, silhouetted against the light from a fan window. It occurred to me that a flair for drama might be a dominant gene.

Even in the bad light, it was evident that the years had not been good to Sean Sullivan. That washboard stomach was gone—or at least buried beneath an avalanche of gut. He clearly thought he was still a looker—his jeans were tight, exhibiting more than should be legal to display, and his sweatshirt had the logo of a university football team. Even though he was about my age, he looked fifty if he was a day.

Maybe there is some justice in this world.

He grinned and raised his hand for a high five, a parody of the sleek jock he used to be. "Hey, big brother, long time no see."

"I wonder why." Nick's tone seemed very dry in contrast.

Sean hesitated only a minute before shoving out his hand, and grinning too broadly. "Aw, come on!" he said boisterously as Nick took his hand with evident reluctance, then hugged Nick.

Nick is not a group hug kind of guy. He never has been. He said nothing but didn't really get into the spirit of the embrace. He certainly didn't participate.

Sean backed off and openly studied Nick. "If you've come for money, I don't have any."

"That's not why I came."

Sean elbowed him, his familiarity at odds with Nick's reticence. And distinctly at odds with the history between them. "Hey, if you're giving out money, I'll be glad to help."

Nick shook his head.

Sean turned on me, clearly hoping for easier prey. To my surprise, he checked me out but never spoke directly to me, turning instead back to Nick. "Nice piece."

I bristled but there could have been heavy gauge steel up Nick's spine. "Maybe you remember Philippa Coxwell."

"No shit! *You're* Philippa Coxwell?" Sean ogled, a past association, however bad, apparently enough to declare open season. "Jesus Jenny, you really have changed." He winked. "Anytime you want to upgrade, Philippa baby, you just give me a call."

Nick's hand landed on the back of my waist but I can fight my own battles. Besides I couldn't keep my mouth shut. "Why? Do you have friends with manners?"

He colored, then gave Nick a belligerent glance. "So what do you want? You're a regular little ray of sunshine today, but then I shouldn't have expected much different."

"To talk. Preferably not in the hall."

Sean thought about it for a minute, then backed away, gesturing to his open apartment door. "You want a beer? Josie! Rock it on down to the corner and pick up a six-pack. We've got company."

A small, dark-haired woman scampered out of the bedroom. She was petite and pretty, her eyes too wide as she looked at him. "I've got to go to work."

She was wearing a plain white blouse and dark pants, as though she waited tables. Her sturdy shoes confirmed my theory.

She was pretty. I figured she'd make good tips.

"Then you'd better hurry up, so you're not late." Sean made no effort to fetch the beer himself, merely ushered us toward his living room.

What was this woman, his servant? I was annoyed on her behalf.

But she hesitated for only a heartbeat, then didn't take issue with his tone. "I don't have any money."

Sean complained under his breath, then dug out his worn wallet and rummaged through it. He threw a ten at her, apparently not caring that it landed on the floor. She scooped it up like a dutiful little dog and ran to fetch his beer.

I felt like tossing my cookies.

Sean gestured expansively to the tatty plaid couch. "Make yourself at home." The reclining chair was clearly his throne and not available to anyone else. He parked himself in it and leaned back while I had a good look around.

The place was reasonably clean, if somewhat down at heel. There was a big pile of empties in the kitchen—Sean's taste seemed to run to cheap domestic brands. Either they didn't keep a fastidious kitchen or he drank a lot.

I eyed his gut and decided that it was the latter.

His smile faded as Nick said nothing. "I suppose you've been out kissing up to Lucia again."

"I haven't talked to Lucia in fifteen years."

It was strange to see how little the two brothers had in common. I'd noticed it that long ago night, but the years had made the differences more acute. Where once they had looked so much the same that they could have been confused for each other—and had been, much to Sean's benefit—now they barely looked related. They might have been the same height still, but Sean looked shorter and was certainly rounder.

And their mannerisms were as different as chalk and cheese. Nick barely moved and certainly was a man of few words in comparison with his gregarious brother. "How is she?"

Sean shrugged and looked away. "We had a big fight—seems the old bitch didn't think I was living up to dear old Dad's memory in the way she'd planned."

He rummaged through the open beer cans on the table beside him. I had the frightening thought that if he did find some dregs in one can, he'd insist on offering it to his guests.

"You always reminded her of him."

Sean rolled his eyes. "What a pain in the ass that was. Jesus Jenny, she could never leave it alone. It got a lot worse after you left, I'll say that. I guess she had nothing else to do once her golden boy was gone but try to remake me."

Nick shook his head. "You were always her favorite."

"Yeah, right. That would be why she ruined my life."

Nick's expression turned impassive, which I was starting to realize was a big clue. I guessed he was angry enough that he wouldn't say anything.

"Ruined your life by taking you in and raising you?" I asked sweetly. "Gee, your own room in one of the biggest houses in Rosemount, along with more money and stability than you can shake a stick at. My heart is bleeding for you."

Sean's eyes flashed. "What do you know about it? She did me no favor, that's for sure. I could have been somebody! I could have gotten in with the right crowd. But no, Lucia had to make sure everybody was terrified of her. Such a goddamn freak. And worse, it rubbed off on me!"

There was bitterness. "It was like she hexed me or something. I didn't get that football scholarship, even though I was way better than that Fergusson kid." He stuck out his chin and glared at Nick. "Do you know what happened to him?"

"No."

"Figures. Princeton. He played quarterback, got picked up in the NFL draft and now he's retired, after making huge bags of bucks. Poor guy. His knee hurts." He rattled the empty cans more impatiently. "I feel so sorry for him in his billion dollar house. And me, what happened to me? I couldn't even get a joe job in Rosemount after high school. Yeah, Lucia did us a *big* favor."

We all knew that there were other reasons, reasons of Sean's own making, that he had been shunned by the good folk of Rosemount.

Nick finally spoke, his voice low. "And everything that went wrong would be Lucia's fault?"

"Obviously! You know they say she's a witch—well, I was her numero uno victim." He snorted. "All because I couldn't be my daddy come back from the dead for her. As if I had a chance of doing that."

"You can't think that you did *nothing* to deserve being ostracized," I said, because I was as incredulous as Nick but not nearly so determined to keep my mouth shut.

"I did one thing. I let this fool"—he jabbed a finger in Nick's direction—"when he was all of eight and filled with the wisdom of the ages, decide that we were going to live with the old bat. One mistake when I was six goddamn years old and I'm still paying for it."

The ensuing silence was awkward at best.

"You have a job?" Nick asked quietly.

Sean shook his head. "Back injury. I'm on comp."

I refrained from asking how Lucia had hexed him all the way to Boston.

"It's running out though, and I don't know what I'm going to do." He studied Nick, obviously making an assessment. "That jacket's nicer than I thought at first. You must be doing okay, big brother."

Nick straightened ever so slightly. "Well enough."

"Don't suppose you could see your way to lending me a few thou?"

Nick's smile was cool. "No."

"Why the hell not? We're blood!"

"You've borrowed all from me that you're going to get."

"You *have* been talking to the old witch! You always took her side."

"Only when she was right."

Animosity sparked between the two of them, then Sean shook his head. He picked up another can, wiggling it hopefully. "Don't know what the hell's taking Josie so long. She's not usually so slow."

"Maybe she left you," I offered.

Sean scowled at me. "She may be a stupid bitch, but she's not that dumb."

"Seeing as you're a prince among men and a good catch?" I just couldn't keep my mouth closed, even when Nick touched my elbow.

Sean shook a finger at me. "Someone ought to rip that tongue out of your head and . . ."

Nick interjected smoothly. "Shut up, Sean."

To my surprise, Sean did.

He fidgeted in his chair, his gaze flicking between the two of us. "Maybe you ought to leave. This reunion doesn't seem to be going all that well." He made a show of stretching his back and wincing. "I didn't get much sleep last night and my back is killing me."

"When did you last see Lucia?"

"What's it to you?"

Nick studied his hands, clearly choosing his words with care. "Something may have happened to her."

"You did come back to kiss up!"

"When, Sean? It's a simple question."

"You came back and she wasn't there. She probably ran away to the circus like she should have years ago. Or flew off on her broomstick." Sean chuckled to himself. "Or maybe she's done with both of us. Hey, maybe if the old bitch up and finally died, she'd leave me some cash, seeing as I'm her *favorite* and all." He leered at Nick.

The joke, if it was one, fell pretty flat. There was no color in Nick's face and his eyes were glittering green.

"She is dead, Sean."

Sean's mouth worked for a moment.

Nick continued with a toneless impassivity that I knew meant he was furious. "Someone stabbed her in the greenhouse, someone who knew I was coming to see her, someone who tried to set me up to take his fall."

He flicked a quick glance at Sean and Sean flinched. "Strangely enough, it made me think of you. The only thing I wanted to know is why you did it, and you just gave me the answer."

"Me? Shit, I would never . . ."

"Save it, Sean. I'll find out the truth, probably quicker on my own than if I listen to you." Nick got up and offered me his hand. "And this time, I'll make sure you don't just walk away."

We headed for the door as Sean bounded to his feet. He loosed a torrent of obscenities fit to curl my hair, nearly shouting down the walls, but he didn't come after Nick.

I guess I wasn't the only one playing compare and contrast.

Nick paused on the threshold. "You never did learn about consequences, Sean, and that was partly my fault." He smiled a chilly smile. "It's time I fixed that."

"You bastard! It was you, it was *you* who made that call last night!" He started hurling empties after us and we ducked out in the hall as they dinged off the trim. We scampered down the stairs as he raged on above us. "I knew no one around here had the balls to call the cops." His tirade degenerated into a snarl of obscenities.

"What's he talking about?"

Nick marched down the stairs. "You don't want to know."

"Well, actually I do." I marched right beside him. "That would be why I asked."

He ignored me, flicking a finger at a woman coming our way. "Is that Josie?"

An expert deflection and one that worked like a charm. It was Josie, emerging from the corner store with a six of Bud. Her face fell when she saw us hurrying toward her.

"Oh, no! There was a line and I knew I would take too long . . ."

Nick smiled for her. "No, Josie, we just left quickly."

She looked up at the muted sound of Sean's shouting and paled slightly, clearly identifying who was yelling. "I've got to go."

"Could you talk to us for a minute?"

Her eyes widened in alarm. "Oh, I don't think so. I need to get to work."

And get the monster his beer. It really irked me how determined she was to keep Sean happy. She might have rushed past us to hurry home, but Nick matched step with her. I fell in on the other side, wondering what he was up to.

"Is he always home?"

"Well, yes, since he hurt his back."

"What about yesterday?"

She hesitated, her dark eyes darting between the two of us. "Why?"

"How's your arm, Josie?"

She flushed then, as red as a candy apple. "I don't know what you're talking about."

"Right there," Nick said softly. He moved so quickly that she didn't anticipate him and she winced at the touch of his fingertip on her upper arm.

She started to stammer, but Nick kept on talking, his voice as smooth as old Scotch.

"Does he always hurt you where no one can see the bruise?"

A puzzle piece clicked into place for me and I was even more appalled than I had been a minute before.

The color completely left Josie's face. "You can't know . . ." She shook her head and shut her mouth. She might not be the sharpest tack in the box but she was cornered and she knew it. "I have to go."

"Yesterday, Josie."

She stopped on the steps to her building, her head down and her hair obscuring her face. "He's a good guy, you know. He's good to me."

"When he's sober?" I asked. "Or all the time?"

"It was better when he had a job." She was so defensive of him that it nearly broke my heart. "He'll come out of this, I know he will. Then everything will be fine."

"Yesterday?" Nick asked, his voice more gentle.

She turned and looked at us, her eyes filled with tears. "He borrowed my cousin's car to go for a job interview. It didn't go well—that's why he's upset." Her features set in stubborn defense. "It's not fair."

"Where can I find your cousin?"

Her eyes narrowed. "He's your brother. You shouldn't be checking up on him."

"Well, I am."

"I forget my cousin's number."

"Do you remember your cousin's name?" I asked.

Her lips set tightly. "No."

Nick made a growly sound in his throat, but I've seen enough cop movies to guess that she might change her mind. I pulled out one of my cards, wrote my home number on the back and handed it to her. "If you remember, give me a call."

"I thought he was the one asking the questions."

She had me there but Nick answered with surprising ease. "Phil will know where I am."

I had a split second to marvel at his certainty of that before Sean roared from above. Josie ran up the last of the stairs, not even troubling herself to say good-bye.

But she stuffed that card into her pocket as she ran.

* * *

Nick was seething. There were little eruption warnings all along the fault line. I could feel it as I practically ran to keep up with him, and could nearly see the steam coming from his ears.

It was worse once we got into the Beast. I started the engine, but Nick just sat and stared straight ahead.

"So, how are we going to nail him?" I asked. I caught the barest glimpse of his anger before he narrowed his eyes and hid it from me.

"*We* aren't going to do anything."

I edged the Beast out of the tight spot and darted into a break in the traffic. The dragon in the passenger seat was not amused by this move but had the good sense to keep his opinion to himself.

He certainly wasn't chatty.

I decided that the ambiance needed a boost. "Why do I get the feeling you have issues with commitment?"

It was intended as a joke, but Nick didn't crack a smile. "I don't have any issues with it."

"You just think you're the Lone Ranger?"

"I like to keep things simple."

"How simple?"

"I commit to what I can carry. No more and no less."

It made a certain amount of sense. "Nothing but a footprint?"

"Exactly. You can let me off here."

"I don't think so." I touched the gas and merged on to a busier street.

"Phil."

"I'll let you out, right after I tell you about a little something about footprints. You're kidding yourself if you think you can skate through life without leaving an impression of your passing."

"Or your fingerprints in a file."

I ignored that. "Do you really think that no one has any memories of you in Rosemount? I've got a few and they're not up for erasure, thanks very much." He turned and watched me, but I played the inscrutable one for a change. "You set my life on another course twice, by something you said or something you did, and I don't regret a bit of it."

"This must make three," he said, his voice a lot less tight.

"Well, the third time's the charm, right?"

He didn't smile. "Do you regret my looking you up this time?"

I stopped at a red and turned to look at him. "No. Do you?"

He smiled. "No." Then he frowned and looked away, drumming his fingers on the car door. "I'm just concerned that you'll be drawn in deeper than you should be."

"Maybe I don't care."

He flicked a hot glance at me. "Maybe you should."

"Why? Because the Sullivan boys are trouble?"

"That's what they say."

"Well, I beg to differ. In fact, I'm starting to think just the opposite."

I had his attention now. He was so engrossed in watching me that he didn't even notice that I turned onto the highway to Rosemount.

"How so?"

"Well, think about it. The first time we met you helped me pick myself up."

"You mean I cleaned up Sean's mistake."

"Call it what you want. It was important to me and I'll never forget it. The second time, you had enough faith in me to encourage me to buck my family's expectations."

"I don't want to talk about the second time."

"Because that's what's at the root of this?"

He didn't answer that but then he didn't really need to. His fingers were still drumming, but his eyes were very green. "And the third time?" That smile toyed with his lips. "How are you going to pull something good out of this, Phil?"

"Easy." I grinned at him. "You satisfied my curiosity."

Oops. Now he'd want to know about what. The cat was out of the proverbial bag.

Me and my big mouth. I drove, feigning tremendous concentration.

"How?"

"Doesn't matter." He was way too interested and I was pretty sure I'd said too much already.

"Sure it does."

"Well, you didn't do it by answering any questions, that's for sure." I decided not to try a different tack. "You know, I think you could be my lucky charm."

He chuckled then and shook his head. "Fat chance."

Inspiration struck in a timely fashion. I snapped my fingers. "You showed up and we went into the black, that's what happened the third time. How could that not turn things in a better direction? All these years I wondered whether we could make it work and now I know for sure."

I had a heartbeat to think he was convinced before he leaned across the great divide and touched my chin. "Curiosity about what, Phil?"

"It doesn't matter."

"You're blushing."

"Just whether the business would ever fly." It sounded more like a question than a statement, which must have been why he shook his head.

"You knew it would or you wouldn't have stuck with it. What were you curious about?"

"I think it's time I let you go without an answer on something." His fingertip slid along my jawline and I know he noticed how I swallowed. I was thinking about those fingertips wandering a little further south and had to focus hard on the road ahead. "Maybe it's also time you hopped into the backseat."

His finger halted, he turned away and then he sat back in his seat. "Why are we going to Rosemount?"

Oddly enough, there was no sense of victory in having surprised him this time. "Because I know something you don't."

"Are you going to tell me what?"

His words echoed with humor and I glanced over to find his eyes glinting with amusement. "There was a brandy glass on the kitchen counter."

He sobered immediately. "Lucia doesn't drink, as a matter of principle."

"So, I was right to think that maybe Sean decided to have a sample of something better, on the house, before he left."

"And there will be evidence he was there. Good thinking, Phil." He touched my shoulder, then climbed into the backseat. His butt was too close to be ignored, so I pinched it and smiled when he yelped.

"I'll get you for that."

I met his gaze in the rearview mirror and sighed theatrically. "Promises, promises."

He smiled the smile of a dragon checking on lunch.

Chapter 9

I had a plan.

What's more, Nick approved of it.

Things were definitely on a roll. I parked in Lucia's driveway, liking how it was getting darker. That hadn't been part of my scheme but it meshed very nicely. Nick wished me luck in a whisper as I got out of the Beast.

Keeping to my cover from earlier in the day, I went to Lucia's door and rang the bell.

There was, of course, no answer. I rang again, giving my best impression of someone stood up and displeased about it. I rang once more, looking around with a bit more impatience.

Mrs. Donnelly's curtain moved. Ha! I had her.

I headed right over to her door and used the brass door knocker. She didn't answer until the second time, then peered around the door with suspicion.

Evelyn Donnelly was probably in her sixties, a pinch-faced woman whose lips were always tightly pursed. Her eyes were so narrowed that no one could have guessed what color they were. If she ever had smiled, no one remembered the event.

And there was no evidence left on her face. She'd always lived there alone, as far as I remembered, and always had an extraordinary number of cats.

I smiled broadly. "Hi, Mrs. Donnelly. You may not remember me, but I'm Philippa Coxwell."

A cat wound around her ankles and mewled plaintively. "I remember you."

I offered one of my cards with a flourish. "I hate to bother you, but I was just on my way to my parents"—an inspired embellishment and one that would ensure the gossip grapevine didn't track my movements—"and I thought I'd try again to get hold of your neighbor." I sighed. "You see, I had an appointment with Lucia Sullivan this morning but she wasn't here."

Mrs. Donnelly fingered the card as she eyed me. "I saw you this morning."

"So, I just thought I'd try her house again, but there's still no one there. I was wondering whether you knew where she was."

She picked up the cat, holding it before herself like a shield. "Lucia Sullivan hardly reports to me."

"Well, I know, but on a quiet street like this, it's hard to not notice things once in a while." I stepped deliberately into her line of vision to Lucia's porch and willed Nick to run for it. "Have you seen Lucia today? You know, just coming or going?"

Mrs. Donnelly shook her head firmly. "I haven't seen her. Not that I would be looking or anything."

"Of course not! But Lucia is such a striking woman that she'd be hard to miss."

Mrs. Donnelly sniffed. "You can say that again."

"But, it's just the oddest thing. She was so definite about the time. She didn't strike me as a person who wouldn't keep an appointment."

"She's a person who would do whatsoever she wanted, everyone else be damned."

"Really?"

"Really." Mrs. Donnelly glowered at me. "I suppose since you're a garden person you're here about that greenhouse. Is she going to build it illegally? I'll fight her all the way to the Supreme Court, you tell her that!"

Playing dumb seemed the way to go. "But there already is a greenhouse. Why would anyone build another one?"

"She wants to make it bigger, as if you don't know all about it." Mrs. Donnelly tried to close the door, but I was ready for her, my foot over the threshold.

Nick hadn't had nearly enough time to get in and out. I needed to stall.

I smiled sweetly. "I really don't know what you're talking about. I'm supposed to update the exterior landscaping, and my goodness, but it does seem to need it."

Mrs. Donnelly snorted. "It's a disgrace is what it is. She's dragging down the property values of the entire street with all those dead beds. It doesn't look so bad now, but you wait until summer when everyone else has lovely flowers. She shouldn't be allowed to do that. There ought to be a law."

"Well, I guess she must agree with you, because she called me. How strange that she didn't keep our appointment." I frowned with apparent concern. "Have you seen her this week at all?"

"No. But then, I seldom do. It's not like I'm watching or anything."

"Of course not. Why a woman like you must have a thousand other things to do."

"Exactly." She opened the door slightly. "What are you going to do to that garden?"

"Well, actually, this is something that I should talk to you about. I was thinking that a lovely hedge would really show off the house, but of course, when it runs down the property line, it's nice to ensure the neighbors think it's a good idea. What do you think?"

"How big of a hedge?"

Fortunately, I had found some books in the back of the Beast. I juggled the three of them, then shivered elaborately. I looked at the light fixture in her hall ceiling. "Oh, that light will be so much better for you to see." Without waiting for an invitation, I pushed into the foyer, barely avoiding the tail of one of her cats.

The house stank of felines, and not particularly clean ones. The carpet might have been any color at all—it was so thick with the hair shed by her beloved creatures that you couldn't see the wool anymore. There were glinting pairs of eyes in every shadow, all fixed upon me.

I cheerfully opened the book and pointed to a red barberry bush. "There, wouldn't that look splendid? It would grow about four feet high."

"It's got thorns!" Mrs. Donnelly nestled her cat closer. "You can't put that up. My cats will hurt themselves." The one she held looked mean enough to fend for itself against a mere shrub.

"Oh. I hadn't realized they went outside. What about a nice boxwood?"

"Got to be trimmed." She shook her head grimly. "There'd be *people* on my side all the time, stepping on things, bothering me, disturbing my babies." She eased the cat to the floor despite its complaints and snatched the book. I was more than happy to help her find her glasses, no less to wait patiently while she pawed through the book for a plant that suited her.

Go, Nick, go.

* * *

It took her fifteen minutes to choose and by then, we were the best of pals. One of her big Himalayans had crept down the stairs to rub itself against my ankles and a cross-eyed Siamese watched me fixedly from its perch on the stairs. The Persian she had put down sat by her feet and continued to complain at her neglect.

Mission accomplished.

I waved a merry good-bye and climbed into the Beast, then turned to ostensibly chuck the books in the backseat. I fully expected a green-eyed devil to wink at me in triumph.

But there was no one there.

Which meant that Nick hadn't made it back yet.

I froze for a moment, uncertain what to do. How long could it take the man to collect one brandy snifter? Had he skipped out on me?

Or had something gone wrong?

Think, Philippa, think. Nick had told Josie that I'd know where he was, which left the latter option. I looked at the house, which wasn't going to share any of its secrets with me, and worried.

Mrs. Donnelly waved from her doorway, clearly intending to wait until I drove away. I started the engine because I didn't seem to have many other options, then let it idle good and long while I stared at Lucia's house.

There wasn't a single sign of life. Not a curtain moved, not a shadow flickered past the windows. Certainly no hunk of man waved madly from the doorway for me to wait up.

What had happened to Nick?

I had a very bad feeling and I know well enough not to ignore those things.

But I waved to Mrs. Donnelly and backed out of the driveway as though I hadn't a care in the world, my mind churning all the while. It was falling dark, but I couldn't exactly return unnoticed in a noisy monster like the Beast. I reached the end of the street and turned on to the main drag before I had an idea.

I couldn't return unnoticed from the *front*.

Lucia's property ran all the way to the shore. And there was a service road that ambled along the coast, running north toward Rosemount. It didn't go all the way to town, but it might even go to the back of Lucia's lot. Or close enough to suit.

It was worth a try. I pulled a U-turn and headed south of town.

Forty minutes later, I'd parked at the end of the road and inched my way toward the hulk of Lucia's house. I stubbed my toe more than once in the darkness but didn't seem to have attracted any undue suspicion. It was a windy night and the trees were rattling their branches restlessly. The air was damp, as though a storm might be coming in, the clouds scuttled across the sky.

As I got closer, the contrast between Lucia's house and the others on the block was more noticeable. First of all, hers was bigger, and more poorly tended. I couldn't discern any gardens or even shrubbery, which was a shame since she must have great sunlight.

But more significantly, every house had a light or two shining out into the darkness, except the Sullivan place. I could see Mrs. Donnelly in her kitchen, telling her cats some story while they sat on the counter and waited for num nums from Mama's fingies. Golden light spilled from the windows of houses further along, shadows periodically moving across them as people went about their lives.

But the Sullivan house stood apart, as well as silent and dark. I thought of one reason the family might have bought it—you could have anchored a boat here and run all sorts of stuff up to the house without anyone being the wiser. The land was so rugged and rife with hiding spots, that even if someone did try to intercept things, they could be evaded. I wished belatedly that I had something warmer than my suit jacket.

It was only when I stood in the shadows at the back of Lucia's house that I had a most unwelcome thought. What if she didn't show the same disregard for locking the back of the house as the front?

That seemed to open the floodgates of negative thinking. What if Nick had left while I'd been bashing up my toes and a pair of flats? What if I never knew what happened inside?

Enough of that. I forced myself to remember that Dame Fortune was on my side and darted around the greenhouse. There was another door to the kitchen, one that opened onto that back patio. The fairy lights were still in the tree overhead, though they weren't lit. The loose plug dangled near the wall, the wind slapping it against the brick. I looked up and the tree branches seemed to form an ominous web overhead, one that held the stars captive.

I shivered and tried the door.

Merciful heavens, but it was unlocked.

I stepped inside, shivered and rubbed my arms as I leaned back against the closed door. At least the house was warm.

Once inside, I realized that there was a light on, its glow casting a light into the kitchen. There were drapes on the windows, not great ones but evidently thick enough to disguise the light. I guessed that Lucia liked her privacy.

I looked for the brandy snifter on the counter but didn't see it. Nick must have picked it up, and I wondered if he knew how to do it without mucking up any fingerprints already on it.

And then I heard the music.

It was faint, as though it came from a distance. I listened and could only discern that it was a woman's voice.

No, a recording of a woman's voice. The sound quality was

scratchy, as though it came from a very old record or a vinyl one that had been listened to many, many times.

I know enough about opera to recognize it when I hear it, but that's about it. I crept down the hall toward the source of both light and music, and that's where I found him.

Nick was sitting in an old red leather armchair, his fingers tented together and his eyes closed. He was so perfectly still that he could have been struck to stone. There was only one light on in the room, a lamp with a stained-glass shade of voluptuous grapes in improbable colors. The light it cast across the room made me think of carnival rides.

It also cast that light across photographs.

On the walls, on the mantelpiece, on every surface, there were framed pictures. They were mostly old, black and white prints, in elaborate wooden frames. Treasures. Memories. I had never seen so many photographs in my life and for a moment, I just stood and stared.

"It's Lucia," Nick said quietly. I looked to find his eyes open, though he was still doing the Mr. Spock. But when he moved to turn off the music, the motion changed the play of light on his face.

His face was wet with tears.

He was mourning. "Leave it on," I said softly. I didn't intend to interrupt any more than I had.

Nick sat back again, watching me over his fingertips. "Iseult was her signature part."

Now, every card-carrying romantic knows the story of Tristan and Iseult, the doomed Celtic lovers whose tale may have inspired Shakespeare to pen Romeo and Juliet. I tried very hard to imagine Lucia as Iseult but failed miserably.

Iseult, I've always thought, was a willowy maiden, one of limpid eyes, dulcet tones and flaxen tresses. Lucia came across as more of an Italian battleship, her breasts making a considerable prow, her manner enough to make anyone lay down their weapons and surrender.

But like I said, I know beans about opera. "She was famous enough to be recorded?"

That smile touched his lips. "It was a small pressing, but she was always proud of it."

She certainly could sing. Even the deteriorated recording couldn't hide that fact. Her voice filled my ears to bursting. It was rich and soulful.

I realized that in this piece, Iseult was mourning something too.

I crossed the room, giving Nick some privacy, and picked up a photo from the mantel. It showed Lucia in costume, younger and more slender, though still not a small woman. The blond wig was a bit unrealistic given her dark eyes and brows, and her dress was a romantic medieval fantasy. Here she was dressed for her favorite role. There was a gleam of pride in her eyes, and her expression was exultant. Clearly, she loved what she did.

I finally realized why her makeup was always so extreme—she'd learned to apply it in the theater.

There were a dozen photos of her before the style of photographs abruptly changed. Here she sat on a lawn chair, a more casual setting though her pose was stiff. A young boy laughed on her knee, the style of his clothing hinting at wartime. He had a smile that could warm a room and I was tempted to smile along with him. Lucia smiled in the photo too, but there was a sadness around her eyes that hadn't been in the earlier photograph.

She looked weary. I touched it with a fingertip and jumped when I realized that Nick must be watching me.

"My father."

I looked closer and saw some resemblance to Nick and Sean in their father's features. "He doesn't favor her."

"He looked like my grandfather." Nick came to stand behind me. He handed me a wedding photo, Lucia in all her maidenly glory, a dapper man in a suit by her side.

Again, happiness mingled with resignation in her expression.

I noticed that there were no more opera poses, no shots of Lucia the diva in roles for older women. "Didn't she keep singing?"

"Only until my father was born. That's when they moved out here."

I hadn't known that. "But she loved singing. You can see it in her face."

Nick shoved his hands into his pockets and stared at the photograph, the one of Lucia in her glory. "Yes. She did."

I wondered how Lucia had felt, giving up the occupation she clearly loved, and had a pretty good idea. Her voice swelled with anguish, the emotion undisguisable even though I didn't understand the words.

There was a lump in my throat.

Maybe Lucia did understand Iseult, that maiden who was forced to learn so much about sacrifice to fulfil the schemes of men.

Maybe she had learned to understand her.

There was a photo of an old building, a print so small that I had to squint at it to make out the details. It looked vaguely familiar and I realized with a start what it was. "That's the movie theater in Rosemount."

Nick picked up the photo, then put it down again, sparing a brush of his fingertips across the frame. "It used to be a real theater."

I waited, but he typically didn't elaborate. "Okay. I give up. Why did she have a picture of it?"

"She owned it."

"Really? I didn't know that."

He shrugged. "It wasn't for long. She had a grand scheme after my grandfather died to make it into an opera house."

"When was this?"

"Nineteen seventy-three."

This was important. I wasn't sure why, but when Nick is precise, I pay attention. He wasn't going to tell me, that much was obvious, but maybe I had a chance of figuring it out.

The largest picture on the mantelpiece was in color and it held the place of honor. It was a school photo, the sweaters on the two boys captured there dating it to the seventies. They were obviously brothers, so similar in looks that only their expressions revealed the difference between them. The smaller one grinned at the camera, cocksure, like the man in the wedding photo and the boy on Lucia's knee.

The larger boy was solemn. Wary.

Nick.

I touched the frame and glanced at him, knowing I didn't have to utter the question.

"The first year we were here."

Typically, there were volumes of subtext to his explanation. My gaze was drawn back to the photograph, the vulnerability in his expression tugging my heartstrings.

I never remembered him looking like that. Did my memory play tricks, or had the camera caught him with his guard down? Had Lucia seen that uncertainty when she chose this photo from the proofs?

"When was this?"

"Don't you remember?"

"Not exactly. You came in primary school."

"It was nineteen seventy-three."

I looked back at the picture of the movie house. "Lucia sold it after you came."

Nick nodded once, then returned to his chair. The shadows claimed his features, though his eyes glittered as he watched me.

Or maybe he was looking at the photographs, so tellingly arranged.

"How did your parents die?"

He shrugged, glancing down at the record spinning beside him. "Car accident."

The recording finished. The record player clicked as the needle lifted, only the sounds of the old house creaking in the wind filling the silence between us. I waited, sensing that he might actually tell me something.

But he slid the record into the sleeve and got to his feet, the album tucked under his arm. "It's ancient history, Phil. Sorry I didn't keep to the plan." He took my elbow, ready to usher me back out of Lucia's sanctuary.

And away from his precious secrets.

I dug in my heels. "Maybe all this history has something to do with her death."

"No, it doesn't. Let's go."

"You don't know that!"

"Yes, I do."

The man had a gift for just shutting down a conversation. It was as though he slammed a door and threw away the key, leaving you looking at a smooth wood panel that you didn't even know could be there.

It made me want to spit.

There had been a time when I had thought it terribly romantic that Nick was this walking enigma, a man of mystery just needing the right woman to unravel him.

Ha. Sadly for him, I'd gotten done with that.

"How can you think that you know everything?" I demanded, flinging out my hands. "How can you imagine that you see every possible angle?"

"We both know that Sean is guilty," he said, the heart and soul of reason. "So, this can't have anything to do with it."

"Well, what about just answering a few questions? You expect me to just troop around with you on good faith? I'm curious! And if none of this is important, would it kill you to tell me any of it?"

My breath hitched in my chest and the words that came next weren't the ones I planned to say. "Why won't you trust me, Nick?" I actually grabbed his shirt and gave him a shake. "What have I ever done to make you think I can't be trusted?"

He studied me and I wondered what the heck he was thinking. "I trust you."

"Wrong. You evade every question I ask you, even the most innocuous things." To my embarrassment, there were tears blurring my vision and I hoped the bad light hid them from him. "You have got to be the most irritating man I've ever known, and I have three brothers to offer serious competition for that honor. That's it, Nick, that's *it.*"

I didn't wait for the sweet talk, just in case there might not be any. I turned and stalked across the room. He didn't say anything, which might have been the smart choice.

I stormed down the hall, thinking that it would be nice if he at least pretended to give a damn that I was leaving, my blood boiling hotter with every step. But I knew where I stood now. It couldn't get any more crystal clear than this. When I got opposite the French door to the greenhouse, I just glanced that way.

And I saw Lucia.

At least, I saw her ghost. Dressed in flowing white with her hair unbound and holding a candle aloft. Her feet didn't seem to be touching the ground, as though she floated there. There was a red gash on her throat and a stain on the otherwise pristine white.

She looked annoyed, for all her ethereal air.

Her ghost took a step closer and lifted one hand as though she would strike me dead on the spot. Or hex me. My mouth opened, but I couldn't have made a sound to save my life.

I didn't hang around for a better look. In fact, I ran so wildly that I nearly broke my ankle in the process.

Phil was right.

As much as he might have preferred otherwise, she had nailed it in one. She had never done anything to make him withhold his trust.

It was just the way he was. Or maybe it was just what he had learned.

He slipped out of the house and clung to the shadows as he rounded the dark side of the building. In the distance, he glimpsed Phil running away, away from him, but he knew she'd never hear him if he yelled. He guessed she wouldn't stop if she did.

He walked along the lip of the sea, Lucia's album tucked beneath his arm. Eventually, he found a quiet road and turned back toward the anonymity of the city.

The air stayed crisp, even tainted with the fumes from fast-food restaurants, its edge clarifying his thoughts. He followed their line back to the city, the crinkle of Chandra's recipe in his pocket and the weight of Lucia's only recording as reassuring as the bite of the wind.

He realized immediately that he had left his pack in Phil's Beast, but there was nothing critical in it. He had his passport, enough cash to get by, and his wits. There was nothing else he needed, there never had been.

For the first time, he wondered. He'd been so careful about not making any ties, not forging any emotional bonds, not needing anyone or letting them need him. But Lucia had been killed and he missed her, all the same.

Despite his efforts, he was just as lonely as when his parents died. He had to admit that his strategy of living showed some serious weaknesses.

And Phil insisted he had left a mark in her life.

He couldn't regret that. He squinted into the distance and tried to guess which light might be the glow from Phil's kitchen window, the one that overflowed with vigorous plants.

She'd probably be washing a stick of celery to eat raw for dinner, or some damn thing. Here he'd tried to apologize to her, to make things better, and he'd just made things worse. He was supposed to erase a footprint, but he'd trampled everything within sight.

He wondered whether he could still pull this one out of the fire.

There was something about Phil Coxwell that drew him like a magnet. There always had been. She was so optimistic, so determined, so good at challenging expectations.

Like today. It had never occurred to him that everyone couldn't just eat what they wanted, when they wanted. He was awed by her willpower, her determination to make herself into who she wanted to be, to look the way she wanted to look.

That must be why he wanted to help her. Right. A knight in shining armor bearing rice cakes.

Maybe her parents' meddling pissed him off enough that he wanted to sweep in and make everything easy for her, for a change. Anyone could see that McAllister wasn't the right kind of guy for Phil.

It was as though they wanted to push her back, to make her into whatever they wanted her to be. Clearly no one cared what Phil wanted, yet what she wanted was so simple.

She just wanted to be herself and make her own choices.

He hadn't realized until today what a gift Lucia had given him when she insisted he be himself, make his own decisions, follow his own dreams. She'd refused to give advice, she'd compelled him to think things through for himself.

There was more than the oddity of their house that the rest of Rosemount's families didn't share.

But then, Phil didn't seem to need anyone's protection. She'd gotten this far without him and would probably make her own way further. He thought suddenly of salmon swimming upstream, never accepting failure.

Was that why Phil was so hard to walk away from? Because he had always been one to champion a noble cause, and hers clearly was? Because he liked to back the underdog, to help those with everything set against them? Because if he was going to make a difference, he wanted it to be a lasting and good one?

Or was he lured back to Phil because she credited him with setting her on the course to her own happiness? Because she made him feel welcome? Because she accepted him as he was, even when it infuriated her?

He smiled. And that was when he knew what he had to do.

First things first. He sauntered past his brother's apartment, saw what he expected to see, made the call he had to make. This time Sean peered into the darkness as he was led away.

Nick waved from the shadows. It was a playful gesture, more showy than was typical of him, but he thought Phil would appreciate it.

By dawn he had made his way to Haymarket. He leaned against a wall, sipping a coffee as traffic on the floor grew. He loved markets, the colors, the smells, the negotiations. The form changed slightly, but the functionality was the same all over the world.

He found them jubilant, practical, reassuring.

Not unlike Phil.

First came the vendors in fingerless gloves and heavy coats, piling their oranges, sorting the radicchio, plunking fresh herbs in water. They shouted at their junior help, who were often their children, a dozen languages filling the air. Trucks were backed up and emptied, then driven away to park. He could smell fresh fish and hear running water as the greens were rinsed to a glisten. Just the sights and smells made him want to cook again.

He'd never taken the time and trouble to invest in a good kitchen, though he'd yearned for one once or twice. It was the act of acquiring stuff that stopped him, the fact that he wouldn't be able to carry it all if he chose to walk away.

But today, he itched to take that step.

Then came the chefs, questioning, fingering, sniffing, choosing with expert assurance. The smell of fresh bread drifted through the chill of the morning. He wrapped his hands around his coffee cup, as though he would stop himself from buying food he had no need for.

The serious cooks filtered in, rubbing elbows with the chefs, carrying cut flowers with their purchases. Then came the grocery shoppers with their pull carts and strollers, and finally the tourists with their cameras and white running shoes. By nine-thirty, the place was chaotic.

There was something unfinished between himself and Phil, something he had to name with certainty before it would leave him alone. His gut told him to seek her out again and he knew better than to ignore his instincts.

They'd saved his sorry butt a few times.

No doubt McAllister would be sniffing around, determined to make the career move of courting Phil. It would only be decent to make sure that lawyer didn't pressure Phil into something she didn't want to do, that her parents didn't short-circuit her plans.

He wanted to be sure that didn't happen. He wanted to know before he left.

He remembered her suggestion that he could have stayed on her couch. Maybe they could make a deal. He could cook for her in exchange for a few days of crashing in her living room. He needed somewhere to stay and she couldn't live on Indian takeout forever. Josie might end up calling and he wanted to be there.

It seemed like something friends might do for each other.

He ignored the way his pulse picked up. He was just going to resolve unfinished business.

Someone dropped a quarter in his cup and he jumped as it splashed in the last increment of coffee. He fingered the stubble on his chin and cast a glance over his dirty jeans.

There was absolutely no guarantee that Phil would even talk to him. A shave and some new clothes were in order if he was going to be persuasive at all.

And groceries. He stepped away from the wall in anticipation. The good thing about knowing that a woman doesn't cook is the certainty that her cupboards and refrigerator are bare. Phil probably didn't have so much as a pot to her name.

He'd just have to buy everything he could possibly need. There was a spring in his step as he set to work.

Chapter 10

So, I'd been joking about Nick being my lucky charm, but everything sure went to heck in a hurry once I abandoned him in Lucia's house. I knew I shouldn't be disappointed that he hadn't been able to confide in me and I tried to tell myself that I didn't care that he was gone.

Again.

Nick had stepped out of my life and this time, he wasn't coming back. I should in fact have been *glad,* though I was no more persuaded of that than that I wasn't disappointed.

I did admit that I didn't know that much about Nick Sullivan. He'd always been a mystery—that had once been part of his appeal—and the kind of guy who didn't tell you what he was really thinking. I had assumed from the beginning of this little adventure that Sean was responsible for killing Lucia.

But I lay in bed that night thinking. Seeing all that money in

Nick's wallet made me uneasy. It wasn't just the question of where Nick had gotten it, though it's not that hard to lay hands on a couple of thousand at least temporarily.

It bugged me just that he had it. Who carried around that kind of cash? No one, in these days of instant tellers and credit cards.

No one, except someone who had been *planning* to disappear. I couldn't have dropped out of sight on a moment's notice, not without leaving a paper trail of bank machine withdrawals and credit card slips, or at least one monster withdrawal. It looked as though Nick had known he was going to find Lucia murdered and that he would need to fade away fast.

Which neatly explained why he had finally come home after all these years. He had had something to do. I shivered and nestled deeper into my cozy bed.

The worst thing was thinking that my parents might have been right. I vowed to never tell them the truth—but then, they were already sure they were right.

On the other hand, Nick coming home to murder Lucia didn't explain why on earth he had bothered to hunt me down, let alone our whole adventure tour package. Had that been just for old times' sake?

Seemed like a lot of trouble to me.

But then, having three older brothers has convinced me that men are inexplicable creatures of whim—even though they like to present themselves as denizens of practicality. At least I know that they don't always plan everything they do and that impulse can certainly rule the day.

Especially a certain kind of impulse. Look where it had gotten my oldest brother, James. Marcia might have been gorgeous in her time, but now that she had two kids, a successful lawyer husband, a big house and a big rock, she didn't bother with appearances much. Looks had faded, or at least ceased to be artificially enhanced, and her personality had become much more of an issue. In short, she's a shrew—and probably most of the reason James is a workaholic.

That kind of impulse would explain Nick's steamy kisses. It didn't feel nearly as good as I once might have thought it would to have Nick following his pecker back to me, but then, I hadn't had a lot of sleep last night.

And I wasn't getting much more. I actually rolled out of bed early, giving it up for lost. I still had a lot of working drawings to fill in for Mrs. H. and figured I might as well get in to the office. I had to go over the plans with Joel today so he could begin scheduling the work for the hard landscaping. The message on my answering machine could wait.

It was probably just Mom, giving me heck for not going to lunch with the eligible Mr. McAllister.

There was a depressing thought. But it was time to get my life back into all its organized little boxes. The most prudent choice would be to just forget that these last thirty hours or so of my life had ever happened. Forget Nick. Forget Lucia. Forget them all and think about a pink accent for that hellebore bed.

As if anything in my life could ever be that simple.

Well, the day started off badly and got worse.

It turned out that the interlock stones that Mrs. H. thought would be perfect for the little retaining wall around the garden beds didn't stack vertically as I had thought. Each layer set back a good three inches, because that's how the block was designed. Joel explained patiently how that would keep the wall from shifting, but I still had a problem.

If we moved the wall out to allow for this little engineering marvel, there would be a garden path wide enough for cats walking single file. Alternatively, if we started the wall where I had planned, the bed at the top would end up in the neighbor's yard. I figured that would be a tough sell and sharpened my pencil. There had to be a way to make this work.

This was particularly problematic as Joel and I had an appointment with Mrs. H. at four-thirty to walk through the grand scheme one last time. Joel left to hunt down other possibilities for the stone while I dove in.

Elaine breezed in and out, up to her eyes in a sunroom that was being added on to a kitchen, though I have to admit I only half listened to her woes. The phone rang incessantly, of course, because the entire world sensed that I was trying to concentrate.

And ye olde sap answered every time . . . hoping. There's something about optimism that is really tough to shake. They should come up with a vaccination for it.

Speaking of things that are tough to shake, Jeffrey called in the middle of the morning to repeat his invitation. I declined the so-called honor, choosing the tactful course of declaring myself busy.

He called again twenty minutes later, taking the time and trouble to explain to little ol' me that our lunch was in his best career interests. When I still declined, he implied that I was the most miserable woman alive for not marrying him and bearing his sons on the basis of that credential alone. Further, his tone of voice made it clear that his explanation was provided since I was so stupid that I couldn't be hoped to work out this facet of his invitation all by myself.

As a tactic intended to charm me to compliance, it was lacking a certain je ne sais quoi.

I told him that I thought arranged marriages had died with Victoria. It was too painful listening to him trying to figure out who or what I was talking about.

"You know," I said helpfully. "Lie back and think of England."

A stony silence was my only answer.

"Because she was the Queen of England and she had to produce an heir, but she was marrying a virtual stranger. That was the advice given to her for her wedding night."

He sniffed. "I hardly think such an anecdote is appropriate under the circumstances, Philippa."

"My point was only that her marriage is pretty much the last arranged marriage that I know about. My father may be trying to fix us up for the sake of empire, but I'm not going to play. I don't want to have lunch with you, Jeffrey, though certainly many other, infinitely more suitable women—ones with far better taste in anecdotes—would."

I paused, then decided what the heck. "What you need is a gorgeous smart woman, like my partner Elaine."

He sputtered. "Never!"

"Really? I could have sworn you two had some history."

He made a pretty good recovery. "Well, if you really want to know, I could tell you over lunch."

I laughed despite myself. "Good try, Jeffrey, but no, thanks."

Even he had the grace to end the conversation after that.

The phone rang as soon as I hung it up and I rolled my eyes. It was going to be one of those days.

I declined an urgent request from one of Mrs. H.'s neighbors to landscape her garden first. Not only was her attitude annoying, but I finish jobs in much the order they come in.

Another neighbor called to demand an accounting of what we intended to do with the fence. He made it clear that if the new fence infringed so much as an inch upon his property, he would take great joy in tearing it down during the night.

I assured him that a surveyor had already staked the lot and suggested that this would be the best time to contest the location of any stakes. Since he hadn't even seen them, I knew they had to be slightly to Mrs. Hathaway's side of the property line—as I had requested—and obscured by the current fence. It was right on the line.

Keeping everything slightly inside the lot line can solve a lot of issues before they start. I think this neighbor was disappointed that I didn't panic—maybe he was looking for a fight or hoping to be able to tear down that fence with his bare hands.

The phone rang again, no sign of a relief pitcher in sight.

"Coxwell & Pope."

"Why do you have to ruin everything?" a woman demanded querulously.

"I beg your pardon?"

"If you have any sense at all, you'll stay out of my house. You've ruined everything!"

The hair started to rise on the back of my neck.

Now, I couldn't have told you what Lucia Sullivan sounded like, because it had been decades since I had heard her voice. But the caller was a woman, she sounded older and she sounded mad. I thought about that ghost I'd seen in Lucia's greenhouse and the dots pretty much jumped into a line.

"Who is this, please?"

But she slammed the phone down so hard that I jumped.

I don't get a lot of calls from dead people, generally speaking. In fact, this would have been a first. But I'd only been into one house uninvited of late. My hand shook a bit when I put the receiver back and I got up to make myself a nice hot cup of tea.

Then I had an idea. I could use one of those nifty phone company codes and obtain the number of the last caller to my line.

But Joel called in first, suggesting that we meet at Mrs. H.'s as he'd gotten tied up.

Grrr. Things had definitely turned against me today.

I couldn't help thinking about that call. Why had Lucia bothered with the phone? She could have just levitated something, written on my mirror in blood or walked through the wall to deliver her message. Maybe she was an amateur in the spooking arts, being so recently dead and all.

Or maybe she wasn't dead at all.

Or maybe someone wanted me to *think* that she wasn't dead at all.

Aha! Someone had gone to a lot of trouble to clean up the greenhouse, if Nick had seen what he said he had seen. I knew I had seen nothing.

The incident might have fit another piece into the puzzle for Nick, but he was gone into the wide blue yonder. He had told me that it wasn't my concern any longer, so he'd never get this tidbit.

His loss.

I shook my head, decided that the Coxwells didn't have an exclusivity on family weirdness, and sighed when the phone rang again.

It had taken my mother until two to hunt me down, although we both knew there was only one place I could be. She was already stinko, as evidenced by her slurred speech.

This was going to be a treat.

"Working, Mom. Can I call you back?"

"Like you did last night? I don't think so, Philippa Elizabeth Coxwell. Don't think I don't know that you're trying to avoid me." She paused significantly, probably for an invigorating sip. "Or that I don't know why."

"Did you call last night?" I feigned innocence, knowing that responding in kind wouldn't solve anything. I turned the drawing ninety degrees, then did it again, muttering under my breath a little that the solution was so elusive.

And suddenly there it was.

The path was serpentine, but from this angle looked like a voluptuous S. I could straighten the curve slightly and increase the size of the beds without sacrificing the width of the paths.

There would be less stone, less curvy walkway, but the illusion of depth we'd been trying to achieve could be kept.

We could plant taller things in the middle beds to ensure that the whole garden couldn't be seen at once. Mrs. H. wanted a sense of discovery, hence the very curvaceous path, but I was suddenly sure I could achieve the same effect without changing the wall material that she so loved.

I tucked the receiver under my chin and scribbled madly.

"Of course, I called last night, Philippa, but you didn't call me back."

"Late night, Mom."

"You're working too much." Her voice chilled. "Or is that really what you're doing? Jeffrey told your father that there was another man there yesterday, Philippa. What haven't you told me? Who is this Nick? How serious are you?"

I started to admit the truth, but demons seized my tongue. It was an evil thought, but then again, it beat being gay.

And what harm would it do?

"Oh, Nick, well, I didn't want to get your hopes up, Mom. We've been seeing each other for a while . . ."

"You should have told me, especially before your father spoke to Jeffrey."

"Well, no one asked my opinion of that before it was done, and as I recall, no one was interested in much I had to say about it."

"Which just shows the value of a little honesty with your family. Your father is humiliated, you know, and he's been impossible to live with since yesterday." I refrained from observing that he's pretty much always impossible to live with. "You've made him look like a fool, Philippa, and it's not a role he relishes."

She had some trouble with that last word.

"Then he shouldn't have set me up without asking me first."

"Philippa!"

"It's true."

"This is all your fault and I hope you understand that there will be consequences." My mother sighed a martyr's sigh. "Not that I can imagine this *man* is worth the trouble. Philippa, Jeffrey said he looked quite disreputable and was rude on top of it."

"He's certainly no Jeffrey McAllister," I conceded, silently thanking the gods for that.

"Oh, this just goes to show what appalling judgment you have, Philippa. I suppose you've *slept* with him. No, wait, I don't want to know . . ."

Her voice trailed off suggestively, because of course, she did want to know.

Sometimes trouble is impossible to resist.

I sighed with apparent rapture. "It's just great, Mom. I could never have believed that it could be so good . . ."

"Philippa! Bite your tongue!" She inhaled mightily, no doubt taking on a flagon of sherry in the process. "If things are that serious, then there's nothing for it. You'll just have to bring him to your father's birthday dinner on Saturday so we can assess whether you've made an acceptable choice or not."

Okay, I'd forgotten about my father's birthday bash—in a classic "forget about it and it can't be real" strategy. But it was the second part of what she said that really made me mad.

"What? It's not up to you who I date."

"Oh, Philippa, don't get foolish with me. Of course, it matters to us and of course we're going to ensure that you make a suitable decision. It's well known that you have the worst judgment possible in men and this certainly doesn't sound like a promising choice. We're talking about the rest of your life, Philippa, and I am not going to stand by and let you cast it aside on a poor marriage."

Now, she had my full attention. "Because you made such a good one?"

Jack Frost danced down the telephone line.

"I beg your pardon?"

I sat back and folded my arms across my chest. It was about time I had my say. Enough of passive resistance—I was ready to make my position clear.

"You know, Mom, I've never understood why you think marriage is such a great institution when yours is so lousy. Maybe I'll never get married. Maybe I'll just take in men like stray dogs and have a couple of dozen kids out of wedlock."

"Philippa!"

"I'll certainly never marry a guy like Jeffrey McAllister, who's more worried about pleasing his boss than who he spends the rest of his life with." I snapped my fingers. "Maybe I'll marry one of these unsuitable men I keep finding, maybe I'll marry Nick just because he looks disreputable."

"Philippa, you had better bring this young man to dinner . . ."

"Maybe I will. Come to think of it, Mom, you probably remember Nick Sullivan. You know, the guy who went to jail? I tell you, there really is something to that bad boy charm."

She sputtered but I tossed the phone back into the cradle and didn't answer when it rang again.

My hand was shaking so badly that I couldn't draw worth a poop. It didn't feel nearly as good as I had thought it would to toss my two cents into the ring. I didn't feel triumphant or proud of what I'd done.

And the truth was, I'd just made more of a muddle of things. Not only had I told my mother—and by extension the entire gossip network of Rosemount—that Nick was back in town, but I'd practically said I'd drag him in like a prize boar on Saturday night.

I wished that I knew where he was, because this was one time that I would have liked to prove my parents wrong.

But that and a buck would get me a cup of coffee. I knew I'd have to get down on my knees and eat some Coxwell crow before this was over. I wasn't, however, going to rush in to dish myself up a plateful.

My family could wait for Saturday night.

Meanwhile, I checked the clock and sketched like a maniac, knowing the gods would have to smile for me to make that appointment at four.

You're probably thinking that I should have told my mother off a long time ago, but that's only because you don't know the whole story.

I told you already that we moved to Rosemount when I was a little squirt, in 1970, and that my mother wasn't happy about the move. But there was more to it than that, although it was years before I knew about it.

My parents didn't fight. They ignored each other, so there was never any chance of overhearing anything particularly good. I vaguely remember one huge argument before that move, but after that, nothing. My father worked longer hours once we were in Rosemount, supposedly because of the commute, and my mother, well, she was always distracted. In fact I have no memory of her being any other way.

My brothers noticed, though, and they whispered about the change in her. I did notice the change in the pretty decanter that I always wanted to touch because it sparkled in the sunshine. It had juice in it once we got to Rosemount. No one would ever let me have any, but I knew, with a toddler's conviction, that someone else was drinking that juice. The amount in the decanter went up and down, up and down. Not fair, by any accounting.

I must have been about ten by the time I was sure where that juice was going. And that it wasn't juice. It was sherry, and my mother wasn't distracted—she was drunk.

My mother is an ugly drunk. When we were younger, she must have had things under more control, or maybe she hid it better. About the time of my epiphany, she must have decided that we could fend for ourselves. And when she drinks, she's a lot less worried about hiding her misery. She either weeps and is inconsolable or she rages, hurling insults like deadly weapons.

My father, amazingly, can ignore this. He looks right through her, as though she's not there or doesn't deserve to be acknowledged. She could be an unfortunate choice of lampshade for all the notice he takes of her. My brothers quickly picked up this trick. There's something surreal about sitting at the dinner table while a drunk rants and everyone else eats as though there's nothing amiss.

I can't ignore her.

I just can't do it.

Her pain is so raw, her disappointment so tangible. It seems rude to brush it aside, as though she doesn't count. I suppose that's what she's raging about in the first place.

Well, my father worked longer hours once she lost it and my brothers stayed late at school and friends' houses. Mom had stopped coming downstairs much and usually got pickled in the little sitting room off her bedroom.

I guess she didn't want to burden any of us with the sight of her.

Sad, isn't it? Our own mother drinking alone in her bedroom, not wanting to embarrass her family with what she had become.

As soon as possible, my brothers moved away to college, leaving you-know-who with the dirty work. Maybe it's assumed in a household primarily of men that the women should stick together, maybe my father finally thought I was good for something.

You don't think I ended up with this hastily feminized name because they were dying for a daughter, do you?

Appearances had always been so important to my mother. That picture of her debut is still on her dresser, like a talisman of a moment when all things were possible, maybe a reminder that anything could go wrong. And both she and my father were determined that our household appear normal, despite all the nonsense going on inside.

Maybe I just played my part in that.

I never bought her booze and I never facilitated her drinking in any way. I just helped her hide the signs. I harvested the bottles from behind the drapes before my father found them. I cleaned up things she'd spilled or broken. And for whatever reason, I got into the habit of hunting my mother down every night and putting her to bed.

It's normal to sleep in your own bed, not facedown wherever you passed out. It's normal to wear your nightgown to bed, not whatever you were wearing when you started to drink midmorning. And it's normal to go to bed clean, not adorned with whatever body fluids have happened to make an appearance.

Now, it's not easy to wrestle a surly drunk into the bathroom, much less into her pajamas. It wasn't unusual that my mother didn't want any part of it or of me. She fought me, she struck me, she swore at me, but those insults and accusations always rolled right off my back.

It didn't take a rocket scientist to figure out that her anger was really targeted at my father. Compared to the things she said then, these telephone conversations are a piece of cake.

But I only found out why she was so angry with Father years later. I was in my first year at Harvard, after nearly killing myself to get good enough grades to be accepted, and I hated every minute of it. I wasn't allowed to live in the dorm—where I might have had some fun—and had to commute.

It wasn't about money, and it wasn't even about my mother. It was about my father's ideas of feminine purity—and his desire to ensure that I kept mine. On the other side of the coin, I knew damn well that Zach was busily spreading the milk of human kindness as far and as wide as he could.

But I was always told it was different for boys. So, I called my little car the Vestal Virgin Express and often took the long way home, just because. I certainly didn't tell my father that if I wanted to lose my virginity, I could have done it any time any place that I so chose, regardless of where I was living. At the time, I was afraid he'd lock me in the basement if he thought of that.

I'm still not sure he wouldn't have.

So, one night I came home to find a single light burning upstairs. My mom's sitting room. My father's car wasn't there, but then, I would have been shocked if it was. James was already married by then, and Matt had moved downtown. Zach was living in the dorm, making merry and getting lousy grades. I'd had a crummy day myself and was having some real doubts about my future as a lawyer. I unlocked the front door and paused at the sound of Mom's sobbing.

Given a choice, I'd take sorrow over rage any day.

I climbed the stairs, knowing there was no use avoiding the inevitable. She was on her hands and knees, and there was a spilled bottle, leaking sherry all over the carpet. At first I thought that's what she was crying about, but she turned when she heard me and clutched something to her chest.

It was a letter.

In fact, there were a lot of letters scattered across the floor. They looked old, the corners of the envelopes rounded as though they had been handled a lot. There was a narrow ribbon discarded on the floor, so I figured she'd had them all tied together in a bundle. The envelopes were almost square, and had a deckle edge on the flap, like invitations or fancy stationery.

Or love letters. I saw that the one my mother held was wet in one corner, the sherry having made a stain. She was trying to blot it out, but she was too smashed to make a good job of it.

As soon as she recognized me, she held out her treasure and wailed, beseeching me to fix what had gone awry. It was a horrible sound, that cry of hers, like an animal in pain, and I was quick to take the envelope from her. Sure enough, it was addressed to Mrs. R. Coxwell in a bold masculine hand.

It wasn't my father's handwriting. He scribbles, prompting jokes from the intrepid that he should have been a doctor.

This was a legible script more typical of an architect. And all the envelopes were addressed in the same decisive hand. The stamp was a commemorative of a laughably small denomination, adding credence to my theory that this was old news.

There are some things you just don't need to know. I willed myself to not look any further, but took the letter and pressed the liquor out of it while my mother watched. Her crying stopped and she followed my every gesture as though fearful that I would ruin her prize.

Or tell on her. I gathered up all the letters and put them back in that little bundle, carefully tying that bow. Then I handed them to her, told her to put them away while I ran her bath.

And I left.

Because if I had known where she put them, then one day I might have been tempted to see what those letters said. You've got to know your limitations and I knew that in a weak moment, I might get curious.

But they weren't my business. I wouldn't go through my mother's drawers—that would be too intrusive—so not knowing exactly where she put them was insurance enough.

When I came back for her they were hidden away. I never saw them again. We never spoke of them. It was as though that night had never happened. Maybe she didn't even remember it.

I did.

And maybe I did idly flip through the book of commemorative stamps at the post office one day, and maybe I did discover that that stamp was from 1970.

Maybe my mother had another reason for not wanting to move to Rosemount. I guessed my father had an issue with Boston that hadn't been mentioned to us. I'll probably never know the whole truth.

But it's because of those letters, whatever they say and whoever the man was who wrote them, that I cut my mother a lot of slack.

We may not have the same ideals of marriage, but my mother, for all her flaws, only wants me to be happy.

Maybe she can't imagine that being alone is any better than being isolated in a marriage. Maybe she thinks the four of us make up for my father's deficits. Maybe she never expected much more.

I don't know. But the fact that she worries about it, about *me*, is the closest thing to love I ever had from my parents.

And that means a lot.

I wasn't lying when I told Nick that I'm a romantic. Those letters made me realize that I came by it honestly.

Chapter 11

Of course, Joel was already at Mrs. Hathaway's by the time I rolled in.

Jez was waiting, ever patient, in the truck, her chin propped on the steering wheel as she awaited "he who fills the dish." She thumped her tail and accepted a scratch of her ears, her gaze vigilantly fixed on the garden gate where Joel had last been seen.

Mrs. H. and Joel had hit it off, at least. I arrived to find him firmly settled in her kitchen, drinking Earl Grey tea, recounting anecdotes and making a dint in her fresh blueberry muffins. He's quite a storyteller, our Joel, and I could see that Mrs. H. was charmed.

Something was going right. My apologies were waved off and we adjourned to the garden when I declined a buttery muffin. Joel glanced at my plans as though checking his memory, then gave me a surreptitious nod of approval. I paced off the measurements and explained the drawings, etching the shape and position of beds with fine chalk dust.

Joel dragged out stone samples and built an impromptu mock wall, butting a few pieces of the interlock for the pathway against it. I suggested leaving out some of the stones in the path, and letting thyme fill the gaps, since greening up the stone would soften the look.

She liked that the hellebores had center stage in the plan. They'd occupy the central bed beneath that hydrangea, which would have to be moved after all. I tentatively suggested adding three pink ones to the collection, to zing it up, but could see that she had to think about it. People get fixed on all white floral beds and it takes them a while to agree to color, even when it adds subtlety.

I left Mrs. H. a catalogue, filled with pictures of hellebores and dotted with a few Post-it notes from me, as well as a copy of the plans and drawings.

It's a good idea, in my experience, to give people a few days to ruminate over things like this—if you press for agreement on the first presentation, you'll probably get it. But then a week or a month later, the client will admit that they wish the path was a little further to the left or something equally difficult to change. It's a good-sized investment and one worth thinking about.

"Brilliant, Philippa. You can hardly tell the difference in the plans," Joel said when we were alone in the street. He playfully punched me in the shoulder. "What a star."

"It was closer than I like. Do you think the paths will be too straight?"

"Nah. It'll be perfect. She'll go for it before the weekend, I bet." I didn't quite share his confidence but waved gamely as he started his truck. "Say hi to Nick for me. He's a keeper, Philippa."

Well, there was nothing to say to that.

The Beast choked on the way back to the office, making a horrible grinding sound that faded into a whimper. I should have known that the comeback couldn't last. I couldn't get the engine started again. I couldn't even get the Beast over to the shoulder and nearly had the door sheared off trying to get out to call for help.

Cell phones suddenly had a certain appeal.

I got took by the tow truck driver, of course, who ruminated over what a big job it was and how far it was to the garage etc., etc. My Visa card started to melt as soon as he had it in his greasy paws. This was only the beginning though, because the mechanic would almost certainly pillage our checking account before he pronounced the job done.

So much for being in the black.

I watched my baby being towed away to oblivion and conceded that it might be a mercy to let it die. There was a depressing thought. I couldn't flag a cab for love or money and there was no one at the office when I found a pay phone and called, so I finally took the bus and walked the last bit back.

A former client phoned as soon as I got in, all in a tizzy because the Japanese maple she had insisted on having wasn't in bud yet. The tree had cost a fortune, because it was old and beautifully shaped. I had advised against it, recommending that a younger tree would be similar in five or ten years and would cost only a fraction of the price. Also, the older the tree, the less tolerant it is of changes in its living conditions.

Like people, I guess.

I bit back on the urge to shout "I told you so!"

I told her that it might just be slow coming into bud, because of the shock of relocation, but that I would come out the next day to have a look. She, of course, wanted a replacement, as though I could: A. conjure a unique specimen from midair and

B. afford to just give it away. Old Japanese maples can set one back a lot of bills—I saw one go for $65,000 last year. Yee-haw.

I left a message for Elaine on her cell, which she still wasn't answering. I begged shamelessly for the loan of her car the next day so I could go and grovel, maybe hex the tree into bud. It was worth a try.

As the shadows fell, I realized that I was back on my familiar turf. Fighting valiantly against adversity, without a hope of winning.

Funny, it didn't feel that comfortable anymore. I felt older that night, a little more burdened and certainly short of optimism. Nick's backpack had been in the Beast and I had scooped it up with everything else before the truck got towed away.

Maybe it would provide some postmortem entertainment value.

I tossed it over my shoulder on my way out the door. The phone rang as I was locking up the office but whoever it was could go stuff themselves. The cab I had called was idling in the lot and I didn't intend to let it get away.

They get nervous around here at night, because there aren't a lot of potential fares. You have to pounce when you have the chance.

I left the phone ringing, and tried to feel some enthusiasm for raw carrots. That was all I had in the fridge and a fine dinner it would be.

Not.

Nick didn't have a single thing that was interesting.

While my carrots warmed to perfect serving temperature—there's an art to consuming a peeled raw carrot—I had unpacked Nick's bag and spread its contents over the kitchen table.

What a miserable display. Two T-shirts that could have been

brand new, a sweatshirt, a plaid shirt and a pair of cords, a fleece jacket, some undies and socks. Everything was neatly folded and fastidiously arranged—heavy stuff at the bottom, wrinkleables on top.

Impersonal and replaceable. He could have packed in an Eddie Bauer store at the airport. A compact shaving kit was nestled at the bottom, including a small bottle of cologne.

I opened the bottle and took a whiff, and my toes curled. Just checking. It was the man's cologne, not him *per se,* that riled me up. That was good information to have. I noted the brand, just to be sure I didn't make this particular screwup again.

I looked into the shadows of the bag, but there wasn't another thing. Its contents were about as intimate as a government voice mail message. They told me zip, and the man who was the closest living replica to the Sphinx probably liked it that way.

I growled a bit and carefully put everything back, trying to make sure it looked as though I hadn't touched it. I wasn't sure why, since I probably had just inherited a couple of new T-shirts for my own. At least they were good thick cotton ones. The teal would suit me.

The phone rang and I picked it up before I thought too much about it.

Otherwise I wouldn't have bothered.

"Did you hear that the post office just recalled their latest batch of stamps?"

Number Three son calling in. "Hi, Zach. No, I didn't, but I bet you're going to tell me why." I leaned against the counter and smiled. Zach has that effect on people.

Well, people except my parents.

"They had pictures of lawyers on them and people weren't sure which side to spit on."

"That's bad," I told him, because he expected it. Zach has the greatest store of lawyer jokes known to mankind.

"How can you tell when a lawyer is lying?"

"I dunno, Zach."

"His lips are moving."

"Ouch."

"What do you throw to a drowning lawyer?"

"Go ahead, tell me."

"His partners."

That one made me laugh, although I'll swear on a stack of Bibles that I wasn't thinking of my father or his newest partner. "How are you, Zach?"

"I'm shocked and appalled."

"Why?" I wasn't sure whether to expect a confession or a punch line.

I wasn't expecting him to break into song. His was a terrible cover version of a Tammy Wynette song, " 'Cause Your Good Girl Is Gonna Go Bad."

He'd changed "your" to "our," just for me.

"The world is a little bit poorer because you turned your back on music to become a lawyer," I informed him, deliberately interrupting the chorus. There's only so much abuse the ears can take.

"I'm not one yet."

"Well, it's just a matter of time."

"Is it?"

Zach had his insouciant tone, which meant he was up to something. "What's that supposed to mean?"

"Never mind." Not only was he not going to confess, but he changed the subject with lightning speed. There must be something in the drinking water, turning all thirty-something-year-old men into clams. "What I want to know is what you've been up to. Father is pitching a fit about this Nick Sullivan thing. Is it for real, or are you just trying to age him a bit?"

The heat was on.

"Why would I lie about something like that? You know what a lousy liar I am." I made the carrots dance on the counter, because I was nervous enough that I needed something to do with my hands.

There was a long silence, sufficiently long to convince me that I had already blown my cover.

"Yeah, and I know what a Goody Two-shoes you are, too." Zach was teasing, affectionate. "You always did have to show me up. Jeez, Philippa, you nearly killed me with the contrast. There you were, every time I screwed up, halo perfectly in place." I smiled. "What did you do, save up your rebellious urges to use them all at once?"

I laughed. "Maybe." He didn't sound unpersuaded, so I got a bit bolder. "Maybe it's true love."

He snorted whatever he was drinking. "Give me a break, Philippa. Tell me what's really going on. There's no such thing as a prodigal daughter and I really don't appreciate you infringing on my official black sheep turf."

"Mixed metaphors."

"So, shoot me. Come on, I want the straight goods."

The carrots began to polka in a drunken sort of way. Hedge, cookie, hedge. "Uh, sounds as though you already think you've got some wild theory figured out. Alternatively, you know, you could just believe me."

"In your dreams. I'm not fooled for a minute, even if everyone else is." My gut went cold—but then, I *knew* I was transparent. "The problem is, Philippa, that if you don't produce Nick Sullivan for dinner on Saturday, everyone's going to know you're lying. Why'd you have to pick someone everyone would recognize? You could have pulled a name out of the air, then dragged in any poor sucker to play the part. As a scheme, this one is a bit shortsighted."

"So maybe it's the truth."

"Not a chance." Zach heaved a heartfelt sigh. "It's just your sorry lack of experience."

I chuckled.

"After all I've tried to teach you about diabolical planning, this is the best you come up with." He sighed again. "Philippa, I'm disappointed in you. It's a shame, a damn shame. Years of brilliant examples of ingenuity were clearly wasted on you . . ."

I hemmed and I hawed, I tried to buttress my lie, but Zach wasn't going to let it go. He was on to me and he wanted a story.

The real story.

I wished it was better than it was. Maybe it was just pride that had me insisting the whole thing was true, because the truth was so lame. I got ticked at Mom, I made something up on the spot that would never hold up in the family court.

He was right to call it inexperience.

When the doorbell rang, I seized the opportunity to get away from an interrogation that was nothing compared to what I'd face on Saturday night.

And just about dropped my teeth to find Nick on my doorstep, burdened with groceries. He looked at me, then looked at the carrot I was still holding and grimaced.

"Figures." He hefted one of the many bags he was carrying. "Could you grab this one? I think it's going to drop."

The bag I snagged held a set of pots, still neatly boxed up. I could see a whisk through the plastic of another bag, the outline of vegetables and bottles of spices.

I looked at him, probably with an expression that matched my incomprehension.

He'd shaved and his jeans weren't either dusty or faded anymore. He was wearing a dark green polo shirt now and looked a bit uncertain of his reception.

And so he damn well should.

"I'm not cooking you dinner," I said, which weren't perhaps the most welcoming words that could have crossed my lips.

He rolled his eyes. "Duh."

I put the bag down, square in the doorway. "I thought you'd headed for the hills."

"Well, you thought wrong. Do I get to come in and put this stuff down?"

"Not without an explanation."

"I don't think I came close enough to setting things right, Phil, so I'm here to finish the job."

It was awfully forthright for the Man of Few Words. When I hesitated, he smiled that smile that made me tingle, even though it clearly didn't come out of that cologne bottle.

So much for that theory.

I still didn't move out of the doorway. "So, you've come bearing gifts? I told you that I don't cook." I tried to hand him back the box of pots, but he didn't take it. Of course, his hands were so full that I don't know how he held on to it in the first place.

"I know that. Fortunately, I do."

"So you've started a cookware collection and intend to store it here?"

He shook his head, then dropped his voice to that husky burr, the one that makes me want to play tonsil hockey. "What do you say we make a deal, Phil?"

"Here we go again." I put the box down again and folded my arms across my chest. "Blend, stir or frappé?"

His smile faded. "What?"

"If I'm going to be a kitchen appliance, then I get to choose what kind. I'll be a blender. I've always thought of myself as a blender. Dump in all sorts of interesting bits and the blender always gives you something pinky-orange and lumpy. It's never what you want, but it's what you get. Blenders are a lot less useful than people think, except when it comes to wringing consistency from chaos." I leaned forward. "And when provoked, they can liquify."

He chuckled suddenly. "Are you provoked?"

"Pretty much."

"Well, here's my suggestion." He juggled the weight of his parcels pointedly, but I didn't leap in to help. Let him sweat. "Let me make it up to you. I need a place to crash for a couple of days. You need a decently cooked meal at least once a day. What do you say I cook for you, in exchange for using your couch?"

I could have felt sorry for him, under the burden of all that stuff, but this was what could only be called an opportune moment.

He had gone and bought it all of his own free will.

And given me a golden opportunity to solve my problem. I knew what I wanted from Nick, but couldn't imagine he'd do it. "You'll have to do better."

Now, he looked grim. "I'll get rid of that McAllister jerk for good."

I shrugged, pretending I didn't like the sound of that. He said it in a protective kind of way that made all the feminine bits of me tingle deliciously. "He might be gone already."

Nick watched me the way a hungry dog watches a ham bone. "He must have told your family that you and I were an item."

"Why would he do that?"

His grin flashed. "Because that's what I told him."

"Why?"

He rolled his eyes and shifted the weight of groceries again. "Phil. Could we talk about this over dinner?"

"No. I want to know why you did that. I want an answer or two. If this is a communicative kind of mood—and I don't for a minute think it is—then I'm not going to abandon the moment until I get some answers. You're the one so hot to not leave any footprints behind—why would you tell him something like that?"

Nick actually fidgeted. He looked out into the street and eased his weight from one foot to the other, clearly itching to evade that question.

Sadly for him, I can wait with the best of them.

"All right. He ticked me off."

"Why?"

Nick made an exasperated sound. "Why do I feel like I'm being interrogated?"

"Because you are." I smiled. "And I've learned from the best."

He muttered something under his breath that I was glad I didn't quite hear. "I didn't like that he was so ready to do what your parents wanted him to do. And I really didn't like that he didn't care what you thought of the whole thing." He glared at me. "Okay?"

More than okay. "Fair enough."

His eyes narrowed. "Did he tell your parents that?"

"Of course."

"Did you admit it was a lie?"

I smiled. "Not exactly. It was a bit too handy to be let go so soon." He smiled back, and we were coconspirators, just like the good old days. His gaze slipped over my sweats and fuzzy slippers—I was outfitted for seduction, let me tell you—in what could only have been admiration.

The man was obviously having vision problems, maybe from lack of food. The packages rustled. "Phil, I'm dying here. Do we have a deal or not?"

I leaned in the door frame and shook a finger at him. "Not yet. You may not want to talk, but I'll let you off easy. There's a Coxwell family dinner Saturday night for my father's birthday. It should be excruciating enough to make fingernails on a chalkboard sound good. You have to attend and keep up the show."

He winced. "Tough call, Phil."

"Those are the terms. You started this rumor and you can smother the flames. Isn't that why you're here?"

He nodded, but not as reluctantly as I might have expected.

"So, look on the bright side. Maybe we could start a food fight and pretend to break up in front of them all. That would provide entertainment value, and maybe inject some levity into the proceedings. It would also give them something to talk about for a few years."

I held the back of my hand to my brow, feeling a lot perkier if you must know the truth, just because Mr. Enigma had turned up again. "I could be so emotionally shattered—or pretend to be—that I never date again. It would buy me at least six months."

He studied me. "Is that what you want, Phil?"

What I didn't want was to talk about *that*. "We'll figure it out. Now, deal or not?" I tapped my toe. "I'm wasting coal-generated electricity while you waffle. It's a very comfortable couch if that's a factor in your calculations."

"And these groceries are heavy. You're on." He would have shouldered past me into the foyer, but I stopped him with one hand. His leather jacket was cold against my fingers, his shoulder firm beneath it.

"One more thing. Why do you have so much cash, Nick?"

He looked perfectly dumbfounded by my question. "I don't have a lot of cash on me."

"Sure you do. I saw in your wallet at Chandra's." I paused. "It looked like you're planning to not need a bank machine."

We eyed each other for a moment, my hand on his shoulder,

and he seemed to realize what was bothering me. "I never use bank machines, Phil. They're a rip-off. I've only got a couple of thousand in my wallet, enough for this trip, including incidentals. That's how I travel." He hefted the bags of groceries, a pointed reminder.

"A couple of thousand? No one carries that much cash."

He heaved a sigh and gave me a hard look. "Phil, mine is a cash-based business. In a lot of the world, American dollars are the terms of negotiation and the means of smoothing the way. The last time I went to Southeast Asia, for example, I had thirty thousand bucks on me."

My eyes must have boggled. "Are you running drugs or little boys?"

"Neither." His eyes flashed and I knew he wasn't lying. But I didn't step away. "I book guides, I arrange for porters, I ensure that space is found in the most popular hotels and that people remember my company name. I prepay for the incoming tours so that there are no problems once the group arrives. They're on vacation, after all, and are paying my tour company to ensure that everything runs as smooth as silk."

"How do you keep from getting mugged?"

"You look the way I did this morning." He almost smiled. "At least, that's what I used to do." He looked into his bags of stuff, clearly avoiding my gaze.

"And now?"

His brow quirked. "I antagonize old friends."

I watched him for a moment, certain the joke had been purely to deflect my curiosity.

But new rules were in force. I decided not to bite. "Why did you sell your business?"

His gaze swivelled back to mine, his eyes cat-bright. Too bright. This was important and he wasn't going to tell me, I knew it right then and there. "I needed a change."

"Liar."

He shrugged. I felt that invisible door slide into place between us, just like it always did when I asked him too much. His tone of voice turned neutral but I was feeling pretty charged up. "Deal or not?"

"No."

Surprised him again. "Phil . . ."

"No. No, no, no. You may love playing Man of Mystery but it drives me bananas. I'm not trying to claim all your state secrets, Nick, but it wouldn't hurt you to answer a simple question or two."

He went very still. "Name your terms."

"Three answers to three questions. Tonight. Or your sorry butt's out in the street, groceries and all."

His words were low, thoughtful. "I thought you needed me on Saturday night."

My breath hitched in my chest as I felt a need a little different from the one he was referring to. "I'll think of something."

I forced a smile before he could ask and propped one hand on my hip. "See, if I let you in and you go incommunicado on me, then I'll have to kill you in your sleep, which isn't going to do much for either of our futures, much less ensure that Sean gets his due."

He chuckled then. "All right, Phil. I think I can handle three answers." He rustled the bags again. "Now, have mercy on me."

I plucked a bag out of his hands and stepped out of his way. The truth is that I'd never expected him to agree.

But then, what else would he do with all this food? I knew Nick was practical—maybe agreeing to my terms was just the most practical solution.

He filled the foyer, shedding bags of stuff as he progressed, a man on a mission. I felt like Neanderthal woman, helping Neanderthal man drag the kill back into the cave. There was a lot of stuff. Really, a lot of stuff. I wasn't sure how he'd carried it all this far. He invaded my kitchen and took it over without so much as a do-you-mind.

I peeked in a heavy bag. "I do have dishes, you know."

"The odds were against it."

It was a little insulting that he had bought everything from soup to nuts, forks to glasses. But then, he wasn't completely off the deep end. The cupboards were pretty barren.

I was sure there had never been so much food in my apartment at once. "How much does Freddie eat?" I grumbled. "I only have one fridge, you know."

He chuckled and chucked his jacket over a chair before I remembered poor Zach. I pointed at the phone, then gestured to Nick. "It's my brother Zach. You talk to him."

"More conditions?"

"Part of your declared mission. He's *skeptical.*" I started putting stuff in the fridge, well aware of Nick's gaze following me and not at all certain he'd do it. But he picked up the phone and tucked it under his chin, making order of his purchases on the counter as he talked.

"Hey, Zach, how's it going?"

I waited for the sound of my brother's sputtering, but it never came.

I turned just as Nick held out the receiver with a shrug. "There's no one there, Phil. He must have hung up."

Nuts.

Chapter 12

There's something seductive about a man cooking for you.

Especially when he won't let you help. I had been banished to the kitchen table with a glass of mineral water, and nothing to do but watch.

I did. There wasn't a doubt in my mind that Nick knew what he was doing—he moved with ease, the entire symphony of preparation planned in his mind to the last detail. He seemed to be concentrating, so I didn't jabber away at him.

He didn't hurry, but then he wasn't the kind of guy who was hasty about anything. His gestures were decisive and efficient. I certainly had never had any similar abilities in the kitchen and would have been all thumbs with a mean knife like the one he had bought.

Maybe I would have had fewer thumbs by the time anything was done.

"How many people are you planning to feed anyhow?"

"Just two." He tugged a bottle of Sauvignon Blanc out of a bag, then tugged a corkscrew from his pocket.

"I don't drink."

He considered me for a heartbeat, then went back to unpacking the last few bags. The wine sat on the counter. "I didn't before either." He stacked groceries with more care than the job required. I could practically hear the cogs turning.

I was all ready for Nick to lock me out again, but he looked up suddenly and actually spoke. "You know, Phil, compromise was one thing I had to learn on my own, after I left here. With Lucia, it was all or nothing, in or out. No half measures and no compromises. Everything was cast in black or white."

I was stunned to silence that he was even capable of stringing so many words together in sequence. Then my heart warmed. The man had taken that promise seriously. He was trying to open up. It obviously wasn't easy for him.

The least I could do was not interrupt, though I knew I should mention that mysterious phone call to him soon. It could wait. I watched as he worked the corkscrew into the bottle, transfixed by his hands and his concession to me.

"Lucia never allowed liquor in the house. She had issues with the source of the Sullivan money. And then, my grandfather couldn't resist the stuff. He died young of liver problems and I don't think she ever forgave him for leaving her alone."

Because she had surrendered everything to him and to marriage. I can believe that would tick her off.

Nick frowned. "But her rule was wrong, because it was too harsh. You and I both saw what came of it. Liquor became a forbidden pleasure, one that had to be enjoyed secretively, one that took on all sorts of emotional overtones. To drink was to defy Lucia, to cast a vote against her edicts. That was probably a big part of its appeal to Sean. And drinking excessively became a signal of defying her excessively."

The cork popped. "The problem is that the pendulum swings too hard when emotions get into the picture." He hefted the bottle. "Lucia's complete boycott of liquor upped the stakes. It wasn't long before Sean could only drink excessively because of the emotional payload. All or nothing."

What he was saying could be applied equally well to food and we both knew it. I thought about the hard lines of my diet, which kept me slimmer but took a toll in sacrifice. It worked, as long as I didn't have a big emotional disaster—because food had been equated with solace for me.

Nick was all too right about snapping to the other end of the scale under duress. When my last relationship ended poorly, I inhaled a carton of double chocolate caramel ice cream without stopping for breath. I'm sure it wasn't a pretty sight. The very memory of that lapse has kept me celibate and single for a long time.

Nick made me wonder if there was another way. He poured some wine into a glass, sniffed it, tasted it, then held it up to the light. It sparkled.

"Wine is just a beverage," he mused. "Juice gone bad. It's not defiance or rejection or even independence in a glass. Our bodies burn food and drink, admittedly some kinds better and more effectively than others, but they're just machines consuming fuel. There's no love in this bottle, no acceptance, no freedom, not even any illusions." He winked at me as he conjured a second glass and poured some wine into it. "And once you get that straightened out, you realize that it tastes good with food."

He handed that glass to me and our fingers brushed in the transaction. "A little moderation never hurt anyone, Phil. And I think that moderation actually prevents those hard swings of the pendulum. Call it a point of balance."

Come to think of it, that chocolate bar a month plan had

come into being after my last romantic disaster. It seemed to keep me on a more even keel and kept the worst of the yearnings at bay.

Great minds think alike. I thought about that as he went back to work.

It was nice silence between us, one that made my kitchen feel warm and cozy. We'd agreed to abandon the twin topics of Sullivans and Coxwells once he got off the phone with Zach—or more accurately, not Zach—so this was a night out of time.

Maybe that was what made it seem so special. I've told you about the emotionally charged silences I was used to, the ones that had me always looking over my shoulder to see who was angry with me.

This was different. I watched Nick work, sipped my water and once in a while my wine, and felt the tensions of the day slip from my shoulders.

He provided me with nibbles as he worked. I was touched that he had bothered to find a low-fat swiss cheese. He sliced it thin thin thin and laid it on grainy crispbread—just about negative calories, those things—garnishing each one with a ruby red slice of pepper. He put some antipasto pickle things on the plate, as well, and some rabbit food from his slicing and dicing.

"So you don't pass out on me," he said with a smile as he slid the plate onto the table. I nibbled dutifully and decided that I could get used to this.

"Where did you learn to cook?"

"Everywhere and nowhere."

A typical Nick answer. His brow furrowed as he surveyed the array of goodies on the counter and I understood that conversation was not welcome at this time.

It was surprisingly okay.

He cleaned the red snapper with the expert strokes of someone who has done that job before. He had it stuffed and ready for the oven before I could whistle Dixie. He chopped a lot of stuff and put it on to simmer in a saucepan before I managed to identify it all, then diced a mountain of vegetables.

Eventually he served up a mixed green salad dressed with a vinaigrette that looked deceptively easy to make but I wasn't fooled. He joined me to have the salad, one eye on the pot.

"Think you've got enough plants?" he asked drily as some of my babies were nudged further across the table to make room for two settings. It's true that the window is full of them and the tabletop is half covered.

Maybe more than half.

"It's not usually an issue. There's lots of room and the kitchen gets good light." I moved my avocado to the floor, silently promising to put it back where it would get sunlight before the morning.

"Where do you get them all?"

"Everywhere and nowhere."

He gave me a wry smile. "People leave them on your doorstep? Like kittens needing a home?"

"No. I grow them. This is from an avocado that had a split pit. And that one's a mango and that's a peach tree, though it'll be a while before it bears any peaches."

His expression was incredulous. "All from pits?"

"Um hmm. I haven't had much luck with apple seeds though. They're probably mostly hybrids."

"Meaning?"

"Hybrids are more resistant to bugs and diseases or adverse conditions, but the seeds are often sterile as a result."

"Hmm. So what happens when the hybrid trees die? It's not so easy to start over again, is it?" He looked really interested, which was all I needed to warm to my theme.

"No. That's a problem. And there's also the problem of what are called heritage varieties of plants disappearing."

He looked up. "How so?"

"People stop growing the original varieties, because the hybrids are easier to grow. So, over time, the originals disappear. Seed isn't good forever—and if no one saves any, then it's all lost." I leaned forward because this was one of my dearly beloved issues and his eyes hadn't glazed over yet. "We've started a nonprofit organization to catalogue and preserve heritage varieties, especially those typically grown in New England."

He nodded approval. "Who's we?"

It was a real treat to be able to talk about something I cared about, without being told that I was wasting my time, or that it was foolish.

"Well, I'm the only garden designer, though Joel donates a couple of Saturdays every spring to play rototiller man. There are some avid gardeners around here who are members, as well as a woman from the historical society and one botanist from the university. And there are a few people from seed companies too. We're trying to figure out a good way to keep track of who's growing what and who's got what, and who's harvested fresh seeds."

"You plant stuff every year?"

"Well, sure. People give us seeds, or we grow some of the ones we've saved. The great thing about plants is that they're always willing to make more seeds. Gradually, we're building up a repository, but we could use some more garden space too. Maybe a database."

"What's needed always comes to good causes."

"Knock wood." I rapped on the tabletop and got more than I bargained for.

"If I'm in town when you plant this year, I'd like to help."

I blinked at Nick before I remembered that he was the king of biosustainability. That explained his interest. "Well, thanks."

"No problem."

But he probably would be gone.

I decided to find out. "We don't plant until the end of May."

Nick grimaced. "Too bad. I thought it might be sooner." He turned his attention to his salad.

How many times did I need to confirm that he was just stopping by? It's not as though the man made a secret of it. I opted for avoiding any further elucidation, returning to the plants at hand. "And that's a lemon tree and that's the orange that started it all."

"How so?"

"The seed had a little root when I ate the orange. I couldn't just dump it in the trash. It was alive already!"

A smile played over his lips. "So you planted it."

"And it grew." We looked at the four foot tall shrubby plant with the glossy orange leaves. It was undeniably vigorous.

"Who would have guessed it could be so happy in Massachusetts? You must have a special touch, Phil." He pointed to the monster in the corner. "And what's that one?"

"An oleander. A pink one. The blooms smell like heaven. It's sulking right now, but will perk up once I put it outside next month. It blooms every summer out in the sunshine even though it's not a fan of Massachusetts winters. I guess it gets temporarily faked out in the sun."

He chuckled, collected the salad plates and went back to work. It wasn't long afterward that he served up the red snapper, now grilled to perfection and dotted with lemon slices. The pot proved to hold a mango and lime salsa that smelled too yummy to be believed. There were steamed veggies and wild rice, the whole thing looking so artful that it seemed a shame to gobble it up.

"Don't worry, Phil," he said as he sat down, obviously mistaking the reason for my hesitation. "There's hardly any fat in it. Eat what you want, and don't worry about waste."

"Because there won't be any?" I eyed his much more generous serving.

He just grinned.

"To Freddie," I said as we clinked our glasses.

The fish melted in my mouth. Not only was it the most divine meal I'd had in a long time, it had been cooked especially for me by a man who made for good rear views in my kitchen. And he had made an effort to ensure that it didn't break my diet. The thoughtfulness of that could have made a lesser meal stick in my throat.

I wondered then what it would take to keep Nick around. He was a bit big to chain to the stove and probably wily enough to escape.

But it might seriously be worth a try.

"Maybe we shouldn't stage a breakup on Saturday," I suggested casually.

He looked up in evident surprise.

"Saturday is only two days away, and I could go for at least a month of eating like this."

He choked on his dinner and had to take a swig of mineral water.

I clicked my tongue and feigned disapproval. "You're losing your edge, Sullivan. I don't remember you ever being so easily surprised."

He chuckled then. "Eat up," he instructed. "There's no dessert and it's a long time 'til breakfast."

We exchanged a smile that should have been harnessed for its electrical voltage, then dug in.

He wouldn't even let me help wash up.

I sat in the living room, nursed my mineral water and alternatively pondered two questions: 1. where did one buy manacles?; and 2. would hitting Nick over the head with that shiny new skillet stun him enough for me to get those manacles on without causing long-term neurological damage?

I was so lost in my ruminations that I jumped slightly when Nick dropped onto the other end of the couch.

He closed his eyes and leaned his head back.

"You look exhausted. You should have let me help with the dishes."

"It's not that." He spoke without opening his eyes. "Two nights without sleep is about my limit."

"I hope the couch is okay."

He slanted me a look through half-opened eyes. The expression made him look sleepy but wary, a bit dangerous. Dragon time. "I could sleep on concrete tonight."

Without even having moved, he seemed suddenly very close, and I swore I could feel a little fan of steam on the back of my neck. I started to move plants out of the way, purportedly so he wouldn't have to worry about impaling himself whenever he got up. There were a lot of cacti in the living room, an inspired choice to my thinking, since it was hot and dry in there. The landlord wasted a fortune on heating, but my plants adored it.

"And tomorrow?"

"What about tomorrow?"

"What are you going to do?"

"What difference does it make?"

"Don't get cute with me. We have a deal."

I scooped up the Christmas cactus, which either didn't have a clue or felt as though it had been deprived of late. It was in full bud, irregardless of the fact that it was spring. But then, most plants will rush to make seeds one last time if they think they're going to die. I fingered the soil and decided I'd been stingy with the water.

"And you're going to waste one of the three on a question like that?"

"You're right. Forget I asked."

He yawned elaborately and stretched out. I might have thought his eyes were closed except for a telling green gleam. "What are *you* doing tomorrow?"

I gave him a perky smile, enjoying that I could throw his words back at him. "What difference does it make?"

"Are you seeing anyone, Phil?"

I perched on the edge of the couch. "I get to ask the questions around here."

"Are you?"

I decided it was time he had a measure of his own medicine. "I'll take the Fifth on that."

He did one of those quick moves that could make me jump out of my skin and was suddenly right beside me. He looked down at me as though my mind was an archaeological site he intended to unearth, labeling each revelation as he went. Short of leaping over the coffee table and its array of spiky plants, there was no escape.

And he knew it. "But you're a romantic by your own admission. Just between great loves at the moment?"

"Perhaps you've forgotten that my mother is setting me up with eligible young men, who are gainfully employed, well-connected and suitably attired."

He didn't smile. "But no one said you tell her everything."

"Why should I tell *you?*"

His smile was smug. "If my presence on the couch is going to have repercussions, don't you think I deserve a warning?"

I heaved a sigh, hating that he had some small point and wishing that he had been curious for another reason. "There haven't been any great romances for a while, so you don't have to worry about a spurned lover charging through the door and bludgeoning you to death. Happy?"

"Because Sean hurt you?"

I laughed, I couldn't help it. "Nick, I just had a crush on him. It lasted all of a month. I was hardly scarred for life."

"Not pining for him?"

"No, not for him." I realized my slip too late to make a save. I met his gaze and realized he hadn't missed a thing.

Uh oh.

Nick lifted one hand and tucked a strand of hair behind my ear, then tipped my chin up with his fingertips. I knew I wasn't going to squirm out of this easily and I didn't really want to.

It was time to lay it all out.

I silently hoped it might turn out for the best.

"Then for who, Phil?"

But, you know, I couldn't say it. I just looked at him, no doubt with the truth shining in my eyes, so I might as well have spit it out. But I seemed to have been struck dumb. My heart was pounding and my mouth went dry. He studied me and shook his head, as though he couldn't believe what he saw.

His voice was hoarse when he whispered my name. He eased closer, giving me lots of room, but I wasn't running anywhere. Then his lips closed over mine. I couldn't decide why his kiss was so gentle, whether he was trying to let me down easy or whether he thought I was fragile, but I didn't care. He might be holding back, but I had no reason to, now that he knew my secret.

I've only ever had one.

I twined my arms around his neck and opened my mouth to him. He made a sound deep in his throat but I was ready to be gobbled up by this particular dragon. His arms closed around me and his kiss deepened, giving me a taste of that volcano fire. I wanted more. I was ready to be the sacrifice that leapt over the edge. I felt his heartbeat and the heat of his skin through his T-shirt for exactly three beats before he pushed me away and stood up.

He paced across the room and shoved one hand through his hair. He didn't turn around. "Go, Phil." His voice was uneven. "Go now and lock the door."

I was shaking as I got to my feet. I swallowed as I linked my hands together. "I'll have one of those answers now." I hated how my voice was shaking. "What exactly would be the problem here? I thought things were beginning rather well."

He turned around, his expression grim. "I won't be your fantasy, Phil. As tempting as it is, I can't be whoever it is that you've decided I am. It's been fifteen years. Everything's changed, we've both changed."

I felt my tears rising, but I wouldn't plead with him.

He heaved a ragged sigh and flung out one hand. "Don't you see, Phil? Do you think I don't see what you want? But I don't do commitment. I don't stay anywhere for long. I don't get involved because every time I have, things have gone straight to hell. If you knew anything about me, you wouldn't want what you think you want."

"There you go, knowing all again."

"It matters to me that we're friends," he said hoarsely. "This would change everything, and almost certainly end badly."

"I thought you were the risk-taker."

"Not when the stakes are this high."

I didn't know what to say to that. It was hard to be angry with him, even though lust was short-circuiting my wiring. "Our friendship is important to me, too, Nick. I just wonder whether it's something more."

He folded his arms across his chest and eyed me grimly. "I'm trying to do you a favor, Phil. We're not the same kind of people. Our families are as different as can be."

"You're the one who told me to buck expectations."

"But Phil . . ."

He looked so apologetic that I couldn't stand it anymore. Everything worked in the hormonal department for him, I'd tripped all his switches but he wasn't really interested in me.

So, now I knew. I guess I should have been glad he didn't take what I offered, that he had done the noble thing. I might have regretted it in the morning.

On the other hand, maybe I wouldn't have.

"It's okay. No means no. Message received. Good night, Nick." His eyes flashed, but I marched into the bathroom, locked the door and made a lot of noise brushing my teeth. I opted for the flannel granny gown, knowing that it was about as sexy as a burlap bag.

Just in case you're not sure, I'm not casual about intimacy. The guy who slips between my sheets next time will be planning to hang around for a lifetime.

Or so I've always maintained. There are these moments though—like the one when I came out of the bathroom to find Nick peeling off his shirt in the living room—when it seems as though the love of my life is taking a long time to show.

I was starting to think that chastity was seriously overrated. Chances were pretty good that one day—say, Sunday—I would hate myself for not jumping Nick's bones at least once before he disappeared.

But he wasn't gone yet. I had two days.

I decided to make them count.

So yes, I looked, then disguised healthy feminine curiosity with a rummage in the linen closet when he turned around. He was completely untroubled by partial nudity or proximity, appearing suddenly in my peripheral vision in nothing but his jeans.

But Nick wasn't even looking at me, so the nightgown must

have evoked its spinsterhood charm. "What is that?" he asked, pointing into my bedroom and not indicating the bed.

I thought he meant the flats of seedlings perched willy-nilly under the window, and halfheartedly started my heritage seeds explanation again. He laid one warm finger across my lips to silence me.

Oh, it worked.

He watched my throat work for an instant before meeting my gaze once more. "No, Phil," he whispered. "That."

To my mortification, he pointed to the corner of the ceiling.

"Oh, well, it's my star." I forced a smile and tried to rush past him, foolishly assuming that he wouldn't follow me into my haven. He didn't quite. He sauntered after me and leaned in the door frame as I should have guessed he would until he had an answer that suited him.

It was absolutely the worst confession I could have to make under the circumstances. He'd think I was still some heartsick adolescent who never grew up. I fussed with the linens and tried to ignore him.

"That's a stick-on phosphorescent star."

If he wanted a medal for naming that toy, he wasn't going to get it from me. "So?"

"Where'd you get it?"

"I begged it off my nephew when he got an entire constellation for his bedroom ceiling." I checked my babies with more concern than they really needed. "Good night already."

"Why?"

I threw him a look that should have been a warning. "You ask a lot of questions, you know."

"Maybe I'm a naturally inquisitive person."

"There's an understatement."

He watched and waited, probably knowing that he was the

only male to have gotten this close to my bed—at least in this apartment—who wasn't blood-related.

And knowing damn well why I had that star.

Which meant there wasn't a lot of point in being coy.

I turned to face him, betting he could outwait me. "Okay, I like to wish on the brightest star before I go to sleep. This way, I don't have to go looking for the star every night. It's right here, the last thing I see before I close my eyes. There, end of story hour." I propped my hands on my hips. "I thought you were exhausted."

"Does it work?" He clearly wasn't going to be easily dissuaded.

"Oh, I don't know." I looked at the star. "The galley slave wish seems to have come out all right."

He chuckled, but didn't turn away. No, he stood there and looked at the damn star, as though he would wait all night to know whatever the heck it was he wanted to know.

"Isn't it time you tucked up on the couch?"

"I remember you picking out a star once."

Oh, so did I. I looked at that star and wished with all my heart and soul that he wouldn't figure out that the memory of that magical night was the reason I had made this a habit.

Nick's expression turned distant, the way it had when he talked about Bhutan. "You've really got to go to Morocco, Phil," he murmured. "There's a place, generously called an auberge or an inn, out by the dunes of the desert. It's near Merzouga."

"Merzouga." It was irresistible to try out the name. It felt as exotic on my tongue as it sounded. "That's the town?"

"Well, a lot of these places are more a feeling than a destination." Nick smiled. "They don't do the New England foursquare corner much. Sometimes there's only one building, sometimes the name refers to a general district, sometimes there really is a cluster that we would call a town."

He looked at me again, his voice dropping low enough to lull me to the land of good dreams. "But you can sleep on the roof of this place when the weather's good. It's miles from anywhere—in fact, I have to hire one of the locals everytime I drive out there.

"There's no road and it's too easy to get lost in the shifting dunes. The only electricity comes from generators and people are pretty tight with it, so it's dark at night, really dark.

"When a full moon rises, it's as though the sun is coming up. It actually casts a shadow. I never knew there were so many stars. You can hardly see the sky for them. They're dazzling."

He shook his head and looked at me, his eyes gleaming, his voice filled with an affection that made me shiver. "You'd have a hard time picking which was the brightest one to hang your wish on, Phil."

We stared at each other across the darkened room and I knew then that he hadn't missed the connection.

But he wasn't going to make me feel like an idiot about it.

"Why did you really sell your company, Nick?" I asked quietly. "You obviously aren't tired of traveling."

He abruptly turned away. "Yes, I am. That part of my life is done. Good night, Phil."

But I had had enough slamming doors to last me a while.

"That's *it!*"

Phil stormed out of the bedroom behind him, an avenging angel in beribboned blue flannel. He guessed she didn't know how the soft fabric clung in all the right places.

He enjoyed the view for a moment, only now accepting that she hadn't befriended him to get closer to his brother. He'd always assumed that was the reason she'd first approached him, never mind the reason they'd become friends. Now he wondered what had led him to that conclusion, let alone what had made him cling to it all these years.

But Phil couldn't lie. And the way she had looked at him had completely shaken the foundations of his universe. She liked *him*. That seemed like a stupid thing to both please and excite a thirty-five-year-old man.

Even though he knew nothing should ever come of it. Even though he knew he couldn't be good for her. He wouldn't be responsible for Phil's inevitable disappointment, or her tumble from her tightrope of control. He cared enough about her to be sure that he didn't ruin her.

He had a certain touch in that department, after all.

Her eyes flashed and she jabbed a finger through the air at him. She was flushed and furious.

"Look, it's a bird, it's a plane, no, it's *Reticent Man!*" She flung out her hands and shouted.

The neighbor upstairs thumped on the floor.

"All right!" she cried at the ceiling, then leveled a glare at him that did not bode well for his future. "Honest to God, Nick, I'm going to get you a T-shirt with a big red R on the front and make you wear it every day as a warning to the unsuspecting people of planet Earth who might just be foolish enough to think that you would actually admit to something!"

She paused for breath but only just barely. "How *dare* you refuse to tell me anything at all? What kind of deal is this? Compared to you, the Great Sphinx is making the talk show circuit—every question I ask, you shut me right out. I thought we were friends! Can't I be curious about the fifteen years you've been gone?"

She huffed.

He shrugged, feeling that anything he said would sound inadequate. "I'm not used to talking about myself."

"Well, we have a deal, in case you've forgotten, and I get two more answers out of you." She folded her arms across her chest. "Ante up."

He sank onto the couch and studied her. Phil's feet were bare, the hem of the gown swinging high enough that he could see the sweet curve of her insteps, the sexy line of her ankles. He laced his fingers together and leaned his elbows casually on his knees, pretending his blood wasn't simmering and his jeans weren't too tight.

Or that he wasn't checking out her feet.

Let alone that it had taken everything within him not to snatch up what she offered.

What he needed was a bit of sleep. Just enough to bolster his legendary self-control.

"You can't leave me in the dark like this!" she retorted, his own little Amazon queen. "It's not fair."

"What's fair got to do with anything?"

"Right! I open my apartment to you, I drive to Rosemount for no reason whatsoever, I try to help you—but you put *zipadeedoodah* into the mix. I am not a charitable organization, all indications to the contrary!"

"No, you're a secret collector and you want one of mine."

That took the wind out of her sails. Her shoulders sagged and she looked smaller suddenly. She took a step back, her expression so wounded that he had to make her smile.

He winked. "Besides, you seem to be putting up with me so far."

That brought her chin back up. "Only because I'm a paragon of tolerance." She gritted her teeth visibly. "You've officially used it all up, Nick Sullivan. The buck stops here. Now give me a decent answer or pay the price."

He deliberately let that threat and its potential innuendo lie. "There's nothing to tell."

"Bullshit."

He blinked, never having heard Phil swear before.

She looked unrepentant. "You think it's fair that you weasel all sorts of embarrassing tidbits out of me, but don't reciprocate?"

"Weasel?"

"Weasel." Phil nodded. "There's definitely something subversive

about it all. You cook for me, just to soften me up, then charm the most embarrassing stuff out of me."

He couldn't help but smile and shake his head. "I don't think I've ever been accused of *weaseling* before."

"Because your friends are too chicken to tell you the truth"—her tone turned cutting—"or because this behavior is something special, just for me?"

He had hurt her, again, without meaning to do so. She hid it well but not well enough to fool him. "Phil, don't go making this into more than it is . . ."

"More than murder?" She lifted her chin and charged on even as he winced at the word. "How am I supposed to know what the real story is? Maybe you're lying to me about the cash in your wallet—maybe you *did* plan ahead to not need a bank machine. Maybe you *did* kill Lucia and I'm ending up being accessory after the fact for letting you stay here."

He gave her a hard look, willing her to agree. "You don't believe I killed her."

But Phil wasn't going to play by his rules now. "Maybe I won't tell you whether or not I do."

She tossed her hair and turned around, flicking her foot in a way that she probably didn't know made him want to pounce on her. He shoved a hand through his hair and leaned his head back, closing his eyes for a heavenly moment. She had to be the most determined woman he'd ever met.

She certainly didn't take no for an answer as easily as most.

And oh, she had him tied up in knots.

"Phil, you wouldn't let me stay here if you had the slightest suspicion against me." He spoke more reasonably than he felt, her agreement more important to him than he liked to admit. "You're too sensible for that."

She folded her arms across her chest. "Flattery will get you nowhere."

He rummaged around and came up with an excuse that sounded somewhat plausible. The truth was something he didn't even want to think. "We're so different that I'm curious about you, that's all. You don't have to answer any question I ask if you don't want to."

"Bull." She sat down on the other end of the couch, making it bounce slightly and he looked sideways at her. She had that stubborn expression he knew better than to trust, though she didn't look as angry. Mutinous maybe. Had he ever met a woman who grabbed his attention and held on as effectively as Phil?

His tired brain wondered whether he'd been running from more than he had thought when he left Rosemount all those years ago.

"It's just the opposite," she argued. "We're so much the same that you're curious."

That made him sit up and take notice. "How do you figure that?"

She ticked her points off on her fingers. "We both had to start our own businesses, we both decided against finishing college, we both bucked our family's expectations. We're both proud of what we accomplished. Though you're more of an environmental nut than me, neither one of us wants the usual suburban comfort package."

He hadn't known that about her until just now. He straightened slightly, intrigued.

She leaned closer, her eyes shining, that little smile tempting him to take just one taste. "But I can't ever imagine selling off my business, Nick, because it's part and parcel of who I am and what I love. And you're exactly the same way. You still love traveling, and don't tell me you don't because I'll know it's a lie."

The fact that she had seen through him should have made him feel more edgy than he did.

He wasn't going to think about that just now.

"I'm starting to miss it again," he conceded warily. "But the rest is unimportant."

The look she gave him was scathing. "How dumb do you think I am?"

He almost smiled. "Not very."

"Gullible, then? Fat Philippa was a sap, but I like to think I've gotten over that."

He did smile then. "You're trusting, Phil. You see the good in people, probably more than they deserve. It's very sweet."

She blushed a bit and he decided it was a good thing that she was keeping her distance. He certainly would have lost sight of his noble urges if she was close enough that he could snag her hand.

"Well, I didn't get that from my family," she mumbled, clearly embarrassed. She pleated the acres of flannel between her fingers. "They won't take anything on faith."

"What is that supposed to mean?"

She looked up as pertly as a little bird. "What do you think my mother is going to ask me about you on Saturday? You know, when she drags me into the kitchen to get all the nitty-gritty details."

He hadn't thought of that. "I have no idea."

"She'll want to know what you do, where your money comes from, where you've been for the past fifteen years."

"So, tell her I run an adventure travel company." He shrugged. "It was true two months ago."

Phil shook her head and the light glinted golden in her auburn hair. "But not now. I'm a lousy liar, Nick, and I couldn't compose a story on the spot to save my life." She sat back, so pleased with herself that it was hard not to smile. "You're just going to have to tell me the truth, that's all there is to it." She snapped her fingers. "Cough it up."

"Just so you don't blow our cover?"

"Mmm hmm." Her smile was pure mischief, the glint in her eyes triumphant. That look alone brought his simmering blood right to the boil. He was thinking of naked skin and legs tangled together, of Phil beneath him, sweet and hot and welcoming.

He was thinking about that kiss and wondering why the hell he'd stopped.

Which was exactly what he shouldn't be thinking. He knew why that was a bad road to travel. But the sensible part of him wasn't getting a lot of air time right now. He reminded himself that he'd screwed up many things and he didn't want to mess this friendship up too. Following primal urges would hurt Phil in a way she didn't deserve.

He frowned and dragged his thoughts back to their conversation.

The scary thing was that her argument made a certain amount of sense. Maybe she would understand better the kind of man he had become after he told her the story she wanted.

Maybe it would do the dirty work for him. He reached down and picked up his T-shirt, giving himself a moment to compose his thoughts.

He hadn't told anyone his real reasons for finally accepting the buyout offer and he supposed it would be good to share the weight of it. And Phil, for all her cocky talk, was the most trustworthy person he had ever known. The story would go no further, a fact that reassured him, Reticent Man that he was.

Who else but Phil would have made such an accusation?

"All right, you win."

She shook a finger at him in playful warning. "And none of this 'oh I changed my mind and that's that' crap. I want the *whole* story."

"Or else what?"

She jerked her thumb toward the door.

He pretended to be shocked. "After I cooked and everything. Why do I feel so unappreciated?"

She chortled with laughter and tucked up her feet, giving him another quick view of those fabulous legs. "Hey, I'm no pushover." She pushed one hand through her hair, leaving it rumpled. She looked young and impish and very kissable. He seriously thought about edging a little further down the couch and making her forget all about the sale of his company.

And not just because he was less than thrilled about telling the story. There was something about Phil that he was starting to suspect wouldn't be easy to walk away from.

Much less forget. He thought about the way she'd kissed him as though she'd swallow him whole, and his jeans got even tighter.

But there was no point in making it harder to do what he knew he'd do.

He stared at the ceiling to get his mind out of the gutter. Phil seemed content to wait all night for him to find the beginning thread.

"I started the company after I'd been traveling around the world myself. I had lots of time and enough money that I didn't have to rush, and I found a lot of places that most vacationers, even the adventurous ones, miss. The idea of helping other people see these places had been running around in my head for a while before I got to Asia."

The words came easily once he started, and Phil didn't interrupt. She'd always been easy to talk to, though he was only coming to remember that now.

"I lingered a long time, checking out beaches, kayaking, wandering through markets. It was beautiful and the culture was so different. I just couldn't explore enough of it. At that time, there was almost no tourism outside of the big cities, so there was an entire world to discover.

"There are always lots of local kids willing to show you something for a price, but they're often scam artists. I usually shrugged them off, but there was one insistent kid where tourists were pretty much a rarity. So, I gave him what he wanted—five bucks or something—and he really did take me to the most marvelous place."

He paused for a moment, reliving that first glimpse. "It was a valley that no one would ever have found on their own. The jungle was thick and there was no path, but this kid knew the way. One minute I was pushing through the undergrowth thinking the kid was setting me up, the next I was standing on a rock where an underground stream bubbled up. It was like stepping through a curtain, the change was that sudden. The stream flowed onward, reflecting sun and sky and untouched perfection."

"Shangri-la," Phil murmured.

"Something like that. It sure didn't look real. And it was untouched. There was no sound but the birds and the running water, the hum of huge insects. I can't even begin to describe the sheer beauty of the place. A naturalist would have had a field day.

"The river went on for about half a mile, then disappeared into the jungle again. You couldn't walk the shoreline though—it was too choked with growth. I finally understood why we'd carried this kayak all the way in. He paddled and I rubbernecked.

"In some places the stream pooled and was as smooth as a river; in others, it gushed and gurgled over rocks. Everywhere I looked there were creatures I'd never seen before, tree frogs and birds and butterflies. It was as though we had stepped into a dream. Paradise. I must have shot eight rolls of film that day.

"Late in the afternoon, he took me back to his village. It was a shock to see how impoverished the people were, despite living near such beauty. He was so proud that he had earned that five-dollar bill—I was humbled by how little it meant to me in comparison. Not that I was flush in those days, but we learn to take a lot for granted."

He looked at an avid Phil. "So it was there, in his village, that I had my idea."

"To start an eco-tourist company?"

"Well, more importantly, to make a difference. The company was just the vehicle. This kid was willing to work, to do something. He was just itching for a chance. He had a huge family and they were getting older. Farming was subsistence at best.

"So, I made a partnership with him—though he probably thought it was bogus at the time. We set rules for visiting the Hidden Paradise—that's what they called it—and limits as to how many people could visit a week. I wanted to make sure that it stayed as pristine and beautiful as it was, that other people felt that same joy of discovery that I had felt that day."

"Leave nothing but a footprint, take nothing but a picture."

"Exactly. That's why the company had the name it did. My new partner hired villagers to be guides and we sponsored a couple of households who wanted to provide accommodation to guests. It was a hefty investment but one I could handle. Barely. I came back to the States and printed up a brochure using some of the pictures I took, then hit every travel show I could talk my way into, spreading brochures on all available surfaces.

"I went with the first tour group to make sure everything ran smoothly and the village laid out a welcome like you wouldn't believe. There was a naturalist on that trip and he took even more pictures than I had. It was a resounding success."

"And they told two people and they told two people."

"Well, not quite as easily as that. Eight happy tourists does not a company make. I had to keep finding more adventurous souls, a lot of them to turn a profit. There were more than a few lean years. The first office was in a warehouse loft where I also lived. Just when I thought it was never going to work, it really started to cook." He smiled. "I remember when we went into the black as though it was yesterday."

Phil smiled back at him. "There's nothing like it."

He took her hand, because it seemed a natural thing to do. Her hand fit perfectly into his, her fingers small and slender compared to his own.

"No. And after that, everything just went insane. People loved the trip but wanted to go somewhere different the next year. They liked the no-impact tourism and the small groups. They liked stepping into another world, and wanted to give us their vacation tour business. That was too good a chance to turn down, so I was on the run, finding new destinations, making partnerships, training guides, booking, hiring office staff, putting together brochures and selling selling selling."

"But you wouldn't have had it any other way."

He shook his head. "Probably not. It was fun in a hectic kind of way. That naturalist was the first one on every trip and found me so many new customers I used to joke about putting him on commission."

He stopped then, because this was the hard part of the story.

She tilted her head to watch him. "So you just got tired?"

"No." He looked at her hand in his, not as certain of how to continue as he had been of how to begin. She waited, and he decided she was more patient than he deserved. "That first place always held a special corner of my heart. It was the beginning of everything and even though I used the same model everywhere, always taking a local partner, always hiring local people, that valley was my touchstone."

"That makes sense."

"But I had a few complaints this last summer about that trip. The first one or two I figured were anomalies—on trips like the ones I arranged, anything can happen. Some people adjust less well than others to the unpredictable. Then that naturalist revisited the valley and afterward he came to see me personally. He was pretty solemn when he told me that I'd better go have a look. So I did."

He shook his head, still unable to accept what he'd seen. "The village was so different, Phil, that I didn't recognize the place. It had grown and prospered, which was good, but it had gone far beyond my expectation. The roads were paved and there was advertising all over the place. The people were wearing jeans and sweats covered with logos. You could have plucked them out of anywhere in America.

"The worst thing though was that there were now six different companies doing the same thing that we were, but doing it without the rules. They had signage everywhere and salespeople prowling the streets. And the valley itself . . ."

He shook his head and shuddered. "It was infested with tourists, all grabbing samples and souvenirs. They were swimming in the river and climbing the rocks, shouting in a dozen languages and leaving litter all over the place. The birds had left, the flowers had been plucked, there were footpaths worn all along the shore. The dream had become a nightmare. My partner looked a hundred years older."

"Why didn't he tell you sooner?"

"He didn't want to worry me." Nick sighed. "More likely, he didn't want me to think he was incompetent. But I knew he wasn't. Maybe he didn't want me to shut the business down, because that would affect the income he'd gotten used to, not to mention his status in the village as the one who'd started them all on the road to wealth. He'd done the best job he could, but couldn't make my mistake better."

"What are you talking about?"

He gave her a sharp look, wondering why she was being coy about something so obvious. "I made a mistake, Phil. I should never have started that partnership. Far from taking nothing but a picture, I took everything from those people. They lost their independence, they're probably losing their culture and the whole world lost a treasure that can never be refound."

"Surely they could legislate . . ."

He didn't let her get any further, though his irritation with himself was starting to show. "Phil. We're talking about third world governments. They're not big on environmental issues, but they are fond of revenue. The tourists have to pay a head fee, so the more the merrier. The locals are consuming more manufactured goods, so they're paying more taxes. The government there is not going to do anything to discourage this—in fact, I'd expect just the opposite. The damage is done."

He rubbed his temples where a headache was beginning to loom. "So I tied up all the loose ends and let my partner decide whether he wanted the business or to be bought out. Then I flew around the world and did the same at all the other partnerships. Most of them opted to stay in the game, but I didn't have the stomach for it anymore."

Her silence made him certain she agreed with him. "Then I took the offer that the competition had been shoving under my nose for five years, albeit with a bunch of conditions. Surprised them, but that's the way it goes. They're a good bunch of guys. Maybe they'll do better than I did. If nothing else, I can't make it any worse."

He kept his eyes closed, waiting for her to condemn him.

"Wait a minute." She eased closer. "You aren't blaming yourself for this, are you?"

"Who else would there be to blame?" His voice rose and he didn't care. "I screwed this up, just like I screw everything up! Here I am, the one person in the world who thinks that rampant consumerism isn't so all-fired terrific, and I manage to export it better than anybody else! I destroyed a local culture and replaced it with nothing worth a damn and started who knows how many untouched places on the same path. It's the worst fucking failure that I could have made of my life!"

He turned away, not wanting to see the censure that must fill Phil's eyes.

So much for his last friend.

Instead, he felt her hand on his arm. He could smell the soft perfume of her soap and feel her warmth close beside him.

"Hey, cowboy, ever heard of free will?"

"What the hell is that supposed to mean?" He risked a sidelong glance to find Phil considering him, no disgust in her expression.

"You don't look like God to me." Her lips twisted. "I always figured he was an older type. You know, flowing grey beard and all that."

"Phil, this is not funny."

"No, it isn't, but you look like you could use a laugh."

"You can make all the jokes you want, but I'll never forgive myself."

She sobered immediately. "But what about them, Nick? Are those people happy with what's happened to them? You're not the grand puppetmaster, you know. You had an idea and they liked it—you're not responsible for the fact that they turned into something entirely different."

"But, I . . ."

She continued firmly, not acknowledging his interruption. "Maybe something that suited them just fine."

"But . . ."

"Don't you think it's important that most of your partners chose to stay in the business? They can't share your view, Nick."

She was a dangerously persuasive creature.

"Maybe they're happy with their choice." She nestled closer, her eyes filled with sincerity. "Do they have better living conditions? Cleaner water? Better access to schooling for their children?"

He didn't know.

"Well? Every facet of Western life isn't bad, Nick. There are good things too. Maybe they're living longer now and having better medical care. Maybe women aren't dying in childbirth and children are getting vaccinations. Subsistence farming is a tough way to get by." She shook his arm. "Maybe they have choices. What could be more precious than that?"

He eyed her warily. "I'm starting to think that optimism should be classed as a lethal weapon."

Her smile flashed briefly and she took his hand in both of hers. She was so intent on casting him as a hero.

And he wanted to take the role more than he'd ever wanted anything in his life. It was different this time—he couldn't accuse her of not knowing the worst of him.

Trust Phil to still turn everything up roses.

"Nick, what if that boy had found someone less altruistic than you? Anyone could have set up tours there and sucked the money right out of the country. They could have been left even more deeply impoverished, used by another company and left without any of the spoils. You did a good thing by letting them not only run the tours but share in the wealth."

"The valley's still ruined."

"Who says it can't be fixed? One of the wonderful things about the earth is how incredibly forgiving it can be. A few paths are nothing compared to some of the stuff we've managed to do in a lot of the world—yet natural places recover quickly once given a chance. I'll take you to a place we've been working on. It was a dumping ground for chemicals and old concrete. It's taken a lot of work, but there are flowers growing there, Nick. It's still got a way to go, but every year, it comes a bit closer."

He looked down at Phil and felt the burden he'd carried ease slightly. Maybe he *could* fix it. Maybe he could go back and help, make an alliance between the competitors. They had to see that the change would affect their business. Maybe all was not lost—maybe they could all learn something from this and make things better in the end.

He held Phil's gaze and decided that the earth wasn't the only one that was forgiving. She smiled that little Mona Lisa smile that awakened all the slumbering passion in him.

"I think," she whispered as he stared at that widening smile, "you need to cut yourself some slack, Sullivan."

When she stretched up to kiss him, the touch of her lips on his seemed the most natural thing in the world.

He could have done the chivalrous thing if she'd jumped his

bones, but this gentle touch was impossible to resist. She offered solace, and hope, and Nick desperately wanted some of each. He kissed her back, a wordless gesture of gratitude for the way she listened, and Phil framed his face in her hands.

The slide of her tongue across his lip changed everything. Their kiss turned hungry, the heat between them crackling with just that small provocation. They were horizontal on the couch before he knew what happened, she was sprawled on top of him, the perfection of her butt was filling his hands. His erection pressed against her stomach and she wiggled on top of him, greedy for everything he had to give.

His good intentions had a hell of a fight to break that kiss. He wanted some of her sunshine more than he'd wanted anything in his life. But he knew, he *knew* that just wanting something wasn't enough.

Even loving someone wasn't enough. He'd loved his parents, but they'd left him. He'd tried not to love Lucia, but he'd lost that battle, and he'd lost her too.

He didn't want to lose Phil.

He caught her shoulders in his hands and held her slightly above him, refusing to look down her gaping gown at her breasts.

"Last chance, Phil." He looked her steadily in the eye, his pulse thumping at the flushed just-kissed look of her. "Kiss me again and I won't be able to stop."

Her eyes widened as she looked at him, and he saw that she was hopeful for a promise he wouldn't make, couldn't make. He speared his fingers through her hair, still shaken by the eruptions she'd caused, and rubbed her cheek with his thumb. She was more than he remembered but it wasn't in him to make impulsive choices.

He had to think.

He had to be *sure*.

He refused to feel guilty when Phil's baby blues clouded with disappointment. He had been honest with her—she deserved the truth, even if she didn't like it much.

Nick closed his eyes, bracing himself for the inevitability of feeling her slip away.

Chapter 13

Well, I've had my face slapped a few times, but this was too much. "So, I'm still too fat for you?" I snapped, took another swat at Nick, then bounded to my feet. I was furious with him for not being able to see beyond the size of my butt.

I expected better from him.

"Phil . . ." He had his Be Reasonable tone which only made me more angry.

I paced across the room, figuring I had nothing to lose at this point. "So, what, you were just playing games with all those steamy kisses before? Giving me a little bonus offer so that I'd help you out?" He got to his feet and glowered at me but I was on a roll. "Hey, you had somewhere free to stay, a few lifts into town. You had to put up with me, mind you, and touch me once in a while to keep me on the team . . ."

"Phil, don't do this."

"Don't do what? Don't speak the truth? It's okay, the jig is up. And don't you lay any more of your charm on me to make it all better." I jabbed a finger through the air at him, disregarding the way his lips had tightened to a thin line. I was pushing the limit but I didn't care.

"I get it already." My voice rose slightly and those stupid tears gathered. "Fat Philippa doesn't do it for you. Fine. Don't let me cut into your beauty sleep any longer."

I left before I humiliated myself any further.

I managed three steps before he caught me around the waist. He spun me around, caught my butt in his hands and lifted me off my feet so fast that I didn't have a chance to protest. I would have said something then, but he kissed me hard and backed me into the wall with a thump.

And I got a good sample of how hot the core of that volcano was.

He lifted his head, his eyes as green as new grass. "Never imagine for a moment that you aren't the sexiest woman I've ever known." He rolled his hips against me. "Does that feel like disinterest?"

I shook my head, surprised to rare silence.

He smiled. "Kiss me, Phil, and let's do something about it."

I did. There was nothing but Nick, his tongue, his hands, and his erection pressed into my belly. I hung on to his shoulders and surrendered to the moment. He moaned when I opened my mouth to him and his hands slid under the flannel to slide over my bare skin.

I shivered, but he braced me against the wall, trailing kisses down my neck as his fingers slipped into my own heat.

Then I moaned.

I was squirming on his fingertips in nothing flat, certain I couldn't stand it a minute longer. He made me wait though, tempting me more than I thought I could bear. When I came, I think I screamed.

I must have, because Joe upstairs thumped the floor again.

But Nick was grinning. He nuzzled my earlobe and laced our fingers together high over my head. His erection nudged against me and my mouth went dry at the size of him.

"What was that about me not wanting you?" he whispered in my ear.

I mumbled something incoherent and he chuckled, then pulled back to look into my eyes. He looked smug, pleased, and very male. "Not true, Phil," he murmured. "I've always wanted you. Only you. I thought you deserved better."

"Wrong," I whispered unevenly.

He eased into me, hot and thick and hard, even as I tried to catch my breath. He held me against the wall with his hips as I got used to the size of him, then impatiently tugged my nightgown over my head and chucked it across the room.

He looked down at me and smiled, his admiration unmistakable. "Beautiful," he whispered. "And don't let anyone tell you differently."

"Lots to love," I said, trying to make a joke.

Nick shook his head. "Perfect." He cupped one of my breasts in his hand, meeting my gaze, his palm fitted exactly around me. "See?" He arched a brow, watching me as he slid his thumb deliberately across my tight nipple.

I gasped and his gaze darkened as he bent closer. "Come again, Phil. Come with me inside you."

I'm not too clear how things proceeded after that, save that it's true what they say—all things do come in threes.

Including me.

I woke to the sound of rain and the smell of chocolate, and a space on the mattress beside me. For a moment I thought I'd had particularly good dreams, then a cheerful voice proved me wrong.

“Up and at ’em, Phil. Daylight’s wasting.”

I rolled over and eyed the man who had kept me awake most of the night. Nick was dressed and shaved, disgustingly bright-eyed and bushy-tailed.

“I thought two nights without sleep was your limit.”

He shrugged. “Live and learn. Some cushy job you’ve got, Coxwell, laying around half the morning.”

I tried to sling a pillow at him but missed. “Be warned that I may bite before I’m fully conscious.”

“Which would be when?”

“Noon at the earliest.” I rubbed my eyes and yawned, wanting nothing more than to dive deep beneath the covers and stay there. I knew I must look like hell, but I peeked and Nick didn’t seem to be making a run for it.

In fact, he looked as though he was trying not to laugh.

“I don’t look that funny.”

“No, you look grouchy and rumpled and about as mean as a goldfish.”

“Don’t underestimate me.” I bared my teeth at him. “I enjoy munching on morning people, especially those who are cheerful and organized.”

He moved closer, feigning caution, and put a steaming mug on the nightstand before backing away with his hands up. “Then consider this a peace offering.”

The chocolate smell got stronger. “Hot chocolate?” A nice gesture but about forty-five million calories. I glared at him. “I hope I’m rabid so you die a painful death after I chomp on you. This is cruel and unusual punishment, you know.”

He leaned down, his tone cajoling, his eyes gleaming. “Maybe you’ve burned off enough calories to have earned it.”

There was that damn blush again. “Maybe not.”

“I can help.”

I laughed, probably a first at that hour.

Nick brushed my hair back with a gentle fingertip. "It's skim milk, Phil."

This was too good to be true. And you know what that means—anything too good to be true usually isn't. I eyed him with suspicion. "Equal?"

"How'd I guess?" He shoved his hands in his pockets and rocked back on his feet. "Maybe it was the fact that the only grocery you had came in little blue envelopes."

The man was becoming positively loquacious. I sniffed as I reached for the mug. I took a cautious sip of the hot chocolate.

It tasted divine. Ambrosia with no aftereffects. "All right. Maybe you can live, after all."

He turned to leave, pausing halfway across the room. "We should have a chat about moderation and synthetic sweeteners, Phil. Real sugar has only sixteen calories per teaspoon and is entirely natural, not to mention a sustainable crop."

I sat up and gave him my best death glare. "I'm changing my mind. You should die after all, preferably painfully and slowly. I'm not much for lectures in the morning."

He folded his arms across his chest. "Such a short memory. I seem to recall someone insisting last night that I was better than chocolate."

I blushed, knowing that I'd said exactly that. "Well, it's morning and all bets are off."

"Is that right?" I could have sworn I saw his eyes twinkling before he turned away. "Drink your chocolate, Phil."

Somehow that sounded ominous.

I figured I was imagining things. After all, he left me in peace. The rain pattered against the windows and I took my time waking up. It was only quarter to eight, close to miraculous for me. There was rustling from the kitchen, as though Nick had hunted down a paper, and a strong smell of coffee. I like the smell of coffee in the morning, even though I don't drink it.

There was another smell too, lingering on the linens. I peeked and discovered that my resident neat freak had straightened and tidied while I slept. All in all, things were deceptively cozy.

I sighed contentment, put my mug on the nightstand and smiled at the sound of the shower starting to run. I really could get used to this man being around if he was going to wait on me hand and foot.

But that wasn't exactly what Nick had in mind. He strode into the bedroom, peeling off his shirt. He dropped his pants and I woke up fast, not that it made any difference. He scooped me up in his arms and headed for the bathroom.

"You've had a shower already!"

"You can never be too clean."

I squealed when we got in the shower, because the water was cold.

"Awake yet?" He turned to adjust the temperature.

"Wide awake, thanks."

Nick smiled a predatory smile. "Good. Now, let's play a little compare and contrast."

"Between you and chocolate?"

He nodded, but I rolled my eyes, cheeky now that I was fortified. "That was very, very good chocolate. You haven't got a chance, Sullivan."

He certainly gave it the old college try.

We made it to the kitchen half an hour later, more or less ready to go. I'd chosen chinos today and a sweater, since I was probably going to have to get intimate with that Japanese maple.

There was an empty box from the bakery down the street beside the trash. "I assumed you didn't want a Danish." Nick was doing up his shirt as he sauntered in behind me. He poured himself another cup of coffee, snagged me around the waist and nuzzled my hair.

"How many did you eat?"

He grinned. "You don't want to know."

"I've got to git me one of them there tapeworms," I muttered.

There was a bowl of fruit and yogurt on the top shelf of the fridge and a pot of herbal tea already made. "You should rent yourself out," I teased and joined him at the table.

"You in the market for a rental?"

I ate a piece of fruit, guessing by the brightness of his gaze that I was on dangerous ground. "I'm a rent-to-buy kind of woman."

He smiled a Mr. Enigma smile and sipped his coffee. "Those kind of deals are hard to find."

If I had expected a pledge of undying love then and there, I was doomed to be disappointed. He was evidently fascinated by his newspaper. I gave him a good look through my lashes while I ate.

Then I noticed that he was wearing one of the shirts from his backpack. I tried to play innocent, not my best trick.

"Oh, you found your pack?"

"Uh huh." He shot me a glance so fast I nearly flinched. "Did you find anything interesting in it?"

It seemed ridiculous to lie, but I tried to hedge. "How do you know I even looked?"

"Don't you think someone who routinely carries a lot of cash would want to know whether anyone had rifled through their luggage?"

"I didn't *rifle*."

"No, you were careful." A smile touched his lips. "Just not careful enough."

"How could you tell?"

Nick watched me over the rim of his cup. "I can't go telling all my secrets."

I snorted. "I don't think there's much fear of that."

His expression turned serious. "Which reminds me. Thanks for listening, Phil."

Oh, he could disarm me so quickly with a look and a couple of words. So, what had that been? A fling? A means of satisfying curiosity?

Or something more?

Fortunately I didn't have to pluck one of the ten thousand questions whirling through my head, because someone rang the bell and hammered on the door without waiting to see whether I answered.

"Philippa, open up! It's pissing out here!"

"Elaine," I supplied before Nick could ask, and hurried for the door.

"Ah, she of the gilded tongue."

"Be nice. She's had a tough row to hoe. If I'd started where she did, I sure wouldn't have made as much of myself."

He smiled at me. "There you go again."

"What?"

"Seeing the best in people."

I spun on the threshold of the kitchen. "Well, she's lending me her car today. What's not good about that?"

He straightened. "What's wrong with the Beast?"

Elaine was in the foyer in time to hear his question. "Sick. Possibly dead. It croaked on Philippa yesterday in the middle of nowhere, faithless piece of crap. Do I smell coffee?"

"There's a full pot," Nick said. He got up and poured, taking Elaine's directions for milk and sugar as she wriggled out of her wet coat.

"Yum yum yum. Too bad you don't have a Danish or two."

"You're too late for that." I went back to my fruit.

Elaine frowned at her mug, then held it up and studied the pattern. "Since when do you have nice dishes anyway?"

I had a piece of melon in my mouth, so I pointed my spoon at Nick. "Ask him."

"You picked this?" Elaine turned the mug, examining its giddy pattern. "Wow. It's so, so *Philippa*."

I did like what Nick had bought—all the pieces were brightly colored and didn't exactly match up. It had a gleeful hodgepodge kind of feel and looked sunny on the table.

Elaine put down the cup and looked between the two of us. "What's up with you two, anyhow?"

Trust Elaine to dig in and come up with the million dollar question.

I was kind of interested in the answer myself. I took my time with that piece of melon but Nick wasn't playing anyone else's game.

"I thought she'd like it, that's all. And you can't say Phil didn't need dishes." He obviously was more interested in other things. "So, what's wrong with the Beast?"

"Who knows?"

"I don't want to even ask," I told him.

"It's gonna be bad," Elaine affirmed grimly. "We're gonna get took."

"Why?"

"It's a chick/mechanic symbiosis thing."

Nick harumphed and sipped his coffee. "Then you should go to a different garage."

Elaine pulled out a chair and I could smell her getting an idea. "Don't suppose you'd mind calling after it?"

"Elaine!"

"What? They'll probably give him a different answer. A *cheaper* answer."

Nick straightened. "That would hardly be ethical."

Elaine squeezed her eyes tightly shut. "Ethics. Auto repair. What do these things have in common?" She shook her head. "I give up. Some of these things just do not belong together."

"Nick, you shouldn't do this. It's our problem."

"It's not an issue, Phil. You've probably got a ton of things to do today. I just have to figure out what to do with that glass." He hefted his cup toward Elaine, then at me. "You can tell me where the Beast is. And then you can tell me where you hid the brandy snifter."

I put down my spoon. "I didn't pick it up."

"Well, of course you did."

"No, it wasn't there. You picked it up."

He shook his head. "No, it was there on the counter. Then I got distracted and it was gone when I left. I thought you had taken it."

"I thought you had already picked it up before I got there." We looked at each other and my hair was doing that standing up thing.

"It was there when I got there," Nick repeated carefully, "but it wasn't there when I left. Which means either you took it, which you didn't . . ."

"Or somebody else did," I concluded.

"Aren't you two getting a bit excited about a glass?" Elaine drank her coffee, looking between the two of us questioningly. "I mean, I'll pick you up another brandy snifter today if you like."

"We wouldn't have heard someone else in the house," Nick mused. "Not with the music playing."

"Especially not a ghost. They tend to move quietly."

"What?" They both looked at me like I was crazy.

"I saw Lucia's ghost, right there in the greenhouse. She was all dressed in white and kind of floating. There seemed to be a wound at her throat. She didn't look very impressed that I was there."

Oops, I had totally forgotten to mention the phone call. Of course, Nick had done an excellent job of distracting me. "And there was that phone call. It was really strange."

"What phone call?" Nick asked.

"It was a woman, she said I ruined everything and that I should stay out of her house."

Nick stared at me. The gears were in motion. He looked down at the paper, blinked a couple of times, then looked back at me. "How could I not have thought of that?" he murmured, then he began to smile. "It's perfectly, utterly Lucia!"

And then he started to laugh.

In fact, he laughed so hard that it took a long time to get him to make any sense at all. Elaine gave her cup of coffee a hard look and put it aside half-finished.

He howled until the tears ran down his cheeks and he thumped his fist on the table. "I told you," he finally choked out, "I told you that she was more likely to kill me than the other way around."

"You mean Lucia set you up?"

"Yes."

"It's a bit extreme, don't you think? Committing suicide just to get even with someone?"

"Who committed suicide?" Elaine looked between the two of us. "I feel like I walked into the middle of a movie."

"No one did. That's the point." Nick leaned across the table and caught my hands in his. "You didn't find her body in the greenhouse, because she wasn't dead. She wanted me to think she was dead, but she isn't."

"*She* cleaned it up."

"Which is why it was cold in there. And was it wet?"

"Well, yes. I thought the sprinklers had just run."

"No, she hosed the place down."

"But Nick, you said she was stabbed."

"It's a stage trick, Phil. I should have looked closer. Lucia knows how to create stage illusions. She probably broke off the blade from the dagger and stuck the hilt to her skin. The rest she could do with makeup and whatever concoction she chose to use for blood. God only knows what it was. It smelled awful."

"But what about the ghost?"

"There are no ghosts, Phil."

"That house is supposed to be haunted."

"Well, I lived there for years and it isn't. You must have seen Lucia again."

I was skeptical. "So, she must really be a witch. How else could she levitate?"

He smiled. "Another trick of the light, one achieved with a mirror. You saw her reflection, which is why she probably looked kind of wispy." I nodded.

Elaine was intrigued, even though she didn't know the whole story.

"She must have been standing to one side of the door or the other. She'd wear white, because the eye is drawn to white, then dark socks, so the silhouette of her feet dropped away in the reflection. It works especially well if the light is high and the lighting is otherwise poor."

"She was holding a candle."

He spread his hands. "See? She's good with this kind of stuff."

Elaine propped her chin on her hand. "But Philippa got a phone call. What's that about?"

"When was it?"

"Yesterday. After I left you at the house in the shrine o' Sullivan."

Nick nodded. "And she said you ruined her plans. That

room was never like that. I don't even know that I've seen all of those pictures before. It was set up when I got in the house, with the light on beside that chair. Her record was on the turntable already." He shrugged. "Now that I think about it, it was kind of contrived, but I just got side-swiped."

I reached out and touched his hand. "It's okay to get caught up in your memories."

Our gazes held across the table and I remembered how upset he had been.

"So what do you think she was planning? To float in on you?"

"Probably to spook the hell out of me, then reconcile." Nick caught my hand in his and smiled crookedly at me. "No wonder she was ticked. You really threw a wrench into the works, Phil."

"Didn't you stay?"

"No, I left right after you."

I didn't want to sound critical but it seemed to me that this had to be said. "Don't you think it was a pretty mean trick? Are you sure she would do this?"

"Oh yes. Lucia has always played hard." He toasted me with his coffee. "All or nothing."

The phone rang and I reluctantly got up. I knew who it had to be at this hour. Elaine started to give Nick directions to the garage. "Hi, Mom."

There was a strained silence on the line. "Is this Philippa Coxwell?" It was a man, with a rough voice.

"Yes, why? Who's this?"

"I'm Josie's cousin, Max. She said you wanted to know about Tuesday, about Sean borrowing my car."

"Yes, I did."

"Well, how am I supposed to tell you if you never answer your phone? I've been calling you all the time and if I hadn't got you this time, that would have been it. Some people think that everyone's got all the time in the world . . ."

"Did he borrow your car on Tuesday?"

Nick looked up with interest.

"No. That Josie, nice girl, but jeez. She's always getting the days mixed up. It was Monday, not Tuesday. I'm telling you the girl's short of a load, if you know what I mean."

I shook my head at Nick and he shrugged, content that his theory was confirmed.

"Well, thanks for letting me know."

"Like I said, this was the last chance. Glad I got a hold of you. Sean, he's a good guy. You need to hire a good guy, you keep him in mind. You gotta always be looking for good guys."

He insisted on giving me his number and I finally realized that Max had my business card. "We're fine now, thanks, but you never know."

"Summer's got to be busy for you garden people and Sean is a good guy. Hard worker . . ."

I declined to comment on that. "Yes, it is a busy time, Max. Thanks for calling. I've got to go."

"See?" Nick said. He got to his feet and stretched. "Mystery solved."

"So, what are you going to do?"

He smiled. "Let Lucia worry about it a bit. I'll bet she's hopping mad. Meanwhile, I'll check on the Beast."

We planned to drop Elaine off downtown en route, where she was meeting a client to prowl for antiques. She was bouncing in anticipation of living vicariously, spending someone else's money on shiny baubles.

Nick lost the argument about his sitting in the backseat of the Geo—as tallest, he won the front passenger seat. I warmed up the engine as he rounded the hood after doing the gentlemanly door thing. I liked that he did those kinds of things and that he never made a big deal about it.

Elaine leaned over the seat and tapped me on the shoulder. "If you throw him back, I get dibs," was all she managed to say before Nick opened the door.

Which got me thinking again about how I could convince Nick to *not* throw *me* back.

Maybe it couldn't be done.

But it was definitely worth a try.

I had a day and a half.

The *Mission: Impossible* theme song began running in my head.

The amazing thing wasn't that Phil drove the Geo with the same aggressiveness as she had the Beast—it was that her driving seemed temperate compared with that of the other drivers in the city. The place was a madhouse. He watched her decisive grip on the wheel and easily imagined her driving an expedition truck across the savannah, dodging antelopes and potholes as adeptly as she outmaneuvered sport utility vehicles and pedestrians.

That would be a cakewalk compared to this.

Elaine jumped out at a busy corner of Newbury Street. "You can drop me here, as well," he suggested, but Phil shook her head.

"I have to show you that bakery."

"Just give me the address."

"Then I'll drop you at the garage."

He argued, but she ignored him, chewing her lip as she merged into the traffic for the Harvard Bridge. Phil made a beeline for Cambridge, exactly the wrong direction that he needed to go. She parked with the expertise he was coming to expect from her, then poked him playfully in the arm. "Come on, help me prove that this Japanese maple hasn't given up the ghost."

"As if I would know."

"Then charm the woman for me. It can't hurt." She slammed the door and darted up the path, obviously confident that he would follow.

And he did.

Even though Phil could charm the birds from the trees without his help. He watched as she re-established her rapport with the garden owner, taking the time to check on the other plants before approaching the tree in question. They cooed over the various bulbs in bloom, Phil touching tiny blossoms with a fingertip in admiration.

He stood back and looked at what she had done. The house had very strong simple lines and Phil had capitalized on its spare beauty, laying out a garden with definite Japanese overtones. The flowers that were in bloom were in clusters, like showpieces, and of clear vibrant hues.

There was a bed of smooth dark pebbles that flowed through the perfectly square lot like a dry river and softened its shape. A round, stone-lipped pool was in one corner, its surface as still as a mirror. Orange carp drifted through the water, providing sudden glimpses of color in the dark shadows.

The Japanese maple was a centerpiece, twisted artfully like a giant bonsai, and surrounded by a path made of square stones. Some reddish groundcover was coming to life around its roots. It was hard to believe that the garden had only been laid out the year before.

Phil definitely knew what she was doing.

He felt a surge of pride in her accomplishments, both this garden and undoubtedly many others. He stood and watched her, the weight of his worries sliding away.

Lucia wasn't dead, he wasn't wanted for murder, he didn't have anything left to prove. He was a man with a sizeable chunk of change, a lot of time on his hands and some living to make up.

He was going to do some of it with Phil. He was going to give his all to this measure of time they had, he would help her out, he would do his damnedest to persuade her family to see things her way.

He was going to have to get a suit for that dinner. It was about time he had a really good Italian one.

Meanwhile, Phil studied the almost nonexistent leaf buds while the anxious owner watched. She dug her fingers into the soil and tugged on the roots. She chose one branch and bent it carefully, then picked off a bud and unfurled it in her hand.

"It's certainly late," she said finally. "But I don't think it's dead. See, this branch is green—otherwise it would have snapped easily. And the leaves inside the buds are green—see? It's not sick, or at least there are no obvious signs of illness, and it's steady in the ground." She smiled for the woman. "I think it's pouting."

"You did warn us that a big tree like this wouldn't like being moved."

"Did you put that tarp over the bed for the winter?"

"Yes, we took it off yesterday."

Phil nodded encouragingly. "Maybe we should spoil it a bit longer. The weather's been a bit cooler this week than last. Why don't we tuck it in again, say for another week? We'll talk then about how it's doing."

The woman twisted her hands together. "Do you really think it will be fine?"

Phil surveyed the tree, then smiled confidently. "Yes, I do. You see—those crocuses in the bed beside it are a bit later than the ones beside your porch. Maybe the wind is chillier here or the sun doesn't linger quite as long. Each garden has little microclimates, so conditions vary slightly all across the lot."

"Do you think we should move it?"

Phil bit her lip, obviously choosing her words with care. "I'd be very reluctant to disturb it again. What difference if it's a week or two later than expected? You'll just have to be indulgent of it in the fall and spring."

"Every year?" The woman grimaced. "That tarp is so ugly. It ruins the look of the garden. I don't care when the snow is over it, but once it melts . . ." She made a face.

Phil's smile didn't waver. "One more week. It's a small price to pay to ensure that this treasure is at its best." She touched the tree with affection, almost as though she gave it an encouraging stroke. "It will probably be less sensitive next year once it digs its toes into the soil here."

He helped spread the tarp per Phil's instructions and weighted it down with a collection of stones. The client obviously thought he worked for Phil and Nick didn't bother to correct her. The woman looked reassured by the time they left.

"You might have been a pediatrician calling on her sick child," he commented once they were safely back in the car.

Phil shrugged. "Do you know how much that tree is worth?" When he shook his head, she told him and nearly stopped his heart.

"For a tree?"

"It's old and beautiful and people are impatient. A smaller tree would have adjusted much better to the transplant but she had to have that one." She cast him a glance. "Pray that I don't have to replace the sucker."

"Do you think you'll have to?"

"No, not if she doesn't whisk that tarp off as soon as we're gone. She's not the most patient soul in the world, unfortunately." She made a little sound of frustration in her throat. "Honestly, what is someone doing in Massachusetts if they don't want to put up with winter?"

Nick had no answer for that. He looked back as they pulled out from the curb, willing the tree to thrive.

Then he picked up Phil's hand. It was time to make some things come right. "Why don't you drop me off and I'll take care of the Beast. I'll meet you at the office later this afternoon, then maybe we can go visit Lucia."

She smiled. "That's a great idea. I don't think she should be left to worry too long."

"Sweet Phil." Nick leaned across the small space and kissed her. "You're better to all of us than we deserve."

He watched her blush, very much enjoying the view.

"Are you going to cook tonight?"

"Of course. I've got to keep my strength up." He flicked a fingertip across the tip or her nose and she swatted at him.

"I'm driving!"

"I know." He sighed heavily. "And it leaves me with nothing to do with my hands." He reached over and traced a circle on her thigh.

"Nick! Stop it." He didn't and she gritted her teeth. "I'll get you for this."

"Oh, I'm looking forward to that."

Chapter 14

Mrs. H. wasn't sure about the pink.

In fact, she'd decided that she so disliked the pink of my suggestion that she was questioning whether we were really simpatico at all.

She was having *doubts*.

TGIF. I danced as hard as I could and she finally seemed persuaded that it was just a suggestion. Hardly written in stone. Even if anything had been planted, I could have dug it up and changed it for her.

There might have been sweat on my brow when I hung up the phone but there is no rest for the wicked. It rang again right under my hand.

That gave me a bad feeling. I was pretty much convinced that my mother had somehow sensed my lapse in chastity and would want all the details.

But I still answered the phone. "Coxwell & Pope."

"How many lawyer jokes are there?"

"Zach, this is really not a good time."

"Three. The rest are all true." He paused for a heartbeat. "Cracking under the pressure, are you? Only one day left to admit the truth, Philippa. Tick tock."

"I've told you the truth."

"Right." He laughed. "I've gotta tell you that you've stolen my thunder here. All they want to talk about is *you*. It's weird not being the center of attention. I don't know what to do with myself."

"Get a pad," I muttered. "I've got a few ideas."

"Touchy, touchy, Philippa. Why don't you spill the real story to ol' Zach? By the way, who was calling at your door so late the other night?"

"Nick, of course. He wanted to talk to you but you'd hung up."

Zach laughed and laughed. "Nice try, Philippa, but you'll have to do better than that. Sure you don't want to 'fess up?"

"Get lost, Zach."

"I'll take that as a no. Don't sweat the heat too much though—I promise to make sure it won't last long."

"What are you up to?"

He chortled. "Oh, something really good." Zach and his wild stunts. He was sure to do something to make the event memorable, especially if he felt his black sheep preeminence was in question.

I really didn't want to know.

"But even with my intervention, it won't be easy for you, Philippa. Sure you don't want to come clean?"

I gritted my teeth. "I have."

"So you say."

"When was the last time I lied to you?"

He clicked his tongue. "Don't say I didn't warn you."

It was the first interesting thing he'd said, but of course, he was gone by the time I tried to ask.

Brothers. Grrr.

The phone rang again. It was seriously beginning to annoy me. I practically barked the name of the company into the receiver.

"Oh, bad time. Sorry, Phil, I won't keep you."

"That's all right." I put down my pencil and took a deep breath, just enjoying the soothing tones of Nick's voice.

"No, it's not. What's wrong? Anything I can help with?"

I sighed, my little sucker heart warming that he'd asked. "I don't think so. Mrs. H. doesn't like my pink suggestions." I realized that he of all people would understand the importance of this. "She might pull the contract."

"Ouch." I could practically hear him thinking. "That's the one that would put you into the black, isn't it?"

"Yes and I was hoping on referrals to some of her friends from this job. The worst thing is that I think she would like it once it was in. It's not as though I can't dig up a plant and change it, but she's just not going to listen."

Well, the floodgates were open. I ended up telling him a lot more about pink hellebores than he certainly needed to know, particularly about the subtlety of their shading. "And she loves subtle, I just know she'd adore them, but she's not listening to me. And I don't know how to fix this."

"Feel better?"

I smiled despite my woes. "Yes. Thanks for listening."

"Least I could do." He thought for a minute. "So, why don't you send her one? Maybe the pictures don't do them justice."

It was such a good idea that I felt like a dope for not thinking of it before. "I don't have a car. Maybe I can find a courier . . ."

He interrupted me crisply. "Consider one found. Where do I

get a pink hellebore, how do I know it when I see it, and what's her address?"

It took me a minute to make any sound at all. "I think I love you."

Then I clapped my hand over my mouth.

But Nick's rich chuckle echoed down the phone lines. "You're just saying that so I really do it," he said, his velvety voice giving me goose pimples.

Saved by the bell.

I told him what he needed to know, plus a lot of instruction on choosing a plant, then remembered that he had called me. "Oh, what did you call about?"

"Right." I heard him snap his fingers. "Pick a color."

"Why?"

Nick made an exasperated sound. "Phil, you've got to be the most suspicious woman I've ever known. Pick."

"You're not going to tell me, are you?"

He didn't even answer that.

But then, I didn't expect much different. "Okay, blue."

"Mmm, Mediterranean azure or twilight navy?"

He sounded like he was reading them off a card or something. "What are you up to?"

"Pick."

"The twilighty one. It makes me think of sunsets and stars coming out."

There was a smile in his voice. "Bright stars."

"I guess. What . . ."

"Gotta go, Phil. See you later."

And I got the dial tone. Men, men, men. They could be an awful lot of trouble, even if they were cute. I must have muttered something to that effect, because Elaine looked up from her drawings.

"Philippa, whenever a man asks, your favorite color should be clear."

"What?"

She smiled. "A little something that cuts glass matches everything."

"Elaine!"

"Hey, if he's buying gifts, it might as well be something you like."

You're probably thinking that Elaine is a calculating little piece of baggage. Mostly she talks tougher than she is, not that I have any experience of that. I respect her, though.

You see, she really came from nothing. Absolutely nothing. Her father doesn't know she's alive because her mother wasn't sure which of her customers he was, and her mother, well, her mother worked the streets until she died with her black, patent leather, stiletto-heeled boots on.

Elaine's mother worked the hotels and the upscale crowd, which I guess is how Elaine got her clothes sense. She also ended up with a nice nest egg, courtesy of Mom's stock picks. She might have been one of the only hookers who didn't do any drugs or drink, but that might have been the issue in the end. They found her dead in a Dumpster when Elaine was twelve years old.

Elaine doesn't talk about it much. She doesn't talk about her mother's family, who shunned her because of her mother's occupation. Imagine, effectively being on your own at twelve. Elaine does talk about the parochial school where her mother sent her, that woman having saved every buck she could toward the tuition.

She told me once that her mother had never set foot on the school grounds, because she didn't want Elaine "tainted."

I guess it was easy to tell what Mom did for a living.

After her mother's death, Elaine went on through private schools, then to art school, working like a little demon even as Mom's capital was whittled away. She was determined that the rest of her family never saw a dime of it—and they were probably glad enough to have her stay away from them to cut loose the cash to a minor.

In the end, her mother gave Elaine the start she had never had, making sure her beautiful daughter had better choices in life. Elaine made good ones. She got top grades, she worked harder than anyone I've ever met. She met all the right people and learned how to mingle amongst them, her roots undetected.

She told me once that it was the very least she owed her mother.

She probably also owed her affection for men to her mother, not to mention her blunt assessments. There were no illusions with Elaine, but that never seemed to affect her popularity. Men came out of the woodwork, like bees to honey, when Elaine entered a room. It was amazing to watch. But Elaine only entered relationships as an equal, with terms stated plainly up front. It might not be a cash transaction, but it sure as heck wasn't going to be love.

Though she never admitted it to me, I know she was crazy about her mother. So, she'd been there and done that as far as getting her heart involved, and she wasn't going back.

We met at a Chamber of Commerce mixer, when I was thinking of starting my own company. Networking intimidated me to death, so I thought I'd start somewhere where no one was likely to bite. Elaine was a revelation. She worked that room front and back, then went back and did it side to side. She talked to everyone, she laughed and she sparkled, and half the place had one of her cards within forty-five minutes.

I caught up to her in the parking lot and asked her to teach me how to do that. It wasn't long until we were friends, and right around the same time, we became partners.

I still enjoy watching her chat up society matrons, wondering what they would think if they knew where she had come from. Truth be told, I've seen more than one husband do a double take when he first glimpsed Elaine.

I always wonder whether those men are remembering someone else.

I hit Elaine up that afternoon for an explanation about Jeffrey, but she stonewalled me.

"You don't fool me," I finally told her. "That one got away. That one mattered, or you wouldn't be nearly so annoyed with him."

I didn't think she'd emerge from under the cone of silence, but I was wrong.

"Okay, you want the story? Here it is." She flung down her marker and stared at me, antagonistic now that she had to surrender a secret. "We went out for a while. We hit my six-date maximum and I told him that was it. He was persistent and I finally caved."

"Why? Because he made you a present you couldn't refuse?"

"No, that's what was weird about it. I liked him. He was sexy." She looked at her desk. "He was a bit uptight in public, but he was smart and sometimes funny. We had a good time together."

"We are talking about Jeffrey McAllister here, aren't we?"

"Don't give me that, Philippa. He looks good. He didn't always walk with a telephone pole up his ass."

"Ah, I'm sensing my father's influence here."

"Maybe. Anyway, he kept breaking my six-date barriers. I don't even know how long we'd been going out when I decided to trust him."

"Big mistake?"

"Go with your gut, Philippa. My mother told me never to trust a man with the truth, and she was right. That was the end of it." Her features tightened and she picked up her marker, savagely untwisting the cap.

"What did you tell him about, Elaine?" I asked the question softly, not wanting to upset her more than she already was.

"Me." She met my gaze steadily, her own over bright. "That was all it took, Philippa, to screw up everything. But if you can't confide in someone, then why the hell would you spend your life with them?"

She went back to work, ducking her head quickly but not quickly enough that I didn't see the tear glinting on her lashes.

I decided that Jeffrey McAllister and my father deserved each other.

Elaine scampered out on a mission midafternoon, leaving me alone with my pink-free drawings. They were taking a lot longer to finish than should have been expected, I guess because my heart just wasn't in it.

The silence from Rosemount was deafening. I hadn't talked to my mother since Wednesday.

It gave me the creeps.

Be careful what you wish for. How many times had I wished that my family would just disappear forever? More than I could reliably recall, and now they mostly had.

Except for Zach, who was more annoying than any brother had any business being. I was tempted to call and make sure the house hadn't been struck by lightning or something.

But I would have heard about that. And they were probably waiting for me to buckle. Tomorrow would be enough fun for all of us. I forced myself to work and tried not to think too much. Job one was a lovely set of reworked drawings of Mrs.

Hathaway's garden, each devoid of the merest hint of pink. They looked deadly dull to me, but she was the customer.

Hopefully.

A pickup truck sailed into the lot about four and I was distracted enough to take a good look. It was brand new, shiny, and a shade of dark blue that could have been called "twilight."

And Nick was driving it.

He looked proud of himself when he strode up to the door, then surprised that I met him right there. I didn't care that he'd bought himself a new toy—I wanted to know where my baby was.

"Where's the Beast?"

Nick winced. "The Beast has gone to the big scrap yard in the sky." He conjured up a paper bag and handed it to me.

It held the contents of the Beast's glove box and the sight brought a tear to my eye. I sat down on the edge of a desk and fingered through the packs of dried out wipes, the registration, the plastic spoons. There was even a little sewing kit from a hotel and a spare pair of panty hose, which must have belonged to Elaine because I was never nearly that organized.

If I'd known they were there, I would have used them. Yep, her size. I couldn't have used them if I'd wanted to.

Nick put an arm around my shoulders and gave me a squeeze. "They wanted $6500 to fix it, Phil. That was too much."

"I thought they'd give you a better deal."

"Maybe they would have asked you two for more, I don't know. But the Beast wasn't worth half that."

Beast in past tense. I'd have to get used to that.

"Besides the engine repair that bill would have covered, it would need brakes and shocks any time now. The exhaust was ready to fall right off. You could have spent ten bills easily and it would still have been an old truck, trying its damnedest to die."

"*My* truck though. Better than nothing." I looked at him accusingly.

Nick shook his head. "It wouldn't have been better than nothing if it left you stranded again like yesterday, and it would have. What if that had been at night? Or out in the country?" He looked grim. "It wasn't worth it, Phil."

His protectiveness did nothing to take the edge off my disappointment.

I was still going to miss the old monster.

"You should have asked me."

"I am. They're waiting for a call." He smiled crookedly. "Consider this my biased assessment."

"I hate when you're right," I muttered and heaved a sigh.

"Someone's got to be a realist around here."

I was thinking about that truck. "Joel and I found the Beast on a used lot about four years ago." I stared into the bag and gave it a little shake. The spare keys jangled in the bottom, a sad little sound since they'd never turn in the ignition again. "It was such a good deal, exactly what we could afford. It seemed as though it was destined for us."

Nick smiled. "Waiting for you?"

"Something like that." But now, my beloved Beastie gone forever. "You may think this is stupid, but I want to say goodbye."

"I thought you might." He touched my cheek, a fleeting gesture of affection that warmed my heart. "And no, I don't think it's stupid. I told the garage that I'd check with you about the Beast's fate and at the very least, we'd come back to get the signage off the doors."

He was being thoughtful, which always confused me. My brothers—and most of Rosemount—were always nice to me right before they played a trick on me. Suspicion is a learned response.

I slanted a look at the shiny new truck and tried to change the subject. "So you bought yourself a truck? Aren't they woefully inefficient?"

"You said you needed one for hauling rocks and plants."

I gaped at him, but he kept looking at the truck, his expression impassive. "You did not buy that for me!"

"No. It's for your business."

"That cost more than sixty-five hundred bucks."

"True. It is pretty basic though."

"So, if we can't afford to fix the Beast, then we can't afford that."

"Put it on the books. Capital investment."

"That won't pay for it."

"It's a better investment than fixing the Beast, Phil. You won't have to worry about it breaking down."

"That doesn't matter. Coxwell & Pope can't afford that truck."

"I know." He shrugged with that casual air that was always a warning. "Fortunately, I can."

"You're not *giving* me a truck!" I suddenly had a very good idea what was going on here and I didn't like it one bit. This was my consolation prize for rolling to my back last night. It would also be salve to his conscience now that the matter of Lucia was settled. He was going to walk away, guilt-free.

There was no point in mincing words.

"If this is for last night, you can take that truck, Nick Sullivan, and stuff it sideways . . ."

He crossed the room fast and caught my shoulders in his hands. His eyes were blazing. "Phil. This has nothing to do with last night. Don't even imagine that it does."

I believed him, even though it left me scrambling for another reason for his generosity. "It's pity, then. But I don't need any handouts to make this company work. We're doing just fine, thanks."

He folded his arms across his chest, his tone reasonable once more. "But you need a truck, Phil."

Nuts. That fact was inescapable. I shuffled my feet for a minute. "Well, yes."

"And you probably don't have the cash flow right now to pay for one outright." He wasn't going to make this easy.

I chewed my lip, thinking of the repercussions if Mrs. H. backed out of her project. "We'll get a used one," I insisted, not at all sure that any fool would give us credit.

Nick shook his head, probably thinking much the same thing. "And the repair bills to match. Phil, you don't need any new troubles." He gestured to the truck. "This has a three-year warranty."

"And let me guess—it's breathtakingly fuel efficient."

He grinned. "Consider it my donation to the preservation of the environment." He held up two fingers. "Two cup holders, just for you."

I was tempted, but that didn't matter. It was the principle of the thing. "You're not giving this to us." I stalked back across to my desk, not even wanting to look at the truck in question. I dumped the Beast's bag of goodies in a drawer.

Of course, Nick followed me and perched on the side of my desk. His eyes were really green, which meant I was in for a fight. "Then you can call it a loan. No interest, pay me when you can."

"That'll be tough, since I won't know where you are."

"Send the check to Lucia."

I studied him, distrusting his easy manner. "What are you up to? What's changed? Am I supposed to drag you into bed and ravish you whenever you show up in exchange for the keys?"

"It wasn't what I had in mind, but . . ." he teased. I looked away, my heart breaking.

Nick caught my chin in his hand, forcing me to meet his gaze.

He wasn't joking anymore. "Phil, I know where you're at with this business. You're on the cusp of making it work, but everything could still go to hell. It's a bad time for your truck to have died and I understand that. I just want to help."

"No one gives away vehicles just to help."

His eyes started to smile. "Maybe they should."

"Don't be nice to me. It throws off my game."

It could really throw my game—I could end up falling for this man and miss him like crazy when he walked off into the sunset. I was already pretty much there and if he kept on confiding in me and being nice to me, I'd be in very bad shape.

Worse than I suspected I was already going to be.

"Are you always so tough?"

"My mother told me to beware of men bearing gifts."

"How about men trying to say thanks?"

I looked up with suspicion but he shook his head impatiently. "Not for that. For showing me a different side of things. I'd been beating myself up about that valley and you convinced me that I'm not as bad a guy as I thought." His lips curved and my resistance melted. "So, let me do something good for you, Phil."

"I don't know, Nick." I looked at the truck. "It's awfully generous."

"And you're awfully overdue. When was the last time someone did you a favor?"

I must have looked blank, because I just didn't know.

"See?" He bent and brushed his lips across mine.

That felt good. "It has to be a loan," I insisted.

"Mmm hmm." He did it again and my knees started to buckle.

"With monthly payments, due on time or else."

"Of course." He had his eyes closed when he eased his mouth over mine again.

"No special treatment."

"None." This time he lingered and I nipped at his bottom lip.

"And . . ."

"Phil, enough talk. Say 'thank you, Nick.' "

I smiled back at him. "Thank you, Nick."

One of his brows quirked. "Care to punctuate that?"

"What about all this talk about moderation?"

"You haven't kissed me for a good eight hours. If that's not moderation, I don't know what is."

I sighed as though being indulgent. "I guess it wouldn't hurt." He didn't need much more encouragement than that to set to curling my toes and pretty soon, I considered myself persuaded.

The truck *was* a nice shade of blue.

"I hope you didn't get air-conditioning," I complained when he lifted his head and I was tingling from head to toe. "I just hate what that freon does to the ozone."

He laughed then and held me tighter. "That's my Phil," he said and I wondered just how far being "his" really went.

Call me a chicken, but I didn't ask.

He drove me to visit the Beast, abandoned as it was at the back of the mechanic's lot. It looked tired and dinged up, rusted and defeated. I hadn't realized how bad it had gotten. It certainly wouldn't make a good impression on anyone who saw me driving it up to their house to make a presentation. Nick made them show me what had to be done, and we poked beneath the hood as the mechanic explained.

I don't know a lot about what goes on in there, but things were pretty corroded. I peeked underneath and saw that Nick was right about the exhaust—it was hanging on by sheer willpower.

The engine wouldn't even turn over. When the mechanic held up his hands in surrender, the Beast gave a little sputter and a sigh, as though it was tired. It seemed to me that it gave it up then, and that maybe it was at peace.

I was ridiculously glad that I'd visited it at the end.

The signage, of course, couldn't be taken off the doors. They weren't magnetic signs, but lettering that had been handpainted by a friend of Joel's. I had taken along a can of the paint at Nick's insistence and painted over the phone number while he watched.

The mechanic gave me a check for $500 for it, for scrap.

I patted the Beast and said my farewells, then turned away with a heavy step. Nick put his arm around my waist and dangled the keys to the new truck in front of me.

"I can't. Not so soon."

"Best thing you could do," he insisted.

"Not in front of the Beast."

"Show it you're moving on." He took the can of paint and got in on the passenger side. He looked about as immovable as Mount Rushmore, so I reluctantly climbed in to the driver's seat.

He handed me the key and when I didn't rush to take it, pushed it into the ignition and turned the key a bit. The truck immediately started to complain that we didn't have our seat belts on and who knows what else. Nick sat back, and I knew he wouldn't intervene.

I moved to start the truck.

"Better step on the clutch," he advised.

Now I must have been really distracted on the way to the garage, because I hadn't noticed that the new truck had a five-speed.

Interest stirred.

"I haven't driven a car with a manual transmission since Zach took me to turn donuts on the ice."

"Really? It seemed like it would be your preference."

It was. In fact, the automatic transmission had been one thing I didn't like about the Beast. It's fun to shift gears and much much better for aggressive passing on the highway. You can slip down a gear for a little lunge forward that sometimes makes all the difference in the world.

So, maybe I'm fickle. It was a feisty little track, with nice tight steering and responsive in a way the Beast had probably never been.

I was smitten before we'd gone two blocks.

And Nick knew it. He smiled as I balanced between the clutch and the gas instead of using the brake at the stoplight. The little engine purred like a well-fed kitten, the gearbox was tight and the clutch clicked in with surgical precision. He sure didn't need me to tell him that he'd chosen exactly right.

"Where to?"

"The dealership. I'm officially on a test drive and the sales guy may be getting nervous."

"And then?"

"You're driving."

I knew then the only place that would do. He had made this transition so gentle for me. The least I could do was respond in kind. There was one place he wanted to go, one rapport that probably wouldn't be easy for him to reestablish. I'd take the choice out of his hands, supply the energy of activation for him.

I'd take him to visit Lucia.

But I would take that curvy little marvel of a back road all the way to Rosemount. Highways, you know, are for people who don't really like to drive.

Chapter 15

Evening was falling when we pulled into Lucia's driveway. Nick hadn't said anything for a long time, though I knew he'd figured out where we were going miles before. I killed the engine and the sound of sea carried through the window he had rolled down.

"I owe you one more answer," he said quietly.

The sense of finality was inescapable. Nick was going back to his grandmother, crossing the threshold into a world that excluded me. The truck was his way of settling whatever debt there was between us.

I couldn't honestly say that I had any regrets about what we had done.

"How about the big one?"

He turned from studying the house to look at me, his features shadowed. "Which one would that be?"

"Why? Why did you ever cover for him, Nick? Why did you do it?"

He leaned back, his eyes narrowed. I thought he wouldn't answer me, but he was just choosing his words.

"I saw my father before he died," he said softly. "Someone called the house in the middle of that night and the sitter got us up to take us both to the hospital. Sean went back to sleep in the car, because no one told us anything.

"But I knew that something was wrong. The sitter was upset and she drove badly, which wasn't typical of her. She was crying and evasive. In fact, she got angry with me for asking questions, which also wasn't her way.

"I remember the nurse who came and took my hand. She met us at the door of the ER, as though she had been waiting for us and knew exactly who we were. She had a kindly face and I remember thinking that she was somebody's mom. She didn't tell me much either, except that my dad wanted to see me.

"When she let go of my hand, I thought she'd taken me to the wrong place. I couldn't connect the man all bandaged up in the bed with my father. A few hours before, he'd been whirling my mother around the living room. He'd been wearing his tux and she was wearing this ball gown that was covered with flowers. They liked to go dancing and that's where they had gone that night.

"But the man in the bed could barely move. I was afraid of him, but the nurse left me there. I might have run but he spoke to me, with my father's voice.

"I went closer, just as he asked, and saw that he had my father's eyes. But everything was wrong. There was blood on the bandages and tubes coming out of him and what I could see of his face had no color at all. I guess he knew that he was going to die.

"He told me that he loved me, though it took a long time for him to make the words. And he made me promise to take care of my mother and my brother. He told me that I was going to be the man of the house."

Nick swallowed as I watched, that memory clearly un-faded by the passing of the years. "I promised, but I didn't know what he meant. Not then. I wanted to ask him where he was going and where my mother was, but he had a convulsion of some kind. He started to choke and blood spurted. The monitors went wild and people came running. The nurse came back and pulled me outside the curtains around his bed.

"But I was eight and I peeked. I couldn't see much, but I heard a lot. I heard him die. I heard the monitors stop. I heard the doctors step away and sigh. And I saw as they pulled the sheet over my father's face."

He looked at his hands. "Lucia told me years later that they had a car accident on a country road. The people in the other car had been killed immediately. My mother had been badly injured and my father had practically crawled to a nearby house to get help. The doctors didn't know how he'd managed it with all his injuries, and the suggestion was made that the effort had cost him dearly."

His eyes clouded with tears as he looked at me. "They never told him that my mother wasn't at the hospital. They never told him that she had been pronounced dead at the scene."

He looked away again, before I could reach out and touch him, his words spilling fast. "I couldn't take care of my mother, but I could sure as hell keep part of my promise to my father. Things were vague for a few days, it wasn't clear what was going to happen to us. I was adamant that Sean and I had to stay together. They might not have listened to me, in fact I'm sure they would have split us up for fostering, but Lucia turned up in the nick of time.

"We had never met her before that. No one talked about her

and I didn't know who she was. We just lived in Connecticut, but we'd never visited Rosemount before.

"Later I found out that she and my father were estranged over something and no one had expected her to step in. But Lucia *did* step in."

He laughed under his breath, his fingers moving as though he turned a cigarette, his profile sharply drawn. "I remember my first sight of her. She was dressed in black from head to toe, veiled and gloved. She blew into our house, where we were staying with the sitter until the funeral, like a diva sweeping onto the stage or a hurricane touching shore.

"The poor social worker never knew what hit him. She shed birth certificates and family genealogies in every direction, talking nonstop all the while. And she blew smoke rings at the ceiling, which impressed both Sean and I. I was convinced at the time that her purse was magical, because it didn't seem to have a bottom. Everything they asked for, she had in there.

"She said she was our grandmother, that she was taking us to Rosemount and that that was that, and if they gave her any shit about it, she'd see that they rued the day."

"She actually said that?"

"Oh yeah. And in those days, people swore a lot less than they do now. She was more than a bit intimidating. And then she left."

"She never spoke to you?"

"Not then. I saw her at the funeral, but I don't think I was supposed to. She was at the back and she was crying, though she tried to hide it behind her veils.

"Some social worker, a very earnest guy, sat down with us to ask what we thought. I knew that the only way we could be together was with Lucia and I had to keep my promise to my father. Even though she was terrifying, seeing her weep made it a little easier to insist. I did insist, for whatever that was worth. Everyone was probably relieved to have things so easily resolved."

He straightened his shoulders. "A week later, the house was cleaned out and put up for sale. Charities had picked up clothing and the furniture had been sold. I remember thinking that it was as though my parents had never been. The sitter, who was the last person we really knew, took us to the airport and handed me two airline tickets to Boston. She kissed us good-bye and told us to be good. That was the last time we ever saw her."

He paused.

I touched his shoulder. "You could look her up."

"I don't even know what her name was." He shrugged. "Dawn or Donna or Doreen. Something like that. No one remembers. I tried a few years ago to find out, just to thank her, but none of those social workers bothered to write her name down."

"But it worked out with Lucia?"

"I don't think it was easy for any of us. It had been a long time since she'd had children around. Sean hated it here. He missed his friends and he didn't like Lucia. He hated the house. I wasn't crazy about it either, but I'd made that vow and I was going to keep it, whatever the price. I was determined to be so good that Lucia couldn't change her mind."

"Surely she wouldn't have."

"I knew that she was unpredictable. I knew that having us around wasn't her first choice. I discovered that she had sold off that theater and taken a loss, because she couldn't pursue her dream and keep us, too. I knew that she preferred to travel on a whim and be carefree, which you can't be with two kids underfoot. I knew that she found sensible meals and doctor's visits and assignments for school a pain in the ass."

I took a guess. "So you minimized how much trouble you were."

"Well, Sean didn't share my goal of being good. He got into everything, I think just to spite Lucia. Maybe he was hoping to go back to his friends and the familiar life we'd had. But I knew we couldn't go back. Lucia caught him once and was so livid that I thought she'd chuck us into the street right then and there. I don't remember what he did but I remember what she said."

"What?"

"That he was just like his father, that he didn't know how to accept that someone loved him."

He studied the house, his features composed. So this was how he had come to the conclusion that Sean was Lucia's favorite.

"After that, I never let him get caught again."

"Keeping your promise to your father."

"Something like that."

"Don't you think she knows, Nick?"

He gave me a sharp look. "If she does, then I haven't done a very good job." He frowned, then pushed one hand through his hair, visibly forcing himself to smile. "I guess I can't put this off any longer. What time should I meet you at your parents' place tomorrow?"

There was a lump in my throat, and it wasn't just from his story. "I should pick you up. It'll look better if we arrive together."

He nodded, we agreed on three o'clock and he leaned over the seat. His pack was there, a bit of planning that I hadn't expected.

So, he'd known this would be it. Maybe the truck was about last night, after all. If you think that didn't take the fizz out of my ginger ale, you're dead wrong.

Nick seemed hesitant to get out of the truck, his fingers drumming on his knee. "Somehow, a thank-you doesn't seem enough."

I would have given anything to hide my expression from him. "Wait until tomorrow," I said a little less evenly than I might have liked. "You'll be sending me a bill if you survive that dinner."

He chuckled and leaned closer, cupping my chin in the warmth of his hand. There was no hiding from that perceptive gaze, though I thought I saw a suspicious shimmer in his own eyes. "Thank you, Phil." His voice was no more than a rough whisper. "For everything."

He kissed me, a chaste kiss that was nothing like what I wanted. I tasted salt, though I couldn't have told you where it came from.

We'd made a deal and all terms were fulfilled, or shortly would be. There was nothing left to do but move on.

He got out of the truck and I sat there as he walked away, just about as low as I've ever been. But you can't compel somebody to stay with you, to take a chance, to reach up and snag a star. When the rubber hit the road, I figured Nick and I were too different.

He didn't want the same things I did. He didn't want anything more than he could carry with him.

And I was still fairly substantial.

Frankly, if he didn't want me, that was his loss. I knew I'd be chanting that theme later, but even then I recognized that you can't make someone love you. I'd given it my best shot, I'd had my curiosity satisfied, and maybe I'd learned something along the way.

That's not too bad of a deal. He'd been honest with me, and he'd told me more than I'd ever expected him to. Maybe we'd both learned something.

Maybe he should have grown up knowing Elaine.

It wasn't much consolation, but it would have to do. One thing was for sure—I wasn't going to dive headfirst into a vat of chocolate ice cream over Nick Sullivan.

Though I might let myself have two chocolate bars this month.

I dashed away my tears with my fingertips and called myself an idiot before I reached to turn the key. I looked up, and Nick was running back toward me.

"Phil, Lucia's been hurt." His knuckles were white where he grabbed the door. "And this time, it's for real."

"Did you call . . ."

"The phone's dead." He was clearly torn between going for help and trying to give some.

I was out of the truck in a heartbeat. "I'll go next door and call 911. See if you can help her."

We both ran.

The gossip mill had enough grist that night to run for a year. I'm sure Mrs. Donnelly was taking notes as I used her phone. The ambulance came quickly, Chief O'Neill and his crew fast behind. Lucia had lost a lot of blood, and even the paramedics looked pessimistic as they did their best to stabilize her condition.

Nick looked positively funereal.

Lucia had been attacked in the greenhouse, apparently with a kitchen knife that had fallen on the gravel. She wasn't even on the gurney before the cops were dropping little souvenirs into Ziplock bags and barking at everyone to not touch anything.

When they said they were going to take her down to Massachusetts General, I knew it was bad. They wouldn't let Nick ride in the ambulance with her, which made it even worse. O'Neill was decent about it—he took everyone's telephone numbers and waved us off.

He had a look of resignation as he surveyed all the potential surfaces for fingerprints. I wouldn't have wanted that job.

We didn't talk about it, but I drove Nick back into town. I

had to go home anyhow and we seemed to reach a consensus without the bother of discussion. I tried to reassure him before we pulled into the hospital lot.

"Don't worry, Nick. They're very good here."

"That's not it, Phil."

"Then what?"

"Don't you see?"

"See what?"

"It happened almost exactly as she staged it."

I hadn't gotten nearly that far. I guess I was thinking that it had been a break-in—or too busy to think much at all—but he was right. The scene was oddly similar to what he had described.

"But the blood was drying. It happened a while ago, while we were gallivanting around in the truck." I patted his hand. "O'Neill can't get you this time."

"No, Phil. It looks like I gave somebody an idea." His lips tightened. "Which is a whole lot worse." He got out of the truck before I could argue with him and strode into the ER, his hands balled in his pockets and his shoulders hunched.

But if Nick thought I was going to let him keep blaming himself for Sean's deeds, then he had another thing coming.

Threes within threes and mystical nines. Magic and myth love a three, or maybe they love in triplicate. Three Fates, three Wyrd Sisters, three Fairy Godmothers attendant at every birth. Three demoiselles beside the fountain. Three goddesses: maiden mother crone. The Trinity: father, son, and holy spirit. Osiris, Isis, and Horus. Odin, Tyr, and Frey. Sun, moon, and stars.

Just read the box—easy as 1, 2, 3. Three wishes to break a spell. Death comes in threes, the third time is the charm, thrice pays for all. If you break a dish, break two more—since accidents come in threes, the others might as well be your choice.

Third time lucky.

Three-ring circuses and three-cornered hats. Three dimensions in space. Tricolor flags, third-class coach, triple crowns and the Three Musketeers. Three-mile limits and three-legged races, threesomes and hat tricks and the third degree. The magic of threes permeates, perpetuates and percolates.

Once upon a time, a certain maiden underwent a transformation in stages of three. That was "one," a first time, an awakening, a beginning of a journey. A call to adventure, if you will, a boarding call to growing up.

Then came "two."

Two is the number of choices, of decisions, of forks in the road. The high way or the low way, the easy way or the hard. It's the number of partnership, of coupledom, of teams pulling in harness together. Of the sum of the parts making more as a whole.

Sometimes magic knocks hard on your door, showing you something you would rather not see, something you weren't sure you needed to know. Sometimes magic's jokes aren't very funny.

Knock, knock.

Who's there?

Yurma.

Yurma who?

Yurmather is an adulteress.

Our heroine, however resourceful she could be, was not likely to sleep that night. Her mission complete, her mother snoring, she left the house and walked. The skies hung low, the stars obscured by a heavy blanket of grey. The air was warm, filled with mist, unseasonable for November. The sea seemed to have invaded the town, filling the air with its water and salt. The town was quiet, only one light burning with welcome.

The diner. She was wet and chilled, more cold from her heartache than climactic conditions. The moment she chose to seek shelter there, the fates had themselves a chuckle.

Alakazam, here comes two.

Because there was only one other person in the diner. She saw him when she shook the mist out of her hair, after he had seen her, when it was too late to turn and run. Their paths hadn't crossed since he finished high school and disappeared. But he was back and he was here and he was making room for her at his table.

Expectant.

After an initial uncertainty, it was like old times. They talked about everything and nothing, who was doing what and what was happening to who. He was evasive about the travel book he'd been reading, less evasive about his determination to leave. She found herself admitting how she hated school, uttering the sacrilege for the first time that she didn't want to go to law school.

And for the second time, he gave her a gift.

"Stop living other people's dreams and live your own."

So simple, so true, as clear as a crystal.

Then he told her about his plan to travel and it seemed a different man sat opposite her. His eyes sparkled with anticipation, he showed her maps and train schedules and pictures of all the places he intended to visit. The world was his oyster in that moment and she was painfully jealous that he could choose his own course.

Until she realized that nothing was keeping her from choosing her own. Nothing but herself. No one else had erected barriers beyond words, edicts, commandments. It was she who had chosen to follow them, to live up to expectation.

And she knew then that she wasn't going to do it anymore.

The diner closed and they had to leave, abandoning their coffee cups for the secretive mist of the quiet street. He took her hand in his, tucked his books under his coat and walked her home. He was leaving and she knew he had to go, she wanted to go with him but she knew it was too soon.

She sensed that they stood at a fork in the road. Everything was tenuous, every choice hung in the balance, anything could happen and might well do so.

And then it did.

His grandmother's car came squealing out of nowhere, his brother driving like a man possessed. The front fender was smashed, his brother was inarticulate.

He was as drunk as her mother had been earlier. He parked crookedly and fell out onto the pavement. He begged for Nick's help in hiding his crime from Lucia, in evading her wrath for his breaking at least two of her rules.

She knew that Nick would do it, though she couldn't imagine why. He kissed her knuckles, a parting salute, then got into the car. His brother could barely stand. There was a mickey of rum on the seat, Nick opened it and drank, deliberately spilling the liquor over himself and the seat. Then he drained the rest.

He looked at her and touched one finger to his lips, a request for her pledge that she was only too happy to give. And then he was gone, driving home in the night as the distant wail of a police siren cut the air. His brother fled into the darkness and she walked the rest of the way home alone.

She was certain she had chosen the right fork in the road, and she clung to it even in the revelations of the ensuing days, even when she was furiously angry with Sean's deception.

But she had made a promise, and she kept it, as all good heroines do. She'd made a choice, and she wasn't going to forget it.

Chapter 16

The ER was chaotic, as I suppose such places usually are. Lucia had already arrived, and was wired up. She was out cold, but the doctor was pleased that she was relatively stable. They checked her in, gave Nick the room number and told him not to worry.

Fat chance.

I tried to talk to him, but might as well have been shouting into the wind. He sat, his gaze fixed on Lucia, and fretted. He was blaming himself and I knew it, just as I knew there wasn't much I could do about it.

"I should have gone down there last night," he muttered finally.

"Where?"

"To Sean's."

I sat down beside him and took his hand. "Because you think he hit Josie again?"

He nodded once.

"You already called the cops on him once . . ."

"Twice."

"Then what else can you do?"

He shot me a dark look. "He's my responsibility."

"No, he's his own responsibility. You can't save Sean from himself and you can't save Josie from her own bad choices. You intervened, you showed her that it didn't have to be that way, and you have to let them make their own choices."

"But I could have saved Lucia, if Sean had been a guest of the boys in blue."

"Maybe today." I squeezed his unresponsive fingers. "There you go, thinking you're God again. You and my father might get along just fine."

He didn't crack a smile. He slipped his hand up my neck though and kissed my temple. "Go home, Phil."

"What about you?"

"I'm staying here."

"What about tomorrow?"

"I'll be there." His gaze bored briefly into mine. "It was part of our deal. I'll call you in the morning to work out the details."

"I guess this isn't a good time to tell you that you'll need a suit. Father's birthday is a comparatively formal event."

A smile touched his lips. "They're hemming the pants for me. I'll have to pick it up tomorrow."

"Maybe I could . . ."

He touched a fingertip to my lips. "Go home, Phil. We'll worry about details in the morning."

We both looked at Lucia, her chest rising and falling as the respirator wheezed. "It's not your fault, you know."

His lips tightened. "Leave it, Phil."

And leave him. The subtext was clear. I picked up my purse,

wished him good night and went home, dragging my heart behind me.

It was incredible to him that he was going to be a guest of the Coxwells.

It added to the surreal sense of the day. He had spent the night dozing beside a strangely frail and immobile Lucia. He had talked to O'Neill this morning, answering his questions about where he'd been the day before, evading any discussion of what he'd done since he got home.

He might not be his brother's keeper but it was a change he had to get used to.

Now, he sat in the most expensive suit he had ever owned, watching Phil's legs as she shifted gears, and marvelled that he was en route to a meal with the Coxwells.

Their home, Grey Gables, had been the hallmark of how things should be for as long as he'd been in Rosemount. They set the standard, and dozens of socially ambitious souls followed their lead. He had always found it amusing to see, for example, how many households waited to see what flowers the Coxwells planted in their gardens before choosing their own.

Beverly Coxwell had always been the maven of good taste, long before there had been television shows and magazines to spread the gospel. He knew that her wardrobe choices each season were scrutinized and discussed by the women in town, everything from the height of her hemlines to the shape of her purse avidly copied.

The Coxwells did not mingle. They were effectively the crown family of Rosemount, by dint of wealth, social position and attitude. They expected homage, and they got it. He imagined that Robert Coxwell's ascent to the judiciary had been less an election than a coronation. It probably was only a matter of time before the judge more actively entered politics.

They were a family whose lives looked orderly, particularly to a boy who had seen so much disorder. They were polite, they were attractive, they sponsored many a local event. Their children proceeded to Harvard, thence to law school, as though there were no other options. It was a kind of normalcy that he had once yearned for, and certainly that he still found intimidating.

But if he was nervous, Phil was more so. He couldn't figure out why. She had a family, a large, established, prosperous family where all events proceeded with mathematical precision.

Maybe it was the rift between them that made her uncomfortable.

Because today, she shifted gears with less than her usual ease and nearly stalled the truck on a perfectly level intersection.

"Is anything wrong?"

She flashed him a look of alarm. "No, nothing. I just hope he likes the cuff links."

So that was what was in the carefully wrapped package she had asked him to hold. "It seems like something he might like." Not that Nick knew, but surely cuff links were a safe bet for a professional man.

"He wears a lot of French-cuffed shirts. I thought they were neat."

"But now, you're not sure."

Her smile was wry. "When it comes to my father, I'm never sure."

"I'd think that having everyone together would be the point, regardless of what gift they brought."

She laughed then. Her laughter had an edge to it, unlike her usual carefree laughter. "That shows what you know about it." She patted him on the hand, her attitude irking him.

"Come on, Phil, it can't be that bad."

"No? You wait and see. It's the annual test. He'll not say a word until he's unwrapped everything, then he'll line them up across the dining room table in order of preference. Favor will be allotted over the coming year on the basis of position."

He looked at her in horror. "You're joking."

"I wish I was. It's not a game I play very well." She parked the truck at the end of the Coxwell driveway, behind an array of shiny SUV's and luxury cars. "To tell you the truth, I think the odds are stacked in favor of those with slightly different equipment than mine."

She wasn't kidding. She made her quip and smiled but Nick knew her well enough to not be fooled.

She was afraid of the old bastard. And rightly so, if that was how she was treated here. The protective urge he'd first felt when she marched into Lucia's house was nothing compared to what he felt now.

He'd rip the face off anyone foolish enough to hurt Phil in his presence.

She was out of the truck too quickly for him to get around to help. She shifted her weight from foot to foot in the driveway and cast more than one anxious glance at the door.

He handed her the parcel and gave her a quick kiss. "You look terrific." It was no lie. She was wearing a trim little navy dinner suit and a white beaded blouse, strappy heels and dark stockings. Her makeup was characteristically light, her hair gleamed.

She looked like a million bucks.

She leaned against him for a fleeting moment. "You too." She took a deep breath and straightened the knot of his tie and he noted that her fingers were shaking. "But I think this was a really bad idea, Nick." She cast a worried glance up at him. "Maybe you should leave now, while you can."

"Chicken." He threw her usual charge back at her but she didn't smile.

"I'm serious."

There was no way he was leaving her to face this alone. "Not a chance, Phil. You're stuck with me."

She took an uneven breath. "Don't expect him to play nice."

"Okay, I won't."

He didn't really think it would be that bad. A part of him couldn't help thinking that this would be a picture perfect family dinner, the kind he'd seen on television a thousand times but never experienced. Okay, they'd be less than thrilled that he was here, but they'd get over it. They'd swallow their objections and be nice.

They weren't like Lucia, after all.

They weren't at all like Lucia, but not in the way he anticipated.

Beverly Coxwell was still a beauty. She opened the door when Phil rang the bell while Nick marvelled that Phil couldn't just walk into a house where she'd lived for years. Beverly smiled coolly at them, her gaze slipping over Nick as she greeted them.

She looked twice at the suit and he figured she pegged its value within twenty bucks. One eyebrow rose slightly, but she said nothing about it.

She was dressed in a full-length sequined gown of exquisite cut and definite expense. Diamonds dripped from her fingers and her earlobes, her chestnut hair was wound into a chignon studded with jewels. Beverly was elegant, poised, well-preserved, and impossible to read.

It was hard to believe that this woman had borne four children. Nick couldn't envision her pregnant, let alone permitting it to happen again. He certainly couldn't imagine her relaxing her composure enough to do the deed that led to those pregnancies in the first place.

Maybe she had just endured.

It was harder to credit that she shared any relation with Phil, the most warm-blooded, generous, passionate and open person Nick had ever known. He looked closely, though, and saw a faint echo of Phil's features in her mother.

He really had to look for it.

Where Phil was animated, her mother's features could have been wrought in stone. Nick was used to being greeted with volume, either enthusiastic hugs and kisses or recrimination—which ended in the same noisy hugs and kisses. But Phil exchanged non-contact cheek pecks with her mother as though she expected nothing different.

Beverly offered Nick her hand, which was very cold. "So, this must be Philippa's rumored date."

It was somewhat disconcerting to not be addressed directly, especially as she assessed him so openly. Phil's tongue seemed to have been cut from her mouth, but Nick smiled coolly. "It's nice to meet you, Mrs. Coxwell."

"Is it?" A smile touched her painted lips and for a minute, there was a light in her eyes. A step sounded behind her and it was gone. She nodded minutely and stepped aside as her spouse joined her.

Robert Coxwell was no less imposing than Nick remembered, perhaps more so close up. He was tall and silver-haired, trim and fastidiously attired. His dark suit was impeccably tailored, his shirt whiter than white.

He didn't even trouble himself to look at Phil, just glared at Nick.

"You've got a nerve coming here, after what you did." He made no attempt to disguise his animosity. "If I'd been on the bench, you'd still be serving time. Hard time. Drinking and driving is a serious offense."

Phil cleared her throat, but her voice sounded smaller than usual. "The charges were dismissed for lack of evidence."

Her father bestowed a withering glance on her. "Don't you tell me my business. Those charges were dismissed because O'Neill is incompetent and Tupper was too much of a sentimental fool to be a good judge. There's always evidence if you know where to look for it."

Nick bristled but would be damned if he would show it. He spoke with deliberate calm. "I always thought a man was innocent until proven guilty in this country."

"Don't quote the law to me." Robert's eyes narrowed. "You got lucky, that's all there is to it. I heard there was marijuana in that car."

The irony of this particular accusation did not escape Nick, especially as the rest of the family hovered in the foyer, listening.

Zach Coxwell had always been untouchable and worse, he had known it. As a result, Zach could always be trusted for a joint or a mickey or just about anything else, no questions asked, cash on the line. He was the youngest of the crown princes of Rosemount, but the only one disinclined to play the regal role.

But no one would ever have nailed him for it. It would have been sacrilege, of a kind.

"You heard wrong," Nick offered with a thin smile. "Unlike some other people, I've never had a taste for pot."

Zach colored but his father never saw it. "A likely story."

"I'm not here to give you an explanation for something that happened fifteen years ago." Nick put his hand on the back of Phil's waist and felt how she was trembling. "I believe this is a social occasion. Happy birthday, Mr. Coxwell." Phil's eyes were wide and she seemed more upset about this exchange than he was.

Which was saying something.

Her father didn't miss the gesture, nor how proprietary it was. He turned to Phil, his tone harsh. "You'll regret this insurrection, Philippa Elizabeth Coxwell. You mark my words. And when you come back, expecting me to forget that you insulted me like this, you'll find that you are very wrong."

He spun and walked into the house, leaving them standing on the doorstep.

Welcome home. For the first time, Nick realized that Phil's warning might have been an understatement.

Even Beverly looked slightly surprised by her spouse's rudeness, but she recovered quickly. "Why don't you come in?" she suggested, standing slightly back as though they were the ones hovering indecisively on the threshold.

"Why not?" Nick muttered under his breath. Phil gave him a quick apologetic smile. He couldn't believe that she had survived so many years in this household, let alone that it hadn't poisoned her sweet nature. He wasn't even in the door and he was ready to take heads.

Phil could never have done anything to have deserved to be spoken to that way. And evidently, it wasn't uncommon, because she wasn't surprised by it.

He was more angry than he could ever remember being.

"I told you not to expect the Brady Bunch," Phil whispered and Nick didn't let go of her waist.

"I should have believed you." He winked for her, rubbing his thumb across her back, and watched some of the tension ease from her smile.

He was going to get her out of here, as soon as possible.

The atmosphere wasn't any better inside, even without Robert visibly present. The air seethed with unspoken tensions as Phil made the introductions. He remembered her brothers, of course, because everyone in town knew who they were. He had never socialized with any of them, even Zach who was his own age. It would have been unthinkable.

They seemed to all be deciding how they should respond to his arrival, and not surprisingly, went with their father's lead.

Eldest was James, a younger replica of his father with the manner to match. He had the same strong profile as his father and the same taste in perfectly tailored clothing. His hair was the same chestnut hue as his mother's but turning silver at the temples. He was a handsome man, who gave the impression of being incisive, impatient and ambitious.

Nick suspected his prime ambition was the role of patriarch. Evidently, James was his father's first partner in the family law firm and holding the reins of power while the judge served his term.

"Nicely done, Philippa," was all James said, his lips so tight that the words barely made it out. He shook Nick's hand as though he might get a disease from the simple touch.

But where James closely followed the paternal model, his wife couldn't hold a candle to Beverly. Marcia might have been pretty once, but her lips pinched with a dissatisfaction that was most unattractive. She looked like a shrew and certainly sounded like one.

She was expensively dressed, but the look didn't pull together well. There were loose threads at her hem, a snag in her bejewelled sweater, her lipstick was smeared, her jewelry could have used a good cleaning.

She didn't seem to care.

"I don't know why you had to ruin everything, Philippa," she whined. "Usually it's Zach that screws up. And at least he's funny about it."

"I'm working on it," Zach joked. "Philippa's just got me temporarily outgunned."

No one laughed.

James and Marcia had ensured the bloodline with two sons. James Jr. and John were handsome boys with mischief in their eyes and defiant cowlicks. They must have been eight or nine years old, and were very close in age. They shook hands politely, oblivious to any subtext, and were clearly hating that they had to wear suits and ties. John wound a finger into his collar and pretended to be gagging, earning a complaint from his mother and a reprimand from his father so sharp that it might have left a scar.

Second son Matt had been less fortunate with the gene lottery and inherited neither his mother's striking good looks nor his father's imposing manner. He stood back from the fray as though he wasn't comfortable with the high tensions of his family. He didn't speak but simply nodded his head in response to Phil's introduction, then flicked a glance to James as though checking that he had done all right.

The man had to be forty years old..Nick would have thought he'd be over such behavior by now. He was also a lawyer, but took some jibes from his brothers for specializing in real estate law.

He didn't even defend himself.

Matt's wife, Leslie, was a scholarly looking brunette who seemed to have all the power in their relationship. She certainly wasn't impressed by the way Matt stepped back from the fray.

"Charmed, I'm sure." She smiled a little too brightly, then pushed a child forward. "This is Annette. Annette, say hello."

Annette declined to do so. She was dressed in ribbons and bows, but didn't speak at all. Apparently, she had inherited her father's quiet manner.

Or she was more sensitive to the atmosphere. Nick smiled for her and she watched him shyly for a moment before hiding behind her exasperated mother.

Zach, of course, was jovial, the life of the party. He was a good-looking guy, which had helped him go far on little more than charm. He was always ready with a joke or a smart comment. Nick thought he was about as deep as cellophane.

"Long time no see," he said, hinting at a friendliness that had never existed between them. "Do you know what you call twenty-five lawyers up to their necks in cement?"

"Not enough cement."

The young boys laughed and repeated it to each other.

Zach cocked a finger at Nick and winked. "Not bad, not bad." Then he leaned closer to add in a stage whisper. "But, you see, the way things work around here, I tell the punch line." He gave Nick a steady look.

Nick wasn't about to play along. "Then you need better jokes. That one's older than both of us put together."

Zach sobered and stepped back, gesturing to a man beside him that Nick hadn't noticed as yet. "I understand you've met my pal Jeffrey McAllister."

Nick knew he shouldn't have been surprised to find the lawyer present. Phil caught her breath and exuded dissatisfaction. And who could blame her? She'd made her opinion clear and no one gave a damn about it.

Jeffrey looked smug, as though aware that he fit into this place better than Nick did.

Nick smiled, determined to outgrace the jerk, and offered his hand. "Yes, I have."

"We meet again," Jeffrey said smoothly, then inclined his head to Philippa. "May I be the first to say that you look wonderful today, Philippa."

She slipped her hand through Nick's elbow and smiled, looking her playful self for the first time in a while. Maybe the heat was off now. "Actually, you can't. Someone beat you to it." She smiled up at Nick. "But thanks anyway."

Jeffrey's lips pinched and Zach gave a low whistle.

Then he shrugged. "Hey, no offense Nick, but we wanted a backup plan. Throws off the seating if you can't boy-girl it all the way around. And no one really believed that Philippa would bring you here."

Nick swallowed a wry laugh. "Now, I can't imagine why."

The silence was deafening.

James cleared his throat and surprisingly provided some relief. "Funny but Zach doesn't seem to have done his part to maintain that seating plan."

"Weren't you going to bring Sandy?" Leslie asked, seizing a neutral topic of conversation with apparent relief. "She's so nice . . ."

Zach interrupted her curtly. "We broke up last night." He didn't look so chipper all of a sudden. Nick guessed that he hadn't instigated the breakup of the relationship.

No one seemed to know what to say. They were stuck in the foyer, mired in a silence that could last all week, the birthday boy amusing himself elsewhere. This could prove to be a very long evening.

"I think," Beverly finally trilled with false cheer, "that it's time we all had a drink."

Chapter 17

It was hell.

I was so embarrassed by my father's behavior and couldn't imagine how I could explain it to Nick. I had expected my father to say *something*, but he'd said a lot.

And now he sat at the head of the table and said nothing at all. He was giving Nick the alpha-male death glare, but Nick, to his credit, was doing a splendid job of ignoring him.

Nick's manners were exquisite. In fact, he showed them all up, but they didn't even know it. I knew he was angry, I could feel him boiling away beside me, but the others never guessed. My mother was watching Nick like a hawk and I could feel her slowly thawing.

She is a sucker for a man who keeps up appearances. If anyone had been keeping score—and I suspect she was—Nick would have been skunking my father at that game.

Of course, she was getting pickled *toute de suite* as well.

Conversation was stilted at best. There was no help. There never is because my mother doesn't want to have to persuade some paid employee to be complicit in her drinking. She doesn't want some woman from town spreading such tasty gossip. It wouldn't look good. So, we women served courses and cleared the table, taking turns.

My mother always started out cooking with good intentions. She was a good cook, but the sherry made her lose her edge. And she imbibed as she worked, so usually the meal degenerated.

Tonight was no exception. The salad was good, the asparagus soup was light and delicious. It's my father's favorite and he was starting to thaw slightly by the time we got up to get the main course. My mother was looking a bit unsteady, so Leslie and I insisted on serving it up.

I like doing kitchen duty with Leslie. She's a no-nonsense kind of woman and she gives me no grief for being all thumbs. She does anything resembling cooking and I get plates and so forth. It works.

So, the main course was roast beef, another favorite of Father's, to be served with mashed potatoes, gravy and vegetables. My mother always stuck a little menu list on the fridge, which was handy because we could just check each course even after she was too far gone to remember.

Everything seemed according to plan. The meat was a bit too well done on the top, but we've read that book and seen that movie, and we were pretty quick to hide the evidence. The platter looked great once Leslie had sliced up the meat and I popped it back into the oven while we got the vegetables. She thickened the gravy and I served up the carrots and peas, and then I realized that we had a problem.

There were no potatoes.

There wasn't another pot, or a dish in the oven, or a casserole in the microwave. We looked high and low, but the best I could do was come up with a basket of un-peeled, unwashed raw spuds from the pantry.

Oops.

"They'll take too long to cook," Leslie insisted, casting an experienced eye over the other elements of the meal, which were rapidly cooling. "We'll have to go without."

We tried to brazen it out.

My father nodded with approval as we set the steaming dishes on the table, only frowning when Leslie and I took our seats again. "Where are the potatoes? Beverly, weren't you serving this with potatoes?"

My mother took a sip of sherry and scanned the table, taking a moment to inventory what had been served. She looked at me, nonplussed. "Didn't I cook them?"

I shook my head minutely.

She smiled and sat up straighter. "Then, Robert, the potatoes are in the pantry. The peeler is in the second drawer to the right of the sink and really, you could use any of the pots." And with that, she drained her glass.

She set it down and tapped the base, and Matt was quick to top her off.

My father nearly inhaled his tie. The words broke from his lips individually. "You. Forgot. To. Cook. Potatoes?" He bounded to his feet. "How could you be so stupid?" Then glared as he cast his napkin on the table. "How could you be so *drunk?*"

She smiled at him, as cool as could be. "How could you be so unspeakably rude?"

His face went red. My father does not do well with public criticism and my mother usually plays to his rules.

But not today.

Something had made her feisty. My father came to exactly

the same conclusion. His gaze flicked from my mother to Jeffrey—who was closely examining the pattern on his plate—to Nick and landed on me. He shook one heavy finger at me. "This is all your fault."

Nick's voice was low and dangerous. "There's no reason for you to talk to your daughter this way."

"You will not tell me how to talk to my family."

"I will not sit here and listen to you insult her for no good reason."

"Then you're free to leave."

"I like this boy," my mother declared and saluted Nick with her glass. "It's about time somebody told you when you were wrong, Robert. And you're wrong a lot." She drank to that, much to the astonishment of my brothers.

My father's hands clenched and unclenched. He was going to blow and woe to anyone in his way.

Leslie and Marcia exchanged a glance, then ushered the children to their feet. "Come on, let's get the cake."

"But we haven't had dinner yet," James Jr. complained.

"Never mind, come on, come on."

My mother seemed to be enjoying herself. She leaned back in her chair, crossed her legs and gestured with her glass. "Zach, what's the difference between God and a lawyer?"

"Um, I don't know, Mom."

"God doesn't think he's a lawyer." She smiled archly at my father and drained her glass once more. The decanter at Matt's elbow was empty. "Jeffrey, be a dear and pass along that bottle, if you please."

He turned to do as he was asked, but my father's words stopped him. "Don't touch it, Jeffrey. You'll only encourage her."

Jeffrey froze, the bottle in one hand, clearly uncertain which was the polite choice. Should he do the bidding of host or hostess?

"Boss" won. He put the bottle down.

The tension sizzled.

Zach braced his elbows on the table and smiled. "Hey, maybe this is a good time to share something with you all. What do you get when a law graduate fails the bar exam three times?"

"Zach Coxwell," Matt said quietly.

"A loser," James contributed at the same time.

"A need to actually study instead of wasting everyone's time," was my father's terse answer.

"Nope, you're all wrong. What you get is a photographer."

If Zach wanted our attention, he certainly got it. We all looked at him in confusion. My mother frowned. "Is that supposed to be funny?"

"No, it's supposed to be good news. You're supposed to all congratulate me on finding my niche in the world."

"You're going to be a lawyer," my father snapped. "We've all known that from the day you were born."

"No, you see, if Philippa doesn't have to do it, then neither do I. I don't think it's my calling. I've been taking this photography course and I'm thinking that . . ."

"Philippa," my father interjected, "has a great deal to answer for today." He took a considerable swig of his wine as he stared down the length of the table at my mother. "But then, it was only a matter of time before what was bred in the bone came out in the flesh, wasn't it, Beverly?"

My mother blinked several times in quick succession. "I don't know what you mean."

"Yes, you do. You just don't think that I know what you did. You think you fooled me, but I've known all along. I've known all along and I've done right by you, despite your treachery, but it all had to come out in the end."

"Perhaps you might share, Robert, since no one else knows what you're talking about."

"You know exactly what I mean. Look around the table, Beverly. Isn't it funny that I only have one child with red hair?"

My gut went cold. I was thinking of those letters tied with that ribbon and my mother in tears. A couple of dots were getting together to make a line.

"Or maybe I don't have a child with red hair at all. Maybe I don't have a daughter who's a bad seed, who shows no inclination to be like me at all, who doesn't look like anyone in my family. Do you think I'm stupid, Beverly?" His fist hit the table and the crystal stemware danced as he roared. "Maybe it's time you explained just who fathered this child?"

He pointed a shaking finger at me and I know the blood was gone from my face. My mother watched him, a little smile playing over her lips. "I never did think you were stupid, Robert, but you've just proven me wrong." She flicked a finger at Jeffrey. "Give me that, please."

He looked away.

They all looked away, as though my mother was invisible again.

And she knew it.

Nick swore. He stepped across the room, took the bottle and peeled off the seal while he made his way to my mother's side. He poured her a glass, then set the bottle down beside her before taking his seat once more.

"It figures that a Sullivan would encourage her," my father sneered.

"It certainly wouldn't be a Coxwell man who acknowledged my presence," my mother retorted. She graciously thanked Nick and sipped as my father fumed.

"It's time you told me the truth, Beverly."

"I suppose it is. Though you should be careful what you ask for, Robert."

"You've told *her* the truth and that's why she defies me.

You . . ." He geared up for a rant, but my mother sat up very straight, her very pose silencing him.

"Well, congratulations, Robert. I never told a soul, but you've managed to tell everyone something they didn't even need to know."

"You were faithless . . ."

"If we're going to have the story, let's have the truth, shall we?" My mother's eyes were snapping. "It's true, I did have an affair. I was young and foolish and unused to men of such passion and poetry. He intrigued me, though his manners were rough, he had no future, and he couldn't have always looked as good as he did then." She looked into the bottom of her glass and smiled. "He could, however, write marvelous love letters."

"Spare us the details."

"You asked for details."

"If you think that I will sit here and listen to you reminisce about an old lover, in front of my sons, then . . ."

"Then you are wrong again. Your sons this and your sons that." My mother rolled her eyes impatiently. "Honest to God, Robert, I'm no adultress. If anyone is not your child, it's James."

James blanched.

My father choked.

Nick covered his mouth with his hand and I'm not sure he wasn't laughing.

"This happened *before* we were married, you old fool. I knew you were the right man for me, I just wanted a bit of romance. You were always so logical, so proper, so good. My parents adored you—do you know how galling that is for a young girl? It went too far once, on one night, but I'm not an idiot. That was enough to show me how foolish I was being."

She paused to take a sip. "I married you because I loved you, Robert. In those days, I was naive enough to think that would be enough."

She set the glass down hard, her eyes glittering with tears. The crystal stem snapped with the force of impact, and the goblet toppled down, spilling sherry onto the linen.

My father stared at her, shocked to silence. It was as though we had all been struck to stone.

There was a sound of childish giggles, then the door to the kitchen opened. The kids came in, Leslie carrying the cake which was adorned with too many candles, Marcia flicking out the overhead lights. Oblivious to what they had interrupted, they started to sing "Happy Birthday" to my father.

I thought things had to improve from here, but I was wrong again. The doorbell rang. Matt went to the door and came back, a familiar shadow behind him.

"It's Chief O'Neill. He wants Philippa to go down to the police station with him."

"What?" I made a kind of choking sound.

"What the hell is this about?" Nick demanded.

My father swore and put his head in his hands.

Chief O'Neill took off his hat, nodded apologetically to my mother for obviously interrupting a family event. "We'd like to ask you a few questions about the assault on Lucia Sullivan."

"You can do it here," my mother protested.

"No, ma'am. We'd like to take a set of fingerprints." He sighed and opened his notepad. "I've got a warrant, if anyone wants to see it. If you need a few minutes, I can wait."

"Arrest her now," my father said crisply. "Blood or not, she's no longer welcome in this house."

I got to my feet with all the pride I could muster, pulling my hand from Nick's grip. "I'm going to need a lawyer. Maybe one of you would like to help."

Then I walked out of the house with Chief O'Neill.

* * *

It was Jeffrey who was finally ushered in to talk to me. I wasn't surprised that my father hadn't come, but I was shocked that neither Matt nor James were prepared to defy his edict, to defend their only sister.

And then I got mad.

Jeffrey smiled apologetically, but looked strained. "I'm supposed to be the voice of reason."

"Does that mean that I have to grovel before my father, begging his forgiveness for my conception which he seems to forget attending, or that I'm supposed to confess to something I didn't do?"

"Take it easy, Philippa. This hasn't been a good evening for anyone."

"No, but I'm the one who gets to spend the night in jail." I got up and paced, but it didn't help. "Will you at least get me a lawyer? No one that you know personally, of course, so my father can't hold it against you in future."

"Philippa . . ."

"Maybe you could call Legal Aid for me. What was in my mind to think that in an entire family of lawyers, one, just *one,* might take my case?"

"Your father is very upset."

"My father is an asshole."

Jeffrey chuckled, as though he couldn't stop himself. "That's exactly what the party line is on the other side of that door."

"Why? Who's here?"

"Nick. He's frothing that they won't let him see you."

Just knowing he was out there, even if he was just trying to set something right that he'd started, made me feel better. Less alone.

"Your mother, who is three sheets to the wind, is insisting that you be released on your own recognizance. She's had quite a bit to say about seasoned criminals walking free while her innocent daughter is left rotting in jail."

I sat down, reassured by this show of support. "I don't think I've been here quite long enough to rot."

"Yeah, well, don't be too optimistic. This could get a lot worse before it gets better."

"They don't actually have a case against me, do they?"

"It's circumstantial, but it's enough to get you some frequent guest points in this place."

"Was that a joke, Jeffrey?"

He grimaced. "Not a good one. What I don't understand is why you're sticking with this guy. He's got a record, Philippa, and everyone knows you're romantically involved. Why are you even in this mess? Hanging out with people like this can only lead to trouble. Why didn't you just stay away from him?"

I propped my chin on my hands and looked at him. He was genuinely puzzled. "Where does it say that the easy answer is the right one?"

"What does that mean?"

"That sometimes you have to take a chance, you have to dream, you have to reach out for something that maybe you haven't got a hope in heck of having. Sometimes you've got to go out on that wire without a safety net, just to see if you can do it. Maybe it's one way to be sure you're still alive."

Jeffrey looked at me like I was insane.

Maybe I was.

But I was going to go down swinging. "Sometimes your heart tells you that something is worth fighting for, maybe worth making a sacrifice for. And even if you know logically that it's unlikely to work out, your heart won't take no for an answer."

I took a deep breath. "I've been crazy about Nick Sullivan since I was fifteen years old and the only way to find out whether he was really the guy I thought he was, whether I really could love him, whether we had any chance of making something good together, was to *try*."

He looked skeptical. "Is it working?"

"Probably not. But the journey has definitely been worth the price of admission."

He studied me.

"So you can go on back to my father and dutifully report that you have tried to talk some sense into me but failed." I patted his hand. "Don't worry, Jeffrey, he'll get over it."

He was far too serious. "Philippa, I'm just trying to keep you from making a mistake."

I smiled at him, appreciating the thought if nothing else. "It's never a mistake to listen to your heart."

He got up then, shaking his head as though he was trying to dump pool water out of his ears. Or something I'd said. He got to the door, then paused. I braced myself for another round of persuasion.

But he surprised me. "I'll probably regret this, but do you want a lawyer?"

"My father will be furious with you."

"Maybe he'll get over it." Jeffrey smiled.

"I don't have much money, Jeffrey. You'll get in trouble over your billings."

"My charitable contributions are down for this year. Let me worry about the billing."

"Then why?"

He frowned at his perfectly polished shoes. "Because I think you're innocent, but I doubt that anyone will have the balls to buck your father on this. Someone told me recently about the merit of trying, even when the odds are long." He looked up and wonder of wonders, winked at me. "And I seem to remember that justice had something to do with the practice of law."

I had to like his attitude. "You're on. Thanks."

"Don't thank me yet." He opened the door. "Let me see whether I can make a difference or not."

* * *

Nick followed O'Neill to his office, not nearly satisfied with how things were shaking out. "You can't think Phil is guilty."

O'Neill turned to face Nick, his expression inscrutable. He was a tall man, built lanky and lean. The chief of police of Rosemount was dressed casually, in cords and a plain blue flannel shirt. What was left of his hair was still a ginger hue. If anything, his face had more freckles than before. He looked younger than the sixty-some odd years he must be.

He gestured to the empty seat facing his desk. "Why don't you come in, Mr. Sullivan." He granted a significant glance to the hovering Beverly Coxwell. "Close the door so we can speak privately."

His choice of words couldn't have been a coincidence. The invitation was verbatim with an offer the chief—then a detective—had offered Nick some fifteen years before. Nick hesitated, noting a shrewd gleam in those brown eyes that he had missed as a teenager.

But he wasn't a teenager anymore. He closed the door with a decisive click and sat down, refusing to be intimidated or impressed by O'Neill's silence.

The officer picked up a pipe from a bowl on his meticulously organized desk. "Do you mind?"

Nick shook his head and O'Neill took his time lighting his pipe, then ensuring it burned to his satisfaction. The smell of the pipe tobacco was soothing and O'Neill eased into his seat as he puffed. "I can build as good a case against Philippa Coxwell as against anyone right now."

He spoke easily, as though they were discussing the weather over a coffee. "I've got her fingerprints at the scene, on the point of entry and throughout the house. I've got eyewitness accounts of her arrivals there this week, both with and without you. She was alone yesterday afternoon, at the time of the crime, by her own admission. And I've got a motive, in her own declaration in front of a witness that Lucia had stood her up for a contract. Her business isn't profitable yet, is it? I'd think that a big contract could make or break her."

"She didn't do it."

O'Neill smiled and leaned back in his chair. "Are you a hunting man, Mr. Sullivan?"

Nick shook his head.

"I am. Bow hunter." He took a deep drag on his pipe. "It's nearly a lost art."

"I'm not sure what that has to do with this situation."

"It has a lot to do with it. You see, I hunt with a bow because I like a challenge, I like to make the playing field level. It's me against a buck, my ability to hunt against his ability to survive. You've got to get close to take down a buck with a bow, you've got to pick your quarry and stalk him." He drew deeply and exhaled. "You've got to understand how he thinks. There's no other way to surprise him."

"I'd think the instincts of a deer would be reasonably easy to figure out."

O'Neill smiled and wagged his pipe at Nick. "That shows you're not a hunting man. They're all different. Some are fighters, some are runners, some are tacticians. You've got to figure out which kind you're stalking, you've got to put together all the little hints to make the complete picture. Where he eats, where he drops his stools, where he beds down, how he responds the first time you see each other. I like to think of it as a study in character."

Nick folded his arms across his chest, but before he could object, O'Neill continued.

"And the job of a policeman in a small town is much the same. Successive studies in character. In a place like Rosemount, there are few secrets. There is time to develop an understanding of individual characters. I've been here my entire career. Some people think that's because I'm not ambitious. They're wrong. It's because I am intrigued by the unfolding of character."

He tapped a bit of ash from his pipe into the bowl. "You, for example. I remember the first time you came here, although you probably don't. You couldn't have been six months old."

Nick tried to hide his surprise.

"Oh yes. Your father was quite the proud papa and took you out to show you around." He mused in recollection. "That was when he and Lucia had their fight. They had it, unfortunately for their privacy, in the bar of the Grand Hotel downtown. Your father was buying rounds for everyone there. He was incoherent by the time Lucia got there, but she wasn't. She had lots to say to him about the responsibility of raising a family."

O'Neill smiled. "I'd just joined the force here and was sent down to straighten things out. Not that I had a chance."

He paused and Nick found himself intrigued by this family tale he'd never heard before.

"Lucia wanted the bar closed down. I guess she figured that if the bartender stopped pouring, she had a chance of getting your father out of there. Of course, they were all a bit gone by then, and the bartender refused. The owner had seen the lump of cash in your father's pocket and wasn't about to cut in on a run of generosity. And the patrons booed her. There was a helluva fight brewing and I was pretty worried about how I alone could stop things from getting ugly."

He shook his head in admiration. "But Lucia did it alone, without raising a finger. I can still see her, standing in the doorway to that bar, the baby that was you cradled against her chest. Now this was one of those old long dark wooden bars, with the glasses displayed in rows, on shelves behind the bartender. I don't know much about music, but she squared her shoulders and hit that note—what is it? High C?—and those glasses broke one after another after another." He snapped his fingers, over and over again, in mimicry of the breaking glasses. "I'll never forget the look on the bartender's face."

O'Neill chuckled. "She told them to go ahead and keep pouring, knowing damn well that they couldn't. People talked about that for years. The hotel owners made some rumbling about suing her, but that came to nothing. More significantly, your parents left Rosemount that night and were never seen here again."

"I never knew about that."

"No, I didn't think you did." His voice dropped. "You probably also don't know, Mr. Sullivan, that your father was drunk the night he died." He looked up, his gaze deadly serious. "Call it curiosity, call it an extension of my study of character, but I checked when I heard about the accident. It wasn't his first infraction."

O'Neill smoked with obvious enjoyment for a few moments, giving Nick time to come to terms with that. Far from being a hero, his father had been the cause of the accident that left four dead. Lucia's refusal to suffer alcohol in her house suddenly made a lot more sense.

As did her claim that Sean reminded her of his father. For the first time, Nick understood that that might not be a good thing.

"It could be said that recklessness was part of your father's character," O'Neill said finally. "And it was clear to me years later that one of that man's sons had inherited that stunning disregard for others, that love of a good time, that need to be the life of the party regardless of the cost." He looked Nick square in the eye. "And that one son hadn't."

The chief watched the smoke curling toward the ceiling. "I know that you thought you fooled me all those years ago, and to be honest, for a while you did. You were always a smart kid, smarter than average, and disinclined to tell everyone what you'd done."

O'Neill lifted a finger. "That's why it made no sense that you kept getting into trouble. I expected trouble from your brother, but oddly enough, he never seemed to find it." The chief's gaze met Nick's steadily.

"But as a student of character, you figured it out."

O'Neill smiled. "Yes. Not that it mattered. Most of it was minor—tipped outhouses on the farms, flattened tires, boats cut loose and nets damaged, stolen bikes that magically appeared on the other side of town pristine. Annoying, but boyish pranks. Out of character for you, but not worth raising a fuss." O'Neill nodded almost to himself. "I just enjoy knowing who's up to what. It's often a good precursor to the future."

Nick had a feeling what was coming.

"But driving under the influence is not a harmless prank." O'Neill leaned forward, bracing his elbows on the desk. "And a hit-and-run accident is no joke, Mr. Sullivan."

Nick held the officer's gaze, his loyalty and his confession under oath not readily sacrificed.

"You gave me lots of evidence, maybe too much evidence. Your blood alcohol was up, maybe not enough to account for your erratic driving, but then, you didn't drink by your own admission. It's hard to guess how alcohol will affect individuals, particularly those who haven't built up a resistance and you were over the legal limit."

He lit his pipe again. "But from the beginning, I wondered who had emptied the rest of the bottles in the backseat. It sure hadn't been you. I had a confession, I had the damaged vehicle, I had your fingerprints all over it and enough goodies from forensics to make the whole thing stick. I had an eyewitness, but you know, that case stunk. In terms of character, it just didn't add up.

He shook a finger at Nick. "If you had been drunk, if you had abandoned the good sense I know you have and had still gotten behind the wheel, if you had hit a pedestrian which I believe you would have done anything to avoid, then you, *you* Nicholas Sullivan, would have gotten out of that car to help. I watched you grow up and you didn't fool me. You would never have driven away."

It was troubling to have a virtual stranger understand him so very well. Nick refused to fidget, well aware that O'Neill watched him carefully.

The chief exhaled a perfect smoke ring, a startling reminder of Lucia. "You certainly would not have let your brother take the fall for you."

Nick didn't know what to say. "I didn't know about the pedestrian, not until it was too late."

"I figured as much. You only helped him because you didn't know the stakes were that high. Another boyish prank, hmm?"

Nick nodded silently.

"I knew who was responsible, but the only person who could have helped me prove the truth wasn't going to do so. It was a very loyal and very stupid choice on your part, albeit a characteristic one, and you could have paid a far higher price than you did."

O'Neill surrendered his pipe. "But someone was smiling down on you. I hope you offered up a prayer once it was all over. The eyewitness identified Wally Long's boy in the lineup, though at the time of the accident, Wally's boy had been serving up burgers under the watchful eyes of a good twenty solid citizens. The victim had only a broken leg and decided not to press charges against such a 'nice young man.'

"The whole thing was falling apart when I went 'round to Judge Tupper and we had a little talk about personality types. Tupper and I—God bless his soul—made a good team. He kept a good Scotch and we had ourselves a number of illuminating discussions. Another thing a small town gives is the opportunity for a bit of discretion. Tupper agreed with me and threw the whole thing out. It didn't have to go that way, Mr. Sullivan."

"Are you saying that I owe you?"

"No. I'm saying that this time, I want that bastard. This time, I want the truth from you, and I want your help. This is no game. Your grandmother could have been hurt worse than she is and I'm not the only one who would regret that." O'Neill leaned back in his chair. "But history tells me that the odds are against your confiding in me."

"So, you arrested Phil."

"Your cooperation seems more likely this way."

"Evelyn Donnelly blames my grandmother for the death of her cat."

O'Neill rolled his eyes. "Because Lucia gave Evelyn the Evil Eye after they argued about Lucia's plans to expand her greenhouse. Everyone knows about that, Mr. Sullivan. The thing is, no one ever saw the deceased cat and frankly, who would know if Evelyn was missing one? There have got to be thirty of the suckers in that house, most of them spawned from a dangerously small gene pool."

He shook his head. "The fact is, she never dug a hole and she never took a dead cat to the vet, which means she either chucked it out in the trash—unlikely given how she dotes on those felines—or its little carcass is still in that house. Though you'd never be sure by the smell, I'm guessing that there was no dead kitty."

"On the basis of character?"

O'Neill smiled. "Evelyn is very fond of stories. She tends to get the truth and her stories all tangled up. It's mostly harmless, since everyone knows how she is. You'll have to do better."

O'Neill thought he had Nick all figured out, but he had one thing wrong. Nick leaned forward to tap a fingertip on the desk. "You're wrong. I'd give Sean to you on a silver platter for his hurting Lucia. But I can't. I've got nothing, though it isn't for lack of trying."

O'Neill's eyes snapped. "Maybe you don't know that your brother paid a visit to Lucia on Monday afternoon. Maybe you don't know that they had a very heated argument that day, that he threatened her if she did not give him money. A lot of money."

Nick eased back and heard suspicion in his own tone. "How do you know this?"

"Maybe you don't know that your brother is on workers' compensation, but that that particular free ride is coming to an end. Maybe you don't know that he's extremely short on cash, which is a very unhappy situation for a party boy."

The chief straightened. "I'm guessing that you don't know just how big the Sullivan estate is—or that Lucia has willed it to both of you in equal parts. Or that she has put in an offer on that old theater downtown. She intends to renovate and start a company, a very, very expensive proposition and one with little prospect of return. Win or lose, it will take a big chunk out of that estate any time now."

Nick didn't have any troubles doing the math. It was now or

never, if either he or Sean wanted to maximize their inheritance. "Maybe you don't know that he hits his girlfriend."

O'Neill's surprise was quickly veiled. "Now that's a very good start, Mr. Sullivan." He picked up a pencil and started to write.

"You seem to know a lot about my grandmother's business."

O'Neill cast his pipe into the bowl, his first show of impatience. "I have a conflict of interest in this case, Mr. Sullivan, but I'll be damned if I let that interfere with my nailing whoever injured Lucia. I'm the best man for the job and I'm going to get your brother, if it's the last thing I do."

That was good enough for Nick. If O'Neill was seeing Lucia, then he had an endorsement that couldn't be questioned. "I don't have anything concrete to tell you, and what I do know, you won't believe."

O'Neill smiled. "Try me. The truth is that since I started visiting Lucia Sullivan, I've become somewhat accustomed to unconventionality."

Chapter 18

Half an hour later, Nick had told all he knew and the two of them were trying to formulate a plan. McAllister came to O'Neill's door, looking haggard and determined. "Philippa Coxwell has chosen me to represent her."

Whatever Nick had expected him to say, it wasn't that, but McAllister continued in a flat monotone. "I want bail posted for my client immediately. She's got no previous record, the evidence is circumstantial, she has a business to run and there's no reason to believe that she would not show up for a hearing." He shoved his hands into his pockets. "I suggest five hundred, tops."

"She should be freed on the basis of her word alone," Beverly interjected.

"It's not up to me and you know it." O'Neill picked up the phone and dialed.

Nick realized belatedly who the presiding judge in Rosemount would be. This was not going to go well.

"You tell that bastard . . ."

Jeffrey touched her arm. "Shh, Mrs. Coxwell, please."

Her eyes flashed and she pointed at Nick. "You tell him then."

Nick smiled. "I'll be delighted, when the time is right. Right now, it could hurt Phil."

Beverly beamed at him. "I'm starting to like you, Nick Sullivan. What are your intentions toward my daughter?"

O'Neill covered the receiver with his hand, sparing Nick from answering that. "He says twenty-five thousand."

"What?" McAllister started to sputter, but then managed to compose himself. "That's completely disproportionate to the offense and hardly representative of Philippa's history . . ."

O'Neill handed him the phone and he repeated his objections, albeit in a more temperate tone. His features tightened as he listened to whatever response he was given. "Yes, she is my client, sir."

O'Neill exchanged a glance with Nick.

"No, it is not my intent to humiliate you publicly, sir."

"He seems to be doing well enough with that alone," Beverly muttered and Nick silently agreed.

McAllister straightened. "That's utterly unfair, sir. My client has no record . . ."

He listened again, then shook his head. "With all due respect, sir, you do have an unmistakable conflict of interest in this case and it might be prudent . . ."

He was interrupted, the roar audible to everyone in the room. McAllister visibly gritted his teeth. "Yes, in fact I *am* questioning your judgment." He spoke tersely. "Sir."

Again, there was a pause.

"No, sir, I do not think that a review at nine-thirty Monday morning would be appropriate." His voice rose. "Your assessment is unreasonable and biased and . . ."

A tirade poured from the receiver and McAllister held it slightly away from his ear until it halted. "Are you finished, sir?" His tone was cutting. "Then please be advised that you cannot fire me because I am quitting."

And he slammed down the receiver.

They all stared at him.

McAllister shoved his hands into his pockets and looked sheepishly at Nick and O'Neill. "So much for that." He took a deep breath and squared his shoulders. "My mother always said I should go out on my own and you've got to start somewhere."

"What's your specialty, Jeffrey?" Beverly asked.

"I've been leaning toward criminal law."

"No." She shook her head. "You'll never meet decent people by consorting with villains. Sooner or later you'll have to defend someone who everyone knows is guilty and then winning is really losing." She patted him on the shoulder. "What you want to do is family law."

McAllister blinked. "Wills?"

Beverly smiled. "Divorces. I'm thinking of a very high profile one that would make your name in Boston." She tapped her fingertips on his arm. "The billing would be considerable. I'm thinking that you might find a personal satisfaction in the settlement."

"You're going to divorce Judge Coxwell?" McAllister demanded.

Beverly nodded. "I've spent the better part of my life trying to live up to that man's expectations and fearing his recriminations. I'm finished with it. Philippa has shown me that it doesn't have to be that way. If you want the case, Jeffrey, it's yours."

"Thank you. I appreciate your trust."

"But what about Philippa?" O'Neill asked.

"I'll finish what I started, and Philippa isn't spending two nights in jail," McAllister said. "Can I use your phone again? Maybe my mother will see her way clear to sponsoring my first client."

"There's no need for that." Nick laid his platinum AmEx on O'Neill's desk with a snap. "I got Phil into this, and I'll get her out."

He met O'Neill's gaze steadily across the expanse of wood. "Whatever it takes."

"I really am starting to develop an affection for this man." Beverly beamed at them all. "Tell me, Nick, what do you do for a living?"

There was something about the relentless grey of that little cinder block room that really got on my nerves, especially when I was left alone there.

Maybe it was the bars. Whatever it was, the reality of my distasteful situation was slowly sinking in.

And I really didn't like the view. My mind went wild, speculating on the fallout. Even if the charges were dropped, people like Mrs. H. might have issues with this dark stain on my history. It could ruin the business, just when everything was starting to go right.

I was going to be bankrupt, a failure, a lifer in Rosemount jail, the subject of family disgust forever. I'd be checking in with my parole officer every Tuesday, I'd be letting down Elaine. My speculation spiraled downward in the gloom of that room, until I just about needed to be scraped off the floor with a spatula.

The keys jangled in the door and I looked up, probably doing a good imitation of Jez hearing something fall into her dish. My mother was somewhat overdressed for a visit to jail, but I was really glad to see her.

"You shouldn't sit on that, dear, you'll mark your lovely suit." She smiled for me, acting for all the world like we'd just met for tea at some posh restaurant and she was chiding me for sitting on a stone bench outside. She stood me up and brushed me off as though I was a little girl again, her protectiveness making me want to cry.

"I'm in jail, Mom."

Her brushing paused for just a moment, then she continued straightening my jacket and passing an admiring finger over the beading on the blouse. "You do have such lovely taste, Philippa. I'd like to think that you got that from me."

I blinked at this unlikely sentiment. "Are you drunk?"

She smiled a little. "Not that much. Something about this place tends to sober a person up."

"Then, where's your pod?"

"I beg your pardon?"

"Would the real Beverly Coxwell stand up? My mother thinks I have terrible taste, in everything from underwear to men."

She framed my face in her hands and looked me in the eye. "Your mother is realizing that she was wrong."

I watched her for a minute, then shook my head. "Did all the molecules in the universe just jump a foot to the left and leave me behind? What do you mean, you were wrong?"

My mother grimaced. "I married the wrong man and I certainly didn't do a good job of fixing it." She turned and walked away. "I've been wallowing for a long time, Philippa, which is no way to solve one's problems."

She tapped her perfectly manicured fingers on the sill of the window, then recoiled from the residue left on her hands. "What a filthy place," she muttered, then turned to face me, brushing her hands fastidiously.

"You've shown me that things aren't always what they seem, Philippa, that people aren't always what they seem to be." She smiled. "That appearances aren't nearly so trustworthy or as valuable as I was taught to believe."

I had been dumped into a new play without a copy of the script. "What are you going to do?"

"I'm going to divorce your father. I'm going to move back to Boston and continue my life as I should have before. I'm going to live again, instead of brood about how I could have lived if everyone hadn't stopped me. I stopped myself, that's the simple truth of it, and I'm going to start myself."

"What about that man?"

She laughed under her breath. "He's long gone, Philippa, and really he never mattered. It was what he represented that intrigued me. He was freedom and passion and spontaneity, things that had no place in my upbringing. I'll be grateful to him forever for introducing me to them, but truly we were as incompatible as chalk and cheese."

"But you kept his letters."

"Because they helped me remember what was possible, what I had sacrificed, what I thought I would never feel or have again." She summoned her social smile, her manner turning brisk. "You needn't worry about me tonight, dear. I have telephoned a friend from years ago who has offered her guest suite to me. It will only be temporary, of course, as I will have to find my own accommodations, but Jeffrey will drive me there."

It was somewhat surreal that she thought I should be so concerned about where she slept, when I was going to sleep on a slab of concrete.

Without my suit touching it.

Then the keys sounded again and everything started to make sense. Nick stood there, his tie loosened, his expression watchful and wary.

"He paid your bail, dear," my mother whispered to me. "And I must say that he shows considerably more promise than I might have expected."

Her voice dropped lower as I stared at Nick. "You know, dear, men usually think that sex is the solution for all ills and the remedy for every situation. I think perhaps we give less credence to that theory than we should." She smiled for me then, actually touched my cheeks with her lips when she kissed me, then took the elbow of Jeffrey who lingered behind Nick.

But there was only Nick for me. Nick and his clear gaze, Nick and his crooked smile. He opened his arms to me and I ran, squeezing my eyes tightly shut when he caught me close. He was so warm and made me feel so safe that I cried like an idiot.

"Tough day for a ray of sunshine," he murmured into my hair, then eased away my tears with his thumb.

"I never cry."

"Of course not."

I sniffled and left mascara on his shirt but he didn't seem to care. He didn't make fun of me or try to get me to smile, he just held me as though he would never let me go.

I really didn't want him to. He said something to Chief O'Neill about the next day but I wasn't listening too well, then led me to the truck. I might have been the queen for the way he helped me in—neither of us considered the possibility of my driving. The world felt big and frightening to me, the future uncertain.

Nick didn't let go of my hand the whole way home, which was a bit tough when he shifted gears, but worth it. Definitely worth it. We didn't exchange a single word the whole way back to my apartment but my heart was pounding as though I'd run a marathon.

Everything felt so tenuous to me, even as I felt overwhelmed with emotion. I didn't dare ask a question or say anything, I didn't want to ruin everything.

I didn't want to lose this sense of expectation.

We stopped in the foyer of my apartment and looked at each other as Nick turned the dead bolt. His eyes were cat-bright, darkest emerald, and he seemed to simmer right before my eyes. But he was waiting, waiting for me.

Even without my mother's advice, I would have reached into that volcano one more time. For now or forever, I didn't care. I wanted everything he had to give tonight.

And I'd give him everything I had to offer.

I barely moved before he caught me close, his mouth on

mine. His kiss was fierce yet tender, controlled yet just barely so. And I understood then that I hadn't loved him all those years before, that I couldn't have loved him before I knew so much about him.

Before I really knew *him*.

We shed clothes all across the living room, I murmured incoherently, he kissed and touched and finally carried me to the bed. We loved the night away as though tomorrow would never come.

Or couldn't be trusted if it did.

And sometime before the sun rose, I told Nick Sullivan that I loved him. He said nothing, but then I hadn't expected him to. He just rolled over and made love to me again.

It was enough.

I awoke to a view of tight buttocks, though sadly, jeans were being pulled over them very quickly. "Don't tell me it's morning yet."

Nick glanced warily over his shoulder at me. So, he had heard what I said and the prognosis wasn't good. "You didn't seem to be worried about sleep last night."

I leaned back against the pillows, choosing my strategy with care. He hadn't made love like a man who didn't care—not that I had a considerable store of experience with which to compare his technique.

Maybe he'd made love like a man doing it for the last time.

That woke me up. "I was planning to linger abed after my unfortunate incarceration, and enjoy the pleasures of the flesh."

He leaned down, wearing only his jeans, and kissed me. It was the kind of kiss you give your mother. He straightened all too soon and picked up his shirt, leaving me in no doubt that I'd peed in the pool. "No rest for the wicked, Phil. We've got to go and see Lucia."

I sat up then, fearful that I had missed something. "Did they call? How is she?"

"No word." Nick looked grim. "But then, they doped her up pretty good." He paused, his back to me as he buttoned his shirt. His tone was too carefully neutral. "O'Neill wants to ask her some questions when she comes around. I'd like to be there."

The very fact that he'd told me about it hinted at his hope that I'd be there, but I was feeling the need for a little reassurance. "Then go. Take the truck with you."

He looked back. "Phil, you know that's not what I mean."

We stared at each other for half an eon. I folded the blankets around myself and pushed my hair back, unable to avoid the musky smell of lovemaking. "Does that mean that you want me to come?"

"You know I do."

I flung out a hand in exasperation. "Then what have you got to lose by asking me?"

He stared at the floor for a minute, then crossed the room very quickly. He sat down on the edge of the bed. "Phil, would you come to the hospital with me and visit Lucia? I hope things are going to be wrapped up this morning"—he actually knocked the wood of the headboard—"and I think you should be there."

"Talk about an offer I can't refuse," I muttered. I climbed out of bed, not giving a damn what kind of view he had. The party was definitely over.

He sobered as I rummaged for my slippers, but I refused to look at him. "Phil . . ."

"Don't." I halted him with one hand. "Don't say anything. Don't even go there. It's bad enough without you saying it."

I walked to the bathroom, feeling his gaze follow me, my heart shattering into little pieces with every step.

Well, now everyone could tell me that they'd told me so. Now, I could tell myself that at least I knew how Nick Sullivan kissed, let alone how he did a lot of other things. I even knew a bunch of his secrets.

Which was cold comfort indeed. I hadn't lied to Jeffrey, I didn't regret a moment of this week and the ride had definitely been worth the price of admission.

I just didn't want it to end. Like a kid at the fair, I didn't want to get off that carousel and go back home, back to boring predictable real life.

I told my reflection that I should be grateful that Nick wasn't going to lie to me. He could have dropped to one knee and confessed undying love before he walked out of my life, which would have made the morning after a lot worse. No, he didn't promise what he wasn't going to deliver.

He'd said he came back to make things right. As soon as Sean was charged for his crime, as soon as the balance was righted, Nick would be gone again. This time forever. He'd never suggested anything different.

I didn't feel very grateful to him though, and there's a shampoo bottle in my shower with a nasty tale of abuse to tell.

All the same, I'd be damned if I'd miss the grand finale.

She'd gone and changed the rules. She'd pulled the proverbial rug right out from under him, leaving him feeling like an ass.

So much for putting things right.

So much for pretending Phil hadn't said what she'd said.

The silence between them was far from companionable and certainly didn't have the sexual charge of the night before. Phil seemed to delight in grinding the gears and she wasn't wasting any time or energy talking to him.

Her confession echoed in his head, confusing him, terrifying him, making a familiar part of him want to run for cover.

But another part of him wanted to hear those three words fall from her lips again. That was the part that replayed the way she had said it, the way the confession had spilled out, as though she'd been trying to hold it back. That was the part that wanted her to say it again and again, just so he could be sure.

That was the part of him that wanted to stay.

He wouldn't make a promise though, not unless he was sure it could be kept. He wouldn't let Phil down in the worst way imaginable. First things had to be resolved first.

O'Neill was waiting for him, as planned. His shrewd gaze followed the way Phil walked away from Nick, as though she couldn't wait to put distance between them. She picked up a magazine in the waiting room and buried her nose in it without troubling to give him another glance.

O'Neill looked at him and Nick felt heat rise on the back of his neck. "I wouldn't have thought it possible to screw that up," the chief murmured, but Nick ignored him.

It wasn't any of his damn business.

Lucia was dozing, just as she had before. She looked pale and elderly in the hospital bed, some measure of her vitality sapped by her surroundings.

Or the tubes running in and out of her. He took her hand, which was less warm than it should be. Her skin felt thin, as though he could slough it off her bones just by trying. Her bones seemed small and brittle in his hand.

The respirator wheezed, the IV dripped. The chief stood slightly back, but his face wasn't as impassive as he probably would have liked.

"Helluva trick, Lucia," Nick muttered, his voice sounding strange and thick to his own ears.

Her eyelids fluttered. It took her a long time to get them open, or maybe it just felt like an eternity because he wanted to see her incisive gaze so badly.

Her eyes were clouded though, her gaze slipping over him without any hint of recognition. Then she frowned, and squeezed his fingers slightly.

"Be a good boy, Nicholas." Her voice was a reedy whisper. "And get me a cigarette."

"They won't let you have one in here." He cleared his throat. "Do you want one badly enough to get better and go home?"

She snorted then, and coughed weakly. "Maybe." She looked across the room and smiled. "Hello, Bill. You better not have finished that brandy on me."

"Not a chance. It's bad luck to drink alone."

She harumphed, a shadow of her usual self. "Worse luck to eat venison without something to wash it down." She looked up at Nick, a gleam in her dark eyes. "Has he made you eat it yet?"

"No. We only just met."

"Hmm. You'll have to get used to it then."

There was a question in her voice and her eyes. Nick smiled for her. "I guess I will. Do you know how to cook it?"

Lucia scoffed weakly. "Not my job."

"Then I'll have to make it mine."

She eased back then, her eyes closing as though this small conversation had cost her dearly. "Guess you learned your lesson."

"Guess I did."

The sound of her breathing filled the room, punctuated by the rhythm of the respirator. O'Neill stepped closer and took her other hand. "Who did it, Lucia?"

But her breath was slowing and her eyes were closed once more.

"Lucia," Nick urged. "Who did this to you?"

She frowned, as though trying to stay conscious but losing the battle. Her grip loosened on Nick's hand.

"What about Philippa Coxwell?" O'Neill suggested.

Lucia smiled. "Nicholas's girl," she whispered. Nick knew he wasn't the only one straining to hear her words.

"That's what I thought," O'Neill commented wryly. Nick ignored him.

"Taught her to dance." Lucia's smile broadened and she lifted Nick's hand to her face. "She's the one."

O'Neill frowned in surprise, but Nick knew they were misunderstanding his grandmother.

"It couldn't have been Phil. Lucia, don't go to sleep yet, please. Tell us who did it."

"No, no, not her," she muttered, her words slurring as the drugs claimed her. "The other one."

"The other what?" O'Neill barked, but Lucia was gone to dreamland.

The other one.

The other what? Lucia wasn't going to tell them any time soon.

They left the room together when the nurse shooed them away. Nick wanted only to pace. At least Phil was exonerated.

"The other partner of Coxwell & Pope?" O'Neill flipped through his notebook. "Maybe this Elaine is in some kind of debt, maybe she needed this contract."

"There never was a contract, that was the point."

They reached the waiting room to find Phil cornered by Sean, who was ogling her legs. She looked hostile, he looked undeterred. Josie stood behind him, her arms crossed, her expression petulant.

Apparently the woman had some limits.

The other one.

Nick halted so fast that O'Neill practically ran into his back. "Not *Nick's* girl, the other one."

O'Neill smiled and shook his finger at Nick, then stepped forward to take charge of the situation. He introduced himself briefly. "Your grandmother's asleep, Mr. Sullivan," he said to Sean. "But maybe I could ask you a few questions while you're waiting."

"Sure! Always glad to help the men in blue." Sean smiled broadly. "What can I do for you?"

"Tell me where you were on Friday." O'Neill got out his notebook and pen.

Sean's smile disappeared. "What is this?"

"It's an investigation into an assault, Mr. Sullivan. If you'd prefer that we chatted elsewhere, I'm sure that a private room can be found."

"Hey, I've got nothing to hide. I was at an interview Friday. Full day. I might even have gotten the job." He jammed his hands on his hips as though defying O'Neill to question this.

"I'm sure they'll have a record of your presence."

"They damn well better."

"Why don't you give me that address, and the name of the person you spoke with. What time were you there, exactly, Mr. Sullivan?"

"Nine to four."

"I guess Max will vouch for your using his car?" Nick asked.

Sean frowned. "No, I took the bus. It was right in town. And how do you know about Max's car?"

Something flashed in Josie's eyes. "I told them you took it Tuesday," she said, "for that other interview."

"Tuesday?" Sean shook his head. "No, that was Monday."

"No, you're wrong," she insisted. "It was Tuesday. I remember."

"Max said it was Monday," Phil supplied.

Josie's eyes flashed. "Max is a liar."

"His car won't lie," O'Neill said quietly. "We'll check it for prints."

Josie paled and sat down hard.

"Phil, do you have Max's number?" Nick asked, watching Josie carefully. "Maybe he'll remember whether anyone used his car on Friday."

"Not me," Sean scoffed. "I took the bus."

Josie dropped her face into her hands and started to cry.

Josie confessed, the whole story coming in dribs and drabs between her tears. It seemed that she really thought that money would solve everything. Sean had told her about his fight with Lucia, and Lucia's plans, and Nick's story had given her the perfect opportunity to do something about it.

Sean had an alibi for Friday, so that was the day she chose. She never figured anyone would look twice at her. She'd insisted that he had the car Tuesday, because she wanted to hide the fact that Sean had been in Rosemount on Monday, arguing with Lucia.

And of course, she'd been late fetching that beer because she'd been listening to our conversation outside the apartment door.

It made such sense and was sad because Sean wasn't exactly appreciative of her efforts.

"Jesus Jenny," he declared while O'Neill read Josie her rights. "I knew she was a dumb bitch, but this really takes the cake."

I stared at him, incredulous that he could be so callous. "What?"

"You heard me. I mean, how could she imagine that she could get away with that?" Sean brushed his hands together and looked away. "Good riddance is what I say. Lock her up and throw away the key."

I was shocked. "She did it for you!"

"Hey, I never asked her to do anything."

"You ape!" And I punched him in the nose.

It was a good right hook, executed just the way Zach taught me. Sean bled all over the place. I had time to be glad that I broke his nose before I realized that my hand hurt like heck. Nick was laughing himself silly.

So, I got charged with assault after all. What with the chief there to witness my dirty deed, he didn't have a lot of choice. He had to run after us though, because Nick practically tossed me over his shoulder to take me down to the ER again.

They were getting to know us down there.

It was almost funny to watch Phil struggle against the sedative. She certainly wasn't going down without a fight. He drove back to her place, keeping one eye on her as she tried to maintain consciousness.

"You just don't want to miss anything," he teased when he helped her out of the truck.

"Go ahead, make fun of me," she charged, her words slurred. She couldn't keep her balance so he scooped her up and carried her into the apartment.

Her eyes drifted closed again once she was on the bed.

She was starting to lose the battle. He undressed her, which was a challenge seeing as she'd gone all rubbery, and tucked her into bed. He would have left her to sleep, but she clutched suddenly at his hand. Her lips worked but no sound came out, a tiny frown of frustration creased her brow.

Her determination made him smile.

"Give it up, Phil," he whispered as he sat on the side of the bed and folded her hand into his. "I promise to keep good notes." He eased the frown away with the pad of his thumb and watched her reluctantly succumb.

She still managed to hold his hand tightly, though, even with that brace on her fingers. And as he tried to ease her grip on him, he realized what it was that she didn't want to miss.

She thought he was going to leave.

And why not? The puzzle he'd asked her to help with was solved, Lucia was recovering and Josie had confessed. Phil's name was cleared and there was no reason for him to stay. He'd made a point of never promising to do so.

He'd left her twice before, by her own accounting, though he hadn't thought of it that way himself at the time. He wondered why he wasn't in such a hurry to pack up now.

It wasn't like him to be content to stay anywhere.

It was like him to take the situation apart and reason out the answer.

He wasn't worried about Lucia particularly, and he could re-establish his relationship with her from anywhere. Telephones were good for that sort of thing. She was on the way to healing and it looked as though Sean would be more involved in her life.

Phil's family would always be screwed up, he suspected, but they appreciated her a bit more. He'd done what he could there and felt that he'd repaid her trust in him.

He had his wits and enough cash to last him a long time. He certainly could have continued the way he'd lived for fifteen years.

Lucia's assertion echoed in his ears. *"She's the one."*

Not the one who had assaulted Lucia. His eyes narrowed as he realized what she had meant.

The one for Nicholas.

The truth was that he didn't have much interest in the nomad's life all of a sudden. He liked cooking for Phil and wasn't ready to stop. He hadn't nearly exhausted his repertoire of recipes, much less watched her taste and discover them all. He hadn't made love to her nearly often enough to know the location of all her moles and dimples, and that seemed a pressing lack.

He watched Phil doze, his fingertips absently stroking her hand as he thought. The brace made her fingers look small and fragile, the pallor of her skin made her look unusually vulnerable. Maybe it was sleep that brought down all her considerable defenses, or maybe this week had just drained her. If he left, he'd never know for sure.

He'd never promised her anything and now he wondered what she would have made of it if he had.

She'd simply given. It wasn't Phil's way to ask for anything for herself and he supposed that was another thing they had in common. He had never expected anything for himself, or expected anything good to last. He never asked either.

He'd never asked her to love him, but she did.

And he was glad.

Her star shone from the ceiling with a faint bluish cast and he stared at it for a long while, the softness of her fingers cradled in his palm. He'd certainly never had the audacity to wish for anything for himself.

Maybe they were too different, after all. Phil spread sunshine everywhere she went, she saw the good in people and wished for the best. She crossed her fingers and knocked wood, she hoped, she believed that her wishes might come true. She was optimistic that good could conquer all.

He'd been wrong when he accused her of not seeing who he really was. She did see, she just didn't view the truth as negatively as he did. She shone that relentless beam of sunshine right into his shadows and found something good in him, something he didn't even realize was there.

She credited him with making good changes in her life, with empowering her to make her own dreams come true. That was pretty heady stuff. She saw the potential good in what he considered his greatest failure. And she persuaded him to take another, more objective look.

He would go back to Asia, back to Hidden Paradise, to see what could be done to retrieve it. But for the first time in his life, he didn't want to travel alone. He wanted to take Phil with him. He wanted to pore over the pictures of what that place had been, he wanted her advice on how to make it better. He wanted her to help him see what was good about what it had become.

Maybe what they did was complement each other. Perfectly. He felt good about himself when he was with Phil, he felt good about life and the world in general. A little bit of her blithe confidence tended to light his path.

It was no wonder he wasn't ready to walk away.

He eased a tendril back from her cheek, content to sit and watch her all night long. The thing was, he was never going to be ready to walk away. Phil had welcomed him into her home, her bed and her heart.

He understood now why he wanted to show her the wonders of the world—it was one experience he could share with her, an adventure he could offer in exchange. He slipped his hand free of hers and peeled off his clothes, sliding into the bed beside her. She nestled against him with a sigh, her curves fitting to his as though they were made for each other.

And they were. He'd known it all those years ago, recognized it that night she learned to waltz and first wished upon a star. He'd been afraid to want anything as much as he'd wanted Phil, so he'd run from her generosity, from her love.

He'd done it twice. But all the women he'd known could never measure up to the one he'd left behind. That was why he kept moving, so he wouldn't have to think about what was missing. So he could lose himself in a deluge of new experience.

Those days of wandering were done. He wasn't going anywhere, not without Phil.

Because Lucia was right . . . Phil was the one.

He'd help her make her company work, offer her a helping hand whenever she wanted it. He'd love her and protect her and try to keep the world from raining on her parade.

If she'd have him.

He winked at that childish star—it was the brightest one in sight—wishing with all his heart and soul. It was the first time he'd wished on a star since childhood, but if sincerity had anything to do with it, his wish would come true.

Third time lucky was what Phil would have said. He kissed her temple and her lips curved, as though she knew it was him.

"I love you, Phil," he murmured, his voice thick with words he'd never expected to utter in his life.

But the lady in question was out cold.

In fact, she started to snore.

Consciousness was as elusive as a stage illusion. Lucia fought against the siren's song of the drugs, willing that boy to hurry. He finally came into her room, with Bill propelling him forward, and with a bandage on his nose. Bruises were starting to rise around his eyes and it looked as though he would soon have a pair of shiners. His eyes were narrowed, not just in pain, but resentment.

But then, she hadn't expected much different from Sean, not after Monday's argument.

"What do you want?" he demanded, obviously not intending to linger long.

"I wanted to talk to you." Her voice wasn't as commanding as she might nave liked and the supine pose did little to emphasize her authority, but it would have to do.

Sean folded his arms across his chest. "So, talk. I don't have all night."

Lucia pulled herself up slightly, his attitude irking her. "So busy as that? Did you get a job?"

He colored. "No. It's not fair, but I'm getting close. I'll get something . . ."

"No, you won't."

That shut him up. "Because you're going to hex me?"

"Because you hexed yourself, fool." She coughed, wished for the thousandth time that she could have just one cigarette, then glared at her interested grandson. She'd have to make this short and sweet, since the drugs were winning again. "When did your luck go bad?"

"Jesus Jenny, I dunno . . ."

"It went bad the night you did wrong and never made it right."

"How do you . . ." Sean folded his arms across his chest. "You're just making this up. Your golden boy is back and you're just making excuses for him."

Lucia ignored his argument. "Your father believed in making reparation for anything he did wrong, one way or the other. He believed that his luck would change for the worst if he didn't."

"I thought that was the court's job."

"Sometimes," Bill interjected, "the courts don't always get their man, even though a wrong has been done."

"If you think you're going to gang up on me and force me to admit to something I didn't do, then you're more wrong than you can imagine."

"I expect nothing from you." Lucia spoke firmly. "And that's what you should expect from me."

Sean paled again. "You can't write me out of your will. I'll contest it."

"I know." Lucia permitted herself a smile. "So I'm going to spend it all instead." The effort cost her dearly and she coughed weakly again.

Bill said what she meant to say, if with less drama than she might have preferred. "Which means that if you want anything out of this life, you're going to have to turn your life around."

"I can't get a job, what the hell am I supposed to do?"

"I'll give you a job. Tell him, Bill."

"The theater needs a caretaker, preferably live-in. The job entails ensuring security, even during renovation and reconstruction, general cleanup after it's done."

"I'm not going to be a janitor!"

"There is the potential for a particularly successful candidate to be promoted to the management of the theater, supervising advertising and PR, hiring and booking of shows."

"Now, that sounds like a job for me. Give the joe job to someone else."

Lucia shook her head. "That's not how it's going to work."

"Your grandmother believes that the manager of the theater needs to know its workings from the ground up."

Sean eyed her balefully for a long moment. "What does it pay?"

Bill named a sum that made her grandson scoff.

"I can't live on that!"

"Of course you can. Your room is on the premises of the theater, so you'll have no rent to pay."

"Still, it's not enough for beer. No way."

"Well, you might have the time to take on another part-time job, one that pays only slightly but could have positive repercussions in your life."

"What the hell is that supposed to mean?"

"An older gentleman called your grandmother a few weeks ago. Seems his health has been failing since he had a small accident some years ago. His broken leg, although it seemed to heal well enough at the time, has become quite crippled with arthritis. He's having a hard time getting around and seeing his errands done."

"Why would he call you?" Sean demanded, his manner belligerent. He truly was not the sharper of the two boys. "What are you, charity central?"

Lucia cleared her throat, disliking that the point had to be made so ponderously. "His leg was broken in a hit-and-run car accident fifteen years ago."

Sean sat down and scowled at the pair of them. "You've got nothing on me . . ."

"And you've got nothing in your future," Lucia snapped. "I used to think you were just like your father, but I was only partly right. You certainly don't understand how to let somebody love you, but you lack the moral integrity to fix your own mistakes. It's not an attractive combination and it's about time somebody told you so."

She fell back against the pillows, exhausted, hating the loud echo of her breath in the room.

"We can blame everyone else for the shortfalls in our lives," Bill said quietly, "but in the end, we each are our own creation."

"Yeah, well, no one ever gave a crap what became of me, that's for sure."

"Is that right? There's a certain young lady who was prepared to murder just to see that you had your chance."

"She did a pretty lousy job of it."

"Lucky for you. You can go to anger management classes together, instead of visiting her in jail for the rest of her life. And your grandmother can give you a job, which she couldn't do if she were dead."

"You've been taking the path of least resistance," Lucia croaked. "Just like piss running into a gutter. Look where it's gotten you. Grow up, Sean."

"Your grandmother's offering you the best chance you're likely to get."

"I don't need to be lectured to for my whole life."

"End of lecture." Lucia's eyes drifted closed despite her efforts.

"It's a onetime offer," Bill concluded. "Take it or leave it."

She heard her grandson hesitate, could imagine him working through the possibilities. "You're really going to spend it all?"

Lucia smiled without opening her eyes. She'd known that would be the persuading factor. A party boy, like his father, he wanted comfort and the luxury of money in his pocket. "I'll probably die owing a fortune."

"And you'll give me that other job, the good one, if I do this shit one first? Guaranteed?"

"There are no guarantees, Mr. Sullivan, but if you do your best, I'll wager that your luck will change."

"Yeah, and get that geezer his groceries."

"It would certainly be the gesture of a compassionate citizen."

Sean snorted and Lucia guessed that he rolled his eyes. She couldn't open her own to check though. "Any other conditions before I sign up?"

"Nicholas's girl," Lucia whispered and felt Bill pat her hand. His touch seemed a thousand miles away. She was losing the battle, the sedative claiming her bit by bit.

"You really want to press charges over that broken nose?"

"Damn straight! She bopped me, right in front of everyone and for no good reason!"

Bill's words were gentle but firm. "Which is different from your striking Josie for no good reason when no one could see?"

Sean made an exasperated sound and Lucia smiled. Bill had a natural flair for bringing disparate elements to closure that she admired. He could keep track of imbalances over the years and gradually ensure that justice was done, one way or the other. She suspected that the gentleman with the arthritic knee hadn't come up with the idea of calling her all by himself, but Bill's gentle meddling suited Lucia well.

It was the mark of any good production to tie up all the loose ends, to mete out retribution and reward, by the time the houselights came up. Bill did a better job than most.

The last word she heard was Sean's reluctant agreement, then Lucia permitted her own curtain to fall.

Chapter 19

You've got to believe that the next week was tame in comparison. Mrs. H. called Monday morning, smitten with the pink hellebore and anxious for us to begin. A sweet little deposit check started the week off on a high note and by Tuesday, Joel and I were walking off the plans again and starting to dig.

She was even warming to the possibility of more pink "since your instincts are so good with these things." Over the weekend, she'd decided that the new sketches looked kind of dull in comparison with the ones she'd nixed.

I wasn't asking a lot of questions about her change of heart. I was excited about the project, particularly about going back to those pinky plans. The brace on my fingers annoyed the heck out of me, but it's amazing what you can get used to.

On the family front, there was definite fallout from the weekend. Zach was going to Venice to take pictures, off on his dream of becoming a photographer. When he called to tell me, I knew that he felt cheated of the family's disgust. I assured him it wouldn't last long. My father would recover himself soon and be outraged all over again.

Zach had that effect on him. Maybe my father didn't believe that Zach would really do it.

Zach, of course, did.

My mother, by the way, called to complain that my father was demanding that James take a DNA test to determine his paternity. James had been shocked by Mom's revelation but this shook the foundations of his castle.

Truth be told, it shocked me. My father was threatening to take away everything James had worked to earn, because of an accident of birth. Forty years later, he was going to disavow the man he'd raised as his son. James had put a lot of hours into that partnership and its success was as much a part of his efforts as my father's.

I was betting that James and Marcia's household wasn't a happy one. They certainly weren't returning phone calls.

All through that week, I kept waiting for the other shoe to drop, but Nick didn't seem too inclined to pack up and disappear. He spent a lot of time at the hospital, sitting vigil with Lucia, but invariably, he showed up at my office in the late afternoon, laden with groceries. He cooked for me, he actually talked willingly, he told me of his travels and a thousand places I'd probably never see.

But he left after the dishes were done, every night.

I thought it was his way of saying farewell, but he never seemed to get to that part. Maybe he was weaning me off. Maybe he was weaning himself off. I didn't worry about it as much as I had thought I would. We had great talks, there was a little simmer of electricity, but I was happy.

I finally decided that he was waiting for Lucia to be released.

He plundered my books on hothouse flowers once Lucia was more reliably conscious and I figured she had demanded he ensure their survival. I didn't offer to do it, and he didn't ask.

At the end of the week, Joel had another worker fade into the great beyond without explanation or apology, but to my astonishment, Nick offered to help.

Which meant I got to watch two fine specimens of masculinity tear off their shirts in Mrs. H.'s garden, laboring beneath my command like slaves before the queen.

They sent Lucia home on the weekend and the first thing she did was light up a cigarette, according to the Chief, who drove her home. But Nick showed no signs of heading out.

If anything, he bought more kitchen gadgets.

Midway through the second week, I figured it out. He knew Mrs. H.'s contract was a critical one for me. So, he was waiting to see this contract through, to make sure I didn't stumble or get tripped by Lady Luck again. Once Mrs. H. wrote that check, he'd be gone. No doubt about it.

The project proceeded without a hitch.

It was done in twelve long working days, precisely three days early, two and a half weeks after Lucia made her acquaintance with Josie's knife. It looked gorgeous, if I do say so myself.

But any triumph was short-lived. Nick left the site early, with nary a word to me, though he shook Joel's hand. He even gave Jez's ears a good scratch, leaving me feeling like the city mouse's poor cousin.

But maybe it would be easier this way.

As if.

Elaine was trying to clear her desk before she went home for the night. The windows were open and the sound of evening traffic carried into the office on the warm winds of May.

She knew she was dallying, but there was something about seeing Philippa and Nick together that cut deep. Elaine was alone, she'd been alone all her life and she was starting to realize that she would probably always be alone.

Her apartment rang hollow to her ears these days, even her new tabby kitten Snickers doing little to fill the gap.

Worse, it was her own fault.

She filed with a vengeance, in enough of a foul mood that she didn't notice the hum of a foreign car parking in front of the little office building. She didn't even notice the shadow of the visitor who hesitated outside the door. When the door opened, she jumped like Snickers discovering for the four hundredth time that his tail was attached to his butt.

"Got a minute?"

Elaine blinked, but it was still Jeffrey McAllister. Not only was he here, but he didn't look pompous and irked as he usually did in her presence. He was carrying something—it looked like a framed print or painting—and she guessed he wanted her to drool over some nifty new Picasso he'd picked up on sale.

She wasn't feeling terribly charitable. Elaine nodded once. "About a minute is it," she declared and started stuffing things haphazardly into her briefcase.

"Got a date?" Jeff looked uncertain.

"Yeah," Elaine lied, then forced a smile.

Jeff shrugged and crossed the office, pausing opposite her desk. "Lucky guy. I won't hold you up."

Elaine regarded him with suspicion, but before she could question his manner, Jeff started to talk. "Look, I want to tell you a little story. It won't take long."

Jeff telling stories. Elaine could just bet that this one had a moral, one that showed the poor quality of her character and the failures of her lineage. "Hurry it up, then. I don't want to be late."

"Fair enough." He unwrapped the package he was carrying and set it on her desk.

To Elaine's surprise, it wasn't a legal document or a fabulous piece of art, but a piece of red construction paper in a cheap frame. Something was scrawled in the middle of it in purple and green, crayon and marker respectively.

Elaine stared at it in surprise for a moment, then looked to Jeff. "Is this a joke?"

He shook his head. "Wasn't to me."

"What is it?"

Jeff pushed his hands into his pockets and gave her a rueful glance. "I don't know."

Elaine half-laughed, then folded her arms across her chest to study him. "This is a joke. It has to be, although I don't get it."

"No, I really don't know what it's supposed to represent," Jeff corrected, "but I do know what it is." He glanced at her, then looked away, as though he was afraid to see her reaction. "It's the first drawing I ever did. It's, in fact, the only drawing I ever did. I don't even remember doing it."

He picked it up and turned it, squinting at the lines. "My grandmother kept it. She said I gave it to her when I was about five, that I told her it was love. She, not surprisingly for a grandmother I guess, framed it and hung it in her kitchen." He looked to Elaine and smiled. "As you can imagine, this mortified me, particularly in my teenage years when she insisted on regaling everyone with the story."

Elaine smiled reluctantly and Jeff held her gaze long enough that her heart went thump.

"But I was never any good at drawing or anything in art class. I used to explain this to my grandmother, but she insisted that what was important was that I tried. And she would not take this picture down, not for any price."

He paused for a long moment, a frown pulling his brows together. "She died a month or so ago and I was her executor. My cousin came to the house and just plucked the picture off the wall.

He handed it to me and joked that this was one thing we couldn't argue about. Everyone had a little laugh. I took it home because I didn't know what else to do with it, but I've found it tough to just chuck it out."

Jeffrey McAllister having a heart. Would wonders never cease.

Elaine struggled to not soften toward him. There had been a lot or tough words between them, after all.

But missing someone was a little too close to the loneliness she was feeling for her to make a joke about it. "Because it reminds you of her?"

"That and a couple of other things." Jeff sighed. "I've been really lucky, Elaine, and I'm only just starting to realize how lucky. Lots of things have been easy for me, lots of good things have come to me without much effort on my part. Opportunities have come my way because of where I was born and who my parents were. I guess I always assumed it was that way for everyone."

He was watching her closely and Elaine felt her cheeks pinken, knowing very well that he was referring to her.

"I was wrong," he admitted, looking at the drawing again.

He cleared his throat and Elaine couldn't think of a single thing to say. "I know that I never really appreciated how hard you'd had to work to get what you have, or how much uncertainty you'd faced while I was having good fortune piled in my lap."

Elaine clenched her hands together and stared back at this astonishingly earnest Jeff.

"Someone recently reminded me that not everything is guaranteed, that sometimes you have to just take a chance." He looked up. "That sometimes, you have to listen to your heart."

His smile flickered tentatively, then died when Elaine didn't respond. "I miss you. For a long time I thought that was some kind of moral weakness on my part"—he shoved a hand through his hair—"but I see now that it was more than that. I miss the way you laugh, I miss how you celebrate everything that comes your way, I miss your sheer bloody-mindedness. I miss how you take everything life gives you and enjoy it to the utmost." His voice dropped. "I miss your perfume on my sheets."

He bunched his hands into his pockets again. "And I miss the way every head would turn when you walked into a restaurant with me."

Elaine stiffened but he hurried on.

"Not because you were some kind of a trophy that I'd won and I wanted everyone to be jealous—though I might have thought of it that way at one time—but because you were the most bright and beautiful woman I'd ever known. And you'd chosen to be with me." He met her gaze once more. "I guess I thought relationships wouldn't require any effort on my part either."

Jeff stared at his shoes. "I got fired last weekend because I decided to do what I thought was right."

"Oh, I'm sorry."

"I'm not. It's a good thing, an opportunity to head out on my own that I might not have taken otherwise. I guess realizing how the odds are stacked against me now made me think of you, of how easy you make it look to get what you want."

Elaine felt her tears rising, but she stubbornly blinked them back.

"I know, Elaine, that I treated you badly. And I know we both said a lot of horrible things. If I could change anything in the world, I'd wipe all of that away." He impaled her with a glance. "But I can't. What's done can't be undone."

He picked up the drawing again and put it down square in front of her. "But I would like to be remembered as someone who tries, someone who makes the effort to get what he really wants."

He walked all the way to the door before Elaine realized he was leaving the only drawing he had ever done with her.

He paused, one hand on the knob, then looked back at her, his heart in his eyes. "And if you ever want to go for dinner with a guy who is willing to try to do better, please let me know."

With that, Jeffrey McAllister walked out of Elaine's life.

And not a moment too soon. The tears that she had fought to hide spilled and it was only quick reflexes that kept his drawing from being soaked. Elaine buried her face in her hands and cried, touched more than she could have believed possible by his gesture.

Someone had finally given her something that wasn't disposable, something that mattered, something that came right from the heart. It was whimsical and romantic and as unlike the Jeff she had known as was possible.

Maybe it was a better view of the Jeff she had glimpsed, the one man she had not been able to forget. Maybe this was what made him special.

The really stupid thing was that Elaine could see love in Jeff's drawing. The squiggles sort of made lazy hearts, as well as circles that could have been hugs. She could imagine it hanging on a doting grandmother's wall, she could imagine a five-year-old Jeff feeling adored by his grandmother, proudly eating cookies in that kitchen under his "art" while his cousins teased him.

She'd seen enough old movies that she could imagine what she had never had. Elaine blew her nose and wiped her tears. She rummaged for a nail and hammer in her desk, then hung that drawing on the wall beside her desk.

She stood back, tilted her head and studied it with a dawning smile. If Jeffrey McAllister could come to her with his heart in his hand and ask for another chance, the least Elaine could do was meet him halfway.

Because she had missed him too.

To hell with her desk. She scooped up her purse, locked the door and sailed out of the office, coming to a full stop in the parking lot.

Because there were two cars there, her own and a silver BMW. The beemer had a certain long-legged lawyer leaning against it.

Jeff smiled ruefully. "I stink at waiting."

Elaine smiled back. "We can work on that." She fiddled with her purse strap, the words hard to say now that he was watching her so closely. "Maybe over dinner."

Jeff's eyes lit in that way that had always thrilled Elaine right down to her toes.

He stood up, but paused. "What about your date?"

"It's about time you got here." Elaine grinned at Jeff's obvious relief, then tossed her keys in the air and caught them. "I'll drive." She wrinkled her nose at him playfully. "It'll give you a chance to see how the other half lives."

But when she would have darted past him, Jeff caught her around the waist, swinging her close enough for a quick hard kiss.

That was another thing she'd missed.

While Elaine was distracted, he stole her keys. "Let me. We're still going to Sabatino's," he declared as he pulled the Geo out into the traffic.

"Can you afford it now?"

He grinned recklessly. "No. Call it a motivational move. This calls for a celebration."

"We can celebrate anywhere."

"Elaine, I want to do this. It may be a while before I can do it again." He captured her hand, giving her fingers an impulsive squeeze. "I want everyone to know that we're together."

Elaine sighed, feeling a niggle of doubt at the sound of that. "Everyone who's everyone?"

Jeff shot her a hard look. "Everyone. Period." He rolled down the window and stuck his head out, his hair blowing wildly around his face.

"Hey, Boston!" he shouted. "Elaine Pope is having dinner with *me!*"

A few drivers commented, a pair of kids on the sidewalk hollered in support. Jeff pulled his head back in and grinned at Elaine, looking disheveled and very, very sexy. "How am I doing?"

She was unable to stop her answering smile. "I think you might just do, Mr. McAllister."

* * *

I took my time going home, driving via everywhere I could think of. I knew the apartment would be empty when I got there and I just didn't want to face solitude there.

Not to mention carrots for dinner.

In the truck, it wasn't so bad. I had the windows rolled down and had chucked off my jacket. My hair blew around my face as I drove down the coast, all the way to Cape Ann, then back. I could be going somewhere.

And I do love to drive.

I enumerated all the good things in my life. The contract for Mrs. H. was a success, the check had cleared. Lucia was home and happy with the chief of police. My mother had found a condo and raided my father's various bank accounts, much to his outrage. She'd called to say she was going dancing tonight, as excited as a kid given a bag of candy.

So, everything should have been right in my world.

You know that it wasn't. The only thing I really wanted was gone—not that I would have had it any other way. The manacle plan would have never worked out. Knowing Nick, he would have gnawed his way free. He could be a wily kind of guy.

And really, who wants a guy compelled to stay?

The end result would have been the same anyhow. He'd be gone, this time for good.

The sun was setting when I finally turned back toward the city. My stomach was grumbling by the time I took the exit home. Thinking about that dark kitchen, I nearly drove around the block, or back to the office, but called myself a chicken. Sooner or later, I had to go home.

Home. The apartment had never felt less like one.

My porch light with its trusty light sensor was on and that was about it. I'd have to tell Matt about my unauthorized leasehold improvement, since he was about the only one in the family who wasn't wound up about something.

But then, maybe he was the lucky one.

I parked the truck beside the upstairs guy's Passat, wondered as always why he had a cheap apartment and an expensive car, then rolled up the windows. I didn't hurry toward the porch, but no one was there to see.

At least that was what I thought at the time.

I was about twenty feet away from the porch when I saw him. There was a man sitting on my porch, a very familiar man. I stopped and stared, but he just smiled the slow smile that made my toes curl.

This time I couldn't blame anything on champagne. I was stone cold sober—and starving too.

"Don't tell me that you haven't got anything to say." He leaned forward, bracing his elbows on his knees, his eyes gleaming.

I hitched my purse further up my shoulder. "You didn't have to hang around to say good-bye."

"I know. I didn't think you'd take so long."

"Lots to do." I jingled my keys and headed for the door, but never made it that far.

Nick stepped forward to intercept me. He closed one hand over mine, silencing my keys. His hand was warm and he must have felt me tremble at his touch. His expression was surprisingly anxious. "Walk for a minute?"

A minute, an hour, a week. I'd take all I could get. I nodded and he slipped his arm around my waist. We strolled away from the house, though I had no idea where we were going. He seemed preoccupied, and I knew he was planning where to go next, what to do, what to make of the rest of his life.

I thought of all the adventures he must have had and the places he had been and I wanted to put my hand in his and go there too. I wanted to unfurl a new map on the kitchen table and pick a destination, any destination, with the drop of a pencil, then go there with Nick.

But he would do the same thing, alone.

"You can hardly see the stars here." His words were whiskey soft.

"Big city lights," I agreed, expecting another tale of his travels.

But he halted at the end of the street, his head tipped back. "Which one's brightest, Phil?"

"Are you going to tell me to make a wish?"

His smile was warm if fleeting. "Why not?"

Why not. I scanned the sky, painfully aware of the echo of this deed in our shared past. I spun around in place, then pointed to the brightest one. "That one."

"Sure?"

"Um hmm."

"Then let me get it for you."

I turned to him in surprise, but he stretched up onto his toes and reached into the night. When he opened his hand, offering me its contents, something glimmered there. It was a star, a perfectly white star trapped on a white gold band, that band caught between his fingers. It glimmered against his skin.

I met his gaze, probably with a big question mark in mine.

"It's the closest thing I could find to a lucky star, Phil." His words were gruff and oddly uncertain. "I thought it was time you got rid of that plastic one."

I stared at him, knowing I'd never seen him so nervous.

"I thought maybe you would wear it, and that then you'd be able to make a wish anytime anyplace."

I couldn't quite believe that he was saying what I knew he was saying, so I just stared at him, a dumbstruck dope. His gaze searched mine, as though he was looking for some kind of encouragement.

"I love you, Phil." He smiled ever so slightly. "I told you before but you were asleep."

I found my voice, though it was husky. "Chicken."

His smile flashed and disappeared. "Something like that." He held the ring between his finger and thumb, turning it so that the diamond sparkled in the light of the city. "Care to make a wish?"

"You first."

He held my gaze, his own intensely green. "I wish that Phil Coxwell would marry me, travel with me, and count stars with me wherever we manage to find ourselves."

I smiled at him and held out my left hand. "It must be your lucky night, Sullivan. I think I can arrange for that wish to come true."

What happened after that is none of your business.

Epilogue

We got married with unholy haste, but there were seeds to harvest and gardens to plant, so we took a belated honeymoon. We ditched the apartment and moved into Lucia's place, which was big enough that we could completely avoid each other if we wanted to. She was getting more frail—though she denied it vigorously—and Nick slept better knowing that she wasn't alone out there.

He and Joel tilled a huge crescent of a flower bed at the back of the lot and I planted heritage seeds out there. The sun was terrific and they grew beyond expectation. Nick donated a computer and database software to the cause and the woman from the historical society had a heyday making that database.

Mrs. H. did indeed refer us to her friends and we were busy all summer. Nick worked a lot of days for us, which was a great help. An added bonus was that he, unlike so many worker dudes, wasn't going to disappear.

So, it was near the end of October when we locked our bikes together on the roof of an auberge near Merzouga. The moon was new, the sunset smeared orange from horizon to horizon.

I curled up beside Nick in the sleeping bags we'd zipped together and he bunched our packs and fleeces behind us.

"Show time," he said with a wink, then uncapped a flask. He poured a measure of something gold into a little metal cup and handed it to me.

"What's that?"

"Brandy. Drink it."

I took a sniff and wrinkled my nose. "Moderation is one thing, Nick, but that stuff is like jet fuel."

"Drink it." He pushed the cup into my hand when I hesitated. "Freddie has friends and family everywhere."

Yuck. I drank and practically coughed up my liver, that stuff was so strong.

He was smiling at me, so I smacked his shoulder.

"Not funny."

"Of course not. Here's your reward." He unwrapped the foil on a slightly melted Swiss chocolate bar, broke off a piece and handed it to me.

I eyed him warily. "You're leading me down the path of temptation."

"After today?" He shook his head. "We biked thirty miles today, Phil. You deserve it."

"My butt will get huge."

He grinned. "Why do you think I've been riding behind you? I've been keeping an eye on it, as part of my marital duties. Rotten job, but someone's got to do it." I laughed at him and he caught me close against his side. "You get sexier every day, Phil, and don't imagine otherwise."

I took the chocolate, and leaned back beside him as twilight slipped across the sky.

He was right about the show. Soon the heavens were thick with stars. Star soup. Star carpets, star-studded. It was awesome and even though I was tired from all that pedaling, I stared and stared, filling my mind with the sight of them. I curled up against him and tried my damnedest to find the brightest one.

It was impossible.

But then, I already had everything I'd ever wished for.

"Find your lucky star?" Nick's voice was a purr in my ear.

"Oh yes." I squirmed around to face him, then snuggled closer. "And I'm not going to let him go."

A confessed romantic dreamer, *USA Today* bestselling author **Claire Cross** has always wove stories in her mind. Since selling her first book in 1992, she has written more than thirty romances. Winner of the Colorado Romance Writers' Award of Excellence and two-time nominee for *Romantic Times'* Career Achievement in Medieval Romance, she has more than two million books in print. She also writes medieval romances under the name Claire Delacroix. She lives in Canada with her husband. Visit her website at www.delacroix.net.